HIGH PRAISE FOR STEPHANIE MITTMAN
AND HER PREVIOUS NOVELS

A KISS TO DREAM ON

"*A Kiss to Dream On* is a historical romance that has the typical Mittman Midas magic: a fun-to-read story line filled with two heart-wrenching, wonderful lead characters. Fans of the genre will immensely enjoy this novel even as they dreamily await more magic from the magnificent Ms. Mittman."
—*Affaire de Coeur*

"Mittman joins the ranks of the greats in this poignant historical western romance."—*Oakland Press* (Pontiac, Mich.)

"A very powerful book . . . Ms. Mittman deserves heaps of awards for writing some of the best Americana romance around. Ms. Mittman brings daily life into focus so well that you feel like you are stepping into these people's lives. The depth of understanding is unbelievable."
—*The Belles and Beaux of Romance*

"Stephanie Mittman has conjured a delightful story of two ~~lo~~vers too blind to see each other's feelings. You cannot help but find yourself feeling happy and sad with them."
—*Rendezvous*

~~ta~~lented Ms. Mittman has written a touching, tender love ~~story~~ of two people trying to make the best of a difficult ~~situati~~on and finding love along the way. . . . The happy ~~ending is~~ just what I want in a book. . . . A highly enjoyable ~~roma~~nce for a quiet afternoon of reading pleasure."
—*Old Book Barn Gazette*

~~beaut~~iful love story that captures your heart . . . a ~~ki~~nd of tragedy along with some good humor . . . ~~touchin~~g and terrific story."—*Romance Reviews*

"KISS ME, HARRY," SHE SAID. "KISS ME GOOD NIGHT."

Harry brushed her forehead with his lips and sat down next to her. "This isn't good, Nan," he whispered.

"Because you don't like me, or becuase you do?" sh asked before she could stop herself.

"You don't even know me," he warned, all the stroking her through her clothes. "What I've done do . . ."

"Do you think I care what you do for asked, moving so that he could stretch out couch.

"Very much," he said. Gently, he own and raised it to his lips. "I sh "Before I make things worse."

Against her chest Nan co rapidly as her own. Agains sire. Against the pale r silhouetted, and watch

"Please don't go

"The t
story
situati
ending is
rom

lo

"A beaut
wonderful ble
a movi

THE COURTSHIP

Dell Books by Stephanie Mittman

A Kiss to Dream On
The Courtship
The Marriage Bed
Sweeter than Wine
Head Over Heels

Head
Over
Heels

Stephanie
Mittman

A DELL BOOK

Published by
DELL PUBLISHING
a division of
Random House, Inc.
1540 Broadway
New York, New York 10036

ISBN:0-7394-0748-1

Printed in the United States of America

When I was growing up, my mother used to say that her heart was like a rubber band—it stretched to encompass my father, both my sisters, and me.

This book is dedicated:

To Barbara Moher, whose heart has stretched to take care of many, many children and who keeps finding a little more give in the rubber band to love still more.

To Bernardine Fagan, who listened by phone to paragraph after paragraph until this became a whole book.

To my husband, Alan. People are always saying that my heroes are such decent men. Alan is the inspiration for every hero I've ever written about. He is my hero in real life.

To my children, for making me so proud that I work all the harder to make them proud in return.

To my sister Shelle, who read through the manuscript and laughed and cried at all the right places.

To my agent, Irene Goodman, who always tells me to "go for it."

And to my editor, Christine Zika, who insisted I fill in gaps, plug holes, and shore up lines until this manuscript became a book I could truly be proud of—

Thank you all from the bottom of my heart.

 # One

Deburle, Ohio
Summer, 1998

On her knees beside a tub filled with two slippery little girls wearing bubble halos, Nan Springfield pushed back the hair from her forehead and inhaled the sweet scent of baby shampoo and clean children. If there was a better smell than that, she surely wasn't aware of it. If there was a better time than bath time, or a better feeling than wrapping a fresh warm towel around a squeaky clean child, if there was anything sweeter than the sound of a three-year-old's giggles, well, she wasn't aware of those, either.

"One more rinse," she told Rachel, the older of the two little dark-haired mermaids. "You be a rose, now, and I'll be the gardener, watering you so that you'll grow." She directed the four-year-old's head under the spray attachment that she'd finally found in a pet shop. The sprayer worked just as well for washing little girls as it would have for the puppy she'd promised her son, Topher, when he'd turned seven.

That had been a mistake, making a promise that she'd been unable to keep. It still grated on her nerves that Phil had vetoed the dog and made her go back on her word. No, it was merely a delay, she reminded herself. She was still working on him, trying to change his mind.

There'd been a time, a million years ago when their marriage vows were fresh on their lips, that she surely could have convinced him that all good ministers have dogs, just as she'd convinced him, once Topher had started school, that they should take in foster children like the girls and poor little Derek James.

Now if she could just make him think that every pastor needed a collie . . .

A dog! What was she thinking? Her marriage needed another strain like a turtle needed antilock brakes. It scared her breathless that unless things changed between her and Phil, there was the awful chance that she could wind up training that dog on some lawyer's separation papers.

"I'm a rose, too!" Robin shouted. "Do me!" she demanded, scooting and swimming about the tub like some little lemming while Nan aimed the hose at her head in the hopes of getting some of the soap out before they all drowned laughing.

"Out you go now," Nan said as she turned off the water. "Roses need to sleep at night so they can bloom in the morning." *And mommies need their rest so that they can carpool and type the church bulletin and figure out how that infernal database thing works and pick up a clean T-shirt for Topher to paint on at church camp.*

She reached down and lifted Rachel out of the tub, setting her feet on the plush bath mat. Robin scrambled out behind her and was out the door before Nan could get a towel wrapped around either of them.

"Mom!" Topher whined from out in the hall. His voice held all the frustration an eight-year-old boy could cram into one word while being streaked by a three-year-old girl.

"Robin," Nan yelled after her for Topher's sake—half-heartedly, because she was sure the imp was already halfway down the hall and heading straight for the front door.

"Naked lady on the loose!" she called out to warn Phil while she quickly secured a towel around Rachel.

"Naked yady on the yoose!" Robin parroted as Nan chased after her, a Little Mermaid towel spread wide like a net to catch her in.

With her head turned back watching Nan and Rachel and Topher, all in hot pursuit, Robin ran smack up against Phil's legs and fell back onto her little behind with a rush of air.

Phil towered over the child. He wasn't a big man—just five nine, but he was imposing in his silence, and they all quieted immediately so that the only sound in the hall was Robin whimpering.

"For Pete's sake, Nan! The child is running around stark naked. Aren't there any sort of rules around here anymore?"

Nan knelt down and, with the towel in hand, wrapped her arms tightly around the little girl for a brief moment, wishing she could hold her forever, wishing she could claim her for more time than Social Services would allow. Rules? She didn't want to give the children rules—she wanted to give them memories.

"It's after nine o'clock." He stared accusingly at Nan, directing his words at her, as he always did. He rarely spoke to any of the children anymore except Topher. Exceptions could be made for their own flesh and blood, it seemed. "Is there no hope of peace and quiet tonight?"

"They're getting into their pj's now," she answered, nudging the girls and Topher back toward their bedrooms and reminding Topher not to wake up D.J., already asleep for hours in the room they shared.

"Okay, synchronize your freckles," she told the children, looking at her watch while they looked at their wrists.

"Meet me back here in three minutes, teeth brushed, pajamas on, foreheads ready for kisses from Dad."

She herded the children without looking back at Phil, who was no doubt grimacing at being called Robin and Rachel's dad. He wouldn't mind being called Father by a whole darn congregation, he just didn't seem to take well to it on a more personal level.

Phil didn't take too well to anything on a personal level anymore.

Not that she didn't still try.

After she'd tucked the children into their beds, kissed them good night, fetched a last drink of water, promised to love them forever, and turned out their lights, she changed into her nightgown and ran a brush through her hair.

She stared at herself in the mirror. Ten years older and seven pounds heavier than when Phil had married her. Should that make enough difference to make her unappealing? Had she changed so much that he just didn't love her anymore? Shouldn't he at least have a physical need for her after nearly ten months with him sleeping on the couch in the TV room while she slept alone in their bed?

She pulled her short-sleeved cotton robe from the hook behind the bathroom door and wrapped herself in its comfortable familiarity. Tightening the sash, she took a deep breath and headed out to try once more to break down the well-fortified wall between herself and Phil. Nearly out the bathroom door, she reached back in, sprayed a little Wind Song at the base of her neck, and then shut the light.

He was sitting at the kitchen table with stacks of papers spread out neatly before him. Sometimes she imagined them being interviewed by Barbara Walters—jeez, she imagined all sorts of ridiculous things!—and Barbara would ask, If they were vegetables, what kind would they be? Phil, she'd say, would be an ear of corn, all his kernels in neat little rows. She, on the other hand, would be a dented can of house-brand succotash.

If Phil were a plant, he'd be a saguaro cactus—no muss, no fuss, just straight and prickly. She'd be a daisy or a petunia or a dahlia, something that needed light, water, deadheading.

High maintenance. If it wasn't her needs, it was the children's. There was always something she needed from Phil that lately he found difficult, if not impossible, to give.

"Still working?" she asked as if there were nothing extraordinary about this night, as if she hadn't come to some sort of decision in her mind about how much more she could stand.

He nodded without looking up.

She reached for the kettle and filled it from the tap. Once upon a time they'd ended every evening with a nice civilized cup of Earl Grey or Royal House Blend. "I'm making some tea," she said softly. "Would you like a cup?"

"Now?" he asked, looking up at her as if she'd asked him to fix the television antenna in an electrical storm. "It's too late for tea now. I'll be up all night."

Once upon a time they could find a way to fill the hours of the night. . . .

"Not that I ever sleep anyway," he added.

Say it! Say it! she demanded silently. *Say because I'm not there beside you. Ask to come back to our bed and our life—or tell me it's time to give up and let go.*

He shuffled the papers and made some notes on a yellow legal pad. "I couldn't find the evening paper," he said. Not *I miss you, Nan.* Nothing so much as that.

"The sprinkler got it," she said with a sigh.

"Great. My life is going to hell in a handcart and I can't even read about it in black and white."

"What are you talking about?" She measured out the loose tea, an art she'd learned from Phil's sister, Eleanor, and poured the boiling water into the pot over the leaves.

"Nothing. Never mind," he said, resting his forehead on the back of his hand. "How was your day? The kids give you much trouble?"

She pulled out the chair across from Phil's and sat down with one leg curled up beneath her, eager to share a casual moment. "Dee and I took the kids down to Paint Creek Lake—"

"All the way over there?" Phil asked. "What's the matter with the creek behind our house? The creek's not good enough for these kids?"

These kids. How that grated. She wanted to ask him just what he meant, but knew the dangers of being sidetracked into an argument, and so she said, "The lake is there, and that little beach, and there's room for rafting." She knew it was the gas to get there and not the destination that bothered him. "And we took Dee's car." Everything these days was about money.

"Did you have fun?" he asked, his eyes on the legal pad in front of him, on which he scratched out a series of numbers, then drew lines with arrows on both ends.

Was he listening? "Oh, yes," she said with enthusiasm she didn't feel. "We all drowned. The funeral is tomorrow."

"That's good," he said, the words a dismissal. As far as he was concerned, the conversation was over.

She'd let him do it to her time and again for the better part of a year. She'd let him tell her that she was just imagining things with D.J.—that the boy's not looking her in the eye, his hating to be touched, meant nothing. She'd let

Phil tell her that his moving out of their room was temporary and personal, having only to do with him.

And he'd forced her to bite at little things—like *these
kids*—to keep her away from big ones. But tonight there
would be no arguments over the children or the lawn or
whether she'd spelled a parishioner's name wrong in the
Weathervane.

"Phil," she said, screwing up her courage so that her
voice came out a bit squeaky. "Patty Murdock told me
there's a guy who does marriage counseling for free over at
the First Methodist Church on Thursday nights."

"Why would Patty Murdock be telling you that?" His
eyes were sharp and she felt them bore into her even after
she'd turned her back on him to strain the tea.

"You know how she's always telling me that First Meth
is a better church than ours," she lied. "She was saying how
they feed the poor, and have Bingo for the old folks on
Wednesday, and how now they have this counselor on
Thursdays."

"Well, those Methodists have a lot more to work with. If
I had their congregation . . ." he said, gesturing for her to
pour him a cup of tea, even though he'd already told her he
didn't want one.

"Maybe we could go—you know, sort of just check him
out to invite him to the Old Deburle Church."

"No."

"*No?* That's it? *No?* You promised me that things would
get better, Phil, and all you can say is *no?*"

"It was a nice try, Nan," he said, scratching off more
numbers with such vengeance that it snapped off the tip of
his pencil. "But I know what you're up to. We don't need a
marriage counselor. Even if we did, it's out of the question.

People come to me with their problems. How would it look if I went running to someone else?"

"*How would it look?* Why is that always the first consideration to everything we do? It would look like our marriage is in trouble, Phil, which is the truth. You promised me you'd do something about it, but as far as I can see, you've done nothing. In the last year, you've spent more time with our checkbook than you have with me."

When he didn't say anything in response, she asked, "Is it our own finances or the church's that have you so tied up?"

He looked up at her as if he couldn't understand what she was asking him. "I am the church, aren't I?" he asked, as if he were truly unable to make the separation.

"I thought you were my husband—the man I married," was all she could manage to answer.

"I am a lot more than that, Nan, and you know it. I'm the spiritual leader of a whole congregation, and there are some problems that concern me that do not revolve around you. It's time you grew up and learned that a minister has to worry about his whole flock. The problems that exist here have nothing to do with you. I wish they did. I wish it were that simple. But I will work it out. I'll find a way to fix everything and then we can pick up where we left off—"

"Excuse me? Did you really just say that our marriage problems have nothing to do with me?" Her heart pounded in her chest. "What does that mean? Is there someone else?" It made all the sense in the world. Maybe he didn't need her physical comfort because he was finding comfort with someone else.

"There is a whole world, Nan. There is a congregation and session and elders. There are bankers and brokers and people that will stand in line to judge me. And there's me. I have to live with myself."

"And which of those people are you having an affair with?" she demanded.

"Didn't you hear me? I have to live with myself. Do you think that on top of everything else I would break my vows to you? That I ever broke them? I have no desire to break them." He looked up at her and then looked quickly away. "I have no desire at all."

"Why not?" she asked, looking down at her sensible robe and scuffs. Was she supposed to wear some black silky teddy and high-heeled mules?

He pounded his fist on the pile of papers that sat on the table. "Because I have work to do and things on my mind. Because I have a million responsibilities—and you on top of them, with all those kids, trying to be your stupid Nanny Annie all over again. Do you know what four coats for those children to wear to church this fall is going to set me back?"

"Maybe I could get some from that charity group. You know, the Columbus Newsies. They give clothing to poor children all the time," she said sarcastically. "And don't you go calling my great-grandmother stupid. Annie Morrow was an incredible woman and I'd die happy if one day Topher gets the same look on his face when he's talking about me that my Grandpa Isaac used to get when he talked about her!"

"If only she'd been a Catholic, they could have made her a saint." He broke a cookie in two, examined one half and then put it back on the tray. "Raising all those brothers and sisters of hers. You'd think all those kids would have driven her crazy. Of course, they were her own flesh and blood, and she was stuck with them. . . . If we had a normal life . . ."

Ah, the same old merry-go-round. The same old ride. She was a fool to board it, but she couldn't help herself. "What's normal? And what's not normal about taking in children whose parents can't love them right now?" she asked him. "You're a minister. You should welcome the opportunity to—"

"Love them *right now*? You don't see the scars on Robin's arms? What's gonna happen when it's time to give them back, Nan?" He pushed all the papers in a pile and came to his feet. "What happens if I'm not here to pick up the pieces you're going to fall into when they pull those girls out of your arms and hand them over to a clean-for-a-day junkie mother?"

"Not here?" she asked quietly. The thought of him leaving had never entered her mind before, and it stunned her so that she spilled the hot tea and nearly scalded the back of her hand. "Are you leaving me? Is that what you're planning with all this financial maneuvering?"

He laughed. It was the saddest sound that Nan had ever heard, sadder than the keening her father had done beside her mother's grave.

"Financial maneuvering, huh? Want to watch the financial wizard at work? Want to see me make some more money disappear?"

"I asked you if you're planning to divorce me," she said, the word tasting funny and unwelcome on her tongue.

"Why do you always want to talk about these things at midnight?" he asked. "No, I don't want a divorce. I want to do some work." He scooped up snippets of papers and bills and receipts. "I'll go into the den so that you can turn out the lights in here and go on to bed."

"Work?" Nan heard her voice crack as she shrieked. "Are you kidding? You talk about leaving and then say you want to do some work? This marriage is your work. Topher and I are your work! Making money for the church is not your work, we are. And you know what, Reverend Springfield? You are in danger of losing your job!"

He stood, his papers clutched to his body all willy-nilly. "I never said I was leaving, Nan. I merely asked how it would be if I were no longer here. There's a difference. Now, why not just go on to bed like a good girl and we can talk about this later, when I'm not so busy."

And then he simply turned on his heel, expecting her to quietly acquiesce, the way she had been doing for nearly a year. What a mistake that had been—thinking that he'd come crawling back into her bed and her life if she just gave him enough space to miss her.

"I can't, Phil, because there is no *later*. I can't do this anymore. Do you know what I thought to myself when I asked you if you wanted a divorce? I thought maybe that wouldn't be so awful. Maybe our being divorced wouldn't be as awful as our being married." She drew in a deep breath and steeled herself to say words she never believed she'd have to say when she married the minister who had replaced her father at the pulpit. "If you won't go for some sort of counseling with me, then whether you want it or not, I think maybe I want a divorce."

"Great," he said sarcastically. "I tell you my life is a mess and your answer is to bail out. Well, I have enough trouble as it is right now. I don't need any more."

"Is that all you can say? Not 'I love you'? Not once in the last year have you said that. Not once have you even said that you missed me or you so much as like my company."

"Is *my* love in question here tonight? Or is yours? Have I

ever not stood beside you, through your sorrows, your joys? Have I stopped you from taking in every stray that's come down the pike? What more do you want from me?" He put his head in his hands. "What do you all expect of me? I'm only a man."

"And I'm your wife. I'd face the devil with you, if you'd let me, but—"

"And no doubt you'd stand up better than I. But then, you've never really been tested—"

The telephone rang, startling them both. She clutched at her robe and stared at the phone on the wall while Phil crossed the kitchen and answered it. "Reverend Springfield," he declared into the phone, as professional as ever despite the hour and the fact that at the moment he seemed to have more troubles than any of his parishioners could have.

"What?" Phil said into the phone. "It's after midnight, Stan. Can't this wait until the morning?"

"What is it?" Nan asked, coming closer to the phone. They had called her at 2 A.M. to take the girls when there was nowhere else for them to go. Emergencies happened at night. She leaned closer to Phil to hear what the caller was saying. He smelled pungent. Sharp. It wasn't an offensive smell, but it was disconcerting. Nan thought he smelled like fear.

"You'd better turn on the radio," she could hear the voice say while Phil tried to back away from her. "Call me when—"

"Nan is here with me," Phil said, pulling away from her so that she couldn't hear what the man said in response. After a moment he sputtered something about not being able to, then something more about waiting until the morning. "All right, all right," he finally agreed, tapping the button on the phone to disconnect the call and then leaving the receiver on the counter.

"Was that Stan Denham?" she asked Phil. "What did he want at this hour?"

Phil fiddled with the radio, his hand visibly shaking. "What station is WCGA?"

"WGCA?" Nan corrected. "Ten-fifty, I think. It's one of those all-talk stations on AM."

"Too much talk," he said as the static cleared and the voice on the radio boomed.

"Jeez! The wheel's turning, but the hamster's dead. Try to concentrate now, will you? I just told you that this thing, this D-linc, is like a walkie-talkie between your home computer and whatever you've got with you on the road—"

"I don't want a link with what I've got with me on the road other than maybe a set of handcuffs," a second voice replied. *"Listen, Suit, for the first time in all the years we've been on radio together, will you just shut your trap and listen? I'm trying to talk to you about my sister's boy's scholarship and you want to talk about some stupid stock."*

Phil's face was ashen. His leg shook impatiently.

"What is this a—" Nan started, but Phil waved his hand at her to stop talking.

"All right, Ross," Suit said. *"We'll just put all the callers on hold and pretend for a minute that I give a damn about your sister's kid's scholarship. Let's make me the patron saint of hopeless causes. I could wear a towel on my shoulder and you and everyone else could cry on it. They could change my name to Harris Terry instead of Tweed and people could cry all over my suit."*

"That has interesting possibilities, Tweed," Ross said.

In their kitchen, Phil rolled his eyes.

"But wet suits aside, the point is my sister's son won this

scholarship back in November—nice because then he could put it all over his college applications. My sister says that sort of thing looks good—awarded the Eastman Annual Scholarship from the Old Deburle Church on the 'awards and honors' line."

Nan stared at the radio in utter disbelief. It was her father's scholarships they were talking about. He'd set up the first one with the proceeds from the fall church fair the year before he died. That one had grown along with the fair every year until this year they'd been able to award ten scholarships with the profits.

"I can just hear everyone out there applauding for your nephew. Quite a din. . . . Oh, sorry. That's snoring I hear. Maybe I better take a call . . ."

"In a second. This is right up your alley, Suit—the kid starts college in two weeks, and no check yet."

"No moola?" Mr. Suit or whatever his name was, asked, apparently very interested now.

"No money?" Nan repeated. "But those checks always go out the first of August."

Phil wiped at the sweat that beaded on his upper lip. She knew he was busy, but the kids needed that money. They needed it now.

"You've a caller on line two from Pittsburgh," a third voice said.

"Put him on hold, Ray," Suit said. *"Ross, I assume your sister called the church?"*

"They promised the money two weeks ago."

Phil turned his back on Nan and looked out the window as rain pelted the glass in the darkness.

"You mean to say that they promised your nephew the money in November and here it is August and the kid still hasn't seen dime one?"

"Well, it's not as if he's supposed to get the check before

the beginning of August," Nan told the radio, as if they could hear her.

"He'll have the money," Phil said without turning around. "They all will."

"*Tell you what I think, Suit,*" Ross said, but Suit interrupted him.

"*No one cares what you think, Ross. It's what I think that matters. And the Suit thinks there's something rotten in the Old Church of Deburle, and it ain't just the box lunches. Smells to the Suit like misappropriation, smells like bookjuggling. Smells like theft.*"

"*Now, Suit, you can't just go accusing a church of—*"

"You certainly can't," Nan agreed, but her voice came out more shaky than indignant, and she wished that Phil would turn around and say how ridiculous the man's accusations were.

"*Have you talked to this reverend?*" Suit asked.

"*Directly. As I said, he promised the check two weeks ago,*" Ross said. "*Spoke to one of the church elders, too, and he said that the reverend took care of the scholarship money himself, so it seems to me that some honest mistake—*"

"*Honest mistake,*" Suit said with a humph. "*Honest my ass. You said the kid still hasn't gotten the check.*"

Phil turned around, his face whiter still, and looked past her at the clock on the wall.

"*Well, no, but—*"

"*So tell me, is this blindness a self-imposed condition or did your mother have herpes?*" Suit asked. Nan expected Phil to look as appalled as she felt, but instead he just rubbed his finger across the counter as if he needed to erase something that wasn't even there. "*I mean, come on, Ross. Surely there is some hanky-panky going on over there. . . .*"

"You see hanky-panky everywhere," Ross said. *"Maybe that's 'cause you aren't getting any anymore."*

"Well, I bet the reverend's getting some. Maybe down in Grand Cayman where your nephew's scholarship is invested in some nice little house with the reverend's name on the mailbox."

"Thirty-five thousand down there would be a tidy little nest egg, Suit. Buy him a happy little housemaid, too," the other man said, followed by a round of snickering. *"Springfield's Inn,"* he added.

"Your idiot nephew won a thirty-five-thousand-dollar scholarship?" It sounded as if Suit has just spit out a mouthful of coffee. *"Shit."*

"It was *ten* thirty-five-hundred-dollar scholarships," Nan explained. Then she wanted to smack herself for talking to a nasty man on the radio when she should have been talking to Phil. "And his must have just gone astray," she said to Phil, waiting for him to agree.

Ross told Suit the same thing about there being ten scholarships. Only then he added that his nephew had checked with the other kids, and none of them had gotten their money.

"Oh boy. It sounds to me like Springfield's in deep!"

"Phil?" Nan asked, feeling for a chair with the back of her legs and lowering herself into it. "Why haven't the kids gotten their money yet?" Phil reached for the phone book, flipping pages until one of them tore in two.

"Are you implying that the minister himself took the funds?"

"The man wins a Harris Tweed Suit!"

"He's a minister, for Christ's sake!" Ross said. *"I never meant to imply that a minister—"*

"And we've all never heard of Jim Bakker, just to drop one name. But if you wanna believe there's just been some oversight and that ten kids' checks all got lost in the mail, well, I've got a

deed in my pocket for the Brooklyn Bridge," Suit said. *"And I'd like your check before your brain engages. My bet's on the house in Grand Cayman. I got three little words for you . . ."* He let a lull build tension, in Nan's heart, in her house, in her town, before adding, *"Guilty as sin."*

She studied the papers that still rested on the table. There were arrows that pointed from *PS* to *ODC* and back again. *Phil Springfield. Old Deburle Church. I am the church, aren't I?* he'd said. "Oh, Phil! You didn't somehow take the kids' money, did you?" she asked as he fumbled with the phone book and squinted at the pages.

"Some jerk you never saw in your life makes an assumption about your own husband and you believe him?" he asked as he found the number for WGCA. Not that calling Suit would help. Harris Tweed was getting the tar melted and the chickens plucked for Phil's congregation while some jingle played about cars and trucks.

"You wanna hear what the public thinks about men of God?" Suit asked. *"You wanna go to the phones?"*

Phil dialed the number, smacked the receiver button, and then dialed the number again.

"Busy. The man slanders me, blackens my name, and then takes the phone off the hook so that I can't explain."

"Explain?" Nan asked. "What do you mean, *explain?* It's true?"

"Before we hear from Jeffrey in Columbus, I just gotta admit that it's hard to blame this reverend guy for looking for a little action. You ever see a minister's wife? I mean, a woman who marries a minister hasn't exactly scribbled 'for a good time call Candy' in any turnpike restrooms."

"Now, Suit, don't go picking on the poor little woman just because your wife—"

"That was my fault," Suit said. *"I thought it said 'for a*

helluva time call Susie.' I only found out later that it said *'hellish'*—*'for a hellish time call Susie.'* And it was."

"Well, I'm sure the reverend's wife—"

"Reverends don't do it with their wives. Nobody does it with a reverend's wife. Eew. Think they burn altar candles by the bed?"

"Turn off the radio, Phil. We'll go see the church elders in the morning and you can tell them your side of it."

"*I* will straighten it out," he shouted, his face red as he slammed his fist on the counter. "Not you. Somehow, *I* will get it all straightened out."

She stared at him under the harsh kitchen lights. And she knew that Suit's words were true, all of them. Even down to the line about reverends not sleeping with their wives.

"You think I've been socking the church's money away. I can see it in your face. So what explains why I fight with you over every grocery bill?" She followed him into the hall, dogging his footsteps, nearly getting her nose crushed when he opened the closet door.

No, she told herself. It couldn't be. This was Phil, her husband and her minister. He would never steal anyone's money, let alone the church's.

"Don't you think we need to talk about this?" Nan asked. It was so like him to just shut her out, as if none of this had anything to do with her. "If you took the money—"

"That Harris Tweed said I stole the money, not me. I never said I stole anything. You just leaped to that conclusion after ten years of marriage," he said, snatching up an umbrella from the corner and heading for the door. "*Despite* ten years. Whatever happened to blind faith, Nan? Is that too much to ask?"

She tried, but the words of faith and trust just wouldn't come. "It's pouring out there. Where are you going?" she said instead.

"I'm going down to that radio station to give Harris Tweed a piece of my mind," he said, throwing the umbrella onto the porch and stepping out into the rain.

"We need to talk when you get home, Phil. I mean it," she said on the top step as he turned up his collar.

"Don't wait up," he said, turning to look at her. He added something that sounded like she would need her rest and then he stepped out into the storm, heading to the curb where his nine-month-old Ford Taurus was parked.

He turned, his hair shiny with the rain, and looked at her as if he was wondering if she'd be there when he got back. She nodded, a silent answer to a silent question.

"I'll be here when you get back," she said softly, unsure if he could even hear her with the rain drumming against the roof of the car.

She repeated it again to no one after she'd closed the door on the night and leaned with all her weight against it. "Heaven help me, Phil Springfield. I'll be here."

Two

The sun had been up nearly an hour when Harry Woolery slipped out of the broadcast booth at WGCA and reached for the Best's Cleaning Service cap that guarded his anonymity. Harry had been scrupulously careful to keep a chasm between his radio persona, Harris Tweed, and himself ever since an irate fan had forced him and his very pregnant wife off the road.

Not *his* wife. Not anymore. Suzanne was somebody else's wife now. Somebody else was tucking Harry's son under the covers and crawling into bed beside Harry's wife. Well, maybe a wife could stop being a wife, but a son would always be a son, and Harry might have had to let Suzanne go, but he would never sever the ties with Josh.

"Great show," Ross said as they headed for the cleaning company's van.

Harry nodded, and got into the driver's side while Ross went around to the other door. Maybe all these precautions were just an ego trip—wishful thinking that anyone cared who the hell Harris Tweed really was anymore.

"You all right?" Ross asked when they'd pulled around some yellow *Police Line—Do Not Cross* tape at the end of Station Road, where the aftermath of an accident was being cleaned up and Harry still hadn't said a word.

When they passed the old penitentiary site, Harry asked, "Think Josh is getting sick of going out to the farm every other weekend?" finally committing to words the worries that had been rattling around in his head for days.

"Your father's place?" Ross asked. "What kid doesn't like a horse farm?"

Harry hadn't. He'd spent his summers hosing down horses while his friends went off to camps and on trips with their parents. He'd spent his autumns shoveling horse shit while his friends played football. He'd spent his winters clearing paths to the stables and making sure the horses' water hadn't frozen as solid as his blood had felt. He'd spent his springs watching foals kick their way into the world, and just when he'd become attached to them, he'd watched his father sell them off.

And now he was dragging Josh out there every other weekend so that they could pretend they were still a family.

"It's just that I think it's important for him to know his grandfather, don't you think?" Harry asked. "I want the kid growing up knowing Nate is his grandpa, not Charles Riteman's dad, even if he's getting confused about who his own father is."

"Josh isn't a two-year-old," Ross countered as Harry took the turnoff to the parking garage where his car, a flashy white Shelby Mustang with red interior, was waiting. "He knows you're his dad."

Harry hoped so. Seven was an impressionable age. His mom had died and his dad had sold Buck when Harry was seven. "I'm just living temporarily with Nate, and as long as I'm there, I think it's good for him to get to know the old man," he said.

"It's nice for Nate, too," Ross said. "He must be happy to have the kid around."

Harry snorted. "The only thing that would make Nate happy would be if I quit the radio and took up shoveling shit again. The man honestly believes that if you don't stink at the end of the day, you haven't put in an honest day's work."

"How about if you shovel shit all night and stink first thing in the morning?" Ross asked.

"Hey, it was a good show," Harry said defensively. "That bit about that crooked reverend sure took off. I haven't seen the phones that busy since the Indians whipped Yankee butt. That poor bastard's sure gonna be doing a lot of explaining to his church come Sunday."

"And well he ought to," Ross said. "My nephew needs that check, and if it turns out that the reverend's got the greed and he's done the deed, well, then he oughtta bleed."

Harry cringed. "You taking lessons from one of O.J.'s lawyers? That's awful."

"Oh yeah. So I guess you won't be using it tonight," Ross teased. Harry probably would, at that.

"You know, I really don't get off bad-mouthing defenseless preachers. Give me a politician and I'll grind him to pulp, but a reverend. . . . Jeez, I like thinking they're aboveboard. Somebody's gotta have morals, right?" The admission embarrassed him. Had he been with anyone but Ross, he'd have never said something so soft bellied. But Ross knew him inside and out, from those first days in Tulsa at KFKU where Harry had been grateful for the graveyard shift on a two-thousand-watt radio station even the FCC probably hadn't heard of. Ross had been the one he'd called when Josh had been born, and Ross had been the one who'd gotten blind drunk with him the day the divorce was final.

"You going out to Suzanne's now?" Ross asked when Harry stopped the motor.

"Don't I go out every morning?" Charles had Josh's nights, but Harry had his days. He drove him to school each morning, went back to his father's place to sleep, and then picked him up at school or camp and drove him to soccer or hockey or Little League. Today was camp until five o'clock. He'd take the boy to Dairy Queen on the way home, probably as much to annoy Suzanne as because Josh would like it.

"Tell the kid to hit one out for me," Ross said as he slid over on the seat to take the van back to the station. Harry nodded and waved as he folded up his body, tucked his knees under his nose and wondered when he'd grow up and get a car that fit him.

He drove for nearly an hour in silence, thinking about his dad, his son, the branches that the summer storm had broken and sent to the ground, and the way his life was turning out. He'd set out to be a "radio personality"—a shock jock like the guys in New York—and turned out to be just one more overnight guy with an obnoxious attitude conversing over the airwaves with other obnoxious guys who would otherwise be alone in the dark. The poor man's psychologist. The Doctor Ruth of people that didn't have sexual troubles because they probably didn't have sex. They, like he, were just too insufferable for anyone to cozy up to.

About a mile from Suzanne's new house, he flipped on the radio.

"*. . . tea. So I'd say that any of them, tablets, elixir, tea, are all gonna help your memory, as long as you're getting fifty milligrams a day of the best ginkgo biloba you can get your hands on.*"

Maybe that was it. Maybe he had too much natural

ginkgo biloba in his system. He couldn't forget anything. Not what Josh used to smell like when he'd pick him up and put him into his crib, not what Suzanne's skin felt like after a bath, not what his father's voice sounded like when he'd come looking for him that day in the barn.

"And in the news, the Reverend Philip Springfield was involved in a fatal one-car collision last night at the corner of Route 33 and Station Road. Police report that the Reverend Springfield was apparently on his way to confront WGCA talk show host Harris Tweed after some of the church's financial dealings were questioned on Tweed After Dark. . . ."

Harry slowed the car and eased it to a stop by the side of the road. It took him two tries to put the gearshift into park, and he fought the door handle as if the devil himself were holding the other side closed.

". . . he leaves a wife, Nancy, and eight-year-old son, Chistopher. Services will be—"

Harry pushed open the door and leaned his head out of the car. He managed to take in one deep breath.

And then he heaved.

☂ Three

Harry stood in the hot August sun watching as the coffin of the Reverend Philip Springfield was borne down the steps of the white clapboard church by six somber men. Following behind them was a woman who looked brittle enough for a good breeze to break her. Instead it just ruffled some blond curls and played with the hem of her dress as if it had no regard for the solemnity of the occasion.

She didn't look like a woman for whom a man would steal, especially from the church. But then, how good a judge of women was he? Maybe all women wanted more than their husbands could give them. Suzanne had. Maybe Nancy Springfield had, too.

Beside the woman, whose features seemed to soften as he watched, was a boy about Josh's age clinging to her arm. There were more children behind them, shepherded by relatives, but apparently happy to be out in the sunshine. They were too young to know about the pain, the loss, the aching that never wholly went away.

He stood by the truck he'd borrowed from his father, knowing that his white Shelby Mustang didn't belong there any more than he did. *Nothing wrong with paying your respects,* his father had said, but Harry didn't believe his respects would be very well received at this particular funeral. Not after Vernon Springfield, the reverend's brother, had called the station and threatened to sue Harris Tweed, Ross Winston, WGCA, and anybody else he could think of.

Ah! Love thy neighbor, and all that religious rot. Was it his fault those scholarship checks never got where they were going? Was it his fault that neither did the reverend?

He shouldn't have come at all, he told himself as he followed the crowd to the grave site, keeping his distance, measuring his breaths to stop himself from yelling out that he was sorry for something that he knew was only marginally, so infinitesimally, his fault.

A man drives into a tree, Ross said, *and it's his fault or the tree's. Not yours.*

Did that pretty lady with the kids surrounding her know that? When she explained to that little boy that Daddy wouldn't be coming home anymore, would she tell him it was no one's fault? Or would she say that Daddy was vilified on the radio and the poor man was on his way to call the coward out?

Just in front of him, a man and his wife walked slowly toward the grave site. "I'm telling you, it was suicide," the man said.

"Stop that, Stanley," his wife replied. "The police don't think so, and it'll hurt Nan Springfield if you say otherwise."

"A little rain doesn't make a man drive clear across the road, does it?"

Harry was glad that the man wasn't talking to him, because he wouldn't have been able to answer any more than he could breathe. He loosened his tie just slightly—not enough to show any disrespect to the dead, just enough to draw a breath. *Suicide?* He felt the sweat begin to drip down his temple, and touched the back of his hand to it.

"I shouldn't have called him at that hour," the man said. "Everything looks worse in the middle of the night."

"Maybe he would have heard that radio show anyway," his wife said. The man looked at his wife as if she were crazy for thinking that the reverend would have been listening to Harry. All pride aside, Harry knew he had plenty of closet listeners, but the idea that the reverend was one of them seemed no more likely to him than it did to this man Stanley.

"It coulda been me," the man said. "So casily, it coulda been me."

"Don't even say such a thing," his wife said. "It gives me the shivers. If he took the money, Stanley, it wasn't your fault. You're his accountant, not his keeper. If he told you he put it in a separate account, what were you supposed to do, ask to see the passbook?"

"I'm the church's accountant, not Phil Springfield's. You and the rest of them shouldn't jump to any wrong conclusions."

"Don't be an idiot, Stanley," the woman said. "Do you think they'll take the children away? Not Topher, of course, but the others? The foster ones?"

"Well, I suppose she'll have to give the church back the house," he said.

Not far away, Harry could see people coming up to the reverend's widow offering their condolences. A thousand people shook her hand, a million people hugged her, and all the while he could see her try to smile even as she swiped at tears.

Reverends don't do it with their wives. My God! Had he really said that on the air?

"This just kills me. Damn Harris Tweed! If it wasn't for him, none of this would have happened."

Two older women, their dresses belted high over their bellies, walked by. "Oh, but this must just be killing Nan," one of them said. "You know if the reverend did take that money, that poor woman will no doubt try to pay it back."

"As if she doesn't have enough to worry about! What bothers me is poor little Topher. Imagine growing up with that over his head, poor thing," the other one said as they hurried to catch up with the group that stood waiting to hear their reverend eulogized.

Harry stared at Nancy Springfield and the boy beside her. He watched her pat the child's hair into place and straighten his tie for him. He supposed she'd put it on the boy herself, explaining the seriousness of the occasion much as Harry's father had done when his mother had died.

He took a few steps closer to the group as someone whispered something to the woman. She nodded, turned, and kissed two little girls and straightened the barrettes in their hair. She kneeled near the smallest of the children, a little boy, took a small toy truck out of her purse and put it on the ground near him, and then stood back up. Then, her son's hand in hers, she took up a spot near the end of the casket and bowed her head.

Harry bowed his, as well, and while he'd be the first to admit he wasn't a religious man, he began to pray. He prayed for Nancy Springfield and the boy at her side. He prayed for the church's accountant, wracked with doubt about how the man's minister had met his death. He prayed for his mother, that she rest in peace. He stopped short of praying for himself, unsure whether he deserved any sort of mercy or forgiveness. He reminded himself that he hadn't caused Phil Springfield's death and finally assured himself that there was no absolution needed.

"Don't say anything to Nan about me thinking it was suicide," the man said to his wife. He wiped his nose again and shoved his hankie back into his pocket. "The woman's got enough on her plate, don't you think?"

Harry saw Nancy Springfield's shoulders shaking, saw her body sway back and forth as if she had no center of balance anymore, and figured that yeah, she had enough on her plate, all right.

As people clustered around the reverend's wooden coffin, perched on stretcher bars above the hole in the ground into which it would be lowered for all eternity, words rang out in the breeze.

". . . man of God now serves at his side . . ."

"Is my father in that box?" At the boy's words, Harry squeezed his eyes shut.

". . . beloved by all who knew him . . ."

"He can't breathe in there!" the child shouted, and Harry opened his eyes to see the sea of people parting and one small boy barreling through them blindly.

He hardly had to move at all to block the child's way, to crouch and catch him and press him against his chest to share his hurt. *I've been there,* he wanted to say. *I know how much this hurts, how deep the blackness goes.* He wished he could say the boy would get over it, put it behind him, forget it.

"It'll get better," he said instead. "I promise."

He patted the boy's back and saw a pair of lady's black pumps crossing the grass, eating up the distance that had kept him away from the bereaved.

He raised his eyes and blinked up toward Nancy Springfield, the sun half blinding him while he tried to make out her face. He winced, not knowing if it was the strong sun or the woman's sad face that hurt his eyes.

"Topher," she said softly, caressing the top of the child's head. At her touch he turned from Harry and melted against his mother's legs, his head buried in her belly, his cries muffled by the soft black cloth. "I shouldn't have brought you," she said, tears streaking her cheeks, while the rest of her children came rushing behind her.

"I don't want him to be dead," the boy said, choking on his sobs.

"No one wants him to be dead," she answered him. "And I'm sure he didn't want to die." She said the last with a certain determination, as if someone else might have hinted otherwise.

"Come, son," a man said, nodding a thanks toward Harry and reaching for the boy's hand. "Your father would have wanted to be proud of you today. Don't make him or your mother ashamed."

Fire flashed in Nancy Springfield's green eyes. She came to her full height, which didn't bring her up to Harry's shoulder, and pulled the child's hand into her own. "I have never been prouder of Christopher than I am right now," she said through gritted teeth. She put her arm around a little girl who had begun to sniffle. "I'm proud of them all." Then she extended her hand to Harry and said, "Thanks for being here. I mean, catching Topher and all."

"I'm glad I was here for him," Harry said honestly as someone came toward them, no doubt to lead them all back to the service.

"Vernon Springfield," the man who had tried to take Topher's hand said, extending his hand and waiting for Harry to explain just who he was and what he was doing there.

"Harry Woolery," he said quietly, pointing vaguely into the distance. "I was just visiting my mother's grave."

"Yes, well. You'll have to excuse Nan," Vernon Spring-field said, gesturing toward the reverend's widow. He didn't elaborate further, just turned on his heel and brought up the rear of the procession.

Harry hated him with a passion, and had the uneasy sense that the feeling was returned. He reminded himself that Nancy Springfield—*Nan*—was going to need someone to lean on and she was lucky to have the reverend's brother there for her.

It didn't make Harry hate him one iota less.

It didn't make getting back in his dad's pickup any easier, or heading off to one of Josh's baseball games any easier, or wondering about the Widow Springfield's finances any easier, either.

Once Suzanne had accused him of hiding behind an on-the-air personality not because he was worried about his family's safety, but because he was ashamed of what he did for a living. Was there some kernel of truth buried in those spiteful words she'd hurled at him?

He sighed and let his shoulders sag. He hated soul-searching. Especially on hot August days that were made for fishing or getting lost in the pine woods.

Vernon Springfield was wrong if he thought that they needed to sue him for the few dollars he had; he'd be perfectly willing to donate to some memorial fund for the crooked reverend. But he'd be damned if he'd say he was sorry.

Unless, of course, he was wrong.

If Nan thought that the funeral was the worst thing she would ever go through, it was only because she was as shortsighted as Phil always said. And even as hard as it was to entertain an entire congregation in her home once the funeral was over, and to receive the tearful condolences of people who loved her while she caught traces of the whispered speculations and accusations of those who apparently didn't, the worst was still to come.

Now, after all the Eastmans and Morrows who were her aunts and uncles and cousins had headed back to Van Wert, she sat in the living room with Phil's sister, Eleanor, his brother Vernon, and Vernon's wife and their two daughters. She felt an emptiness so complete, an abyss so wide, a chasm so deep, that she just knew, deep in her heart, deep in her soul, that there was no hope of surviving it.

Vernon was ranting about Harris Tweed and the nerve he'd had to send flowers to the funeral. Vernon had sent them back without even asking Nan. Not that she disagreed for a moment. After all his help, she would have to be eternally grateful to Vernon. The man had dropped everything and come flying in from Pittsburgh to complete the funeral arrangements she'd only begun. He'd finished making the calls. He'd commandeered two ladies from one of the church circles to watch all the girls, assigned his wife the task of greeting mourners, and then directed Eleanor to oversee the setting out of the offerings of Deburle into a spread the likes of which the town had never seen.

"This is such a shame," Vernon's wife, Adele, kept repeating as she smiled sadly at Nan. "Phil had so much to live for, so much more to do. And you were such a help to him. A team. You were a team and now—"

"And now, on top of the hurt and the pain, the agony of her loss, she's up a creek financially. It would have killed him! I won't stand for it. I'll sue that Tweed's house out from under him," Vernon said.

Topher's head snapped up. "Then where will he live?"

"I'll ask the ladies to take the children out into the yard," Nan said, but Vernon put up his hand.

"Send them outside for the neighbors to see them playing on the same day we've buried Phil?" He shook his head. "Eleanor can take them into their rooms for a rest."

"I'll take them," Nan said. She wasn't sure whether she hoped to give them comfort or to receive it. She only knew that she couldn't sit with Phil's family and accept their kindnesses as though she'd been a perfect wife.

"You'll do nothing of the sort," Eleanor said. "You will eat some dinner and change out of that awful dress and lie down yourself."

Sweet Eleanor, who for all her trying could never hide her sadness. Nan could hardly look at her without hurting for her, wishing she could heal the wounds that cut her sister-in-law so deeply.

Nan's father always said that the mistakes we made followed us wherever we went. Eleanor's mistake didn't have to follow her—she carried it with her in one small box which she'd brought with her to Deburle shortly after Phil had taken over the ministry of the church—a box that contained her daughter's birth certificate, the adoption papers she'd signed giving her away, one tiny lock of her hair, and all the guilt one woman could bear.

She'd taken a small apartment and gotten a job caring for elderly people who couldn't take care of themselves. Outside of work, she devoted herself to Phil and Nan and the kids, and any spare time she had was spent berating herself and licking her wounds.

And Nan understood now that Eleanor's spirit ached in a way that Nan couldn't hope to heal.

Because now Nan herself was beyond helping, too.

"I'm all right," she told Eleanor.

"You're better than all right," Eleanor said warmly, squeezing her shoulder just enough to keep her in her chair. "Always were, always will be in my book."

And with those kind, sweet words, Nan felt herself slip right over the edge. Tears leaked out from behind tightly shut eyes, sobs escaped through tightly bitten lips.

"I wonder if that brother of mine had even the slightest inkling as to how lucky he was." Eleanor perched on the arm of the well-worn club chair and pulled Nan against her. Topher threw himself into her lap, suddenly younger than his eight grown-up years. The girls hung back in the doorway, eyes wide and bright, Rachel holding on to Robin as if she sensed that they weren't part of this family tragedy, which only made Nan all the sadder.

"They were both lucky," Vernon pronounced before Nan could deny it.

Oh yeah, lucky. Is that what you called it when you had a wife who believed the worst of you because she heard some loudmouth on the radio make some outlandish accusation that in the light of day certainly couldn't be true? Is that what you called it when your wife demanded a divorce because you had other things on your mind besides sex? Is that what you called it when three foster children didn't satisfy your wife and she wanted more, more, more, and she wanted you to take time to play with them and hold them and dress them and feed them and worry about their health?

"Where's D.J.?" she asked Topher, rubbing his head gently and lifting his face from her lap. He was such a good older brother that sometimes it broke Nan's heart to think ahead to the time they'd have to say good-bye to Robin and Rachel and little D.J. and imagine how hard it would be for

Topher to understand. Almost as hard as it would be for her.

As always, Phil had been right. Taking in the children was a mistake.

"Raina's playing with him," Topher said, wiping his nose with the back of his hand while Nan searched for a clean tissue in the folds of her pocket.

"Who's Raina?" Adele asked, and Nan felt something deep inside her tighten. Raina was Phil's secretary. She handled all the church crises and many of the ones at home. Nan often joked with her about how she worked as much for Nan as for Phil.

"A friend," she answered softly, wondering what their relationship would be now that Phil was gone, now that she wasn't the *reverend's wife*. What would her relationship be to all the women of the church? To the new minister and his wife? Where, exactly, would Nan fit into the church now that she wouldn't be Phil's extra hand?

"Come," Nan said, urging Topher toward the hall, where she found the girls on their way out to find her. "You too, sweeties," she added, encouraging them all to go into the room Topher shared with D.J.

"How're you doing?" Raina asked her when she turned toward the doorway. "You going to let me watch these kids now so that you can get some rest?"

"It was nice of you to come," Nan said softly, watching D.J. stare at a top that Raina was spinning for him.

"He sure loves this thing," Raina said. "And I don't mind watching them, Nan. To tell you the truth, I'm not so sure what else I'm supposed to be doing."

Nan nodded her thanks. She supposed she should enjoy whatever help she was offered for as long as it came. She doubted it would be nearly as long as she'd need it.

The kids gathered around Raina, and Nan watched for a moment or two to make sure that they were settled fairly contentedly before going through her bedroom and into her bathroom.

Phil's toothbrush hung in the ceramic holder the way it had every day for the last ten years. His razor lay across the soap dish. She pulled open the mirrored medicine cabinet and studied the contents, finding it harder and harder to breathe as she looked at the row of medicines that settled Phil's stomach, cleared his sinuses, eased the pain in his lower back.

Her hand trembled as she reached out for the first little brown bottle and let it go into the wastebasket beside the sink. Naprosyn, the next label read. It fell into the wastebasket with a thud, followed by the Benadryl for his itches, the Vicks for his cough, the Old Spice he wore to church.

How dare he go and die like this, without giving her a chance to say she trusted him? she thought as she threw the Pepto-Bismol into the trash. Was he thinking, as he hit that tree, that she had asked him for a divorce? Had that been his last thought?

She gripped the bottle of Listerine tightly and then threw it against the wall above the bathtub, the shards of glass flying off in every direction, the golden liquid running down the bright white tiles.

"How dare you leave me like this?" she spat out at what was left in the medicine cabinet, grabbing up his hair tonic, his eyedrops, his foot salve, and throwing them all at the wall. "With this on my conscience?"

Canoe, the fragrance of their courtship, of the early years when Topher had been conceived, sat alone on the shelf. She stared at it long and hard before smashing it with

all her might against the wall just as the door opened and
Eleanor could hear her say how much she hated the man
she'd married. "I won't ever, ever forgive you for this," she
was shouting at the mess in the tub, the piece of glass that
had rebounded off the wall and come back to pierce her
bare arm, the hairbrush that still sat patiently waiting for
Phil on the tank of the toilet.

"Are you done?" Eleanor asked softly, a small sad smile
teasing her lips. "Or should I come back in a while?"

"I don't think there's anything left to throw," she admitted, relying on the wall to hold her up. "I don't know why
I'm so angry. It's not like it was Phil's fault."

"Been there, done that," Eleanor said sympathetically as
she examined Nan's arm and pulled the curved shard from
just above her elbow. "And from experience, I'm guessing
that you're not angry at *him*."

"Well, I don't have Harris Tweed's aftershave handy,"
she said with a sigh that turned into a sob.

"Just so long as you aren't mad at yourself." Eleanor
found a Band-Aid and covered the pinprick of blood with
it. It reminded Nan of a blood test, and marriage licenses
and babies—they all flooded her mind and started the tears
flowing all over again.

"Myself?" she croaked out.

"I was here the morning the police came, Nan. I saw the
blanket and pillow on the sofa," Eleanor said.

The police had asked her if there was anyone they could
call for her, and she'd given them Eleanor's number. She'd
forgotten about the bed she'd made up for Phil in the TV
room that night, as she had all the other nights. And then
the linens had disappeared. "Oh. So it was you that put
them away." Nan avoided Eleanor's questioning eyes. "I

was just waiting up for Phil to come home. I wanted to hear him right away."

"Mmm," Eleanor agreed. She didn't mention that the TV room was at the far end of the house, that Nan would have heard him sooner in the bedroom, or surely the living room, than she would have in the TV room. She didn't mention that to wait up, people didn't usually make up a bed complete with sheets and pillows.

She just put her arm around Nan and led her out from the bathroom to the queen-size bed Nan had once shared with Phil. On one nightstand there was her mother's little blue vase, her jar of Oil of Olay, a frilly box of tissues, and the clock. On the other there was nothing at all.

Eleanor didn't mention that, either.

Instead she said, "You were a good wife, Nan. Phil told me as much, many times."

"He was a good husband," Nan said, forcing herself to remember the good times they had once shared. In the light of day the accusations seemed ridiculous, unfounded, impossible. "He deserved better than—"

"He deserved better than to be accused of something immoral and illegal on the radio, to have his memory sullied and his reputation undermined." Eleanor sat down on the bed beside her and put an arm around her. "But Vernon just loves this sort of thing. He'll see it set to rights. Don't you go worrying about it."

Nan shook her head. "I'm the one who's got to fix it, Ellie. So he knows that I didn't believe it of him."

"He knows that, honey," Eleanor said, crossing the room and drawing the curtain closed. "If he knows anything, he knows that. Now, you get some rest, all right?"

Nan nodded, but didn't lie back. The bed was hers alone, as it had been for the past several months. Only now

Phil's pillow graced the other side of the bed. As she had every night since his death, she buried her face in his pillow.

It smelled of Head & Shoulders shampoo.

And there was no solace there.

Four

She had to be the meanest, nastiest, most vindictive, un-forgiving woman he had never really met. And who was suffering for her pride, her anger, her hatred? Her children.

Well, her children and Harry.

Who ever heard of sending back flowers from a funeral? Returning a check to a memorial fund? How was he supposed to keep the promise he'd made Christopher that it would get better when she wouldn't even accept the cleats Harry had sent over for him?

Of course, Harry had to admit that the next week Topher did have on brand-new cleats for the game, even if they didn't have the Nike logo every kid wanted.

He sat behind the opposing team's bench, watching her. It was the first game she'd come to, and she had her hands full with three kids in the stands. He supposed that was why he'd seen Topher with "Aunt Ellie" at the other games. The girls were all over Nan, hanging on her arm, climbing in and out of her lap. One of the girls had a pigtail on one side and a mess on the other. And she was the neater one. And the little boy—now, he was really something. He had a bath towel pinned to his shoulders, flowing like a cape down his back, and she held on to the end of it, every now and then reeling him in closer to her. But she never touched him, never took him around, or plopped him on her lap like a loving mother ought to do.

Of course, despite reports to the contrary, despite hearing that she was working twenty-five hours a day on some church fair, and seeing to the needy, and serving on several church committees while still getting all the children from pillar to post, he wasn't convinced that she had a loving—or charitable—bone in her body.

No wonder that kid of hers was having such a bad game. He was absolutely worthless at bat, the kind that looked for four-leaf clovers instead of at the batter when he was in the outfield. Despite it, the group cheered him on, the Widow Springfield—it was how he'd come to think of her, *the Widow Springfield*—harassing the youngest child into clapping, and sending one of the girls down toward the bench with messages for Christopher that made the boy smile and turn to wave.

As if the kid didn't have enough trouble concentrating.

By the seventh inning Harry had moved behind her, out of her line of vision, but well within hearing range of her and the kids.

"Tell him we'll borrow Dee's video camera next time," she told the older girl. "So he shouldn't worry that he's saving his good stuff."

Harry choked back a laugh. The kid's good stuff was locked in the vault.

"The ice cream man! The ice cream man," the younger girl yelled before Harry even noticed the bells ringing out on the breeze. "Ice cream! Ice cream!"

"I scream, you scream, we all scream for ice cream!" the Widow Springfield sang back to the little girl.

"Now!" the little girl answered back, scrambling down the bleachers faster than her mother could catch her.

"Grab her, please," the widow said, coming to her feet and following carefully, what with the boy attached to her by his cape. "We have ice cream at home," she said to the little girl while she pleaded with the boy to come down the steps.

"Now!" the girl repeated, stomping her foot.

"We have ice cream at home," the Widow Springfield said tightly. "We can have it after you've had your dinner."

The younger girl's lower lip grew until it drooped over and nearly touched her round little chin. Didn't the woman know that ice cream from the store didn't taste nearly as good as Mr. Softee's did?

Harry added *tightfisted* to his list of adjectives for the good widow. *Tightfisted* and *rule-abiding*—two traits he hated in a parent.

If he were the kids' dad, he'd argue her out of it. But these kids didn't have a dad, thanks to him, and so he strode over to the Mr. Softee truck and pulled out a couple of bills.

"Free ice cream for every kid here," he directed the boy who was just opening the sales window of the truck.

"You want me to just yell it out?" the kid asked. "Free ice cream for everyone?"

Harry reached into his pocket and handed the kid three twenties, which he figured would more than cover the whole lot of them. "Anyone but that blond woman over there," he said, gesturing at the widow with his chin.

"You mean Mrs. Springfield?" the kid asked with obvious amazement, as if no one could possibly harbor an angry thought about the good widow.

No doubt the reverend had made her look good.

Harry nodded and turned to look once more at the widow. The littler of the girls was hanging on her leg, the

older one was pulling on one of her sleeves. The boy was a
million miles away in the stands, and she was yelling, "Run,
Topher!" for all she was worth.

"Oh, hell," he said, disgusted with himself. "Give 'em all
free ice cream."

She was a hard woman to hate, even when she was hating him.

How was it, Nan wondered as she stood in the kitchen
roasting a Thanksgiving turkey, that Little League had already ended and soccer had taken its place, that summer
had somehow melted into autumn without her noticing and
now winter was waiting in the wings? And how was it that
the pain was still there, sharper than ever?

"It was all that work you did on the fair," Eleanor said.
"It's taken all the strength you have."

It hadn't been easy, working on this year's scholarship
fund with last year's hanging over her head. This time all
the money—half of what they'd made the previous year—
went directly into the church's account. It had been hard,
and embarrassing, and she felt as if somehow her father's
memory, his wonderful legacy, had been sullied. But if Eleanor thought that was what was bothering her today, she
was dead wrong.

"And then there's the holidays," Eleanor said, coming up
behind her to watch Vernon's family climb out of their
Lexus loaded down with Tupperware containers bursting
with stuffing and gravy and cranberry relish. "And Phil not
being here to share them. Believe me, that's what has you
so weepy. And the holidays will pass and so will the tears."

Nan shook her head. She wished it was as simple as that.
She handed all the children cookies, gave each a kiss even
though D.J. threatened to shriek, and sent them off to the

TV room to wait for their cousins to arrive. Not that they were looking forward to seeing Vernon's girls, but then again, she hadn't exactly been counting the minutes until she saw Vernon and Adele, either.

"It's more than that, isn't it?" Eleanor asked her in that way she had that made Nan feel like Eleanor was sharing in her sorrow without even knowing the source.

"Mrs. Price called this morning." Nan wiped her hands on a dishtowel and threw it toward the counter beside the sink. She missed, but thought it only fitting with the way things were going. "She's coming to pick up D.J. so that he can spend the weekend with his parents."

"Am I supposed to be glad about that or sad?" Eleanor asked, giving Nan one of those stares that pierced all the armor Nan had so carefully donned. "I don't know how this is supposed to work, Nan, this foster mothering of yours."

"It's good that his parents want to see him," Nan said with as much conviction as she could muster. Talking about letting go of children, of a parent's love, was always hard with Eleanor. What she'd done all those years ago still festered. Nan wished she could help Eleanor put the past behind her, but if all it took were a few kind words, then her sister-in-law wouldn't still be hurting so. "Maybe they're getting ready to take care of him again now that his sisters are bigger. Maybe they'll have more patience this time and not lose control when he—"

"Is that why you look like one of the kids has his foot caught in a bear trap? Because D.J.'s family might be more patient with him this time?"

Nan brushed her hair off her face and pasted a smile on. "So it's not easy," she admitted. "It's what I do."

"You take 'em in, give 'em your heart, and then lose

pieces of it when they go." Eleanor touched her arm gently. "How can you do this to yourself?"

It was the same thing Phil had asked her when she'd agreed to take in Robin and Rachel just weeks after she'd given up Tony—and the boy had disappeared with his family a few days later. It was the same thing she'd asked herself when she knew that D.J.'s parents would want him back before she was ready to let him go. "Because if I don't, where will the children go? Yeah, it's hard for me, but think what it's like for them. They have no safe place to live—where they can just be children. Right now they need me."

The bell rang and before Nan could head out of the kitchen, Eleanor yelled for Topher to open the door. Then she turned to Nan and stared at her good and hard. "You better get out the rest of it before Vernon comes in and takes over the place."

Nan shook her head. The rest was too awful to put into words, especially with her brother-in-law standing in the hall. And then again, it could be nothing—just a frog in Mrs. Price's throat—and not the truth that was choking the woman.

She heard Vernon asking Topher where his mama was, Adele fussing at her husband to take off his coat first, heard the children whining because Nan no longer had cable and they'd be missing some show.

"Don't let him bully you," Eleanor whispered just as Vernon pushed open the swinging kitchen door. "In other words, do as I say, not as I do," she added with a rueful laugh, passing Vernon without touching him and obeying his silent message to leave them alone in the room.

"You sign those papers yet?" he asked. No *Hello, Nan. How are you doing? Holding up all right? Anything wrong?* Lord, but the Springfield men had been cut from the same cloth—probably sheet metal, cold, with no give and no warmth.

"Not yet," she admitted, refusing to be cowed by her brother-in-law.

"Nan, dear, that insurance money isn't going to last forever." He shrugged out of his coat and leaned over, poking a nose into her oven. "Looks to me like it's already running out. That is one puny bird, lady."

"Would you rather have eaten the one that Harris Tweed sent by?" she asked before she could censor herself.

Vernon's eyebrow went up, but he let her comment go—only for the moment, Nan was sure. "Personally, I'd like to see him rotting in prison for killing my brother, but that's not going to happen. So after that, what I'd like to see is you on Easy Street, at his expense. If I can't make him pay with time, I'll have to settle for money. He got you into this mess and I'd like to see him get you out of it."

"Well, if it would bring back Phil, I'd sue him to kingdom come, but no lawsuit is going to do that, Vernon." She glanced into the oven. He was right. She'd seen bigger pigeons land on the church's steeple.

"Did the church start pressuring you to get out of the house yet?" he asked, examining the loose handle on the cupboard and doing nothing to fix it.

"Of course not," she snapped back. She'd been part of the Old Deburle Church her whole life. They were her family almost as truly as all the Eastmans and Morrows, right back to Nanny Annie and Great-grandpa Noah. They wouldn't desert her now. Not if she could prove that Harris Tweed was wrong about Phil.

"Well, what's holding you up?" Vernon all but demanded.

Faith, she thought, *and little else.* But the truth was that she wasn't about to start some lawsuit that called Harris Tweed a liar until she could shove the evidence down his scrawny little neck and make him choke on it.

"I haven't made sense yet out of the records he kept," she admitted reluctantly. It was hard to look at them, the neat handwriting that began to blur and get messier and messier until she could hardly read the notes he made that last night.

"I don't need any damn records to know that my brother wouldn't steal from his own church." He looked at her accusingly. "Do you?"

"No, but if I had those records, I could get back the money I gave the church for the scholarships," she said, knowing the instant she'd said it that it was a mistake. Vernon would never understand that in her own way she was telling the church that she knew Phil would never steal from them—that she knew she'd find the account where it was safely waiting to be doled out to the students and she'd be able to get her money back.

Although, truth be told, it wasn't looking that way. She wasn't one iota closer to that money than she was the day Phil had died. Oh, she found money in and money out, but where it came from and went to, she couldn't guess. Except the five thousand dollars that had gone to Vernon for a portion of his loan to Phil. And the two-thousand-dollar deposit on the nine-month-old Ford Taurus that Phil had wrapped around a tree. Hardly the thirty-five thousand dollars that was missing.

"What money you gave them?" Vernon asked. His voice was quiet, but it didn't hide his anger from Nan.

"I gave the church what they needed for the scholarships. After all, the money was promised and the scholarships bear my father's name on them. And as soon as I can find where Phil invested it, or deposited it, I can turn those accounts over to the church and they'll give me back the money I—"

"Are you mad? Have you freaking lost your mind with grief? Where did you get thirty-five thousand dollars?" he boomed.

Adele popped her head into the kitchen. "Where do you want me to put all this food?" she asked Nan before Vernon grabbed the shopping bags from her hand and pushed her back out of the doorway.

"Stay out of here until I call you," he bellowed.

"Phil's insurance money," she said pretending to be very busy with all the plastic containers Adele had brought with her.

"Well, you've made your bed now, Nan Springfield, and you can just lie in it all by yourself. Don't you go expecting me to bail you out after throwing away your security like that—"

"Mrs. Price is here," Eleanor said, coming into the kitchen and giving her brother a look that could ignite a stone. "I think she needs to speak to you."

Nan covered her eyes with her hand, squeezing at her temples. She didn't know when the headache had started, but it was a doozy.

Had she asked Vernon to bail her out? She didn't want his money, the insurance money, the lawsuit money, or any other money that didn't belong to her. She just wanted everyone—Vernon, Mrs. Price, the church elders, and Harris Tweed—off her back. She wanted her life back.

Ah, if wishes were horses . . .

"Nan! How nice it is to see you!" Patty Price came into the kitchen bearing a sad-looking potted plant in her hand. "For the holidays!" she said, pushing the dying bit of greenery into Nan's hands.

Nan thanked her and made the perfunctory introductions. It appeared that Vernon meant what he said about letting her lie in her bed, as he excused himself with a huff and went out into the living room.

"I put this off as long as I could, Nan," Mrs. Price began while thunder roared in Nan's ears. "Of course, if it were up to me, the girls and D.J. could stay here forever. But you know I'm not the one who makes the decisions."

Liar! Liar! Nan thought. "No, of course not," she said instead. "But they're happy here," she said in her own defense. The words came out like a whine.

"I'm sure they are. It's just that with the reverend gone . . . well, to be perfectly frank, Nan, you have no visible means of support, do you? Is there something I'm unaware of? Some source of income?"

"I have Phil's insurance," she said. Or what was left of it.

"Is it enough to buy the house?" Mrs. Price asked. "It's just that Millie Fenwick is my sister's mother-in-law and she says that the church is going to have to ask for the house back before much longer because the new minister—have you met him? He's quite charming, and his wife is lovely, with four of the prettiest little girls. . . . Well, anyway, it's really all about the money issue, Nan. It is absolutely against policy for you to live off the stipend the state gives you for the children. You know that, don't you? I mean, if people could live off foster children, who knows what kinds of creeps would take in—"

"I'm fine, financially," Nan lied. "I'm sure you know that I'm receiving Social Security death benefits and I've also been doing a little typing for the Food Bank and the Annual Clothing Drive."

Mrs. Price's brows rose.

Nan couldn't ask the Old Deburle Church to pay her for

getting out the *Weathervane*, when she'd been doing the newsletter for years for free. But her friend Dee could—and did—ask the Food Bank to start paying Nan, and then the Food Bank had suggested that the clothing drive would be able to make use of the same list, so why not have Nan do that, too?

"And then there's the insurance, the help my family's been giving me . . . Well, we'll certainly be moving to a smaller place, but that'll just mean less expenses. And that works all down the line—less electric, less gas." She was babbling now, desperate. Finally she swallowed around the lump in her throat and said, "I'll support the children, Mrs. Price. You can count on it."

"Well, it's a hard time of year to place anyone, what with the holidays coming, and I would hate to ruin Christmas for the girls, so if you're sure that you can keep them through the holidays . . ."

One reprieve at a time, Nan thought. One at a time.

"I told you, Mrs. Price. I'm sure by the new year I'll be financially sound." Of course she didn't mention that was on the condition that she won the Ohio State Lottery. "When will you bring D.J. back?"

"You've got to sue him," Vernon said after Mrs. Price had left with D.J. and they were all gathered around the dinner table, Vernon in the chair that was always Phil's.

"I don't want that man's money," she said, dishing sweet potato pie onto Robin's plate and promising her she'd like it if she just tried it. "I don't want to hear his name, be reminded of him, know he exists."

"You're letting him off too easy," Vernon argued. "The man has got to be made to pay. My brother died in ignominy—"

"He died in Columbus," Eleanor said dryly.

There was a moment of silence before Vernon continued, signaling them all that they were expected to ignore Eleanor's comment.

"He dragged my brother's name through the mud, left you barely hanging on by a thread, with only me to see to you—not that I mind watching out for you or Ellie—but I can only do so much. . . ."

"No one is asking you to take care of us, Vernon," Eleanor said. "Nobody's asked you to—*ever*—but that never stops you."

"And you'd know better than anyone that it's a damn good thing it doesn't, wouldn't you say?" he snapped back at her.

"Just leave Nan alone," Eleanor said, but the wind was gone from her sails. "She's never done anything wrong."

"And she won't, if I can help it. None of this charity from *Boss* Tweed." He shifted his gaze to Nan. "He send over anything besides a bird that hopefully was bigger than this one?" He held his fork aloft, waiting for her answer.

Anything else? Well, the obnoxious, loudmouthed, accusation-flinging, insensitive Harris Tweed had sent a fruit basket two days after the funeral. He'd sent tickets to a ball game for Topher, Halloween costumes for all the kids, checks that she supposed totaled a good five thousand dollars, a note of condolence, cleats for Topher, someone to mow the lawn, and a very mean note that said she was being spiteful and shortsighted at the expense of her child.

She had sent everything back—the checks and notes torn to shreds. Eleanor had told her she was crazy, but she didn't want Harris Tweed to think that her husband's life wasn't worth more to her than some money and a pair of children's shoes.

"You haven't taken anything from that bastard, have you, Nan? Not the guy who impugned your husband's reputation? Who killed him!"

"Watch your language, please," Nan said, gesturing toward the children, who had been remarkably busy down at their end of the table. It was amazing what a plastic tablecloth and a bunch of those Colorforms could accomplish during a meal. "And no. I wouldn't give him the satisfaction of letting him off the hook."

"Which is why we have to sue the pants off him. We've got to stand up in court and point the finger at the man who caused Phil's death. I asked my attorney about the chances of getting him charged with manslaughter, but he said it wouldn't fly. . . ."

He droned on and on, but Nan's mind was elsewhere, figuring out what she could do to earn enough money to keep the kids and stay in the house, at least until after the holidays. If Eleanor would help . . .

She looked over at Eleanor, who was tapping her lip with a ragged fingernail and seemed a million miles away.

Maybe they could kill Harris Tweed and sell his organs on the black market. Or kidnap him and sell him to pirates.

All she really wanted to do was hit him, again and again, but that wouldn't let her keep the girls, or feed Topher. And on top of that, Christmas was coming. Mr. Encizo always gave them a tree, but that was when Phil was the reverend. Parishioners always dropped off presents for the children, but if Thanksgiving was any indication, the only one who'd be sending gifts for the children would be the one person in the world she'd never accept them from.

Chicken Little was right.

The sky was falling.

Five

"**D**on't be an idiot," Eleanor said, dropping the first of many cartons onto the faded rose carpet in her sister-in-law's living room. "If that nice new reverend is going to let you stay in this house a few more months, I'll be damned if I'll be the one to kick you out of your bedroom. I'll be perfectly fine in the TV room."

"Absolutely not," Nan said stubbornly with a wave of her hand, as if giving up her bedroom was no big deal. "If you're going to be kind enough to share expenses with me, you ought to at least have a bedroom where you can get away from the children."

"But I'm hardly ever home," Eleanor argued. She supposed that just maybe Nan wanted to be out of that bedroom, to put the memories, good or bad, behind her, and so with a big sigh, she nodded her consent, hefted the carton once again, and headed down the hall.

"Did you take care of having your mail forwarded and your phone and things like that?" Nan asked, gathering up her own things to make way for Eleanor's.

"Of course," she said, though she had been tempted not to, just to see if there was a person in the world who would notice she'd moved and bother trying to find her. *Stop it!* she yelled at herself. This move wasn't just for Nan's sake.

Somehow it was Eleanor's last chance at a life of her own—a clean slate, a fresh start, with people around to boost her spirits and bolster her confidence.

"I'm glad you're here," Nan said, holding open the door for her as she went out for another load.

"Me too," she said, truly meaning it. And then she pulled the door closed behind her to keep the cold out where it belonged—out of Nan's house, out of Nan's life.

Eleanor's Chevy Malibu was old, a castoff from Vernon, who'd made a big deal out of giving it to her when he'd bought the first of his imported I-have-arrived cars. Apparently one couldn't "arrive" in a domestic car. Not that Eleanor cared. It got her around well enough, and no one wanted to hire a practical nurse who drove a fancier car than they did. No one begrudged her her fees when they took a look at what she drove.

But what was good enough for her wasn't good enough for Nan Springfield. For one fleeting moment it made Eleanor wonder if maybe Phil had felt the same way and been compelled to misappropriate some of the church's money.

"Lord almighty, Ellie!" she mumbled to herself in the crisp December air. "Some Springfields do have standards! They don't all compromise their morals to do what's easiest."

"You say something?" Nan asked, running up behind her in a gray sweatshirt that, under the spatterings of paint, proclaimed the wearer part of Habitat for Humanity. If Eleanor didn't do something, and quick, Nan might need to apply to Habitat for a house of her own.

"I'll go over to the grocery store when I'm done and pick us up some supplies," she told Nan, reaching into her trunk for the few odd things she'd bothered to hold on to—her mother's Bible, pictures of her with her brothers when they were all young and carefree, hospital records she knew it was time to throw away.

"I can afford to feed us," Nan said, that smile of hers flashing as if she hadn't a care in the world. "Stan Denham, the church's accountant, says that with the Social Security benefits, your share—thank you, Ellie!—and the typing I'm doing for the Food Bank, and now for Ohio Cares, too, I could probably rent a three-bedroom apartment on Peace Street and still afford to eat."

"Three bedrooms for six of us. That ought to be really cozy." Eleanor leaned the box against the side of the car and took a close look at her sister-in-law. Nan had probably lost ten pounds in the four months since Phil's death. Eleanor doubted she slept much with four kids who always had colds or coughs or nightmares. "I can handle these. Why don't you go in and make yourself something to eat?"

"I'll make us some nice potato leek soup when we're done," she said, that bright smile still pasted on her face.

"No, you go on in. Open a can of something easy and put your feet up for five minutes, will you?"

Nan ignored her, reaching for the box in her hands. "I'll get this one, you unload the backseat."

For all that she tried, Eleanor couldn't loosen her hold on a lifetime of memories and regrets. She'd come as much to help Nan put the past behind her as to help her out financially, and here she was, lugging her own past with her like some albatross. "Go inside," she all but ordered Nan, refusing to relinquish the carton.

"I'll just go around back and peek at the kids, then," Nan said, fidgeting with her hands and finally tucking them up under her armpits. "It sure was nice of Vernon to think of sending money to pay Raina for today!"

"Leave the kids alone," Eleanor said, knowing that if

D.J. saw a carton, the screaming would start again. It was why she'd called Raina and made the arrangements in the first place. But she knew darn well that what Nan would be willing to accept from Vernon, she'd never accept from her, and so she'd told Raina that Vernon was paying for it. Heck, ten bucks for a Saturday afternoon was a small price to pay for your sanity. Even if Vernon got the credit. "Yeah, Vernon's a peach all right."

"You don't realize how lucky you are to have had brothers, Ellie. Someone to turn to when the world turns away . . ."

"No one's turning away from you, Nan," she said, nudging her sister-in-law back toward the house. "Even Harris Tweed is trying—"

Nan put her hands over her ears and hummed loudly. "I can't hear you," she said in a singsong voice.

"You could use his help," Eleanor said so loudly she was sure that Nan could hear her. "Christmas is coming, Nan. You know, 'Peace on earth, good will toward men'?"

"Someone bigger than me is going to have to forgive that man," Nan said, raising her eyes toward the darkening skies.

"How many ways does the man have to say he's sorry?"

"He doesn't have to say he's sorry at all," Nan said, holding the door open for her and closing it against the gray December day. "In fact, he'd make me a lot happier if he didn't say anything at all. Not to me, anyway—I'd be happy never to hear his voice again, unless it's to announce to the idiots that listen to his stupid program that he was wrong about Phil big time and let that poor man rest in peace."

"I don't think he thinks he was wrong," Eleanor said. She'd heard him a few days after the funeral, and the man was obviously shaken by the whole series of events. "He did say he was sorry about what had happened to Phil, and that people shouldn't take what he says as fact and that they ought to learn for themselves what the truth is." Actually he'd said that people who believed what they heard without checking the facts were all fools, and he was the biggest one of all. But when Ross asked him if that meant he was wrong, Harris Tweed had said, "Only time will tell." It had made Eleanor wonder.

"Was that supposed to be an admission that he was wrong?" Nan demanded.

"What if he wasn't wrong?" Eleanor asked quietly.

"He was. And if he wasn't, which I'm telling you he was, he didn't know he wasn't, and he just vilified my husband for a laugh."

"Sometimes people do bad things, Nan, but they can still be good people."

"No, they can't," Nan said simply, as if that was that, slip-slap, done deal. She headed for the kitchen, but instead of following her, Eleanor flopped down heavily in Phil's old easy chair.

"Yes, they can," she said more to herself than to Nan. And sometimes they just needed the chance to rectify their mistakes.

All right—maybe some mistakes could never be rectified; the world moved on and it was impossible to turn it back. But maybe forgiveness wasn't quite out of the question.

At least not in this particular case.

six

By the time he found himself on the Widow Spring-field's front porch, Harry was feeling like there was a hand grenade hidden in the sack he'd brought with him. Oh, he'd thought it positively brilliant to pose as Santa Claus in order to bring the reverend's kids some Christmas cheer. And he was pleased as the proverbial Christmas punch that he'd thought of the disguise, too, after some anonymous woman had called the station just after the show was over one night and suggested that if he was really so worried about the Springfields, he might, as she put it, "try not shoving his name down their throats."

Actually, when he thought about it, he'd even enjoyed himself shopping for the four kids, despite the crowds and the jacked-up-holiday prices.

But it could still all blow up in his face right there on the good reverend's front porch.

On top of that, the red velvet costume had needed less padding than he'd expected; he was now sure the saleslady was wrong about those skinny dolls being what the pudgy little girls would want; and for someone who earned a living talking, he suddenly had no idea what he was going to say once Nan Springfield opened the door.

He didn't even know if she would let him in. She probably didn't even let those kids have Christmas presents. Probably just took them to church for the day, being minister's kids and all. It was why he'd chosen just the gifts he had. Because children needed a certain amount of freedom. And mothers, especially ones like Nan Springfield, needed a little comeuppance every now and then.

He stamped the snow off his boots and caught the movement of the window curtains out of the corner of his eye.

Now or never, he thought, mentally pulling the pin from the grenade while he shifted the pack on his back and hit the doorbell with his elbow.

There was scurrying behind the door, shouts and squeals and children yelling about Santa coming. The boy, Topher, pulled open the door. Behind him, behind all the children, stood a very disheveled woman in a ratty-looking robe that should have been left in a Goodwill bag on the porch. She bit at the side of her lip as if she wasn't sure what he wanted at her door early on Christmas morning.

What *did* he want? Absolution? Forgiveness? It was a frigging eight degrees outside. He'd happily settle for a cup of coffee.

"Ho, ho, ho!" he bellowed in his best imitation of the jolly old elf himself, looking at four sets of sparkling eyes. No, make that five sets—the widow, for all her tough-broad tactics, was looking almost as pleased as the kids.

"What in the world . . . ?" Aunt Ellie—he'd heard she'd moved in with the widow, probably to help with the kids and the expenses—came in from the kitchen with two steaming mugs and stopped dead in her tracks. "Santa Claus?" she asked, her jaw slackening.

"You were expecting someone else at this hour? On this

day?" he bellowed back, trying to look absolutely affronted at the notion.

"Well . . ." Eleanor drew the word out, shrugging and looking mighty uncomfortable in her pink polyester robe and matching slippers. "I hadn't really expected . . . I never thought . . . That is, I thought you might have forgotten us this year. Lord knows it wasn't looking like much of a Christmas before this minute."

"You shoulda asked Mommy," Topher said, pulling at Harry's sleeve to guide him into the warm hallway. "She'da straightened you out. Santa never forgets!"

"That's elephants," one of the girls corrected. She was bouncing on her toes, making Harry dizzy with her energy.

"*He's* a elephant," the other little girl said, poking at his belly. "Only red!"

"Is that any way to talk to Santa?" Harry asked, glaring down at her and knitting his white cotton brows. "Maybe I'm not at the right house. You're not a very good little girl, are you?"

Jeez, but he didn't mean to really scare her, to melt that precious smile. Before he could take it back and assure her that Santa was only joking, the widow put her hands on the little girl's shoulders.

"These are the best children you'll ever find, Santa," she said, and he could hear tears in her throat, choking her words. "Please, oh please, come in. Can we get you something? It's brutally cold out there. Coffee? Tea? Hot reindeer milk?"

"Angels in the snow!" one of the girls shouted. "Get the angels for Santa!"

"Angels!" the littlest boy yelled. "Angels! Angels! Angels!"

"I'll get them," Eleanor said, disappearing into the

kitchen while he was pulled and pushed into the living room and nearly thrust into a comfortable armchair that had an old cabbage rose fabric draped over it.

"Oh, wait! I'm re-covering that," she said apologetically. "I hope you've got lots of padding in there—there might be a pin or—"

"Ow! God da—" He saw her eyes get big as saucers. "—dangle! Gosh oh gee, but Santa found one of those pins of yours, right in his . . . astronomy."

Her hand flew to her mouth to stifle a laugh. He decided that the bathrobe she wore wasn't really ratty, but instead well worn—kind of like the smile that played at her lips as her hand came down and cinched the sash around her waist. Both the robe and the smile had obviously seen a great deal of use. And both had seen better days.

"I can't believe you're here," she said, her voice nearly a whisper, so that he could hardly hear her over the shouts of the children as he loosened the drawstring on the laundry bag he'd pressed into service as Santa's sack.

"Well, well, well. What have we here? I see there's a gift here for someone named Robin." He looked around at the four children. "Are there any birds here?"

"Robin's a girl!" the older girl said, giggling as she pointed at her sister.

"Me! Me!" Robin sang, looking first to Nan Springfield for approval, then reaching out for the fancy wrapped box.

"And here's one for Rachel," he said, handing a similar box to her.

"Celebration Barbie!" He'd expected the girls to be excited, but it was their mother's voice that quivered with joy. "And Christmas Barbie! I never saw two such lucky little girls in my life!"

She was clapping her hands, and damned if it didn't

make old Santa laugh at the reverend's widow, who just couldn't contain her excitement and was all but flapping at him to give Topher and D.J. their presents, too.

He'd have laid odds that she wouldn't be so happy with those.

And he'd have been wrong.

She thought the laser pistols would be great fun in the dark, though despite Topher's pleas she ruled out the attic because of the stairs. Santa said that was reasonable indeed and the begging stopped immediately. Clearly they had all been feeling the absence of a man in the house.

Topher loved the hockey skates and surely seemed excited when Santa assured him that it wasn't too late to join the team. D.J., decked out in a Mylar cape and cowboy boots over his pajamas, seemed fascinated with the sounds that the blaster made, and insisted Santa die, not once, not twice, but nearly a dozen times before someone finally managed to stop the kid. The girls held a beauty pageant for the dolls and insisted Santa choose which one was the prettiest—a very tricky situation that was saved when Springfield's widow reminded them all about the angels in the snow.

Actually, Santa had no great desire to go back out into the cold and fall on the thin layer of snow that barely coated the brown grass, but he supposed that it came with the job. Coming to his feet, he reminded the children that there were still more presents and dumped out the rest of the contents of his sack.

"Can you stay for a few minutes?" the widow asked him. "Just for the children? My angels in the snow are legendary, you know."

He pictured her lying on a bed of white snow, waving her arms, flakes in that mess of blond hair . . .

"Course he knows," Topher said, pulling him toward the dining room, where Eleanor was laying out plates and cups on a bright red cloth. "We leave 'em for him every year, don't we? And didn't Grandpa, and Papa Isaac?"

"Well, Santa gets a lot of cookies," she said, fussing at the collar of her robe as if she'd only now realized that she was entertaining him in her nightclothes. Or maybe she'd read his thoughts.

If you could call what he'd been doing *thinking*. Surely it hadn't involved his brain.

"Not like Nanny Annie's," Topher said, as if the idea that anyone else's cookies could compare was just ridiculous. "Come on, Santa! Just one?"

"Angels in the snow are Santa's favorite!" Robin chirped, and D.J. echoed her sentiments. "He has time, right?"

They all turned to stare at Santa, who nodded his head knowingly and said, "So, these angels in the snow are Nanny Annie's cookies. Why didn't you say so? Santa always has time for Nanny Annie's cookies."

And then he winked at Nan Springfield.

Just like that.

Harry didn't know what the hell Santa Claus was thinking.

Nan Springfield must not have either, as she reddened to her—could it be?—naturally blond roots. Harry hadn't met a natural blond since 1980.

"See how the angels are walking in the snow?" Robin asked, pointing to the fancy white iced cookies that were sticking up from a bowl of pudding.

"Mommy's great-great-great-great-great-grandma used to make 'em," Rachel added. "Or cowboys on the farm or other things, too."

"Mommy's not that old," Eleanor corrected. "Her great-

great-great-whatever-number-grandmother would have been making cookies over an open flame by some cave."

"Well, she's that great, anyways," Topher said. "Right, Mom?"

The red hadn't left Nan Springfield's cheeks. If anything, it deepened as she explained. "I thought that when they called my Nanny Annie a great-grandmother, they meant that she was a great grandma, and that my other grandmas were only so-so," she confessed, then shook her head at her silliness. "I'm sorry. You don't want to know this," she added, dishing out the pudding and placing a cookie on each serving.

"Santa wants to know everything," he said, watching the slight tremble of her hand as she handed him his plate.

"Santa *does* know everything," Topher corrected.

"I know you're going to make a fine hockey player," Harry told him. "If your mom says it's all right for you to join the league."

"Actually, Santa, it looks like we're going to be moving, so I'm not sure that I—"

Harry's eyes swept the room and noticed cartons as if he'd been blind until that moment. "Moving?" he asked. "Where are you going?"

Topher kicked at the table leg, and milk sloshed from his glass and from Santa's hot chocolate. "You know about my dad, Santa, right?" he asked.

"Yes, son, I know," Santa answered.

"Last year we built a snow fort in the backyard."

Santa smiled, unsure what to say.

"But he got too cold and had to come in. Do you think it's cold where he is?"

The widow was biting her lip. Aunt Ellie was twisting a napkin to shreds.

"No, son," he said softly. He'd been fooled by all the joy into thinking that the mourning was over and that they'd gotten on with their lives.

"Then why did Uncle Vernon order a grave blanket for him?" Topher asked.

Ah, but the widow's life was more complicated than Harry had ever imagined, he thought, as he searched for an answer.

"Those blankets are to keep *us* warm," the widow said when Santa remained silent. "They comfort us because they are a way to show we haven't forgotten and that we still love those who are gone."

"Like Daddy," Rachel said.

"Yes," Nan Springfield agreed. And then she tried to return to her conversation with him. Almost apologetically, as if it were her fault, she said, "Well, Reverend Michaels— he's the new minister—has been very nice about allowing us to stay in the house, but the church does own it, and they feel that it just isn't right for his whole family to be staying in a motel all this time—they're right, of course, but I—"

"So where are they putting you?" Harry demanded. The words he'd heard at the funeral echoed in his ears. *The church will want the house back, I'm sure.*

"Ungrateful wretches," Eleanor said, biting the head off an angel with a vengeance. "And that Denham character is the worst of them, if you ask me. He's the accountant—he ought to know where that money is. Not that they care anymore. Now they just want it behind them and they want her out.

"Six months they gave her. You know how little she gets from Social Security? It's a good thing I came when I did. At least that way I can help her get this place ready. They expected her to make this whole move herself. Imagine! You know—"

"Eleanor! It's not his fault," Nan Springfield said. "Let's not ruin the day with problems we can face tomorrow."

"They'll still be here tomorrow," Eleanor said. "Unless someone does something about them." She raised an eyebrow at Harry as if to demand that he prove himself Santa Claus.

He looked at the two women. He looked at little D.J., who hadn't said more than a few words and seemed to be in a world of his own. He looked at the girls, who were busy making their angels do pirouettes on their pudding, and at Topher, who seemed to have some inkling of what was going on. He wanted to hit a wall with his fist.

"Maybe something can be done," he said tentatively. "Surely something can be arranged."

"I *knew* the elders would forgive him," Nan said, tears welling up in moss green eyes. "I knew that they'd realize that Harris Tweed was the villain here, not Phil. I wish Mr. Royce had come along with you, but you must tell him that I thank him from the bottom of my heart—"

"Mr. Royce?" The awful knotting in Harry's stomach wasn't just a result of hearing Nan Springfield utter his name with such contempt. He had a bad feeling that the poor widow had mistaken him for someone from the church.

"It wasn't Mr. Royce who suggested that you not slide down the chimney in the middle of the night the way you usually do? Was it one of the other elders from the church? Mr. Welch? Oh, I bet it was Stan Denham's idea! Gosh, but that man has taken all of this so personally. Of course, he and Phil were very close."

"Oh, yeah. Mr. Helpful," Eleanor said with a grimace.

Harry had only seen Stan Denham at the funeral, but already he didn't like him. He hoped the incompetent accountant would stay the hell away from the widow. She had enough trouble.

"He bothering you?" Harry asked menacingly. Then he realized that it sounded like something out of a B movie from the forties. "I mean, is there something—"

"Why don't we go see if Santa left anything in your stockings while your mama thanks him?" Aunt Ellie asked the children, pulling out the chair for the littlest one and shooing them all from the room so that he and Nan Springfield were alone with nothing but a stupid white cotton beard and moustache to protect them both.

Nan studied the man in her dining room who looked like the Spirit of Christmas Present in some glorious Technicolor adaptation of *A Christmas Carol*. His white cotton moustache had hot chocolate rimming its bottom.

"Have they found someplace else for me to live, or"— she clasped her hands in prayer and looked toward the ceiling —"hope against hope, will they let me stay here?"

Her private Santa was silent.

"I can't stay here, then," she said sadly. "It's not that I mind for me, but D.J. doesn't take change very well and . . ." She let her voice trail off. D.J. wouldn't be an issue much longer. No doubt Mrs. Price would take him away after the holidays. And the girls, too, if she lost the house.

"Is there something wrong with the boy?" the man in the Santa Claus suit asked. "I don't mean to criticize him— I mean, it's a nice change to find a child who isn't hyperactive these days—but he seems, well, not all there."

"The doctor says he's fine," Nan said, taking offense at first, but then letting her shoulders sag. This man must know all her financial problems; why not confide her worries, too? It was kind of easy talking to Santa, after all. Nan wanted to climb into that big lap of his and ask for the world, or at least for a safety net under the tightrope she seemed to be walking.

"You don't think so?" He blew on the hot chocolate and fingered the cookie again. "Too pretty to eat," he muttered more to himself than her.

"It gets soggy from the pudding anyway," she said. "You might as well go ahead and eat it. But thanks. Nanny Annie would be proud of me," she added.

He shrugged and continued to finger the cookie.

"And no, I don't think he's fine. But he's a foster child, and no one wants to look for little problems with those kids, since the big ones are leaping out of every dark corner." Like fathers in jail, like mothers on drugs, like violence and indifference and a hundred other reasons that children like D.J. and Robin and Rachel wound up in other people's homes.

"I might know a guy who knows someone who could take a look at him," Santa said. He looked uncomfortable about it, but then, who was ever eager to get involved in someone else's problems? "If you'd like, I'll ask."

"I'd like," she said, watching him try to get a sip of cocoa without drowning himself. "You might be more comfortable trying to drink that without your beard," she suggested.

"Oh, I don't think so," he said, shaking his head. "Is there anything else you need? I feel like some really lousy Santa Claus, not bringing you a gift."

"Not bringing me a gift? Just bringing the kids those toys was a gift and a half for me. You can't imagine how much I want to give them—how much love, how much joy.

I'm not really supposed to, you know. They don't like the children to get too attached to you. They make them free-float, and then they wonder why they don't learn how to find their way. I want to hold them all tight forever—not let go even after they've walked down the aisle with their spouses. I want them to keep coming into my bed forever. I want—" She put her hands on her cheeks and felt them flame. "I want to shut up. That's what I want. I'm really sorry. It's just that I've been so worried about giving up the house. And the kids . . ." She couldn't even give voice to that thought.

"I'm divorced," Santa said. It seemed rather incongruous for a man in a jolly red suit to say such a thing. "That's not a come-on. I just mean that I know how hard it is to let a kid go."

Nan studied his eyes. They were deep, deep brown and held a sorrow that she understood too well.

"D.J. keeps killing me," Robin whined in the doorway. "And he's bothering me and I can't find Celebration Barbie's shoes."

"I put them on the mantel so that D.J. couldn't reach them," she told Robin.

"Yea!" She scurried off, yelling to Rachel that she *told* her she hadn't lost them.

"Yea!" Nan agreed, hugging herself. Maybe they wouldn't be able to stay in the house, but thank heaven the church was putting the past behind them and reaching out a hand to her. Why else would they have sent Santa Claus over on Christmas morning? "I can't remember when I've been this happy. It has been a long, long time."

"Since the reverend died?" Santa asked.

She looked away, but it was too late.

"Longer, then," he said, nodding almost smugly, as if he'd supposed it all along.

"You never said if they found me a house," she said, uncomfortable with the subject of Phil. How was it that even after death he had the power to drain a room of warmth?

"I'll see if I can't get them to let you stay right here," he said.

"Don't let that Santa suit go to your head," she warned him.

"You don't believe in Santa Claus?" he asked, pretending to be offended.

"I'd believe in the tooth fairy if she'd leave a key to a house under my pillow," Nan said glibly. "It was the goodness of man I was just beginning to doubt. Thanks for restoring my faith in human nature."

"That's an awesome burden, Mrs. Springfield," he said, glancing at his watch and rising from the table. "And Santa's got several other stops to make. It is Christmas, you know."

She smiled at him. The broad grin felt vaguely familiar, and more than welcome. "I don't know how to thank you and the whole congregation," she said softly, feeling small in the face of such generosity.

He looked her over from head to toe, and she pulled her robe more tightly around her as he did. "Up this close you're just a bit of a thing, aren't you? Not nearly as big or strong or tough as I thought."

"Excuse me?"

"I had a very different picture of you . . . from what that Mr. Royce said," he mumbled, waving his hand as he did. "You know, you never should have opened that door this morning. You don't even know who I am. What if I'd been some robber dressed up as Santa Claus to trick you into letting me in?"

"Then the trick would have been on you," she said, gesturing around the room to show how little of value she owned. "You'd have been very disappointed."

"Fine," he said with a grimace. "What if I'd been a rapist, then?"

She looked down at her old chenille robe, her silly Oscar the Grouch slippers that she hadn't realized she had on until then, the torn bottom of her old flannel gown. She remembered how Phil hadn't sought her out for all those months when he'd slept a room away from her. "I suspect you'd have been disappointed then, too."

He looked only half as shocked at her words as she was.

"Don't you go letting just anyone in here, Mrs. Springfield," he warned. "It's not a nice world out there."

"I've lost my husband because of some creep on the radio, I'm going to lose my house, probably three of my children, and you're warning me that it's not *nice* out there? My heart's already broken, Santa, and I don't have anything else of value."

"I can't do anything about the reverend," he said almost as if it were an apology. "But I'll do my best on the rest of it, I promise."

And if she'd doubted it before, this time she was sure. Santa, a soft look in those twinkling dark eyes, a grin half hidden by his silly cotton beard, lifted her chin with a white gloved finger, and winked.

 *seven*

"So, what was she like?" Nate asked him after he'd related how much the kids liked all the gifts and what it felt like to play Santa Claus to kids who treasured the smallest kindnesses.

"Who?"

Nate just rolled his eyes. "All prissy and tight-assed like you figure a minister's wife would be?"

"Not so tight," he said, remembering the softness that surrounded Nan Springfield.

"You've got a funny look on your face there, Harry," his father said. It sounded more like a warning than an observation.

Harry shrugged his eyebrows. "I gotta get a lot done before Suzanne gets here with Josh," he said, putting his mug on the table and kneeling down to pick up the scattered newspapers.

"Took you longer than I expected over there," Nate said, pretending that it was merely idle chatter and not nosy-bodying that was going on.

"Deburle's a good fifty miles from here."

"Hour there, hour back . . ."

"Santa had to eat some cookies," Harry said, pushing the

newspapers into the trash with a lot more noise than was necessary.

"Damn it all, son. Why do you always have to go looking for trouble?"

Harry turned his back to his father and washed his hands carefully in the sink. "I'm not looking for trouble," he muttered, hoping to heaven it was true.

"The hell you're not," his father said, poking holes in the box he was wrapping. "You're making it a goddamn career."

He was saved in the nick of time from an argument with Nate when Charles's car come barreling down the gravel drive, spitting stones that clinked merrily in the frigid air.

"You ready?" he asked his father, as if they had any choice in the matter.

"Best turn up the radio," Nate said in answer. "Or it ain't gonna be much of a surprise."

Harry switched on WGCA and cranked up the volume. Twenty-four hours of Christmas music meant his first day off in close to a year. Not that he couldn't have taken one, or two, or even a whole week if he'd asked for it. But without Josh, without Suzanne, what was he supposed to do with a whole night to himself? Watch *Bonanza* reruns with Nate? Go get drunk somewhere with Ross and pick up women who couldn't find anyone better than the likes of them?

Without bothering to throw on a jacket, he headed out to the car, his breath trailing behind him like the cloud a jet leaves behind it. Josh had the back door open and was looking like the Monday after summer vacation.

"Problem?" he asked Suzanne, leaving the *honey* epithet off since he wasn't in the mood for a confrontation with Charles.

She shrugged and the bright red bow she always wore in

her hair at Christmas bobbed against her neck. He remembered her neck, the way she liked to lift her hair off it and have him rain tiny kisses against it.

He shook off the thought. That was then, and this was now.

"Wanna check on Cherokee?" he asked Josh, ushering him out of the car. Cherokee was Josh's own pony, paid for by Harry so that Nate couldn't sell the horse out from under the boy the way he'd done to Harry. "Make sure his water isn't frozen and that he's got enough hay!" He shouted the last as Josh hurried toward the barn. After he was out of hearing range, Harry leaned against the car and stooped so that his head was close to Suzanne's open window.

"It's cold," she said, clutching her collar more closely around her neck and adjusting the heat, which Harry figured, knowing his Suz, was already up to the max. "You'll bring him back tomorrow?"

Harry nodded. "What's bothering him?"

Suzanne looked accusingly at Charles, who studied his fingernails. Finally her new husband looked sheepishly at Harry's old wife, not unlike the way Harry imagined he often looked at her himself, and whined, "I didn't know. The kid's seven, Suz, and smart as a whip. I thought he'd figured it out by now."

Suz. It grated, hearing that name from Charles's lips. "Figured what out?" he boomed into the Range Rover with the leather seats that were heated to keep *Suz's* fanny warm.

He supposed that Josh must have walked in on Suzanne and her new husband at some inopportune moment, and it made his skin crawl. He rubbed at his arms and noted how cold it really was around him.

Suzanne looked at him with those big brown eyes that

had melted his heart nine years earlier, and he hated the hold they still had on his gut. "It was bound to happen eventually. No one believes in Santa Claus forever, I suppose," she said and placed her gloved hand not over his own, but over Charles's, where it was resting on the gearshift. And then, leaning her body closer to Charles's despite the console that separated their seats, she said over her shoulder to Harry, "Not too early tomorrow, Harry. Bring him after lunch, okay?"

She was as subtle as a mare in heat, and Harry backed away from the window, hit the top of the Rover in a gesture of farewell—or maybe more like *Go to hell*—and watched the truck as it backed up and then flew down the road, strewing bits of his already decimated heart behind it.

"I think Cherokee wants an apple or a carrot," Josh said, coming up behind him and slipping his small hand within Harry's big one. Harry looked down into big brown eyes that duplicated Suzanne's and which begged for assurance that his daddy was all right.

Harry gave his son's hand a good squeeze. It had snowed more out here than in Deburle, and he gestured at the pure white field that stretched out in front of his father's house. "You wanna make some angels in the snow?" he asked. He had a sudden vision of happy faces gathered around Nan Springfield's dining room table and dancing cookies in a chipped white bowl. She had a smile . . . well, if Deburle was a port, they could use her as a lighthouse.

"Too cold," Josh said, raising up his little shoulders.

"Is it?" Harry asked, a foreign warmth curling in his stomach. "Then you wanna race me to the door?"

"You gonna hop, or run backwards?" Josh asked, humoring him when it was clear that the boy was hurting.

"Hopping backwards with one hand on my head," Harry said. "Now!"

Nate was waiting at the door when they got there, holding it open and laughing just as hard as they were.

"Make it snappy, before the snow Santa tracked all over here melts," Nate said when he could muster a voice that sounded gruff.

Josh's face fell.

"Look," Harry said, unwrapping the scarf from around his son's neck. "Maybe Santa doesn't come to Charles's house, but he was sure here. I think his sleigh crash-landed in your grandpa's living room."

Josh's gaze scanned the loot he could see through the doorway and then settled on the snowy tracks that led the way. He looked at them with more skepticism than hope. "How come the snow didn't melt in here? It's hotter than thirty-two degrees."

"Ah," Harry said, inordinately proud that a boy as young as Josh, a boy his first grade teacher had dared to call merely *average*, knew how cold it had to be to snow. "This isn't Ohio snow, Joshy-boy. This is North Pole snow. It's so cold where Santa comes from, it may not even be melted tomorrow!" He sent a stern look at Nate, warning him that they would not be vacuuming up the spray snow until after Josh had gone home.

"Charles says—" Josh began, his voice a little more tentative.

"Charles is an idiot," Nate said, and Harry failed to stifle his laugh, stopping only when Nate added, "So's your dad. Everyone under sixty-five is an idiot, but they don't realize it until they've hit that mark. Then, when they're smart enough to know that the rest of them are . . . oh, never mind! You better see what Santa brought before he decides *he* doesn't believe in *you*, either."

Josh seemed to consider his options and decide that he wasn't about to take chances with a stack of gifts that was bigger than he was.

All right, so maybe Harry had gone overboard. Maybe he hadn't wanted to be outdone by Charles, be the second-class dad in the second-class home.

"I guess Grandpa doesn't hear so good," Josh shouted over the radio, which was drowning out anything else that just might happen to be making any noise in the room. He approached the tree and the treasures that surrounded it almost reverently.

"You better start with this one," Harry said, pointing to a box that looked like it had fallen off Santa's sleigh back at the North Pole and been kicked all the way to Ohio. Nate was no Martha Stewart when it came to wrapping. "Santa had trouble getting the paper on it, I guess."

"Well, maybe *Santa* didn't want to turn it upside down," Nate said testily while Josh sort of poked at the ribbon.

"Just rip the paper, Josh," Harry said. "And for God's sake, don't shake it!"

Josh's eyes widened even before he'd torn off all the paper and lifted the puppy from the box.

Maybe it had been a mistake, getting the ugliest runt of a dog they had at the pound. Spiting Suzanne at Josh's expense seemed petty suddenly as the stupid-looking dog crooked his head at Josh and Josh crooked his head right back. He'd have never gotten the boy an Afghan or some other fancy dog that Suzanne could have been proud of, but this . . . this . . .

"Wow." Josh's voice was a whisper of awe. "Oh, wow,"

he added after a while as the dog burrowed around in the boy's lap and they sniffed each other's noses.

"If you don't like him. . ." Harry began, and let his voice fade away. *Then what? I'll take him back to the North Pole and ask Santa for a different one?*

"That Charles is a jerk," Josh said as he lay back against the worn carpeting and let the mongrel maul him. "He'll have to believe there's a Santa Claus now!"

"Of course there is," Nate agreed. "No one else would get you a dog that looks quite like that."

"He's the prettiest dog I ever saw," Josh said, thinking that he was agreeing with Nate. "And there must be a Santa, 'cause I heard Daddy promise Mommy that he wouldn't get me a dog."

Harry refused to meet Nate's gaze.

"My other dad's allergic, you know," Josh added.

Any satisfaction of besting Charles vanished with Josh's words. *My other dad.* Harry wasn't sure he could breathe, wasn't sure he wanted to.

"What's his name?"

"Only one thing to name a dog like that," Nate said. *God Awful* came to mind.

"Chuck," his father said, and Harry risked a glance at him. Nate winked. He had been adamantly opposed to naming the dog after Charles when Harry'd suggested it earlier. "Santa stood in that very doorway, suited up in red from head to toe, and told me that this dog's name was Chuck. Isn't that right, pooch?" he asked the dog, snapping his fingers above the dog's head.

"Up, Chuck!" Harry ordered, and the three of them laughed as Chuck promptly rolled over and put his paws in the air.

"It's a name that can grow on you," Nate said. "Like mold."

The dog pawed at the pile of gifts, reminding them there were plenty more to open. "Think Santa brought you something, boy?" Josh asked. "He is a boy, isn't he, Dad?"

Harry tilted his head to catch a glimpse of anything below the dog's tail.

"Isn't he? Santa didn't go giving us bachelors some she-dog, did he?" Nate asked, lifting the ugly pooch by the tail and looking accusingly at Harry. "I suppose Santa was so hell-bent on picking the goddamn ugliest dog that he didn't even bother to check."

"Hey, Lassie was a girl and they don't come better than Lassie," Harry countered.

"Technically, Lassie was a boy, they just called him *she*. I don't suppose Santa gave a thought to Josh's mom's white carpets when this little lady goes into heat, did he?"

Harry smiled. He wished he *had* thought of it. He couldn't really say why, but for no good reason he thought of Nan Springfield again, imagined her tut-tutting the dog for bleeding all over her about-to-be-re-covered armchair. If he was looking for a woman (which he wasn't), and he were to take note of Nan Springfield (which he sure as hell would never even consider doing), he'd have to notice that she and Suzanne had as much in common as a piece of fancy stationery and a warped two-by-four. They both might have come from the same tree, but they sure as hell had parted company early on.

"Think there's something for you in there, fella?" Josh said as the dog nosed through a pile of store-wrapped gifts. "I mean, girl," he corrected. "She could have pups one day, Dad! We could have a dozen dogs, couldn't we?"

"Sure," Harry said. Of course, he wouldn't live to see

them because Suzanne would have chopped him into very small pieces and ground him in her Cuisinart by then, but sure, Chuckie the female mongrel could breed.

"Hey! New skates!" Josh shouted. "I hope these fit better than the ones you bought me, Dad. Those were for a baby."

"Is there room on your team for another player?" Harry asked his son.

"Trouble, trouble, trouble," Nate chanted, shaking his head.

"The boy doesn't have a father to look into this sort of thing," Harry said. "And it's my fault he doesn't."

"Who doesn't have a father?" Josh asked.

"Trouble, trouble, trouble," Nate repeated.

"No one," Harry said, but just the same, he'd call George Usdin tomorrow and see if there was room on the Riverside Carwash team for one more player.

"How was it your fault?" Josh asked.

"It wasn't your father's fault," Nate said, raising an eyebrow at Harry and warning, "Little pitchers have big ears."

Harry nodded. He'd been grateful none of this had touched Josh.

"I forgot to tell you Ross called," Nate said. Harry had the sense that he was just trying to fill the quiet that had fallen on the room like a heavy layer of soot, darkening everything. "Something about a woman calling the station and leaving a message."

"Why didn't you say so before?" Harry asked, pushing the half-opened package off his lap and assuring Josh and Chuckie that he'd be right back.

In the front hall he picked up the receiver to the old black rotary phone that had sat on the table there for as long as Harry could remember, and dialed up the station.

"Yo, Ross," he said into the speaker. "Merry Christmas."

"For you, maybe," Ross said. "You're not giving the weather and traffic together on the eights all day." Harry heard a giggle in the background.

"Not to mention the score," he said.

"There's nothing like hitting a home run on the holidays to warm a man's heart. Listen, a woman called down here and said to tell you 'Thank you.' What with you never doing a kind deed for anyone, I was kinda curious."

"She give her name?" Harry asked.

"Said she was just a friend of a friend," Ross answered, before murmuring something that Harry wasn't meant to hear.

"Soft voice?" Harry asked trying to remember anything distinctive about Nan Springfield that could be detected over the phone. "Sort of . . . awed?"

"No," Ross said. "Definitely not a chickie. Oh, and she said to say that they fit."

Topher's skates. It had to be her. "Not soft?" Harry asked again. "Like melted butter, or a pink angora sweater or—" He stopped before he finished making a total jackass of himself.

"You actually went over there, didn't you?" Ross asked, hushing the woman he was with and giving Harry his full attention.

"Aunt Ellie! Older? A little riled? Jeez, I'm stupid! Did she—"

"It was just a thirty-second call, man. Keep your fly zippered. She musta been some piece—"

"She was nothing." The wheels inside his head were turning at a frantic pace. Eleanor, outraged by what the world was doing to her sister-in-law, would surely stick her neck out for Nan and the kids. And she'd surely not tell Nan what she'd done.

Or what Harry'd done, either.

She'd known who he was the minute she'd come in from the kitchen, he was sure of it.

"Call the boss at home and ask him how we go about a charity telethon on the air. Tell him I want to raise a hundred thousand dollars for a widow and some kids. Tell him—"

"Okay, big guy, take it down a notch, huh?" Ross asked.

"Is that Harris Tweed?" Ross's twinkee asked.

"Tell her no!" Harry shouted into the phone. "Tell her Harris isn't a big guy. He's a little twirpy thing. Smaller than you. Tell her Harris Tweed makes you feel like a goddamn gorilla!"

"No, honey," he heard Ross say. "This is some psychopath. The Suit is obnoxious, but he's sane."

"And short," Harry yelled.

"And he's real, real small," Ross said, agreeing with Harry like he was on some bridge about to jump. "You know the Big and Tall Man's Shop? Well, Tweed's got to go to the Rank and Puny Store."

"Dad?" Josh stood next to him in the hall. Harry's father hung back in the doorway. "Why are you shouting at Uncle Ross?"

"He's getting hard of hearing," he answered, replacing the receiver on the hook and ruffling his son's head. "Sorry. I didn't mean to take so long."

Josh was trailing a ribbon and the mutt of a puppy was chasing the end of it like a kitten might. Maybe she was part cat, too, along with every other breed that must have had a turn with her mother the night she came into being. "Who's Harris Tweed?"

"Somebody Uncle Ross knows," Harry said.

"You don't like him, do you?" Josh asked.

Nate coughed loudly.

"Your grandpa doesn't like him," Harry said with a finality that Josh seemed to accept as they wandered back into the living room to open more gifts.

"What's the matter?" Harry asked when Josh just fingered the ribbons and bows and showed no interest in opening the big red gift that Nate had put in front of him.

"That kid with no dad," Josh asked. "Does he have a place to live?"

"Yes, Josh, he does," Harry said, vowing to himself to keep it that way.

Josh studied him, still just playing with the ribbons of his gift. "Does he have a mom?"

"Yes, Josh," Harry said, moved by his son's ability to hurt for someone he didn't even know. "A very nice mom," he said reassuringly.

Josh nodded, apparently appeased. At least Harry thought he was, until the boy added, "Does she know what happened is your fault?"

Eight

Nan hated the cold. She hated watching her children struggle and she hated sports. So to say that she wasn't having the best time sitting on a wooden bleacher in the cold with two complaining little girls and D.J. in a snit beside her, watching Topher try to master the art of staying up on ice skates, was probably an understatement.

Of course, the fact that everyone was staring at the poor charity case that stupid Harris Tweed had made of her, when he started begging for donations on her behalf on the radio, wasn't improving her mood any.

And then there was the awful truth that despite her pride and her anger, she was reduced to praying that the infamous Suit would collect enough money to allow her to keep the kids in the only home they'd ever known—heck, the only home she'd ever known. Apparently she couldn't exactly rely on the church to bail her out. Heck, they wouldn't even officially admit to sending Santa. Just last night Mr. Royce had pretended to have no idea what Nan had been trying to thank him for since Christmas. And he'd implied that it would be best if she'd just drop the whole thing, as if he wanted nothing to tie him to any kindness extended to Phil's widow. If she'd let herself believe for a moment that the church had given up its grudge against Phil and the cloud he'd hung over the Old Deburle Church, she'd been wrong.

Well, what else was new?

Aarrgh!

"First time here?" asked a man who was settling himself on the bleachers a few feet away from her. His face was hidden by the grocery bag he carried, a box of chocolate-covered marshmallow cookies peeking out of the top. He had with him, in addition, a padded seat, a blanket, a thermos, and the *DeBurle Gazette.*

Nan fastened Robin's top button and wished she'd thought to bring along any one of the things the professional dad had with him.

"Just joined the team," she said, pointing to Topher, who was inching his way hand-over-hand around the railing of the rink.

"Really," he said, looking at the rink. "You'd never guess." It didn't take seeing his full face to recognize him. He was smaller without the Santa suit, but he still seemed big. Larger than life.

"Oh, well, he's a quick learner," she said as Topher once again polished the ice with the seat of his pants. "Gordie Howe, watch out, because Topher Springfield's hot on your tail!" she called toward the rink as Topher picked himself up.

Harry stifled a laugh.

"He *is* a hockey player, isn't he?" she asked.

"Was." Topher fell down yet again. "And he's probably in a nursing home drooling with fear that Topher's gonna beat his record."

"It could happen," she said, sticking her nose in the air. "Stranger things happen every day. Like for instance you could be sitting on a bench in the cold and run into a famous person whose name I'd best not mention."

She thought he paled slightly, despite the bright cheeks that the cold had given his nicely rugged face.

"Don't worry. I won't give away your secret in front of everyone," she promised, holding on to D.J.'s latest cape—this one red with a big *D* on it—as he sat on the bench in front of her.

Santa, sans beard, sans suit, turned to look at her. He looked guilty as an altar boy caught with his hand stuck in the poor box. Maybe he was just realizing what he'd gotten her into by getting Topher on the team.

"Too bad you can't use that 'better be good, better not pout,' threat all year," she said, watching him smile and nod at her recognition of him. "Honey, you've got to stay between your sisters and me," she told D.J., slackening the death grip she had on his cape. He immediately sidled over toward Santa. Who could blame him? Santa still had all the goodies, and a face that drew you in, made you want to sit next to him and feel the warmth of his arm around you.

That is, D.J. no doubt felt that way.

Nan's life was already like some computer's motherboard gone haywire—she didn't understand how it had ever worked, what was wrong with it now, and hadn't a clue as to how to fix it. All she knew was that it wasn't working. And she didn't need any more parts that could go wrong.

Like a man. Especially an unhappily divorced man, like she suspected Santa was.

She had taken in her last poor soul with D.J. Why, she was barely keeping her own head afloat, never mind a stranger who kept looking at her like she was some life preserver and the *Titanic* had just been struck.

"I'd like to thank you again for what you did," she said.

"I tried to thank Mr. Royce, but he played it like *Mission Impossible*—disavowing any knowledge of the whole thing."

The man shifted in his seat. "Yeah, well, you know secret agents—if he told you, well, then he'd have to kill you, I suppose."

"Accepting charity under any circumstances isn't easy. Under these . . . well, if you'd just pass on my thanks—" she started, but he interrupted her.

"How's the kid doing?" the man asked, gesturing toward the ice as he turned the lid of his thermos. Steam rose and coated his sunglasses with a thin fog.

"Well," Nan said with a shrug, her eyes on that thermos full of something warm, "he's smiling. I'd have crawled off the ice by now, but Topher's no quitter."

"I don't imagine you're a quitter, either," the man said, pulling several Styrofoam cups from one of his many pockets and handing one to D.J. while he reached for the hot chocolate.

Styrofoam was one of those things that set D.J. off, along with slimy things and coarse things and a bunch of other textures that seemed to make the poor child just go crazy. His howl was ear-splitting. It rang off the frozen trees and the ice and echoed down from the overcast sky to ring all over again. Robin and Rachel covered their ears dramatically while everyone who had only been staring at Nan covertly turned with wide eyes and dropped jaws.

"Stay with Mr. . . ." she looked in the nice man's direction with vague misgivings. He'd already been in her home, given her children presents. She would just have to trust him. "Stay here!" she told the girls as she grabbed up D.J. and ran as quickly as she could to the car.

Twenty minutes later she was damp with sweat, the windows of the secondhand Toyota she'd bought with the insurance money from Phil's car were fogged over, and a limp little boy was asleep in her arms. Every third or fourth breath was a shudder as he fought demons even in his dreams.

He'd found someone to take Robin to the bathroom, stuffed Rachel with cookies, and cheered Topher's turn around the rink on his skates instead of his behind.

Still no Nan.

After the girls had asked where Mommy was for the millionth time, he finally headed for the parking lot with both girls in tow. He knocked gently against the driver's window, soft enough to ignore, if she wanted to. Not that it mattered, with the girls yelping for her to open the door.

Slowly she cranked down the window. Her hair clung to her face, damp, limp. D.J. lay against her chest, his mouth open but his fists clenched. Harry hushed the girls with a stern voice which they immediately obeyed.

"You all right?" he whispered.

She could have been sarcastic and said, "dandy," or "just peachy-keen." She could have been honest and told him that "no, she most certainly wasn't all right and it was his fault for signing Topher up for the team," which was really only a tiny part of it. She could have lied and pretended that it was nothing, that he'd imagined the scene D.J. had caused.

Instead she just nodded, tears clinging to the bottom rim of her eyes and begging to be released.

"I'll give that guy I know a call," he said, his voice low so that he wouldn't disturb the little guy's sleep.

"Thanks."

"I guess hockey wasn't the best idea," he admitted while

the girls kicked at the caked-on snow behind the Toyota's tires. "I just thought the kid would enjoy it."

"There's no reason for Topher to suffer just because D.J. is having a hard time," she said. When she said it, somehow it made sense.

"So *you* suffer," he said, pushing the hair out of her eyes for her because her arms were held prisoner by thirty pounds of terror.

"I'll survive," she said. She shifted the child and arched her back a little.

"Can I ask you something?" she said, transferring the boy's head to her far shoulder to create an intimacy between them that made him uncomfortable. Or maybe it was just not knowing what she might ask.

"I'd be happy to take Topher to practice with Josh," he offered.

"No, it's not that, though I really would appreciate that more than you know." She smiled, luminescent.

He swallowed thoughts that stuck in his throat like bits of glass, choking him.

"Do you know how soon the church will make me leave my house?" she asked.

"The church doesn't tell me its plans," he admitted honestly.

"Do you know how Harris Tweed found out about me having to move?"

His tongue was thick in his mouth.

"I was just wondering because this, this, this charity thing on the radio started after we spoke." She looked embarrassed.

"It would be hard to move all the kids," he said as a way to avoid the question.

She kissed D.J.'s head. "Especially this one. I don't

know how much Mr. Royce told you, but Harris Tweed hurt my family irreparably, and to take anything from that man stings my heart like acid on a wound. I know you didn't mean any harm, but I—"

"The money he's raising isn't from him, Nan." It was the first time he'd called her by her name. It felt too good and he warned himself against doing it again. He *was* Harris Tweed, and just because she didn't know it *yet*, didn't make it any less true. If anything, hiding his identity from her this way made it worse. "It's from the people of Deburle who care about you." It seemed that all the people of Deburle cared about her. There were letters with the money. He read each one, and was in awe that one small woman could mean so much to so many people.

"I used to make up the baskets for the poor with my father and mother. Last week one turned up anonymously on my front porch. This end of the stick is hard," she admitted. "If it weren't for the children . . ."

A Range Rover pulled into the parking lot and he warned the girls to stick close to their mother's car, shifting his body to make sure they stayed put.

"Harry!" His head whipped around at Suzanne's holler. Before he could cover the distance to her car, she was laying on the horn like nobody's business.

"Shut up!" he said, reaching into the driver's seat window and pulling her hand from the horn. "There's a kid sleeping in that car."

"And there's a puppy peeing in this one," she said angrily. "You've got two choices. You can take the dirty beast and bring it to your father's, or I can drop it back off at the pound. Choose the second and you have two more choices. I can tell your son there is no Santa Claus, just a friggin' idiot whose promises don't mean a goddamn thing, or I can tell him the stupid dog is dead." She took a breath. "Your call."

"He really wanted a dog," Harry said, watching Nan's car to see if she could hear Suzanne's words. She was talking quietly to the girls. From what he could tell, it looked as if she was playing Simon Says with them. "You don't want the dog? Fine. I'll keep her at Nate's. We'll just tell Josh that his mother cares more about her carpeting than about her son."

"Oh, puhleeze," Suzanne said, drawing out the word. "This from the man who cared more about his radio program than his wife or his son. Just get the mutt out of the car. And make sure she isn't under the tires when I pull away, because the temptation may be too great."

Harry opened the back hatch and unfastened the leash that Suzanne had attached to a hook beside the window. "Come on, Chuckie," he said deliberately. "That's a good little Chuck—"

Before he could get out the name again, Suzanne was back to laying on the horn, to drown him out, he supposed. He tucked the ugly puppy under his arm, slammed down the hatch, and smacked the top of the car.

As she drove away, he asked the exhaust fumes if she wasn't going to stay and watch Josh's hockey practice. "I guess that's a no," he said to the cloud of smoke that Suzanne left behind her.

"A doggie!" Robin shouted, and Harry bit the inside of his cheek. It wasn't enough that he'd killed the reverend. He just had to keep making things worse.

"Is it for Topher?" Rachel asked. "Mommy promised him a puppy a long time ago."

Nan Springfield rolled her eyes. She'd apparently been trying to get D.J. back to sleep, but all the excitement of the dog had him trying to climb out the window. When Harry went to lift him, Nan shook her head quickly.

"Let him get out himself," she cautioned him, gesturing that they could have another fit on their hands otherwise.

"Is it ours?" Rachel asked.

"Oh, don't I wish," Nan said as if she really, truly meant it.

Harry took another look at Chuckie. She had one ear up and one down. Her fur was not quite curly, not quite straight. Her different-colored eyes made her look cock-eyed. He wondered what dog Nan was looking at.

"Isn't she the most adorable thing you've ever seen?" she asked her girls.

"She's ours, right?" Rachel asked again.

Harry wondered how arsenic tasted.

"No, she belongs to Mr.—" Nan Springfield looked at him questioningly. When he stood there mutely, like some idiot who didn't even know his own name, she asked. "I'm sorry. Do I even know your name?"

Harry took a deep breath. "Woolery," he said as evenly as he could get it out. "Harry Woolery." It was, after all, the truth.

"She's Mr. Woolery's dog," she said trustingly.

Harry felt sick to his stomach.

"Why can't we have her?" Robin whined.

"Because she already has a home," Nan explained patiently.

"She could be a foster dog!" Rachel shouted.

He and Nan exchanged a glance, almost as if she were asking, almost as if he were offering. Jeez, he'd given her enough trouble already.

"Maybe you could come and visit her," Harry said. "My father has a horse farm in Mercer and if your mama thinks it's all right, maybe one day you could come and visit her and the horses."

"And you!" Robin added.

A dagger to the heart would be quicker and more efficient than poison.

"Horses! Oh, that would be lovely," the unsuspecting Widow Springfield sang out.

Harry crouched down amongst the children and the dog, wishing he could get smaller still, until maybe the ground could just cover him up. "Practice ought to be about over," he said while the children all petted the puppy.

"I guess we ought to get back to the rink," she agreed, bending down to scratch the scruffy dog behind her upright ear.

"I could pick up the kids some Saturday," he offered half-heartedly. He could just hear Nate now: *Why do you always have to go looking for trouble?*

"Well, I could give you my number," she said, fumbling inside her handbag.

"I'm sure I can find it," Harry said. He already knew it by heart, had almost dialed it half a dozen times.

"Of course, we'll probably be moving soon . . ." her voice trailed off as if she were afraid that the kids might have heard her.

"I think your neighbors will come through for you, if you let them," he said, watching Rachel reach into Nan's pocket and pull out a tissue without asking, as if of course it would be there.

"I don't think I ought to count on that," she said, and shirked her shoulders.

Incredibly, the coffers were nearly halfway there, but he could never explain how he knew that, or how moved he'd been by all the notes and letters praising Nan Springfield which had accompanied the checks. Nor could he tell her that he'd do whatever it took to make up the difference.

How could he explain that one to her? Or to Nate?

It was guilt, pure and simple. And a promise to a kid made on the day his father had been buried.

He knew Nate would say otherwise.

And it scared the bejesus out of him to think that Nate could, for the first time in his life when it came to Harry, be right.

Nine

"That's a relief," Eleanor heard her sister-in-law say as she came into the kitchen to find Stan Denham, that no-account accountant with his chair—and his thigh—pressed up against Nan's, their heads bent over Nan's bank statements. "I'm not really used to doing this yet. I guess I hit a wrong button on the calculator or something."

"Nothing some Wite-Out can't fix," Stan said, painting out Nan's figures in her check register. Eleanor thought about all the things she'd like to simply Wite-Out herself—documents and decades, mistakes and memories. Stan Denham. Now there was something Eleanor would like to paint right out of the picture in Nan's kitchen. "I told you I'll be happy to help you look after your finances as long as you need me."

"I really think I've got the hang of it. It's just that Phil always—"

Eleanor thought about the way Nan had always been controlled by someone else—no doubt Nan would have considered it being *looked after*. Well, Eleanor had been looked after too, once upon a time, and she wasn't going to let Nan be crushed the way she'd been. She cleared her throat and Stan jumped three feet away from her sister-in-law.

"Ellie! I didn't hear you come in," Nan said, looking up and giving her a smile. "Good news! We can eat for the rest of the month."

"Kids asleep?" Eleanor asked, putting down her shoulder bag and emptying out the insulated lunch bag she took to work with her.

"Mmm. I promised them you'd go in and kiss them when you got home."

Eleanor nodded. She was becoming attached to the kids, and they to her. If they lost the house, it would be the first step on a slippery slope that would land them all in a pool of misery.

"What about the house?" she asked Denham. Against Nan's better judgment, she'd agreed to put their packing on hold when Harris Tweed had started his campaign to save *the Widow Springfield* (as he referred to her nightly) from losing her home, on top of losing her husband. Tweed was good—not too sappy. He made it sound like a matter of doing right by a good neighbor, not like an act of pity.

"What if Tweed raises enough money for her to buy the house?" Eleanor asked. "What then?"

"She'd probably be best off just buying another house with the money—*if* she gets any," Denham said. "Move on with her life and—" He shrugged his shoulders. "I'm trying, but Mr. Royce and the others just want to get the whole matter behind them, and giving Nan the house would imply certain . . . well . . . ." Again he shrugged and a funny little chill ran up Eleanor's spine.

"Oh, but they don't mind her being part of all the women's circles, doing the *Weathervane*, helping with Sunday school, do they?" Eleanor asked. "What does that imply?"

"She's still a part of the church," Stan said. "A member. She'll always be welcome there, whatever . . ."

Wimp! Stan Denham was going to be about as much use to Nan as four flat tires. He was going to get her nowhere. Eleanor abandoned any notions that Stan could be the one to help Nan out of her troubles.

"Have you found something in Phil's records?" she asked. Almost before she had the question out, she had her answer.

"No."

No was what he said, but his cheek twitched and his eyes didn't meet hers. Nan apparently had no clue, but then maybe it took someone who'd made mistakes and tried to hide them herself to recognize someone else dancing the same jig.

"It just doesn't make any sense," Nan said. "There are all these deposits and withdrawals and—"

"I explained that to you already," Denham said with exaggerated patience. "Sometimes the reverend would take the church receipts and put them into his own account and then transfer them over to the church's later."

"Why?" Eleanor asked, waiting to see just how deep a hole the accountant would dig for himself. Apparently Phil's had been six feet, if she was reading between the lies correctly.

"Oh, it was all very aboveboard. Nothing out of the ordinary. If I missed services, for example," he said, trying to seem offhanded. "Or forgot to bring the deposit slips with me—it's not safe to just leave cash lying around, Eleanor, and the reverend—"

Either he'd discovered Phil was stealing and didn't want to expose him—certainly not to the man's widow—or Denham himself had something going on.

"No, of course not," Eleanor agreed, certain they weren't going to get the answers they sought from him and anxious to see the man leave so that she could take a look at the books herself. Not that she had hopes of finding anything Nan herself couldn't find. Between the two of them they could make a dress faster than they could figure out how much they were saving at a 25 percent sale.

"Would you like a cup of coffee and some pie?" Nan offered Denham, rising and going to the cupboard for dishes.

The phone rang and Eleanor answered it, keeping an eye on Denham as she did. The man had been nothing but helpful, but she just didn't like him—she especially didn't like him here in Nan's kitchen, the heart of her house.

"Is this the Springfield residence?" It was a man's voice.

"For the time being," she said sarcastically.

"This is Harry Woolery. I'm looking for—"

"Harry." Lord, when she made a mess, she sure did a job of it. And this one didn't seem to be going away.

"Mrs. Springfield?"

"No, it's Eleanor. We met at Christmas?" And, she didn't tell him, she was the one who had made the anonymous phone call that had prompted Harry to don his Santa suit and walk right into their lives.

"Yes," he said, sounding stiff, wary. He needn't worry, she wanted to tell him. Nan wouldn't be any happier with her part in it than with his.

"She mentioned seeing you at the ice rink," Eleanor said, hoping Harry could hear her disapproval while a big smile spread across Nan's face.

"My son plays hockey, too," he said. "Can I speak with her? Is she home?"

Eleanor held out the phone to Nan.

Smiling apologetically at Stan as she stretched the phone cord to reach the coffeepot, Nan took the phone, tried not to sound as nervous as she felt, and said, "Hello?"

"Nan? This is Harry Woolery. We met at the hockey rink?" His voice jiggled, like his leg was shaking or something.

"Yes, I remember. With the wonderful dog."

"He has a dog?" Eleanor asked with obvious disapproval, as if that were a strike against him.

"She's getting his belly rubbed as we speak," Harry said.

Ah, the jiggling. For some inexplicable reason she'd supposed it was nerves. She almost said, Lucky dog, but was afraid it would sound like she wanted her belly rubbed, too.

"I was calling about the doctor for your son," he said.

"Yes?"

"Sounds like that *Power Rangers* is almost over," Eleanor warned her, raising her eyebrows toward the TV room as she served a very slim piece of pie to Stan Denham and filled his coffee cup only halfway.

"I spoke to that friend I told you about and got the name of a pediatric neurologist."

"I don't suppose he'd be willing to be paid in pies," she muttered, wondering how in the world she would pay for a specialist for D.J. when Social Services was insisting there was nothing wrong with him.

"His fees have been taken care of," her private Santa Claus said.

"Harry, I couldn't let you—"

"Let him what?" Eleanor asked.

To Nan it felt as if no one thought she was capable of running her own affairs. True, she'd gone right from under her father's wing to under her husband's. But now she was flying on her own, and at thirty-two, it was about time. She was beginning to wish that, well-meaning as they might be, they would all just get out of her way.

"Oh, I didn't do anything," Harry said quickly. "I just told him a little about the boy and he said he was interested in seeing him. He's doing a study and the boy would be a possible subject, so he wouldn't charge anything for the consultation. Then, depending on the outcome, things can be arranged."

"I don't know what to say . . ." She could feel the tears in her eyes welling up. So much for flying solo. She covered the mouthpiece and sniffed.

"Would you like to come to dinner Friday night, Mr. Woolery? It's not much, but I'd really like to show you how much I appreciate your making the arrangements for the doctor."

Eleanor smacked her forehead, as if a man as nice as Harry Woolery, a man with the blessing of the church, could misinterpret what she was saying.

"No thanks necessary," he said curtly. He had stopped jiggling the dog. Maybe he had misinterpreted.

"I really do make a mean pot roast and my apple pie is first class," she said.

"I'm sure you do, Mrs. Springfield. But Friday night is bad for me."

"Oh. Well, would Saturday be better?"

"Actually, I work nights," he said. "It leaves my days free to see Josh."

"What do you do?" she asked.

Dead silence.

"Not that it's any of my business," she said, retracting the question and watching Stan Denham strum his fingers on the table. "I really ought to go. I have company and I—"

"Denham's done. He can go anytime," Eleanor said,

taking away his plate while he glared at her. Nan supposed that her sister-in-law had good reason for distrusting men, but Nan didn't share those feelings. She appreciated Stan Denham's help. And whether he wanted her to or not—and it seemed pretty plain that he didn't—she liked Harry Woolery.

"Be talking to you," Harry said as if he were in a rush to get off the phone.

Quickly she asked, "Would Sunday be easier for you? For dinner, I mean?"

"As I said," he started.

"Yes, you work nights. We could have it in the afternoon," she suggested.

"Maybe some other time," he said. There was a pause. Then he added, "But thanks, anyway."

"Anytime," she tried to sing into the phone, hoping her voice didn't sound as flat as she felt. It wasn't like she was trying to seduce the man, for heaven's sake. She just wanted to pay him back the only way she knew how.

"The doctor's appointment is for next Thursday at three o'clock. Is that all right?"

"If it was at midnight in Fairbanks, Alaska, I'd be there," she said and was rewarded with a laugh.

"I bet you would. It's in Columbus."

She thought for a moment about how D.J. got himself out of his seat belt every twenty minutes, forcing her to pull over, refasten him, and sometimes give him a scolding. She'd have to leave before noon.

"Problem?" Harry asked.

"No," she said, wondering about taking Topher out of school early and bringing all four kids and . . . well . . . "No problem at all," she said again.

"Would it help any if I drove you?"

Say no, she told herself. The man's done enough. He doesn't have to have four screaming kids in his car for hours and miss seeing his own son's hockey practice and no doubt have to listen to more of your problems.

"I'd be happy to," he added. "I'd really like to make sure that little fellow is all right."

It felt as if she'd been carrying her own burdens forever, long before Phil's death.

"I'll pick you up at one-thirty, all right?"

"One-thirty," she agreed.

"Are you making a date with him?" Eleanor asked, chewing nervously on the inside of her cheek.

"And, Nan? Could you maybe bring a slice of that pie for me, if it isn't too much trouble?" he asked. She could picture his smile, and it produced one of her own.

"No trouble at all," she said.

"Before I hang up, could I speak to Eleanor again, please," he asked.

She held out the phone to Eleanor, who looked at it suspiciously.

"Yes?" Eleanor said when she had accepted the phone and listened for a while. "Oh, sure, yes. That's nice of you. I'll find someone. Okay then. Do you want Nan back? Okay then. Bye."

Nan put the pie back in front of Stan Denham absentmindedly. He made a careful incision with the knife and evened off the edges, helping himself to seconds. "What was that all about?" he asked.

"You know the man I told you the church sent at Christmas? He just made some arrangements for D.J. to see a doctor," Nan said.

"And for a sitter to stay with the girls," Eleanor added to Nan's surprise.

"Mr. Royce assures me that the church never—" Stan began.

Nan was tired of the game, and didn't want to play. She was too excited at the prospect of help for D.J., and so she said, "Fine. Well, then Santa himself is making arrangements to get me some help for D.J."

"Is the boy sick?" Stan asked.

Nan didn't answer, and Eleanor said, "Wouldn't it be funny if he turned out to be Santa Claus?" And then, as she helped herself to a generous slice of pie, she got a broad smile on her face and added, "And wouldn't old Vernon just burst an artery over this!"

When Friday night found Harry across from Josh at McDonald's trying to wedge his grown-up body into one of those little orange benches obviously meant for people his son's age, Harry wondered why he'd been too afraid to accept the Widow Springfield's innocent invitation. It wasn't as if anything would have come of it. He wasn't likely to get drunk on her pot roast and ravage her. Now, if she was making boeuf Bourguignon . . . "Think Chuckie'd like a burger?" Josh asked him. "We could bring her back one, couldn't we?"

Harry tousled his son's hair and pulled a five-dollar bill out of his pocket, which wasn't easy in the too-goddamn-small booth. "Get her fries, too."

"You think she'd like a shake?" Josh, still a tiny bit of a thing, was on his feet and stuffing the last of the fries into his mouth as he spoke.

"I think we ought to pass on the shake," Harry said and checked his watch. He had to drop Josh at Nate's, which was an hour out of his way in each direction, and then get to the radio station before midnight. "It's almost time for us to be shoving off."

"Okay," Josh agreed, heading off at a run and nearly trampling two small girls in his way. Two small, familiar girls. And their older brother.

And Nan.

Jeez. Now he remembered why he'd said no to dinner. He'd complicated her life enough. Too much, to be thinking the thoughts he had around her. Like whether she was as sweet before her morning cup of coffee as she always seemed to be. Like whether she was as soft to the touch as the eye. Like whether she was missing a man after five months of being a widow.

He was a pig. Pure and simple.

But it didn't stop him from wondering.

It had been a long time since he'd been with a woman. A long, long time. Longer even than he could remember with any detail. Which explained why his heart was creeping up his throat at the sight of a woman who looked like she'd been run over by a Fisher-Price truck.

She spotted him immediately and that brilliant smile lit up the fast-food joint like fireworks.

Shit.

He had it bad.

The smile faded quickly and she pulled back the girls with her free hand while D.J. whirled his cape around himself dramatically.

"Hi," Harry said as casually as his hormones would allow. At least his voice didn't squeak.

"Hello." She was cool, trying to give him a polite smile that fell far short of the automatic one that he'd received at her first sighting. "I thought you had to work tonight." It was the closest he imagined Nan Springfield came to a rebuke.

"I do. We were just finishing up. Then I've got to run Josh over to my dad's and get to the station."

"The station?" she asked.

He kicked himself to Columbus and back while she waited.

"You take the train to work?" While she asked, D.J. crawled under the table to start banging with his fist on Harry's feet. He figured that it was probably hurting the boy more than him, and so he ignored it in favor of saying hello to the girls and introducing himself to Topher.

"Hey," Josh said by way of greeting to Topher when he returned to the table. They high-fived each other and then Josh said that the burger and fries were for his dog.

"Can I buy you guys some dinner?" Harry offered.

"I thought you were leaving," Nan said, pulling some crumpled bills from the pocket of her down jacket and handing them to Topher. "Four Happy Meals and an extra fries," she told him. Josh took off with Topher as if buying food was the most exciting thing in the kid's life.

"You're going to have fries for dinner?" he asked, *tsk*ing at her.

"I was going to have pot roast and pie," she said, a hint of a smile playing at her lips.

"But I blew it."

She looked embarrassed. He was amazed by how endearing her discomfort could be.

D.J. had moved up Harry's feet and was now socking away at his shins.

"I'm sorry," Harry said. "I didn't want to have to eat and run, and you—"

"—and I'm making a federal case out of it. I'm the one who's sorry."

"If anyone should be sorry—" he said, tipping the top half of his body to look under the table at D.J., who was karate-chopping his kneecaps.

Nan bent, too, and gasped, grabbing D.J.'s cape and yanking him toward her. The boy howled. And howled. Rachel and Robin climbed onto the bench across from him and stood on it, covering their ears. Topher and Josh came back with the Happy Meals.

No one was happy.

With obvious difficulty, Nan managed to lift D.J. and capture his arms with her embrace. "Bring the food and the girls," she said to Topher, hurrying toward the door, to the entire restaurant's relief.

Harry managed to follow her and hurry ahead just in time to open the door for her and shepherd the girls out.

She smiled her thanks and headed for the hunk of metal that passed for her car.

She took something of his with her. Sympathy? Admiration? He couldn't put his finger on it. He only knew that he wished he didn't have to get to work.

"Nan?" he yelled over D.J.'s screams.

She looked over her shoulder at him, questioningly.

What did he want to tell her? That he was sorry? Sorry about how hard her life was and how much harder he'd made it? Sorry that he couldn't be the one to take away the pain?

D.J. was squirming in her arms. Her jacket was half on and half off, revealing the stretched-out neckline of what appeared in the neon lights to be a faded green sweater. Her hair was a wreck, and there was something crusty on the shoulder of her jacket. Still, there was something, something . . .

"Yes?" she said, not a touch of impatience in her voice, as if all she had to do was stand there and wait for him to remember what he'd wanted to say.

"You look really pretty tonight," he called out.

Yeah. That was what he'd wanted to say.

Ten

Nan pulled on the pink angora turtleneck that her Aunt Kate from Van Wert had sent for Christmas. It stretched to her hips, over the top of the navy challis skirt with the pale little flowers. She wondered if she looked too soft and sweet, and searched Eleanor's eyes for the truth.

"That one looks good, too," Eleanor told her with a sigh. "They all look good. I didn't realize you were so interested in Mr. Woolery."

"I'm not worried about Mr. Woolery," she said, leaning close to the mirror to make sure there was no lipstick on her teeth. "I don't want that doctor to think I'm not a good mother, or that I'm a charity case, or . . ."

Eleanor looked relieved. Ever since Nan had told her about meeting Harry under the golden arches, Eleanor had been warning her about the unlikelihood of a knight on a white charger coming to Nan's rescue. As if Nan thought that there were white knights, or that she was in need of being rescued.

She had survived Phil's death. Social Services hadn't swooped down yet, and she was learning to get by on computer skills, her wit, and a lot of pasta.

She'd mastered databases. She did not need rescuing.

But she hadn't minded when he'd called out to her in

the parking lot and told her she looked pretty. Of course, when she checked herself in the rearview mirror, she had to wonder if McDonald's had started selling liquor . . .

"Now, I've left a snack for the girls in the refrigerator," she reminded Eleanor for the third time. "Isn't it just awful of me to think it was a stroke of luck that the sweet old lady you were taking care of had to go back into the hospital? What a selfish person I am! Forgive me, Lord," she said, raising her eyes to the ceiling and then continuing with her preparations. "And remember, Matthew's mother is dropping Topher and Matthew at hockey and—"

"I know," Eleanor told her, watching D.J. as he bounced on the bed. "Will you stop worrying?"

"Maybe I should wear—"

The doorbell sounded in the hall and she shrugged.

"Guess I'm wearing this. Come on, D.J.. We're going for a ride with Mr. Woolery."

"Now?" D.J. asked.

"Yes, now."

"Not now," D.J. said, and stamped his foot.

"Yes now," she said in what she hoped was a take-no-prisoners voice.

It worked.

D.J. followed her to the front door and she opened it to find Harry waiting on her porch, filling her doorway like he had on Christmas.

He looked at her for a minute before he said anything. Clearly, oh, so clearly, she had settled on the right outfit. He cleared his throat, almost as an alternative to saying something that she could only guess at. Finally he asked, "Everybody ready?"

"I'll just get our coats," she said, beckoning him into the house and then opening the hall closet for the boy's ski jacket. She laid the jacket on the floor, collar closest to his feet, and watched as he put in his arms and flipped the jacket over his head. Then she told him again that they were going for a ride, that she would be sitting with him, that they would see the river and the city and she would sit beside him the whole time. Thankfully, he seemed no more upset than any of her other children might be. For a moment she almost believed she was making too much of his behavior, that this whole trip was unnecessary and that D.J. was just fine.

Dents in the hallway wall from D.J.'s toys, his fists, his shoes, convinced her otherwise. She got up slowly and reached into the closet for her Sunday coat, which Harry took from her and helped her into. It had been so long since someone had held a coat for her that she had trouble finding the armhole and Harry had to guide her arm into it for her.

He had a very gentle touch for such a big man. Phil's movements were always so deliberate, so brusque. Not that Harry Woolery could hold a candle to Phil. And not that she didn't miss Phil. Just not his touch. Not really. And not the way he could fill the air with raw discomfort. And not the way he glared at the children sometimes, as if they were purposefully trying to set his nerves on edge, when they were just being children.

Which was not to say that she didn't miss him, every day, all the time. What kind of wife would she be if she didn't miss her dead husband? What kind of person could—even for a moment—be relieved? Whatever kind of person it was, it wasn't her.

She offered her hand to D.J. and, wonder of wonders, he took it and followed her out of the house. Eleanor stood in the doorway biting her lip as she saw them off. Harry took

Nan's elbow to guide her down the slippery steps to his car, where the engine was still running so that the car would be nice and warm.

Her father used to do that for her on cold winter mornings when he'd take her to school.

The gleaming white car at the curb looked like one of those Mustangs that the boys in high school were always trying to fix up and get back on the road, only this one was fixed up and then some, with a silver stallion at the rear. *No, Nan,* she reminded herself, *there are no knights on white chargers.*

"There's a car seat in my car," she said, but Harry opened the door, pulled forward the front seat, and there it already was.

"Got it," he said, letting her buckle D.J. in. "You know, you really ought to lock your car."

"Oh, no one wants my car," she said, backing slowly away from D.J. and assuring him she was just going around to get in the other side.

Harry shook his head at her as he accompanied her around the back of the car. "You're entirely too trusting," he said as he steadied her on the ice. She held on to the back of the car, just above where the silver letters said *Shelby.*

"No, it's just not a nice car. This one is beautiful," she said, waiting while he pushed forward the driver's seat so she could climb into the backseat.

"It's just a car," he said, but from the shine, despite the recent snowfall, she could tell it was a lot more than that. "Gets me from here to there."

"Is it new?" she asked him after he'd gotten into the front seat, offered to make it hotter, colder, faster, slower, or have it sprout wings.

"Nineteen sixty-eight Shelby GT," he said, stroking the

steering wheel possessively. "It's a customized Mustang. And everything on her is original. She was my dream car way back before things like seat belts and shoulder harnesses." He grimaced at the restraint as he buckled himself in.

"You don't like safety?" she asked.

"I don't like messing with perfection," he said. And then he turned around, looked over his shoulder, and winked at D.J. "Know what I mean, kid?"

D.J. fussed beside her, reaching out and fingering the sleeve of her coat.

"I see you do," Harry said, giving her a quick once-over before turning around and giving his full attention to his car.

Nan unfastened her top button and made herself comfortable. She handed D.J. his Rubik's Cube, which he threw to the car floor. Great. It was going to be one of those trips. She knew the game well enough, so she held one hand on the car seat fastener while she reached down for the toy with the other. She came up instead with a hat.

"Blue," D.J. said. "I like blue."

"Best's Cleaning Service," she said, fingering the cap and letting D.J. investigate it. "Is that where you work?"

The back of Harry's neck colored. He was a maintenance man. A janitor. She realized that at night when she was home in bed, he was cleaning other people's offices. It didn't suit the picture she had in her mind, but honest work was honest work.

D.J. traced the seams of the cap with his first finger.

"Hey, I type letters asking people for money for the poor," she said with a shrug of her shoulders. "We can't all be Donald Trump."

"I don't—" he began. "That is, it's sort of temporary. I—"

"You work hard and you get paid for it," Nan said. "It's not something to be ashamed of. It's something to be proud of. Good physical labor is honest work—not like men who just sit around all day or all night on their bottoms living off everyone else's hard work and pain."

"You sound like my father," Harry said. "He thinks if you don't stink at the end of the day, you haven't worked hard enough."

D.J. began to moan softly to himself, turning the hat over and over and over in his hands.

"Is he all right?" Harry asked.

"For now," she said. D.J. could turn the hat for hours or throw it and start to scream in a second. Both made Nan crazy. "I really want to thank you for arranging things with this doctor," she said, leaning forward slightly so that she could talk to the side of his face.

"No problem," he said, changing gears with his right hand as they got onto Route 62.

"Do you do this doctor's building?" she asked. "Is that how you know him?"

"I don't 'do buildings,' Mrs. Springfield," he snapped. His cheek twitched.

"I'm sorry," she said softly, leaning back into her seat and wishing the soft leatherette would simply eat her up.

"No, *I'm* sorry," Harry said, wishing he had the guts to tell her the truth, wishing that if he did, she'd still let him take D.J. to the doctor, cheer for Topher when he made it around the rink, tease the girls about how pretty they were. "I'm too touchy about my work."

"Why? I mean it's good, honest work. What's there to

be ashamed of? As I said, it's not like you're sitting on your bottom ruining other people's lives and getting paid for it."

"Like Harris Tweed," he said, looking at her in his rearview mirror.

"Now that would be something to be ashamed of," she said, poking his shoulder with a finger.

He pulled off his leather gloves and turned down the heat. "Warm enough back there?" he asked.

"Mmm," she said, her voice as soft as that pink sweater that made her look like cotton candy—good enough to eat.

Now where had *that* thought come from?

"Actually," he said, glancing at her in the mirror again to gauge her reaction, "I'm in management."

Well, he was in with two feet now. Up to this point, technically, he hadn't told her any lies. A few sins of omission, granted, but he hadn't out and out lied to her.

"So that's why your father doesn't like your job?" she asked.

Jeez, it wasn't going to be easy keeping everything straight around a woman like Nan. "He does measure success by a sweat-ometer," he said. "How's the boy doing?"

"He likes your hat," she said, and they fell silent for a while.

"I like your hat," D.J. repeated. "I like your hat. I like your hat."

Every now and then he looked back at her as she chattered away with the kid. Twice he almost pulled over, to tell her who he was and that he was sorry about what he'd done to her life. But both times she was smiling and he didn't want to interrupt her happiness for his own sake.

"Mr. Woolery?" she said, leaning slightly forward.

"What happened to 'Harry'?" he asked.

"Well, actually, I wanted to ask you a favor and I didn't

want you to feel funny about saying no, and so I thought if I didn't seem to be playing on our . . ." she stumbled around for the right word and made this sort of I-give-up face that was irresistible.

Shit. *She* was irresistible.

"What's the favor?" he asked, glad she had not called their relationship a friendship, because at that very moment he did not want to be Nan Springfield's friend.

"Are you any good with books?" she asked. A glance showed her nervously picking lint off her good coat. A good coat, a fancy sweater and skirt—she was interested in him, too. He gripped the wheel tight enough to turn his knuckles white.

"I can read, if that's what you mean," he said, trying to make it sound offhanded.

"I meant financial records."

He waited.

"My husband's records."

He honked at the car in front of him for going only fifty-five, then peeled out around him and accelerated.

"I'm having difficulty finding some investments," she continued. She couldn't have been more careful if she'd been walking on eggs.

Someone coming from the other direction flashed his brights, and Harry slowed down to watch for the cop in waiting.

"And I was hoping that maybe you could look over his books with me and—"

"Don't you have an accountant?" Harry asked, remembering the man at the funeral. "Or the church's accountant? Couldn't he help you?"

She sighed. "Well, he's tried, but either I'm really dense

or he isn't being candid with me. Eleanor thinks that he's not, well, that he isn't totally—"

"—honest," he finished for her. The woman couldn't even spit the word out, the concept was so foreign to her. He held the wheel in a death grip.

"He's really been wonderful to me," she said softly, a slight quiver to her voice. "When I got the bill for Phil's funeral, he insisted on helping me with it, and he's tried to convince the church to let me stay in the house and he's just been a godsend, so I hate to say this, but, well . . ."

"So what do you want from me?" Harry asked.

"There's money missing and I need to find where it is," she said with determination, that cute little chin of hers jutting forward. "Naturally the church hasn't accused Phil of actually stealing the money, but I know that's what they believe . . ."

"And they want it back," Harry added. Scumbags parading as good pious Christians going after a widow with four little children.

"Oh, no. They'd never ask for it. But just the same, I already gave it back," she said, and Harry nearly collided with the car on his left. "Although I think that was probably a mistake because now that they have the money they don't want to investigate, they don't want to find out the real truth, they don't want anything but to put the whole thing behind them and move on with the new reverend—in my house."

"You gave them back the money?" Harry could hardly breathe, let alone talk. "How? Why?"

"I used most of Phil's insurance money. I had to. I mean, for one, the scholarships bear my father's name and I couldn't let all he'd done—all the church had done—be ruined. And I know that Phil would never have actually taken the money, so it's got to be safe somewhere. And as soon as I find it, I can vindicate him, get my money back from the church, and maybe even sue Harris Tweed for slandering his good name."

Harry eased his car onto the shoulder, put it into park and turned around so he could look Nan Springfield in the eyes.

"Let me get this straight," he said. "You want me to help you find proof that your husband didn't steal thousands of dollars from his church so that you can sue Harris Tweed?" He took two level breaths while he waited for her answer. He wished he was noble enough to want that for her more than he wanted absolution for himself.

"I want the world to know that the Reverend Philip Springfield would never have stolen a penny from anyone." Her gaze was steadier than his, her eyes so green a man could lose his way in them.

"And what if you're wrong? What if he did steal it?"

"He didn't." God, she was sure. To believe in something, or someone, that steadfastly just amazed Harry, astounded him. Humbled him. He couldn't remember believing so blindly in anyone since the tooth fairy—and how had that turned out?

"I can't help you." He might not have been the most honest man in the world, but that didn't mean he could take advantage of a poor widow woman's trust and go rifling through her dead husband's belongings just to assuage his own conscience. He was honest enough to admit to himself that he'd be looking for Springfield's guilt, not his innocence.

"You *won't*. That's not the same as can't." She looked at D.J., and he followed her eyes. Somehow the child had managed to loosen the threads that held the cap together and had neatly separated all the pieces on his very small lap. Harry was sure that proved something, but beyond the fact that his life was unraveling, he wasn't sure what.

"Oh, I'm so sorry!" she said, staring at the disassembled cap.

"He could be guilty, Nan," he said gently, ignoring the stupid hat. "I wouldn't want to be the one to have to tell you that."

"I told you, he isn't," she said firmly, as if the idea were impossible. Quietly, apologetically, she added, "And I never got the chance to tell him that."

"Tell him what?" Harry asked, but she shook the question away and he didn't press it because he could see the pain of it all on her face.

"Ellie thinks Stan Denham is somehow involved, and he might have duped Phil and that's why I can't get anywhere with him. He explains every deposit and withdrawal, but there's something I'm missing and I don't know what it is. I can't make sense of the records myself and—"

"What about the reverend's brother? What's his name?"

"Vernon. And I don't want him involved until I can prove that Phil is innocent. Maybe not even then. I want to do this my way, not his. I will not start a suit against Harris Tweed until I can prove Phil didn't steal anything. Ever."

"All right." He was sorry the moment the words were out of his mouth. Sorry because he knew that if it meant searching through every scrap of Philip Springfield's life, if it meant airing the linens that the reverend slept on with Nan, combing the crevices of the man's being, he would prove Phil Springfield did just what he'd accused him of and then be able to get on with his life. "Just remember," he told Nan. "It wasn't my idea, and don't say I didn't warn you."

"I don't know how to thank you," she said, sighing with relief she didn't have any right to.

Why was it every time he heard the reverend's name in his car, he wanted to leave his breakfast on the sidewalk?

"Don't go thanking me," he said, turning around and putting the car back in gear.

There is no medicine, no operation, no cure for what we group as Pervasive Developmental Disorder, Not Otherwise Specified. There is treatment and therapy and care.

Nan held the sleeping child tightly in her arms and let Harry guide her steps to the car. D.J.'s behavior had a name. And D.J. had a label. For life.

"He's heavy, Nan. Let me take him," Harry said, trying to pry D.J. from her arms, but she held him fast. "Poor kid's exhausted."

Nan couldn't say anything in response. She was still trying to get her tongue around the word. *Autism.* D.J. was *autistic.* She practiced it in her head like a litany, as if somehow he wasn't D.J. anymore. He sobbed in his sleep, his breath warm against her neck, and she kissed at the sweeps of his hair.

He didn't stir when she slipped him into the car seat, didn't fight her when she buckled the strap and backed away, didn't startle when Harry shut the door.

"Sit in the front with me," Harry said, lingering by the passenger door. "I'll pull over the minute he wakes up, and you can move into the back with him if he needs you."

"I'm all right," she told him—a bold-faced lie that neither of them believed.

Just the same, Harry said that he knew she was. They could talk more quietly if she sat up front, he suggested.

"Unless, of course, you'd rather not talk," he added, his hand on the handle to the door.

"I'm all right," she said again, this time with more confidence, throwing back her shoulders and breathing deeply. She gestured at the door and Harry opened it and took her hand as she lowered herself into the bucket seat.

He didn't let go. Not while she settled herself in, not when she reached for the seat belt with her other hand, not until he took it from her and clicked it into place around her. Metal into metal, like a lock and key, like a dead bolt slid into place to protect her from . . . from what? Further calamity?

He kneeled by her open door, his face, his body, all saying *I'm here if you need me.*

"I'm fine," she said again, only this time there were tears rolling down her cheeks. She caught them with her tongue and swiped at them with the back of her hand.

He reached beneath his coat until he could get to his back pocket and produced a clean white handkerchief.

"Men don't carry handkerchiefs anymore," she told him, letting him wipe her tears and dab the end of her nose.

"Well, don't tell the housekeeper who keeps stacking them in my underwear drawer so I can't miss 'em, okay?" he said, handing the now limp square to her.

She nodded, crushed that he had a woman to look after him. As if she wanted to be the one to wash his things and prepare his meals and do the hundred other things a wife does for a husband. Lord, she must be missing Phil something awful to want to go back to the kind of life wherein a man could be justifiably annoyed if he ran out of clean underwear.

"I know you're all right," he said, a little grin playing at his lips, "but are you all right enough to let go of my coat? My knees aren't what they used to be."

She looked at her hand as if it were attached to someone else's body. It was clinging to the pocket of Harry's coat, balling it up and turning the fine camel cashmere into some sort of chamois. Without saying a word about it, she let it go so that he could stretch out to his full height, his head lost above the roof of the car.

Then he closed the door and hurried around the front end of the car, staying in her line of vision, keeping eye contact, smiling tentatively at her as if he were gauging her "allrightness."

"All set?" he asked after he was ensconced in the driver's seat, his belt securely fastened.

She nodded.

"Maybe he's wrong," Harry said after they'd pulled out of the parking lot and onto the main road.

"I didn't think you were the wishful-thinking type," she replied.

"There are other doctors," he said, taking his hand off the gearshift and covering her own. "We could see another specialist."

"Do you doubt what he said?" Nan asked. She didn't. Somewhere in her heart she'd known it all along.

"Well, there's that therapy he was talking about—behavioral modification . . ."

"I know that," she snapped at him, only to find him give her hand a squeeze and then a reassuring pat. "It takes a lot of patience, or money, to pay for someone else's patience," she added.

"Ah," he said with a nod.

And then they said nothing, as if there were nothing left to say.

He took his hand off hers to change gears when they got on the highway, and when he replaced it, he sighed deeply. "Do you suppose that the boy's parents will want him back, now that we know—"

"This is not some puppy who peed on the rug," she said indignantly. "This is a child. You don't simply get rid of a child because he has a problem. I didn't take him in thinking it would be a picnic to have another child around. I took him because no one else wanted a handful who still wasn't toilet trained at three and who could stare at nothing for hours on end and then break his little fist banging it into a wall. If you think that I would just ship him off like some piece of defective merchandise—"

"Could you just take a breath?" Harry asked, maneuvering his way through the beginnings of rush hour traffic. Jordan Winston had taken hours to test D.J., and had then patiently answered their hundreds of questions. It was late, and she knew Harry had to get back to the city—without his Best's Cleaning cap.

"I never said you should send him back," he said, his words clipped and short.

"You asked if his parents would take him back, and that's the same thing in my book," she answered just as snippily.

"If I meant it the way you took it, yes," he said patiently. "But I meant that mightn't it be likely that they'd agree to let you keep the boy rather than face a lifetime of—"

He stopped before describing what she would face with D.J., what anyone would face with D.J.

"—hard work for maybe very little reward. Maybe I'm wrong to even suggest it. It's just that I can see how much you love the boy, and you've already lost so much. But your life is hard enough as it is."

"Losing D.J. wouldn't make it easier," she said softly,

looking into the backseat to see her little boy sleeping peacefully.

"What would make it easier, Nan?" he asked, pulling his eyes from the road for a moment to look her full in the face.

You, she thought, biting down on her tongue to keep from saying it. "Oh, keeping my house, I suppose. Having D.J.'s parents allow me to adopt him. Knowing that Robin and Rachel are happy somewhere, maybe even with me— maybe not. Finding the facts so that I could sue Harris Tweed and exonerate my husband . . ."

Harry's shoulders sagged.

"You think I'm just being vindictive, don't you?" she asked, wondering sometimes if that wasn't too close to the truth for comfort.

"I think you have to do what you have to do," he said softly. He patted her hand, but then returned his own to the steering wheel.

"Do you think they might let me keep him, Harry?" she asked him after a while.

He raised his eyebrows as if to say he just didn't know.

"Don't you think something has to go right for me?" she asked, and then, embarrassed to be feeling so very sorry for herself, she added, "I mean, things'll turn around now, don't you think?"

Eleven

For the rest of the week he'd thought of nothing else but looking over the Reverend Springfield's books. He'd figured it ten ways to Sunday, and for Nan's sake, he didn't want to find that the man was guilty. For his own sake, he did. And he felt like a cad letting Nan trust him to look at all, which, to be truthful, he didn't even want to do.

So what he was doing on her porch Saturday morning with his pencils sharpened and his brain dull, he couldn't say.

She answered the bell with a dishrag and a smile, waving him in to the kitchen—where his nose would have led him without the encouragement.

"We're making spring," Robin explained, elbow-deep in yellow frosting.

"Crocuses," Nan explained, pointing at the sheets full of cookie flowers waiting to be frosted. "When the sun came up so gloriously today, I guess I just couldn't wait for winter to be over."

"Mine are purple," Rachel added. "Crocuses come in white and yellow and purple, so we could pick any of those. Topher's gonna make the grass with pistachio pudding."

Nan was washing up at the sink. He watched her straighten her hair in the window's reflection, and his heart swelled just a little that she cared how she looked for him. He took a deep breath and set his shoulders back a notch. He could tell the minute she felt his eyes on her, saw the way she got self-conscious and just a little clumsy, knocking a spatula into the sudsy sink that threatened to overflow if she didn't pay it some mind soon.

"Ah, spring in Ohio," he said, coming to the sink and reaching over her to shut the water off. "Gotta watch out for the floods."

Her hair smelled freshly washed, and he lingered behind her longer than he should have. Long enough to feel a tug of desire—not just for her, but for it all. For kids and cookies and some ideal he doubted still existed until he was standing in the midst of it, watching this patchwork family function the way his own never had. He wondered what they were doing over at Suzanne's place now. What kind of life was Josh having without him?

"Where's D.J.?" he asked, backing away from Nan and temptation and things that could never be.

"He's helping by napping," Robin told him. "Mommy says that's his job."

"What's Mr. Woolery's job?" Rachel asked, painting not just the cookies, but the tin sheets and the vinyl covering the table.

"I'm an official taster," Harry said, sticking his finger in the bowl and licking off his finger while Nan watched him. Suddenly, somehow, it became a sexual thing, fraught with meanings he didn't intend and making him damned uncomfortable.

"Is it good?" Robin asked him.

He nodded, his eyes still locked with Nan's. *I want this. I want this with all my heart and soul,* he thought. "Yeah, it's good," he said, but the words came out hoarse and gruff.

"I put all Phil's records on the dining room table," Nan said, breaking the spell. "It's so wonderful of you to be willing to—"

"Look," he said, interrupting her, floundering around for something, anything, that could get him out of the quicksand he'd leaped in to. "It's too pretty to stay inside today. What do you say we go to . . ."

"—the lake!" Robin shouted, frosting flying off the spoon she held in her waving hand. "We could go swimming and—"

"It's too cold to go swimming," Rachel told her as Topher came into the kitchen buttoning a shirt that must have been his father's over his clothes.

"I don't see why I have to wear a smock," he complained. "Dad never wore a smock."

Nan ran her hands lovingly over her son's shoulders, over the shirt that had once clothed her husband. "Dad never cooked," she said, turning the cuffs over and over until she found the boy's hands.

"Because boys don't cook," Topher answered back. "Do they, Harry?"

"*Mr. Woolery*," the boy's mother corrected.

"*Harry*'s fine," Harry said. "I keep looking for my dad when you say Mr. Woolery."

"You have a dad?" Topher asked, and the girls' eyes widened to saucers. "A living dad?"

Harry nodded, a twinge of guilt rushing through him. "My dad's dead."

Silence entered the kitchen like some ghost, like the Reverend Springfield's ghost, and they all made room for it and stood sheepishly waiting for the moment to pass.

"I'm sorry about that, Topher," Harry finally said. "But I think you'd like my dad."

"He must be a hundred years old," Topher said. "Can he still walk?"

Nan covered her mouth with her hand, and Harry gave her a stern look.

"How old do you think I am?" he asked the children.

"Ninety?" Rachel offered.

He shook his head.

"Higher or lower?" Topher demanded.

Nan wasn't bothering to hide her smile anymore.

"You think this is so funny?" he asked her and then turned to the kids. "How old do you think Mommy is?"

"Twenty," Rachel said as if that settled it.

"Can your dad eat?" Topher asked. "Or do they have to feed him through a tube or something?"

"Topher! Where did that come from?" Nan asked.

"I keep telling you that you're missing stuff on TV," Topher said.

"He can eat and walk and talk and rope and ride better than I can," Harry said honestly.

"Rope and ride?" Topher asked.

"Horses," Harry said, and then added, "Tell you what. If you pack up the cookies and get your coats on, we'll go up to the farm and you can see for yourself."

Spoons flew, cookies fell to the floor, and hell broke loose in the Springfield kitchen as the children fought each other to get through the doorway first. Nan looked more surprised than annoyed as she surveyed the damage.

"I guess I should have asked you first," he said, waiting for her to call him on the carpet for inviting the kids like that. "You probably had plans . . ."

She smiled that smile that flipped his stomach. "My plan was to keep them out of your hair so that you could look over the papers, but that's under the bridge. Even if I said they couldn't go, they'd drive you crazy now with questions."

"Let's put off the books a bit. In fact, let's throw caution to the wind and forget everything just for today." He took the towel from her hands and threw it toward the sink. "Let's just throw that old caution to the wind," he repeated, feeling better than he had in six months or longer, feeling good enough to swing Nan around in his arms like he was Fred Astaire, and head her toward the hall.

"Go get cleaned up and wake up D.J. I'll find something to put the cookies in and then give my father a call so that he'll have time to hunt around for his teeth and his cane before we get there!"

They stood together in the barn as closely as they had been packed into Harry's car—the girls joined at the hip, D.J. hanging back near Nan's legs, Topher stuck to Harry's right leg—all of them staring at the enormous creatures who snorted and pranced at the sight of them.

"Love company," Nate said, smacking the side of a deep brown horse that could have crushed him in return. Instead the horse nuzzled his nose against Nate's chest. "Looking for this?" Nate asked him, producing a handful of sugar cubes from his pocket.

"We made cookies," Robin said. "Will he eat cookies?"

"He'd eat the stove you cooked them on, given the chance," Harry said. "Let's save those cookies for us."

"You want to feed 'em?" Nate offered, sticking the handful of sugar out toward the entire pack of them.

There was only one thing Nan hated about being a mother. And it wasn't the diapers, the sleepless nights, the endless cooking and cleaning and explaining and consoling.

It was setting a good example, she thought as she reluctantly put out her hand and took the cubes of sugar that Nate offered.

"Like this," Harry said, cupping her hand in his and stretching it out to the horse. "Okay, Malomar, be gentle now. Leave at least one of this nice lady's fingers so that she can still turn the oven dial to Bake."

It tickled when the horse took the cubes and snorted a thanks into her hand. Behind her there were nervous giggles. Glued now to Nan's leg, D.J. watched, his little mouth an O, his eyes soldered on the horse.

"I read somewheres that they're using horses for kids like her little boy," Nate told Harry, putting a cube into D.J.'s hand without a fight, and then guiding it gently toward the horse's mouth.

"Again!" D.J. demanded when the horse had eaten his offering.

"One more," Nate said. " 'Cause that's all I got with me. Then you'll all help me fill up their bins for lunch."

D.J. fed the horse the second cube.

"Again!"

"Not again," Nan told him, amazed at how he took the instruction, and then amazed all over again when he stroked the horse's long nose and touched the rim of the nostril.

"Why don't you leave the kids with me so we can get some work done around here," Nate said, crouching down beside D.J. and pointing something out to him beyond the horse.

"Leave them?" Nan asked, looking around to see the girls petting a kitten and Topher talking to the adorable puppy they'd met at the hockey rink.

"Does she ride?" Nate asked Harry.

"I don't know," Harry said, snorting at his father a bit

like Malomar had done. "But she does talk. You can ask her."

"I can?" his father said, raising an eyebrow. "Thought I wasn't supposed to so much as—"

"Do you ride?" Harry asked her, cutting his father off.

"No. At least I never have."

"I got Maresydotes saddled up," Nate said to Harry before turning to her. "Harry'll take you over by the river. A ride over there and you'll never be the same."

"Does it take very long?" she asked, watching the children as they all ignored her. Even D.J. seemed content by Nate's side.

"Depends on Harry's mood," Nate said, guiding D.J.'s hand down Malomar's nose. His eyes stayed on his son as Harry crossed the barn. "Sometimes it would take forever and sometimes we were back in a wink."

"Do you two ride much?" she asked, trying not to think about climbing up onto the back of one of those giant animals and pretending she was Dale Evans or, more likely, Calamity Jane.

"It's been a long time," Nate said, a shadow crossing over his face. "Before his ma died, we'd ride together nearly every day. After that, we tended to exercise the horses at different times."

"Have you always raised horses?" she asked him as Harry warned the children to stay out of the way and led two horses out of the barn.

"No," Nate said and gave her half a smile. "Once I raised a mule."

Harry brought out the step stool rather than simply lift her onto the horse. After all, Nate was watching and frowning and saying things under his breath like "I suppose it's too late to warn you not to do anything stupid." Then again, mounting up independently tended to make a rider a little less fearful of the whole riding experience.

It had nothing to do with the fact that he was attracted to her, because that was just loneliness, pure and simple. And it was best not to touch what he didn't really want.

She sat on the horse looking like she was ready for the noose around her neck.

"What are you looking for?" he asked her, watching her look cautiously behind herself at the cantle of the saddle, as if she were afraid that any sudden movement might send the horse galloping away despite the fact that Harry held the reins in his hands.

"The seat belt?" she asked, her voice a thin thread in the early spring air. Harry shook his head at her. "Oh. All right. I can do this. I think I just need some music."

He whistled some western-sounding tune and she tried to smile. "If you're too scared, we don't have to go," he said, waiting for her to answer before he mounted up.

"If I never did anything I was afraid of, I'd never get out of bed in the morning," she said, taking the reins he held up to her. "Never answer the phone," she mumbled as if it were some sort of litany. "Never start the car. Never—"

"I'd whistle that 'Whenever I Feel Afraid' song, but I'm afraid you've heard my entire repertoire."

"The only song you know is . . ." She thought for a minute. ". . . the theme from *Bonanza?*"

He shrugged. He knew all the commercial jingles they played on WGCA. He knew heavy metal from two years in the eighties when he'd worked at KOOL in Harding, Iowa, where no one was cool and no one listened.

"Well, Hoss Cartwright, let's head on down to the

Ponderosa." Her face was white, her body stiff enough to paste wanted posters on, but she was forcing a smile.

He gave Wayward's rump an easy kick and clicked at Maresydotes to follow along. After thirty-eight years of dealing with horses, he was convinced that they were stupid creatures who would follow each other right off a cliff.

At the moment, he didn't think they were any stupider than he was, and he had a bad feeling he was headed for that same cliff.

It was amazing what guilt and loneliness could do to a man—make him think he felt things he didn't really feel, make him think he could change things, or forget them, or pretend they'd never happened.

Funny how the things he didn't want to wipe out—six years with Suzanne, for example—were gone in an instant with a judge's decree, and other things he was desperate to put behind him just wouldn't go away.

"You doing all right?" he asked her, slowing down so that the horses were neck and neck.

"It's wonderful!" she exclaimed, her cheeks rosy and her smile bright. "It's incredible. I feel like I'm in some old movie."

"You want to try to go a little faster?" he asked.

She bit at her bottom lip, but nodded.

"Okay. Now, this is a little like se—" He caught himself before he said it. The minister's widow, for Christ's sake! There must be something else you rocked your hips for, but his mind was blank. Blank for anything but that, for rocking hips in general and Nan Springfield's in particular. "Go with the flow, honey," he said in desperation, and kicked Wayward into a trot.

She was all over the saddle when he turned to see how she was doing. Her right hand gripped the horn; the left one held the reins willy-nilly as she tried to keep her balance. Less than gracefully, and before he could get to her, she slid out of the saddle and onto the wet, cold ground.

Shit! What kind of idiot takes someone out trotting their first time on a horse? It was as if, one way or another, he was determined to destroy this poor defenseless woman. "Are you all right?" he called, sliding off Wayward and running back to her. "Nan! Oh my God!"

Her coat was big and bulky and he could see it shaking as he fell to his knees beside her.

"Don't move," he told her, then quickly added, "Can you? Can you move?"

She rolled over onto her side. There was mud covering her pretty red parka, mud in her sandy blond hair, and mud on her face. She stopped laughing long enough to say, "I hope you're impressed," and then went back to it, not even stopping while she winced as she tried to sit up.

"No, but I'm insured. What hurts?"

She tried to wipe the mud from her mouth, but her hands were no cleaner, and so he pulled out his hankie and brushed at the dirt on her face with it.

"Just my pride, I think. It was more fun when I was on the horse."

"Oh, was it, now?" he asked, brushing the hair off her face, easing the strands away from her eyelashes, where the mud was pasting them. "I'd peg you for the type that liked making mud pies."

"I was younger then," she said, arching her back and squeezing one eye shut as she did.

"Broken or bruised?" he asked, putting one hand where she could rest her back against it and shooing Marseydotes away with the other.

"Old," she said as his hand began—purely on its own

accord—to gently massage her back through her down jacket.

"You?" Harry asked, using his hankie to rid her lips of any trace of mud. God, they were soft. And pliant. And there for the taking.

The horses found a patch of grass and ignored them, as if what was happening between them were of no import at all, as if his world weren't suddenly off-kilter and spinning out of control.

"Harry?" she asked softly as he pulled her closer, mud seeping into his own jeans as he went from squatting to sitting, from patting to holding, from imagining to kissing.

It was wrong. It was unfair and inappropriate. He was taking advantage of that trusting nature of hers, and even knowing that, he couldn't stop himself. One hand held her head, tipping it to fit perfectly against his own, his lips tasting the sweetness that was Nan. The other hand fiddled with the zipper of her parka.

She was kissing him back—tentatively, timidly, but kissing she was, and he felt the fire in his chest spread through his body and burn what was left of his brain. What else explained why he opened her coat and reached in to touch her breast like he was some teenager copping a feel?

She made him feel like a teenager—anxious, excited, on the verge of something out of control.

She made him act like a teenager—fooling around in the mud and worrying that someone might come along and catch him doing something he shouldn't do.

She made him need like a teenager—like nothing would ever be enough, not now, not ever.

Beneath his skilled fingers he felt her nipple pebble in response to his touch, felt the shiver run through her, and knew that it was stop now or never stop at all.

"I'm sorry," he said, backing away, reluctantly releasing her breast, nervously closing her jacket. "I had no right to do that."

"I was as much in the wrong as you," she said, color flooding her cheeks where they peeked out behind the mud. She swallowed so hard that he could almost hear it, a sad, embarrassed sound. Marseydotes nudged at her with his nose, clouds coming from his nostrils, and she backed away like a crab in the sand. She smiled apologetically. "I guess I'm a little scared."

"Well, you know what they say about falling off a horse," he said, rising to his feet and offering her a hand getting up.

She took his hand and looked at him with innocent green eyes that hid nothing of how she felt. His father, damn the man, was right. He'd gone looking for trouble, and he'd found it.

"Best thing to do is get right back up there or you may never get on again."

She pulled some dry grass off the elbow of his jacket. "Are we talking about horses?" she asked.

He didn't answer, just helped her up onto Maresydotes, enjoying the bittersweet feel of her body in his hands, knowing it would be the last time that he would ever hold her.

After all, how many times could he wreck one woman's life?

 *Twelve*

Eleanor was waiting for them when Harry and Nan finally came home. She watched as Nan went into her bedroom to change out of her dirty clothes. She hadn't missed the smudges of dirt on Nan's sweater, but she waited until she was alone with Harry to ask him about them. "So, I suppose you were just checking for broken ribs?" she said, her eyebrows raised.

"It won't happen again," the man told her as he stood stiffly in the living room waiting for the children to change into their pajamas before they thanked him for the day and said good night.

"She needs help, Mr. *Woolery*," she warned him, emphasizing his name so that there would be no mistaking what she knew and didn't know. "And you're in a position to help her."

"I know that," he said. He ran his fingers through his hair and looked thoroughly disgusted, but Eleanor wasn't sure whether he was annoyed with her or with himself. And frankly, she didn't much care.

"And it seems you're in a position to hurt her, as well," she continued. "And I won't allow it. Not you, not Vernon, not Stan Denham or the whole damn church. All those ladies in all those circles ought to be able to do something to help her. If they can't, I don't know how I'll stop any of this. But I do know a sure way to stop you, don't I?"

"Stop what?" he asked, his body tensing visibly and reminding Eleanor that they were on the same side—at least in some things.

"Mr. Royce stopped by here while you were out molesting my sister-in-law." His jaw worked furiously, but he didn't deny it. "He left a letter for Nan from the church's lawyer."

"How soon do they want it?" he asked.

"How soon does who want what?" Nan asked, coming out of the bedroom in fresh brown wool trousers and a pink sweater. Her hair was wrapped in a towel and she glowed from the shower.

Eleanor looked at Harry Woolery and cursed herself for ever calling him in the first place. Nan was losing the house anyway, and worse, she was losing her heart.

And clearly the feeling was being returned.

"I'll make some coffee," Eleanor said softly, backing out of the room and nearly running over Robin and Rachel on her way.

"Good night, Uncle Harry," Robin said, kissing the back of his hand because it was the right height for her to reach.

"Uncle Harry, is it now?" Eleanor said from the doorway. What did the man think he was doing, bursting into their lives the way he had? If Nan wasn't positively radiant, Eleanor would have happily shown him the door. "Say your good nights and off to bed," Eleanor told the girls. She wished Nan was young enough to order about the same way.

Topher led D.J. and made a pretense of kissing Harry just for D.J.'s sake. They all made quite the picture there in Nan's living room.

Of course, it wouldn't be her living room much longer, and the picture would surely have to change.

"So," Nan said, after the children were kissed and carried and tucked. "What's the bad news?"

"Bad news?" he repeated evasively.

"Someone wanted something?" she reminded him. Oh God! No reprieve, no call from the governor. "They want my house, don't they?"

"It's just a house," he said, looking around at what probably seemed to him to be a cluttered, shabby room. Of course, he wasn't seeing Nan's father in the recliner, or her mother sitting beside the lamp to see her needlepoint better. He didn't know the tallest marks in the closet in the children's bedroom belonged to her, her father measuring her every year until the marks stopped moving.

"But it's *my* house," she said, heaving a very deep sigh that might have had a tear in it. "I've never lived anywhere else, Harry. Everyone I've ever loved has lived under this roof. Even Nanny Annie stayed here before she died. I saw the lightning hit the old church from my bedroom window."

"The old church?" Harry asked, as she fondled the fireplace mantel and the framed picture of her parents' wedding that sat there.

"The original one. It used to be next door. My mother always said my father had one foot in the church and one foot at home. It burned to the ground when I was eleven. Then they built the new one on Maple Avenue."

Harry's brows came down hard over his deep brown eyes. She could almost see wheels turning in his brain. "Why'd they move it?"

"Parking. Remember that song about paving paradise to

put up a parking lot? Well, they moved it so they could have a bigger lot. My father hated being so far from the church, especially after my mother died."

"Was it difficult for your husband not to be next to the church?" he asked.

"He didn't know any different," she said quickly, walking toward the kitchen and beckoning Harry to follow.

Eleanor handed her the letter. Without opening it, she handed it to Harry.

"How long do I have?"

"You're not dying, Nan," Eleanor told her. "And we're not down for the count just yet."

Harry opened the envelope. "Two weeks," he said solemnly. "Not a heck of a lot of time."

"Do you happen to know how much that obnoxious Harris Tweed has collected for Nan's house?" Eleanor asked him.

Nan was about to ask how Harry would know something like that when he said, "About forty-eight thousand."

"Well, he sure as heck could do better than that. It's his fault she's in this pickle, after all," Eleanor said.

"Is that what you think?" Harry asked her as if it were petty and small of her to think so. Maybe it was, but to Nan's way of thinking, if it weren't for Harris Tweed's unfounded accusations, Phil never would have run out of the house, never have hit the tree, never have died, and never have had to be replaced. And she wouldn't be losing her house on top of her husband.

"I don't believe any of this would have happened otherwise. So, yeah, I think so, too, Mr. Woolery," Nan said.

"And none of this is the reverend's fault?" he asked.

"Why would it be? He didn't take the money," she said, slamming his coffee mug down in front of him. "Sugar?"

"Plenty," he answered. "Then you better bring me those records to look over."

"Make sure you remember what you're looking for," Eleanor warned Harry, drying the table with a dishcloth before Nan put down any papers.

"I believe all of this was *your* idea," he shot back, reaching into his pocket for a pair of glasses.

"I was sure you'd want to help." Eleanor was glaring at Harry and he was glaring right back.

"What do you two know that I don't?" she asked.

Harry's eyes were glued on Nan's sister-in-law, but Eleanor said nothing.

"Well?"

Harry took the rubber band off the stack of envelopes containing Phil's bank statements for the past year. He didn't answer her as he unfolded the statements and stacked them neatly into a pile.

"Ellie?"

"You want a sandwich or anything?" Eleanor asked Harry. "I have a feeling this could be a long, long night."

It was a long night, all right. The longest in Harry's life. Longer than any Harry had spent at the station, where he ought to have been. It was a damn good thing that Ross was willing to cover for him, though he did make a crack about Harry's making these absences a habit.

According to the papers for the car, the down payment of two thousand dollars was made in cash without any withdrawal from any bank account, any checks to a financing company, or any loan fees. Nothing but a check made out to the Commissioner of Motor Vehicles for registration fees. He asked Nan twice when the car was bought and how it was paid for, but didn't let on about his suspicions.

"Did Phil have any other accounts?" he asked as off-handedly as he could. After six hours in the man's personal papers, including his insurance bills (he was actually hoping to find that he'd borrowed the money for the car from his insurance, but the loan came later), his financial dealings with Vernon (who had been charging his own brother 14 percent interest on a loan that went back to the eighties), the stocks he had received as gifts when he graduated from the seminary (with excellent grades according to Nan), Harry was now on a first-name basis with the Reverend Springfield.

"No," Nan said. "That's what I don't understand. There isn't any place the money could be. He didn't spend it. He didn't save it. And even if he wanted to, which I can't figure a reason for, there was nowhere he could have hidden it."

"How about a safe-deposit box?" he asked.

"It's not there," Nan said, plunking a shoe box on the table. "Everything that was in there is right in front of you or in this shoe box."

Harry fingered the few things in the box. A hospital bracelet with Nan's name on it.

"Topher's birth," she said softly.

He felt like some voyeur, pawing through memories that weren't his.

A small jewelry box.

"His baby teeth," Nan said, her cheeks flushing. Where were Josh's teeth? Where were all the important things he'd been forced to abandon without even noticing?

He left the box unopened.

A medal for high school oratory. Another for chess. He could have guessed what they were for without even turning them over. Phil had no secrets left. Except, of course, what he'd done with the thirty-five thousand dollars. *If* he'd taken it. It would just kill Nan if it turned out the man was a thief after all.

And after going through everything, it was the only thing Harry didn't know about the man. He knew the brand of cigars Phil preferred and just what he paid for them.

"Nan's got a house account at the dry cleaner's?" Harry asked Eleanor at close to 3 A.M.

"Phil always wanted to look just so for Sunday services," Eleanor said. "He thought appearances were very important."

He stared at Eleanor, and she stared back, both of them sizing up the other and wondering where the truth was in all of this.

"What do you think?" he asked.

"I think that appearances are overrated," Eleanor said. She pushed at the coffee cup in front of her as if the whole subject irritated her. "And that people should never do things for appearances' sake—or anyone else's sake for that matter."

Well, he'd asked. And she'd answered, cryptic though the answer was. Apparently Miss Eleanor Springfield had a few secrets of her own. Hey, they all had secrets, even him. Well, all but Nan, whose head rested on her outstretched arm, her mouth open just slightly, invitingly, a very slight smile on her lips, as if she were having the pleasantest of dreams.

"Vernon's not going to be happy if you can't clear Phil," Eleanor said, stifling a yawn, snapping his attention back to the papers on the table.

"And that's my goal in life," Harry said sarcastically. "I'll just work a little longer. You can go on to bed."

Eleanor looked at Nan, left, and came back with an

afghan from the den, which she threw over Nan's shoulders. "I'd wake her, but she's slept longer at the table tonight than I've seen her sleep in months."

"She doesn't sleep?" he asked, rearranging the blanket to
cover her better.

"Nightmares," Eleanor said. "Courtesy of Harris
Tweed."

"That's not fair, Eleanor," he said softly, not wanting to
disturb Nan's rest.

Eleanor's laugh was harsh. "Who ever told you life was
fair?"

She'd been dreaming about riding horses. Harry was on
a big black stallion, and she had D.J. on a small reddish
horse with her. Topher was riding out ahead, graceful as
could be, laughing over his shoulder at his slowpoke
mother. But there was this feeling as if just over the hill
something awful was waiting for them all, and she wanted
Harry to hurry and stop Topher before it was too late.

So she was glad when Harry shook her shoulders. "I'm
awake," she said, wiping at her mouth and the damp spot
on her arm. Great. She'd been drooling at the table where
Harry could see her plain as day under the harsh kitchen
lights.

"How long has it been since anyone carried you to bed
the way you do the kids?" he asked, wrapping her in the
afghan and slipping an arm beneath her knees.

"Five hundred years," she said. She didn't fight him
when he lifted her and carried her out into the hall.

"Where do you sleep?" he whispered, holding her as if
she were just one of the children.

"The den," she whispered back like a coconspirator. "At
the back of the house."

He smelled of wool and warmth and she allowed herself the luxury of burrowing against this man who made her feel like it would all, somehow, be all right. From the moment he had come into her life she had felt a power—not from him, but from herself, to bear what had to be borne and not just survive, but flourish. Somehow, in some way, he gave her that power, that strength.

Because—the thought made her smile against his sweater and nuzzle there—for the first time since her father died, she didn't feel alone.

"Kiss me, Harry," she said as he laid her down on the sofa and tucked the covers beneath her chin. "Kiss me good night."

He brushed her forehead with his lips and sat down in the curve of her body. "This isn't good, Nan," he whispered.

"Because you don't like me, or because you do?" she asked before she could stop herself. *Too direct*, Phil always called her. No tact, no diplomacy, no easing into subjects that probably shouldn't be spoken of at all.

"You don't even know me, Nan," he warned, but his breath was warming her cheek as he spoke.

"I know you're good to children and dogs and your father," she said while her fingers began to tangle in his deep brown hair, as if she could grasp his heart with her hands. "All good qualities."

"There are things about me," he said, but he was stroking her through her clothes, unhooking her bra with the flick of a finger, cupping her breast, pressing his hip against her belly. "What I've done. What I do . . ."

"Do you think I care what you do for a living?" she asked, moving so that he could stretch out beside her on the couch, half on her. His hand rested on her belly, inched lower.

"Very much," he said, rubbing her through her woolen trousers until all she could hear was her breathing echoing in her ears.

He kissed her lips, her cheeks, the hollow of her neck. He breathed hot and heavy through her sweater until her breasts hurt with desire. Fighting for control, she reminded herself that her children were sleeping only steps away, that her sister-in-law was only down the hall, that she was a widow in mourning less than a year. None of it could stop the feeling, the incredible release of letting this man love her. None of it was strong enough to stop her from pulling at her sweater, trying to lift it to feel his lips on her skin.

Gently yet firmly he stopped her hand, took it in his own, and raised it to his lips.

"I should go," he whispered. "Before I make things worse."

Against her chest she could feel his heart beating as rapidly as her own. Against her hip she could feel his desire pressing through his jeans despite his words. Against the pale moonlight she could see his head silhouetted, and watched as his shoulders sagged. "Please don't go."

"We'll both be sorry if I stay," he said, twisting around until he was once again seated in the curve of her body.

"We could watch TV, or talk, or I could make you something to eat," she offered, one hand tracing the muscle that tensed in his arm. "Please, Harry. Stay."

She watched him struggle with himself, head thrown back, jaw tight, eyes closed. "I couldn't do any of those things if I stayed now, Nan. You're too soft and warm and inviting in the dead of night, and life's been rotten enough to you without me taking advantage of your loneliness."

She squirmed out from beneath the afghan and managed to sit up beside him. "Do you suppose that's what I'm feeling for you? Just loneliness?" Was she so bereft that she was reading things into their relationship that weren't there? Was she mistaking sympathy on his part for affection? Was she mistaking her own gratitude for love?

"I'm not going to be able to prove your husband didn't steal that money, Nan," he said abruptly, running his hands through his hair. "At least not before they take this house from you."

She sighed. "Well, you did the best you could, anyway. You can't hold yourself responsible for my losing the house or anything else that's wrong in my life."

"I'd change it all if I could. You know that, don't you?" His eyes glistened in the darkness and she rested her head against his arm, felt him shift that arm around her and hold her tight to his chest. "I'll fix everything, Nan. I promise."

He didn't have the power to do it. No one did. Phil was gone, the house was next, and surely the girls and D.J. would follow hard upon that. But she didn't correct him. She didn't tell him that his promise was worthless, because just the fact that he had promised took the sharpest edge from the sword that hung over all their heads.

"I'll call you in a few days," he said, putting her back down on the couch like a little doll, tucking the covers beneath her chin once again, and giving her a kiss on her forehead.

He stood way high above her, looking down, for a minute or two.

"Aw, hell," he said, and sat back down on the couch, lowered his lips to hers, and kissed her hard on the mouth. This kiss was rough, his lips pressed firmly against hers before it softened and he nibbled at her lower lip. He teased with his tongue until she opened her mouth, and then he slid it inside, declaring possession. She had no sense of time or place. She floated, drifted, inhaling his scent, being scratched by his stubble, losing her way.

She had no idea how long the kiss went on, only that when he finally pulled away, her lips felt swollen and stung.

"I'll call you as soon as I've made any progress," he said, his voice ragged. "Don't give up hope just yet."

She smiled at him and nestled deeper under the covers. Giving up hope was the farthest thing from her mind.

 *Thirteen*

"So you went through her things while she was sleeping?" Nate asked him, shaking his head as if he didn't expect any better from Harry.

"She gave me the box," Harry explained again. "She told me that was what was in their safe-deposit box and we went over the contents. She fell asleep—"

"Well, what in hell were you doing there until three in the morning?" the old man growled, dunking his hard roll into his coffee.

"—and I was just fiddling with the box of baby teeth"— he left out the part that he was wondering about Josh's teeth—"and I heard it."

"You heard a key?" Nate's eyebrow seemed to think that was impossible.

"Teeth don't clink. I shook the box and it clinked."

"And you just had to open it."

"She asked me to look for proof. Don't forget that. None of it was my idea."

"And then she chained you to her kitchen chair and brought out the whips . . ."

"She needs to know, Dad."

"So then you told her?" Nate asked, one eyebrow raised as if he already knew the answer. He shook his head and took a swig of coffee. "So . . . *she* needs to know? Or you do?"

Harry rolled his head to ease the kinks. He hadn't slept all night, not even after he'd gotten back to the farm and taken a cold shower. Not even after a hefty shot of whiskey.

"So, what are you gonna do with it?" Nate asked.

"Four choices," Harry said, pushing the yellow pad with his columns toward his father. He could give the key he'd found to the police. After all, he couldn't get into the reverend's second safe-deposit box himself. He could give it to the church's elders—Mr. Royce or whatever his name was. After all, it was the church's money and the church's problem. He could tell Nan—set her free from her dead-husband worship, exonerate himself without exposing the reverend's sins to the public, and maybe even find some money in there she could use to live on.

"Now you're talking. I vote for that last one."

"That's not the last one," Harry said. "Number four. Forget I ever found the damn thing."

"Are you crazy? What good is that gonna do? You're still on the hook and she's still sure her husband's a saint."

"Maybe he was," Harry said. He doubted it—now more than ever—but until he got that box open, there was still a chance that Nan was right, that her husband was honest and upright. And while that box was still a secret, she wouldn't have to face the truth as he thought it would pan out.

"And just how long you think you can live without being sure?" Nate asked, picking poppy seeds from his teeth with the edge of a matchbook.

"As long as it takes her to get ready to hear the truth—whatever that may be," he said.

Nate wiped his hands on a napkin and balled it in his fist. "You sleep with her last night?"

"What kind of question is that?" Harry asked, trying to pretend that the thought hadn't ever entered his mind, that he hadn't been uncomfortable the entire ride home, that he hadn't lain awake wanting her until dawn.

"Normal question about a man in love with a woman," Nate said, pushing back from the table.

"I am not—"

"Don't bother," his father said, standing up with difficulty. The moist, cold days of early spring played havoc with the man's arthritis. "Save it for someone who'll buy your horse manure. I got enough of my own waiting in the barn." He threw the napkin onto the table.

"I didn't sleep with her," Harry said quietly.

"Good. Then you'll be telling her about her husband the crook."

"You don't know what's in the box, not for sure. And I am not in love with her. A man feels sorry for a defenseless woman and the world thinks he's head over heels. She's a nice lady in a bad situation that I—"

"I've seen her, Harry. Your speech mighta worked last week, but I saw those green eyes of hers looking at you like you were some hero up on a movie screen. I saw the mud on her sweater, and I see the way you can't think of nothing else."

"Talk about enough horse shit," Harry said, gathering up the plates and mugs from their breakfast. "You ought to leave that stuff in the barn."

"You gonna help me out there today?" Nate asked. He was standing by the door waiting to see just what excuse Harry had today.

"Can't," Harry said. "Gotta take care of something in town."

"Would that town be Deburle?" Nate asked. "That *something* have anything to do with the Widow Springfield?"

Harry rolled his eyes at his father. "Nan Springfield is not the only thing in my life that needs attention."

"Right," his father said and stepped out onto the porch. He reached in to shut the door. "We ought to keep a couple of shovels in here, don't you think?"

Things seemed different to Nan in the light of day. For one thing, Harry Woolery was obviously not interested in her or what she had to offer. Not that she blamed him, a widow with even more problems than she had children. But it didn't hurt any less to know he was justified in running from her open arms.

And the idea that he could save her house—now, that was a good one!

"You're gonna break those dishes," Eleanor warned her as she wrapped her mother's fine china platter in newspaper and placed it in the open carton on the dining room table.

"It's my china," Nan snapped at her. "Let me worry about it."

"Okay," Eleanor answered, watching as D.J. lined up all of the spoons from the good silver, followed by all of the forks. "You worry about your china and I'll worry about your life."

"What's to worry about there?" Nan asked, so bad at hiding her real feelings that she couldn't even look at her sister-in-law.

"How late was he here?"

Nan busied herself wrapping up the gravy boat. "Who?"

"Oh, please!" Eleanor said. "I do have to get to work

today, so can we just drop this game? Did he find anything about the money?"

"No."

Eleanor tapped her chin thoughtfully. "It probably wasn't a good idea to have him looking through Phil's papers anyway. He's got his own ax to grind."

"Has anyone ever told you that you're paranoid? First you thought Stan Denham was hiding the truth. Now you think that Harry has some personal agenda."

"You don't think they have agendas? Both of them? Men especially, but everyone has agendas but you."

"And you," Nan added.

"Let's stay off my case and concentrate on yours this morning. I noticed he stayed very late," Eleanor said as Nan took the spoons from the beginning of D.J.'s row and handed them back to him so that he could continue the row around the room. On Thursday, Harry was taking them back to the doctor for some references and some advice about D.J.'s behavior.

"Yes, he did," Nan agreed.

"And?"

"And nothing," Nan said, tugging D.J.'s Superkid cape and motioning him toward the kitchen.

"You sound disappointed," Eleanor said, following her there.

"Am I ugly?" Nan asked, pouring D.J. a glass of juice and handing it to him. She stood in front of Eleanor with her arms at her sides and her heart in her throat. "Is there something about me that makes me completely resistible?"

"Mommy's pretty," D.J. said. "Like a horse. Like Uncle Harry's horse."

"Great," Nan said sarcastically.

"So, he kept his distance?" Eleanor asked. "I give him credit for that."

"Apparently it wasn't any harder for him than for—" She stopped herself. Eleanor was Phil's sister, and truthful as Nan was, tactless as she was, she still thought that there were times and places she ought to hold her tongue.

Eleanor put her arm around Nan and squeezed her shoulder. "My guess is that last night was the hardest night of Mr. Woolery's life. So far."

There it was again, that sense that Harry and Eleanor had some history, something between them that they wouldn't share with Nan.

"What are you doing today, anyway?" Eleanor asked, obviously trying to change the subject.

"I've got an appointment to look at an apartment on Pearl Street," Nan said. She told D.J. to hop up into his chair and called out for Rachel and Robin and Topher to tie up their horses and come to the table. The old expression she'd used a million times took on a new, wistful meaning after their visit to Harry's home.

"Don't sign anything yet," Eleanor said, taking her by both arms and looking into her eyes. "Including those papers that Vernon's lawyer sent over."

"What papers?" Nan asked as all the children galloped into the kitchen, full of noise and excitement.

"Oh," Eleanor said with a wave of her hand as if it were nothing important. "They came last week sometime. Didn't I show them to you?"

"No, you did not," Nan said. Even if she had absolutely no intention of suing Harris Tweed until she could present incontrovertible proof that Phil wasn't swindling the church, she did think that she had a right to look at the papers Vernon's lawyer had prepared.

"Well, they're around here somewhere," Eleanor said as she slipped her arms through her coat and picked up her lunch bag. "Don't look so annoyed, Nan. You wouldn't want to sue Tweed before he turned over the money for the house, would you?"

"Who wants French toast?" she asked the children, glaring at Eleanor rather than answering her.

"And there's a chance that maybe not even then," Eleanor added before slipping out the door.

"Remember, let me do the talking," Ross said as they parked the Shelby Mustang on the lot and headed for the door of the dealership.

"This really has nothing to do with you," Harry said. "I don't even know why I let you come along."

"Because I'm less emotionally involved," Ross said simply, holding the door open for Harry.

"Why does everyone keep accusing me of being in love with Nan Springfield?" he asked, wondering what made everyone think that it was impossible for a man to simply be nice to a woman without wanting to climb into her panties.

"I was talking about the car," Ross said, watching Harry out of the corner of his eye as a salesman approached and asked how he could help them.

"He's here to see what he can get for that white car parked outside," Ross said simply, gesturing with his head and clearly enjoying the look on the salesman's face when he zeroed in on just which white car Ross had in mind. "And I'm here to stop him from doing something even more stupid than falling in love with a woman who hates his guts."

"Excuse me?" the salesman said, blinking at the car as

saliva drooled down his chin. "Isn't that a Shelby Mustang? From the sixties?"

"How much?" Harry asked.

"Such finesse," Ross mumbled at him before clearing his throat and addressing the salesman. "He's thinking about possibly selling it. Nothing definite, mind you, and the price would have to be right."

He needed thirty thousand dollars. That, and the cooperation of the church and the Prills, who lived next to the new church, and he could pull it all off.

"I'll get my boss," the salesman said, backing away as if they were royalty. "Don't go anywhere. It'll just be a minute."

"Are you sure you want to do this?" Ross asked him for the millionth time. "I can get you close to ten grand in a couple of weeks if I liquidate—"

Harry smiled at him. He'd already checked with the bank, and while his credit could eventually get him enough money, these things, as the bank manager said, took time. And he didn't have any. Nan didn't have any. "I want to sell the car. Today."

"That's my point. Today you want to sell the car. What about tomorrow when you wake up and realize your heart is in a lot on James Road and Route 70?"

"I can hardly fold myself up into the thing anymore. Where am I supposed to put a bunch of kids in there?"

"You aren't supposed to put a bunch of kids in there, man. You don't have a bunch of kids."

"Josh has friends. I pick him up from soccer and want to take them all out for pizza, and what am I supposed to do? Tie 'em to the roof?"

Ross nodded. "Josh's friends, huh?" he said without the decency to even pretend to believe him.

"That's quite a car you have out there," the manager said, extending his hand and introducing himself. "Just how serious are you about selling it?"

"Just thinking," Ross said.

"Dead serious," Harry answered at the same time. He'd worked out quite a complicated deal, offering to buy the Prills' house so that Reverend Michaels could move in there, thereby freeing up Nan's house so that the elders could allow her to stay there. Who knew how long the Prills would be willing to sell? He'd hit them in their hearts when he'd told them about Nan being forced out of her house. They'd watched the church go up next to their house and they had a soft spot for the little girl they'd watched march in and out of it every Sunday.

He noticed it wasn't soft enough to come down thirty thousand dollars so that the nearly seventy thousand Harris Tweed had miraculously collected would be enough.

"It runs nicely?" the manager asked.

Harry handed over the keys. "Try it," he said. "And take a good look under the hood. The paperwork's in the glove compartment."

"You can't buy forgiveness," Ross said quietly beside him.

He wasn't trying to. He just thought that for nearly a hundred thousand dollars he might just get a little peace of mind.

Fourteen

"**So it's all a shell game,**" Eleanor heard Harry say over the radio in the privacy of the bedroom she'd stolen from Nan. "*This campaign reform business. Like three-card monte, and I don't like being the stooge.*"

"*Hey, it's a dirty job, but you're so good at it,*" Ross said. Eleanor was beginning to find Ross really irritating. He was always criticizing Harry, like when Harry refused to let callers discuss Nan on the air, saying the woman was entitled to her privacy even if the caller's intent was only to praise her. Nan Springfield was not, he insisted, an object of pity. Lately Eleanor had noticed Harry taking other honorable stands, much to his sidekick's chagrin.

And the more she disliked Ross, the more her heart softened toward Harry. Tonight she hated Ross, which was not a good sign. Not a good sign at all, she knew too well.

"*You know, you raise funds and people have a right to know that their money is going where they intend it to go,*" Harry said. Eleanor could hear the indignation in his voice.

"*Oh, so if you pay for warm fuzzies, you ought to get warm fuzzies? Is that the deal?*"

"*Jeez. I hope you've got the emergency brake on in your brain, 'cause it ain't in gear and it's rolling down the hill backward.*"

"That's not what you're saying?" Ross asked, pretending to be offended.

"And it's gathering momentum . . ."

"You aren't saying people are mad because they were paying for fuzzies and—"

There was the sound of a crash, and both men laughed.

"Right into the tree," Harry said. And then there was silence. Eleanor sat in the bed, shaking her head, knowing what Harry was thinking and wondering how he was going to get away from that car-into-the-tree image.

"Man, this coffee is hot!" he finally said, and she could hear him cough and clear his throat.

"Do I smell another Mickey Dee lawsuit? Disc jockey's career ended by scalding coffee?"

"You are just asking for it tonight, aren't you?" Harry asked.

"I never ask," Ross said. *"But if you want to talk about campaign reform and warm fuzzies, I'd like to know where your little campaign fits into all of this. Are you any better than the politicians when you get on the radio and beg for money for some cause or other? Aren't you just—"*

"Hey. Every dollar sent in here is going straight to help out the Reverend Springfield's family—and my books, unlike the reverend's, are open to public scrutiny at any time. The account's in National City Bank and we could use a few more dollars in there, so open up your pocketbooks and put your money where your mouth is if you believe that stuff you're writing in those letters to me."

"Great. Time for the 'appeal for widows and orphans' portion of the program. How about we take a call, Suit?"

"Before we open up the lines, I just want to assure everyone that contrary to what you might do with money coming in from people who don't need to buy brownie points for heaven

because they've already got their tickets, I'm making sure that their money is going to prevent the outrageous actions of the Old Deburle Church against Nan Springfield. It says a great deal about the community, and the widow, when enough money can be raised to provide her with a home."

Enough? Did he say 'enough'? Eleanor covered her open mouth with her hands and took deep breaths, trying to calm herself down. It had been a great many years since she'd believed in Santa Claus the way she was believing in him tonight.

"And if you want to argue with that, you can go suck on your exhaust pipe while I tell you why the city fathers have suddenly decided that the Deburle County Park System needs to spend twenty-six thousand dollars sodding the golf course when they've been crying that there's no money to hire lifeguards for the pool this summer."

As she dialed the station's number she thought how odd it was that she and Harry had developed, by silent agreement, a rule that called for her to communicate anonymously with Harris Tweed at the station while she entertained Harry Woolery at her house on an almost daily basis.

"I'd like to know if Mr. Tweed has actually concluded any deal regarding the Widow Springfield's home, or if he's just blowing off more hot air than usual," she asked the man who answered the telephone.

"He'd rather not say," the man on the other end replied. And then he added, "And he told me to tell you that he'd rather you didn't either, until it's a done deal the way he wants it."

"It's not much of a secret now that he's announced it on the air," Eleanor said.

"Good secrets are easy to keep," the voice—she was sure

it was Ross Winston now—said. "It's the bad ones you gotta worry about."

Eleanor hung up the phone and pulled her hand away from it as if merely touching it could do her harm. Was the good that Harry Woolery was secretly doing enough to overcome the fact that she was helping the man lie to Nan? She'd been down the for-your-own-good road before, and knew it wasn't a decision that someone else ought to make for you. She'd never forgiven Vernon for taking the decision out of her hands. And now here she was, doing the same thing to Nan.

Nan was a zombie at the breakfast table, but at least she looked good. Eleanor had gotten her out of bed at six, insisting that she get herself together, harping about how Nan was letting herself go. And why shouldn't she? Since the night on the couch nearly a week ago when she'd thrown herself at him, Harry hadn't called her, except quickly on Tuesday to postpone D.J.'s appointment.

So maybe she hadn't washed her hair since then. Maybe she'd spent the week packing in her pajamas. And maybe she had planned to go out and sign the new lease today in her old sweats, since it wasn't exactly a champagne occasion.

But Eleanor had read her the riot act, reminding her how the children picked up on her every mood, harping at her that things could get better at any moment.

Yeah. And the Publishers Clearing House Prize Patrol was on the way.

"Does soccer start today?" Topher asked her as she drizzled maple syrup onto the girls' steaming oatmeal and reminded D.J. to stop lining up his silverware and eat his cereal before it got cold.

"No, next week," she told him, making a maple syrup *T* for Topher on his oatmeal just the way she had been doing ever since he'd learned his letters.

The doorbell rang. "Oh, I wonder who that could be?" Eleanor said, leaping up from her seat.

"In a pig's eye," Nan muttered at Eleanor's lack of guile, while all the children cut her off and ran to the door along with Eleanor.

"Ah, Miss Springfield," Arthur Royce said, standing in the doorway smiling at all of Nan's little hooligans as if he weren't about to turn them into homeless urchins. "Good morning, children."

Eleanor stood on her side of the storm door until Nan came up behind her and unlatched it to let Mr. Royce in.

"Come in, Mr. Royce," Nan said. It had been years since she had called him Uncle Arthur, when he'd been her father's good friend and a fixture around her parents' house. This house. She supposed that was what had kept her in the house this long and had to be grateful, however reluctantly.

"I've just come from Reverend Michaels's place," Mr. Royce began, handing his hat to Eleanor and patting each of the children on the head like they were good luck charms. Nan rescued D.J. from the tap on top before he could react badly to it, and showed Mr. Royce into the living room while urging the children to go eat their breakfast. She planned to be brave, but just in case, she didn't want them to see her with anything but a smile on her face.

"Can I get you anything?" she offered. Eleanor still stood in the doorway watching for someone better to come along. "Eleanor? Could you get Mr. Royce a cup of tea or coffee?"

Eleanor turned with a Chesire cat smile splitting her

face in two. "Sure," she said, her arms folded across her chest. "In a minute."

"Stop fussing, Nan," Mr. Royce said. "As I said, I've come from the Reverend Michaels, and I've some good—"

"Well, look who's here! Mr. Woolery!" Eleanor shouted. "Harry!" she yelled out the door. "Hurry up!"

Harry hurried into the living room. His cheeks were glowing and his sleeves were rolled up to his elbows. "Stop packing," he said with a smile.

"What?" Nan asked, looking from Mr. Royce to Harry and back again. "What are you talking about?"

"That's what I've been trying to tell you, Nan," Mr. Royce said.

"Really?" Harry asked, glaring at Mr. Royce. "And who the hell are you?"

"Harry!" Nan said, feeling the warmth crawl up her neck. "You must know Mr. Royce. From the church?"

"Oh, sorry," Harry said, extending his hand. "Harry Woolery. Nice to meet you."

Arthur Royce shook Harry's hand. Nothing was more clear than the fact that the two men had never met.

"It's done, Nan. Cleared with the new reverend and better than we'd even hoped for," Harry said, showing her a smile so bright it was nearly blinding.

"I knew it," Eleanor said.

"Knew what?" Nan asked. "What does everyone know that I don't?"

She could have sworn Harry looked at Eleanor before he looked at her.

"Your Reverend Michaels is now the proud owner of the house at 164 Maple Avenue, right next to the church, where he belongs," Harry said.

"Mr. Royce! How did you ever manage that?" Nan asked.

"Harry Woolery?" Mr. Royce said, looking Harry over. "Are you the real estate agent?"

"This is so wonderful," Eleanor said, taking Nan's hands. "Let's go tell the children."

"Don't you know Mr. Woolery?" Nan asked Mr. Royce. "The man you hired to play Santa here at Christmas?"

"I've told you before, Nan. The church did not—"

"So someone else hired him," Eleanor said. "Who cares? You can stay here, Nan! The kids can stay! We can tell old Mrs. Price to get back on her broom and keep riding! We can start unpacking the cartons! We can—"

"Where'd the money come from?" Nan asked, afraid that she already knew the answer. "To buy the other house for the reverend, Mr. Royce?"

"From your neighbors and friends," Eleanor said. "From everyone that loves you."

"How do you know?" Nan asked. "Why does everyone in this room but me know what's going on?"

"Everyone just cares about you," Eleanor started.

"The money came from listeners to *Tweed After Dark*," Harry said solemnly. "Are you going to spite those children of yours, and yourself? Are you going to leave every memory you have behind you because of something—"

"Oh my God. Did Harris Tweed have anything to do with you coming here at Christmas?" Nan asked. She held her breath waiting for the answer.

Finally Harry nodded.

"*Tweed After Dark?*" Mr. Royce asked. "Harris Tweed?"

"Yes," Nan said, feeling betrayed and hurt at Harry's deceit. "My guess is that Harris Tweed is a good friend of Harry's."

"Nan—" Harry started, but she didn't want to hear it.

"All right," she conceded. "Not *friends*. Harry works for Mr. Tweed, don't you, Harry?"

"Well, you refused to let—"

She cut him off again. "Yes, I did. I refused to let him get rid of his guilt with a few dollars. But he saw you in the building and thought, *There's a man who could make a fool out of Nan Springfield*, and he hired you to come play Santa Claus to my children."

"So what?" Eleanor said, leaping to Harry's defense as if deceiving her wasn't worthy of note. "Don't the girls love their dolls? Doesn't Topher love his skates?"

"And was putting Topher on the team his idea or yours? Was it some way for him to keep track of me? See how I'm doing?"

Mr. Royce rose from the chair in which he was sitting. "Now, Nan, honey," he said, taking her hands in his. "No reason for you to go getting yourself so upset over nothing when you've got something to thank the good Lord for. It's not like you to lose sight of the goal. If Tweed had something to do with you getting to keep this house, I say more power to him for trying to earn your forgiveness."

Nan pulled her hands away. "My forgiveness. The man slandered an honest man, made him so upset that he had an accident and died. There isn't anything he could ever do to make up for that."

She blinked back tears as she looked at the man she'd thought was her hero. "And hiring a spy to keep tabs on me doesn't raise him any in my book."

"I've never spied," Harry said.

"It wasn't because of you that Harris Tweed found out about me losing the house and started asking for charity on my behalf?" she demanded.

"And now you have your house," Eleanor said. "Was that so awful? Has it hurt you or helped you? You're over-reacting, Nan, and it isn't like you."

"Well, excuse me, but I don't know the widow rules very well. I can't help hating the man. I don't even want to help hating him."

"And that hate is going to eat you up, Nan," Mr. Royce told her. "Remember your Bible—to err is human, to forgive divine."

"That's Alexander Pope, not the Bible," Harry said. "And Mrs. Springfield doesn't seem ready yet to hear the truth, so I'll just be on my way. I'm tired and disappointed and—"

"And you need your sleep so you can go in to work tonight and report back to Harris Tweed," Nan shouted as Harry walked toward the door. "Tell him my staying in this house doesn't get him off the hook. I love this house, but I'd live in a hut if it would bring my husband back, and unless he can manage that, I don't intend to ever forgive him. Tell him that."

"Nan Springfield, I have never seen you behave so poorly. Your father would be ashamed of you," Mr. Royce said, taking his leave along with Harry, hurrying to catch up to him as Harry stormed toward his car.

"That man," Nan said, thinking of how she'd kissed him on the same couch where she had sat with Phil and choking back tears, "is even worse than Harris Tweed."

Eleanor covered her mouth with her hand. Her eyes were wide. "Oh my God!" she said in a whisper. "You've fallen in love with him!"

Nan shouted something about Eleanor being ridiculous, and fled to the bathroom.

In love with Harry Woolery!

In love with Harry Woolery?

She watched in the mirror as tears coursed down her cheeks.

What was it they said about the truth hurting?

Eleanor got the children cleaned up from breakfast, all the while telling herself that Nan would get over her anger and forgive Harry. She was that kind of woman—gentle, understanding. Eleanor bet that Nan could forgive nearly anything. Hadn't she, the moment that she'd learned about how Eleanor had given away her baby, forgiven her for what she'd done?

And how ironic that it was Nan, after all, who'd given Harry the way out, the back door, contained the damage to his having maybe told Harris Tweed Nan's troubles.

And Harry hadn't even admitted that much to her.

Quite convenient, Harry's lie about the maintenance service was. Nan just assumed that WGCA must be the building that Harry cleaned in Columbus every night. How neatly it all fit.

But lies, as her mother used to warn her, had teeth, and would come around and bite you. Lies, and half-truths, and secrets.

The phone rang, and Eleanor picked it up while shooing the children out of the kitchen.

"If that's Harry, I don't want to speak to him," Nan shouted in from the dining room.

Rather than argue, Eleanor picked up the phone.

"Hello?" she said, figuring that at nine in the morning, it had to be Harry. Or, of course, AT&T, Sprint, or MCI.

"Good morning. I'm looking for an Eleanor Springfield," a no-nonsense voice said.

"Who's calling, please?" Eleanor asked, pulling her

sweater around her as if the room had suddenly gotten colder, a chill running down her spine.

"Is this Miss Springfield? Eleanor Springfield, originally from Pittsburgh?" the woman asked.

"Yes," Eleanor admitted hesitantly. "What is this about?"

"This is Susan Levine from Birthright. We're an organization that helps to reunite willing birth mothers with children that—"

Eleanor couldn't breathe. She tried to take in a gasp of air, but her lungs refused to cooperate.

"She's looking for me?" she finally forced out as the room blurred through a haze of tears.

"Yes," the voice said softly, gently, as if she had some sense of Eleanor's pain, as if she could possibly know what it was like to pick up the phone and find her past on the other end. A past she regretted. "Your daughter's a lovely woman and she's hoping—"

"If I say no," Eleanor asked, "will it just end here? I mean, will you not tell her you've found me if I say I don't want you to?"

"Eleanor." The woman said her name as if they'd been friends for years and she could be honest with her. "If you tell me to, I'll go away. But you were easy to find, and now that she wants to find you, she'll just hire a detective who will find you even more easily than I did."

"Why now?" Eleanor asked. "She's twenty-six years old. What does she want from me?"

"She says there is a hole in her life, Eleanor, and I'm betting you know just what she means."

It had been twenty-six years. Any hole would be too big for some day nurse who drove a fourteen-year-old car and lived in her sister-in-law's house to fill. "I can't," she said. "I just can't face her."

"Why don't I tell her that you need some time to get used to the idea?" the woman asked her.

Reject her twice? Eleanor couldn't do that.

"Miss Springfield?"

Still Eleanor could say nothing.

"How about this. I'll tell her that you've left the Pittsburgh area and that I'm sure I'll be able to track you down. And then I'll call you back in a day or two. How would that be?"

Eleanor just shook her head. A hole in her life, the girl said. A hole in her heart was more like it, Eleanor thought.

"Her name is Marissa Jane Broder," the woman said, while Eleanor wanted to yell out *No! No! Don't tell me!* "She's got a wonderful job as a creative director in an advertising firm and she raises those cute little fluffy white dogs with the French name."

"Bichons," Eleanor heard herself say. Now how had she known that? Because once she'd wanted to own one, before she realized that she wasn't the kind of person who could be trusted with caring for a helpless being that would depend on her.

"Yes, I think that was it. Can I call you tomorrow, Eleanor? Would that be too soon? I know Marissa's on pins and needles waiting to hear from me."

"Tomorrow?" Eleanor heard the terror in her own voice and felt doubly ashamed.

"The next day then, all right?" the woman asked.

Eleanor nodded, swallowed, and then whispered, "All right" into the telephone before she hung it up. She stood with her face toward the counter, her hands grasping its edge, forcing herself to breathe in and out, in and out.

"Well, if that Mr. Suit or whatever his name is thinks he can use good people's money that doesn't even belong to him to buy his way out of his responsibility, he's got another thing coming," Nan said, barging into the kitchen and banging open cupboards and drawers until she found what she was looking for."And that, Mr. Suit, is that," she said, slapping down the lawyer's complaint next to the phone. "Can you mail that for me when you go out?"

Eleanor couldn't answer, couldn't speak. She couldn't do any more than count to herself as if after some magic number things would be all right.

"Ellie? You're white as a sheet! What is it? What's wrong? Who was that on the phone?"

"Birthright. They've found me, Nan. What the hell am I supposed to do now?"

"Well, what do you want to do?" Nan asked rationally, as if the earth weren't moving, the sky falling. As if Eleanor even knew what she wanted to do.

"How am I supposed to meet a child I gave away more than twenty-six years ago? What am I supposed to say to her—'What's new'?"

"You could explain to her what happened," Nan said.

"Right. Tell her why I gave her away? Tell her I wanted to be a doctor and she was in the way of that?"

"It wasn't that simple, I'm sure," Nan said.

"Nothing is simple except the regrets," Eleanor answered.

"So why don't you agree to meet her?" Nan asked. "Aren't you tired of all the regrets? You could explain it to her—"

"The explanation isn't even good enough for me. How can it be good enough for her?"

"Maybe she just wants to see you, to know if she's got her mother's eyes. To ask if she's got her father's nose. Don't you want to see her?"

Eleanor ignored the question. She didn't want to see Mitch's sparkling eyes staring out at her from a young woman's face, accusing her of never finding him, telling him, of not keeping their child and raising it for him the way he'd have wanted her to do. And it scared the bejesus out of her that Birthright had found her, and that even if she told Susan Levine that she wasn't willing to be found, a detective could find her just as easily.

"Maybe it's time for me to do some traveling," she said, thinking that there were places she could lose herself, be lost forever. "Maybe take a cruise somewhere for a while. Now that the house is yours free and clear, and you really don't need me to kick in on the rent, I think I'll just move on out and let you have your privacy again."

"I needed more than your rent, Ellie, and I still do," Nan said softly. "And you know what they say about running away not solving anything. We're a family. We could help you, if you'd let us."

"Like you don't have enough troubles of your own," she said, when the truth was that there was nothing in the world she'd like more than to stay with Nan and the children—especially the children. But not if it meant facing Marissa Jane Broder. "And I've never seen the ocean, you know, or been to another country where the people don't even speak English."

Nan looked at the phone, knowing full well what was driving Eleanor from her home. "I would never tell the people from Birthright anything you didn't want me to," she said softly.

Eleanor tried to picture Nan lying for her and then just shook her head.

"When?" Nan asked her, resigned.

"Soon as I can make arrangements," she answered.

And then she flung herself into Nan's waiting arms, and cried.

Fifteen

He kept trying to see it from Nan's point of view, and all Harry could think was that he didn't blame her a bit, and that it all served him right. What did he think he was doing anyway, kissing her under false pretenses, messing with the woman's mind and her heart?

But as much as she might hate him, she loved those kids of hers, and so he dialed her number even though he wasn't sure the words would get past the lump in his throat.

"Hello?"

"Nan? It's me, Harry Woolery," he said, his voice cracking on his name.

"*Me* would have been enough," she said, and he could picture the reluctant smile on her face. At least he hoped she was smiling. Putting a smile on her face had been his very first instinct. Another job he hadn't done particularly well.

"D.J.'s appointment with Dr. Winston is Friday at one o'clock."

"Friday at one," she repeated. In the background he could hear the children buzzing about her, asking her to tie something "the good way."

He forged ahead. "I realize you aren't particularly pleased with me, but I don't like the idea of you driving all that way with D.J. in the car, so if you wouldn't mind, I'd like to take you." There. He'd said it. There was silence on the line. "Nan?"

"I'd appreciate it."

"Really?" Jeez! He hadn't meant to say that aloud. "I mean, good. I'll pick you up around eleven-thirty?"

"Thanks. I don't really want to be alone when he tells me . . . I could ask Ellie, but—"

"It won't be bad news, Nan," he said, wishing he could make it so.

"I suppose not after last week, huh?" she said. She'd taken the diagnosis like a trouper, but then, he doubted she'd let on her fears.

"After last week, this is a piece of cake," Harry assured her. There was a pause, during which he patted Chuckie's head and scratched her behind the ear that stood erect. "So, eleven-thirty then."

"You aren't a spy, are you, Harry?" It sounded more like a plea than a question.

"No," he said, wishing he had the guts to tell her the truth and get it over with. "I'm not a spy."

"I didn't really think so. I'll make arrangements for the children," she said. He heard the sounds of wet kisses at the other end of the line, and a plea from Nan that the children "go play."

There were so many things he wanted to say—*I'm sorry. Let me in. Everything you thought that I felt I do feel. I didn't mean to hurt you. I love you.* The last one took him by surprise, but he didn't doubt it. And none of those words would help, because when she found out the truth, having said any of them would just make things even worse.

Whoever the guy was who said that love meant never having to say you're sorry must have been living in some dream world. The best thing, the safest thing, would be if he just backed away and let her go on with her life.

"Unpacked yet?" he asked, trying to be satisfied with having kept her house for her, hoping that in the end it would be enough for him.

"Mostly."

He didn't dare offer to help her with the rest, to touch things that mattered to her, to watch her household take shape without him.

"Thank you, Harry," she said in the quietest of voices.

"My pleasure," he said and had never meant anything more.

"Would you like to stay for supper on Friday?" she asked, her hope so obvious he could see that face of hers right through the phone lines.

"Can't," he said and bit down hard on the inside of his lip. "Gotta work."

"Is Harris Tweed paying for D.J.'s therapy?" she asked and then quickly added, "We'll still go. I just want to know."

"The doctor isn't charging anything," Harry said honestly. "He's the brother of a friend."

"Oh, yes. Well, I appreciate it. Maybe with the house free and clear I can find a way to pay him. I've got a lot of work coming in."

"What kind of work?" he asked, hating the thought of her staying up nights after the kids were asleep and doing other people's typing.

"Oh, database stuff," she said, and he could hear the pride in her voice. "I finally mastered that sucker, and now I'm doing mailings and things for Ohio Cares and for the Food Bank. So far I'm what Ellie calls the Solicitor General, but I'm going to offer my services to a bunch of the businesses in town, too. I've got client lists and I'm going to do a mailing for myself, offering my services now that I'm such an expert."

She laughed at herself, and Harry mentally listed half a dozen people he knew who could give her work.

Even with that, a week of Nan's pecking away at the computer probably wouldn't cover the cost of a single session with Ross's brother. "Dr. Winston would probably enjoy some of your home cooking," he said, knowing how much he would himself, anyway.

"I could keep him in pies for life," she said, and he knew they were dragging out the conversation, neither of them wanting to hang up. "I have all Nanny Annie's old recipes, and no one could make a pie like she could."

"I'm sure yours are just as good," he said, when he wanted to say so much more. "So I'll see you on Friday, then."

"At eleven-thirty," she agreed.

"Tell Eleanor I said hi," he added when he should have just hung up.

"Eleanor's talking about moving out."

Don't ask. Don't prolong this conversation. Don't get involved in her life. It's none of your business and it can only get you in deeper.

"She says she wants to travel, but there's more to it than that. I guess I should be happy to get my bedroom back . . ."

Definitely not a place he wanted to go—not in the conversation and not in real life. He did not want to imagine watching her get ready for bed, brushing her curls, washing her face. He didn't want to see her with one of those mud masks fighting the inevitable and he didn't want to be waiting in that bed of hers while she slipped a nightgown over her head that he would just as quickly slip her out of.

"You there, Harry?"

"I'm there," he answered and then sputtered a correction. "*Here.* I'm here."

"Well, I guess I'll see you Friday."

He nodded, realized she couldn't hear that, and cleared his throat. "Friday," he agreed.

"Okay then. . . ."

"Topher going out for soccer?" he asked. What the hell was so difficult about hanging up the damn phone?

"He's on the Sunny's Pizzeria team," she said. "I do their postcards for free pizza whenever we want it."

He didn't think she'd buy the fact that Josh's being on the same team was merely a coincidence. "He'll probably need new cleats," he said, avoiding the subject of teams.

"Got 'em," she said and he was actually disappointed. Now, how stupid was that? "He went up a whole size since last fall."

"Josh too," he said. At least he supposed Josh had, from looking at the boy's feet. He'd put off taking him for new shoes because he was hoping to take Topher with them.

"In a second, Robin," she said before he heard crashes and clunks and had to hold the phone away from his ear. "Sorry!" he could hear her yelling. "Dropped the phone," she said more softly after a moment.

"Guess I better let you go," he said. The words hit home and it was a wonder his grip didn't bend the receiver.

"Thank you, Harry," she said before the dial tone replaced the calm that was Nan in the chaos that was her household.

"For nothing," Harry said quietly, replacing the phone in its cradle and nuzzling Chuckie against his thigh.

It was hard to tell who was happier that Raina was baby-sitting the children. Robin and Rachel were showing her every drawing they had made for the last six months, and Raina was beaming like a lighthouse beacon.

Nan, on the other hand, was significantly more subdued. She had been mad at Harry—justifiably, genuinely, no-kidding-around mad at him. He'd deceived her and taken advantage of her. And yet the sound of his voice just melted her like butter in the sun. When she thought about it, he hadn't really taken advantage of her at all. In fact, he'd walked away from her advances, saved her house, and not really gotten anything for his troubles.

Oh, it was Harris Tweed's money, but it was Harry who knew how much this house meant to her and who had managed to convince Reverend Michaels to take the house next to the Old Deburle Church.

It was hard to be mad at Harry. Somehow he just made things seem easier. Like when she'd told him how funny she felt at church, how hard it was to show her face among the people who doubted her husband's honesty, and how she didn't know quite where she belonged because she wasn't the reverend's wife anymore, and Harry had made her feel like a shining example to everyone of how to hold your head up above the fray and retain your dignity. And he'd told her she belonged in every circle of the church she wanted to remain in, because it had been through her own goodness, through who she was, that she'd participated before, and that that hadn't changed.

And the truth was that they wanted her there, the women, because Mrs. Michaels taught third grade at Center Street School and was too busy to worry about whether there would be enough pepper jelly for the fall church fair.

At eleven-thirty she was waiting on the porch with D.J. so that the girls wouldn't see Harry and hang on him for half an hour. When the silver Volvo wagon came slowly down the street, she barely paid it any mind. When it stopped in front of her house, she was surprised to see Harry get out of the driver's seat. He came up the walk and took the car seat from the steps, next to where she had stacked the pies she had baked—two for the doctor, two for Harry.

"Hi." He was awkward standing there, shifting his weight, putting out his hand for D.J. to give him a high five which the boy did. "Good boy!" he said. D.J. did it again.

And again.

"Not again," Nan chided.

Which didn't stop Harry or D.J.

"Not again," she repeated, and at least Harry listened this time.

"We better go," she said, hurrying to the car.

She stood by the back door waiting as Harry fastened the car seat. Next to the car seat, and within easy reach of its occupant, were a Cleveland Indians cap, an abacus with shiny beads, and a sealed-in-plastic picture of Harry on a horse, his name clearly written against the sky. D.J. hardly noticed being fastened into the seat. He gripped the abacus that Harry handed him and stared at the photograph on the seat beside him.

"Okay if your mommy rides up front?" he asked D.J., taking the pies from Nan and finding a place for them in the space behind D.J.'s seat. The boy's hands ran the beads over to the other side, one at a time. "Do you care if Mommy sits up front?"

Clearly, at that moment D.J. didn't care if Mommy went to the moon, and so she went around the car and got into the passenger side. Harry shut the door for her and hurried around to his side.

"Is this a new car?" she asked him when he was seated and belted in securely.

"Not exactly." He looked about the car as if he were assessing it. He shrugged as if he were satisfied but not pleased, and put the car in gear.

"Is it yours?"

"Mine and the bank's," he said, pulling away from the curb.

Nan looked behind her. The backseat would hold three kids comfortably. Beyond that was that little seat which would hold two more children and which she had wanted in the new car that Phil had bought.

"What happened to the other one? The Seashell?" she asked.

"Shelby," he corrected. "Time to move on."

"I thought you loved that car," she said, but he just shrugged.

"Outgrew it," he said with a finality that made it clear that he really didn't want to talk about it.

So she asked, "How's your father?" and turned to check on D.J., who was thoroughly engrossed in moving the beads on his abacus.

"Ornery," Harry answered. "The man was born too far east to be a cowboy, but he hasn't let it stop him. Has to do everything himself. Shovel sh . . . shin-deep manure, fix fences, haul hay."

"Well, at least he's alliterative," she said with a laugh.

"You have the most wonderful giggle," Harry said. "It's like marshmallows popping over a campfire."

"That's gooey," she said.

"But you want more and more of 'em, don't you?" Harry asked.

His hand covered hers.

"I'm really sorry about the other day," she said, entwining her fingers in his. "I had no right to assume—"

"Let's just forget the other day," he said, putting his hand back on the wheel. "Let's forget everything for today and just enjoy ourselves."

"You say that every time we're together," she told him.

"Do I?" He took his eyes from the road to look at her. "Well, then we ought to do it. No past, no future. Just here and now."

She had a past, and she wanted a future. And she was smart enough to know that when a man said that they should just enjoy the moment, he wasn't looking for a wife and four kids and a station wagon.

So why was he hanging around? Why had he traded in his dream car for a used station wagon that held five children?

"What happened between you and Josh's mother?" she asked.

His jaw tightened. "I was young, she was young, and we mistook one another for kindred spirits. Turned out in the end that we wanted very different things from life."

"You have a way with words," she said. "Have you ever thought of doing something like writing or—I don't know—public speaking? I could listen to you talk for—" She stopped herself before she said *forever*. He wanted no past and no future. "—hours," she tacked on.

"Trust me when I tell you that no one listens to me. I'm boring as all get-out," he said. "On top of that, I work all night, sleep all day, and play chauffeur when I'm not eating. Any of those pies back there for me?"

"Maybe," Nan said coyly. "I doubt you'd like them. There's just plain old apple, apple with raisin, apple with pear, and an apple custard tart."

He licked his lips and then smacked them. "You know, you should quit the typing and bake for extra money."

"Health laws," she said. "They make it too hard these days. My Nanny Annie used to can fruits and make pies and all that stuff until she was well into her nineties."

"She must have been quite a woman," he said, putting his arm on the back of the seat so that his hand rested against her neck. "Not unlike her great-granddaughter."

"That was a nice thing to say. I always wished I could be like her, you know. When I was growing up, we'd play make-believe and all my friends wanted to be Marcia Brady or Fonzie's girlfriend, Pinky Tuscadero. Me, I'd be a grandma, baking pies and kissing babies and loving her husband to pieces."

"Did Nanny Annie marry a minister too?" he asked. His hand was playing with her earlobe and making it hard to think.

"No, but my grandfather once told me that she jilted one! She married a teacher named Noah Eastman, and most of the Eastmans since have been teachers, too."

His fingers worked their way to that spot where her neck met her shoulder, and she giggled. "Why, Nan, you aren't ticklish, are you?" he teased, trailing his finger lightly while she squirmed and stifled her laugh.

"This is very dangerous, Mr. Woolery," she warned him, adding that he was driving a car, before he read more into her words than she meant.

"So you bake and raise babies," he summed up. "And you've never yearned for more?"

Ah, a peek into his first marriage, she supposed. "What

could be more important than that? What I do every day will matter as long as the children I love have children, and those children have children. Someday some little girl might want to be . . . Eew! I'm gonna be Nanny Nannie."

"That thought never occur to you before?" he asked.

"Nanny Nannie," she repeated, interrupted by another giggle when he went after that spot on her neck again. "If you weren't driving, I'd tickle you right back, you know."

"Promise?"

"That was supposed to be a threat!" she whined, feigning indignance.

"I'm shaking. And tell me, Nan, what else would you do to me?" he asked, his voice low and heavy and warm enough to start the fire burning in her belly.

She glanced back at D.J., who was still fingering the beads. "I'd stuff you with pies," she warned.

"Is that the worst you can do?"

"I'm not done," she said. "After I tickled you and stuffed you with pies, I'd tie you to a chair and hold an icy cold glass of milk just out of your reach and for hours I'd stand there tempting you until you'd beg me to come closer. . . ."

"You sure know how to torture a guy, Nan Springfield," he said, resettling himself in his seat and putting both hands on the wheel.

"And don't you forget it," she said, wagging a finger at him.

"That's not likely," he said, but he didn't smile as he pulled his eyes from the road and looked at her. "I don't doubt for a minute that—under the right conditions—I'd beg you to come closer."

Nan felt the heat creep up her neck and suffuse her cheeks.

"I didn't mean—" she began.

He pulled into a parking lot and pointed across the street at the Topiary Gardens. "We're early. Wanna stroll around the 'painting park'?"

"That's a great name for it," Nan said, looking at the trees that were all shaped to look just like the ones in Georges Seurat's paintings. "Why don't we take a pie with us and indulge?"

"You're quite the temptress, Mrs. Springfield," he said, getting out of the car and opening D.J.'s door. He let D.J. wiggle down from his seat, the boy clutching the picture of Harry on the horse. "You're lucky you've got this strapping young lad to defend your honor."

She let the comment float in the wind and wrap around her. Her strapping young lad was more defense than she needed.

Or wanted, when it came to Harry Woolery.

"So, how's our boy?" Ross's brother asked them once they made their way over from the park to Children's Hospital and were all seated in the doctor's office.

"It makes a difference just knowing," Nan said.

"Usually does," Jordan Winston said, staring at Harry. "Nothing like knowing the truth to put things into perspective."

A jab here, a jab there, but Jordan had kept his promise, and since he'd never called him anything but Harry, had never had anything to do with Harry's job beyond the fact that Ross worked with Harry, it went smoothly enough without much effort on either of their parts.

"I've been reading everything I can on . . . autism."

She'd struggled to face the truth, and Harry had nothing but admiration. Well, he had admiration and a hard-on the size of Texas, but a cold shower—another cold shower—would take care of that.

"And you have more questions than answers, no doubt," Jordan said.

Nan nodded her head, blond curls dancing around that sweet face of hers. The reverend had been a lucky, lucky man. Theirs must have been a marriage truly made in heaven.

"That's because there *are* more questions than answers. A list of symptoms longer than my arm and only an inconsistent smattering of them in each of the children."

"I'm worried about his future," Nan admitted. "I can still carry him when I need to, still hold him in my arms to stop him from banging his head against the wall, still lock the door so he can't run away. What happens when he's ten? When he's twenty?"

Then I'll stop him, Harry thought, pretending he could always be there for Nan, that she'd want him to be.

"Valid question," Jordan said. Harry had drunk beer with him until they were both under the table. He'd cruised for women with him and tossed a football with him on the Mall in Washington, where they'd all gone to protest some war or other all those years ago. Now Jordan sat in his tweed sport jacket with the suede patches on the sleeve playing erudite doctor. Harry wished he'd just get real with them, tell Nan the truth and get it over with.

He humphed to himself. He was a fine one to be annoyed with Jordan for dancing around the truth.

"I'm going to recommend intensive therapy for D.J. I'm going to demand that your insurance pay for it, or embarrass a few colleagues into doing it out of the goodness of their hearts and because I know where they spend their off-hours and am not above a little blackmail.

"It's not going to be easy and the progress may be slow. But because he's so young, there's a better than good chance that D.J. will live a . . . close to normal life."

"What's close to normal?" Harry asked.

"He'll probably be a neat freak—lining things up carefully, washing his hands more often than the rest of us. He'll like order, and there'll probably be diet patterns— eating the same three or four foods—"

"He does that now," Nan said. "Oatmeal is his mainstay. Oatmeal and hamburgers. Oatmeal and juice. Oatmeal and a few other things, but always there has to be oatmeal at each meal."

Harry hadn't noticed that. Irrationally, he resented that there were things about D.J. that Nan hadn't told him.

"And what else?" Nan asked. "What about the other things?"

"I can't promise," Jordan said, "but this is not pie-in-the-sky dreams I'm handing you. Kids with his symptoms have improved enough to attend public school, have friends, have a life like anyone else's."

"Only neater," Harry added as they all watched D.J. evening out the books on Jordan's shelves.

"Really?" Nan asked Jordan, clearly wanting the absolute, unvarnished truth.

"Really," he told her, taking a card from D.J.'s file and handing it to her. "This is the therapist he'll start with. She's not too far from Deburle and she's very good. She delivered a seminar at the hospital here in Columbus about six months ago."

Harry rubbed his thumb against his fingers. "Big bucks?"

"Sherry's a close friend," he said with a wink at Harry before turning to Nan. "She'll be patient while the paperwork goes through. We'll do everything we can for your little boy."

"Well, he's not really—" Nan began.

Harry saw the horse manure heading for the fan and tried to cut it off. "That's great, Doc," he interrupted. "Now, is there anything she's supposed to be doing at home?"

Nan had waited politely for him to ask his question. Now she held up a finger to indicate that Jordan should wait.

"D.J. is a foster child, Dr. Winston. I can't even say for sure how long he'll be able to stay with me. And I'm not sure that his parents will continue his therapy once he's back with them." Her back was as straight as her words.

"He's already been thrown away once," Harry told Jordan. "Nan, you, me . . . we're the only chance the kid's got."

Jordan shook his head. "I should have known that if you were involved, Harry, I'd find myself doing some unconscionable thing like blackmailing my colleagues."

They all smiled.

And then, a smile on D.J.'s little face, too, he tapped one of the books he had carefully arranged on the shelves.

And, like dominoes, book after book fell from the shelves until they stood in ragged, page-bending, spine-breaking piles around him.

Nan looked at the doctor and bit at the side of her lip. "A neat freak, huh?" she asked, and covered her giggle with her hand. "Soon?"

Jordan clasped his hands behind his head and raised one eyebrow in mock surrender. "Apparently not soon enough."

☂ sixteen

They stopped for a quick bite to eat at North Market. The kid behind the counter looked at Harry like he'd lost his mind when he asked if they had any champagne. The other diners stared at Nan, who spent half the meal giggling and the other half praising D.J. for the simplest things.

What a course of therapy! Praise! Dr. Winston had told her that the therapist would go into more detail, but for now the best thing she could do was break down each task into its smallest parts and praise D.J. when he complied with them. *Keep him in this world, in the here and now, with you. Don't let him zone out. Talk to him and ask for responses. If he doesn't want to talk, he can nod. He can point for now. Just so long as his mind is focused.*

Nan could do that. She proved it at dinner, when she instructed D.J. to pick up his fork, stab the french fry, put it in his mouth, chew. And she cheered each command he obeyed as if he'd come in first in the Columbus Marathon.

And during the car ride home she or Harry talked to D.J. "Look—a red car! Can you point at the car? Listen—a truck honked its horn. Can you make that noise?"

When he fell asleep, she and Harry played the game with each other.

"Look," she said. "There's my house. Can you stop at my house?"

He pulled up to the curb. "What, no praise for that perfect park?"

"Very nice," she said, but she was looking at the house. Only the porch light was on.

"I'll carry him in for you."

"Thanks," she said, pulling out her keys. "I wonder where everyone is."

Inside, while Harry carried D.J. to his bed, Nan headed for the kitchen. There, on the table, was a note from Eleanor saying that she'd taken the children out for dinner and a movie.

"Everything okay?" he whispered, coming into the kitchen.

"Do you have to leave for work just yet?" she asked, opening the cabinet above the refrigerator and trying to reach behind the platters there.

He came to where she was standing and looked down at her. "Why don't you tell me what you want?" he said, his deep brown eyes intent on her.

Oh, but there were so many things she wanted, and all of them tied themselves to Harry Woolery. "I think there's a bottle of champagne back there," she said instead, pointing toward the left side of the cabinet. "I'm so relieved that D.J. could be all right that I just feel like celebrating. Can you stay a few minutes?"

He pulled the tall box from the corner and eased it out above the plates. "For a little while," he conceded, dusting off the top of the box.

It looked as if it had been a long time since she'd done any celebrating.

"Open it," she said. "I'll get the glasses."

There was the requisite pop, the spilling overflow, the laughter, but it was all underscored by something else. Being alone in the house, together in the semidarkness, flirting with danger, was even more intoxicating than the champagne.

After a few sips, toasts to D.J. and Dr. Winston and predictions for a wonderful life for little Derek James, Harry suggested she show him the house that meant so much to her. He grabbed the champagne bottle by the neck and followed her out of the kitchen.

"Well, you've seen the kids' rooms," she said, leading him down the hall. "And the TV room. This is where Ellie's staying. It was my parents' bedroom." She turned on the light in the bedroom, and he stepped inside. Eleanor, who never bothered to make the bed, had done so tonight. She'd left it like a hotel, with one corner turned down in invitation.

"Pretty color," Harry said, staring at the walls and then letting his gaze drift to the carpet.

"Wedgewood," Nan said. Her mother had painted the room blue after someone from the congregation had gone to Amsterdam and brought back a little vase for her. It still sat on the nightstand beside the bed.

Harry looked at the various frames that lined the wall beside the window. He leaned close to the lowest one and Nan joined him, crouching beside him to study his face as much as the painting. "Is this . . ." he started.

"Right on the wall," Nan agreed, taking another gulp of champagne and letting him refill her glass. "I painted it when I was little and my father built the frame around it, hoping my mother wouldn't notice what I'd done."

"Was she very angry?"

"Never. Not once in all the years, no matter how I tried her patience."

"What's this?" Harry asked, standing in front of a walnut case containing two blond braids.

"Mine and my mother's," Nan said, fingering the glass. "We cut mine when I was nine, I think. My mother said hers wasn't cut until she was close to thirty. My father hung them both."

"Jesus," he said, his voice raspy. "You're like a dream I never even knew I was dreaming." And then he took her glass from her hand and put it on the doily that was on the nightstand.

"When do you have to leave?" she asked.

He sighed. "I should have left as soon as I put D.J. down. I should leave now," he added, but his hands were in her hair and he was pushing her gently with his body toward the bed.

The last strands of daylight were filtering into the room through her mother's lace curtains. If she'd ever made love with Phil in the daytime, she didn't remember it. And she knew, as her legs touched the bed and Harry eased her down, that lovemaking was what they were about to do. And suddenly she was starved for it, needed it to breathe, and she put her arms around his neck and told him with her body that she didn't want him to go.

"Does the door have a lock?" he asked, tracing her lips with his fingertip. She nibbled at the end. "Oh God!" he said as if he were about to go under. "They could come back and I wouldn't want—"

"Lock it," she said, pulling back the blankets while he hurried across the room.

"I can't believe you're real," he said when he crawled into the bed beside her. He looked as though he'd thought about her just the way she'd thought about him. He touched her face, ran his fingers through her hair, and she twisted against his hand and reveled in his touch. "I shouldn't be here, shouldn't be doing this to you—"

She pulled at his shirttails until they came loose from his pants, and then managed to run her hands and arms inside his undershirt and against his warm skin. The hair on his chest was soft and curled around her fingers. She explored him beneath the cover of his clothes, listening to the labored breathing that was warming the top of her head. He tensed when she found his nipple, and heady with champagne, she teased it as she hungered to be teased herself. And his groan told her all she needed to know about what a woman could do to a man with a simple caress.

He eased her out of her sweater and played with the skin that overflowed her bra, finally pushing away the fabric and releasing one breast. He toyed with it just the way she had toyed with him, then lowered his head and teased it with his tongue.

And she was his.

Limp with the pleasure of it all, she let him unbutton her skirt, let him shimmy it down over her hips, let him rid her of her pantyhose and her panties and her bra. She reached for the covers, but he stayed her hand.

"I'm going on a diet," she said, trying to cover her fleshy stomach, the stretch marks from Topher, the extra pounds that the years had settled around her hips.

"You look just the way a woman is supposed to look," he said, running his big hand down her midriff, spanning her stomach, burying his fingertips in her curls.

She didn't notice when he took off his trousers, only that they were gone. He lay beside her, lazily running his fingers up and down her side, tracing the swell of her breast, dipping by her waist, pressing against her hipbone. And then it wasn't his fingers pressing anymore, and she spread herself and took him in.

Just when she thought it was over, when the warm glow that had spread through her body had caught fire and she'd screamed out and he'd stilled, he rolled them over and set her atop him to begin all over again.

When his groan drowned out her own and he called out her name, she collapsed against him.

"In case you were worried, I haven't been with anyone since Suzanne," he said, dreamily playing with her hair. "I'd never have put you at risk."

The threat of AIDS had never even occurred to her. "There was only Phil," she said and felt the laughter in his chest.

"That's a relief," he said. "Until now I was really worried about the others!"

It was fully dark now, and she knew they should get up and dressed and that Harry should leave. She knew, too, that she had been well loved. But had he?

"You didn't think—" she gestured futilely with her hands at their bodies. She could never ask him, didn't even want to know the answer. "Never mind."

"What?" he coaxed, brushing her hair out of her eyes.

"You didn't notice," she began again, "while we were . . . it didn't occur to you that the drapes needed to be washed or the ceiling needed painting, did it?"

He didn't laugh. He held her tenderly against him as if he knew why she had asked. "Honey," he said, stroking her back. "I didn't know you *had* a ceiling."

"Thanks, Harry," she said, allowing herself another minute of the sweetness of his embrace.

"Oh, no," he said, kissing the top of her head. "Thank *you.*"

"The point is that the guy lied, and that's the bottom line," the caller told Harry and anyone else who was listening in Columbus. "It doesn't matter that he was young and stupid when he got arrested. It doesn't matter that he got arrested. What matters is that he lied, and I can't abide a liar."

"So all the good work the congressman's done counts for nothing?" Harry asked Jerry from Parma. "The fact that he got the strip joint on Fourth closed, the fact that he hasn't missed an important vote in six years . . . all of that pales in the face of a stupid mistake he made when he was sixteen?"

"A liar is a liar is a liar," Jerry said. Ross just looked at Harry with his eyebrows raised as if to say *See?* But Harry didn't see—didn't want to see.

"And a moron is a moron is a moron, " Harry countered.

"Now, Suit," Ross said. "The man has a point."

"Then he should wear a hat so no one sees it," Harry said, swigging a gulp of coffee that had gone cold.

"The man is obviously intelligent—"

"Intelligent? The man would be out of his depth in a parking lot puddle," Harry shouted. "Did anyone ever ask the congressman if he was ever arrested? If he spent any time in juvey?"

"It was his obligation to tell—" Jerry started.

"So the congressman never lied, did he?"

"Maybe not in your book, Suit, but a sin of omission is still a sin in my book," Jerry said.

"Well, your book ain't gonna make it to the best seller list, old buddy. And in my book, if you don't ask, then you can't go blaming someone for not telling something they'd rather you didn't know."

"That sounds awfully convenient," Ross said. "Like let's say you were seeing some woman—"

"We're talking about a congressman here," Harry said, signaling Ross to shut up. "And we've got Mike from Findlay on the line when we come back."

Music flared up and Harry took the headphones off.

"Mike from Findlay?" Ray, Harry's beleaguered engineer, asked.

Harry just answered with a shrug and turned to Ross while they ran a commercial. "It's not that way with Nan. She doesn't have that sort of attitude," he said.

"Except about Harris Tweed."

"She'll get over that," he said. "Believe me, she's softening. I can tell."

"Buddy, I don't think you've got as much chance as a blind chicken who wandered into a fox's den."

The red broadcasting light went on and Harry put his headphones back in place.

"So, Jerry here was saying that a lie is a lie. Anybody want to respond to this ignoramus?"

Sue from Columbus did, and while she prattled on, Harry flipped the mute button on his mike. "She just needs time," he told Ross.

"A week ago she just needed a house," Ross reminded him. "And then you were outta her life."

"And thank you, Sue," he said into the live mike. There was a knock at the glass window, and Harry looked up to see a man in a rumpled raincoat pointing at him. "Is that not Columbo?" he asked Ross. "I swear, ladies and gentlemen, there's a guy here who could be the detective's brother. You remember Columbo? You know . . . 'Just one more thing, Mr. Murderer.' "

"That guy could park in Peter Falk's parking spot, Suit," Ross said. "And no one would blink."

"Go invite him in," he told Ross. "I wanna see what this loser wants."

Ross opened the door and the man in the trench coat stepped into the studio.

"I'm not interested in any dirty pictures," Harry said, explaining to his audience that the man was holding a large white envelope.

"You Harris Tweed?" the man asked. All Harry could think in response was *Shit!* He felt naked and vulnerable and wondered what he'd been thinking.

"We're just foolin' around here," Ross said. "You know, when the cat's away . . ."

"You saying you're not Harris Tweed?" the man asked.

Harry switched off his mike. "Tweed stepped out. We were just fooling around," he said, coming out from behind the desk and putting on the new Best Cleaning Service cap that matched his shirt. *Please,* he prayed. *Don't let him have a gun under that coat.*

"You got someone here who can accept service for the charming Mr. Tweed?" he asked, accepting Harry's story, or not caring whether or not it was true.

"How'd you get in here?" Harry asked him.

"Even security guards have to take a leak after a box of donuts and a thermos of coffee," he said with a shrug. "Is there a manager or someone who can take service?"

Ross beckoned him over. Harry supposed his audience was listening to a long commercial interlude. Only one phone line was blinking. Not a flattering indication of how many listeners he had.

"I'm Ross Winston. I'll sign for it," Ross said.

"Great. I've been up since six A.M. and as soon as you sign for it I can go home and get some sleep."

Ross signed some papers and showed the man to the door.

Harry took his seat in the booth once again and flipped on the mike. "Okay," he said. "Whadda we got?"

"There's Vernon from Fox Chapel over there in Pennsylvania on line two," Ray said.

Harry's backbone turned to mush and he slumped against his seat.

Ross came over and dropped the envelope on his desk.

"You there, Tweed?" Vernon Springfield's voice came over the lines loud and clear.

"I'm here," Harry said, opening the envelope and finding a familiar blue-backed bundle of papers like the ones that had broken his heart once before.

"Just calling to find out if you got them," Vernon said cordially.

Nan Springfield, Plaintiff.

"I got 'em," Harry said, tracing her name with his fingertip.

"I wanted to be sure you got the thank-you for saving my brother's house," Vernon said.

"You really didn't have to go to all that trouble," Harry said, leafing through the pages until he came to the *Whereases.*

"No trouble at all," Vernon said.

Whereas, as alleged in Count One of the complaint, defendant has slandered plaintiff's decedent and caused irreparable harm to plaintiff's reputation and good name;

Harry pulled the earphones off and leaned back in his chair to stare at the ceiling.

And whereas, as alleged in Count Two of the complaint, defendant has slandered the plaintiff's decedent and caused severe emotional distress to plaintiff's decedent's next of kin, plaintiff prays for judgment against defendant in the amount of one million dollars.

And Harry had prayed the guy in the trench coat didn't have a gun.

Just showed how stupid he was.

Again.

 *Seventeen*

G reat. Now he was becoming schizophrenic.
       The part of him that was Harris Tweed was mad
as hell that some conniving, greedy little slip of a thing had
the audacity to sue him for a million dollars. And the part
of him that was Harry Woolery was cheering her on for
standing up for herself. The woman had driven him crazy.

He wanted her. He wanted her body, yes, but that was
the least of it. He wanted her affection, her respect, her
admiration. Damn it all to hell and back, he wanted her
love.

And he hated Harris Tweed nearly as much as she did
for wrecking her life. Of course, if Phil were still around,
there'd be no room for him—him being *Harry*—in her life.
Not that Harry held Harris responsible for Phil's death.
Not really.

Jeez! He *was* Harris. And Harry. And, he thought as he
rubbed Chuckie's ears, one sick puppy.

"You gonna read those papers again or give me a hand
before you go on up to bed?" Nate asked him. "You look
limp as an empty udder."

"I bet no one ever told *you* that you had a way with
words," Harry muttered as he pushed himself up from the

table and followed his father out to the barn in the rain, Chuckie winding around his legs as he walked.

"A day inside wouldn't hurt them, Dad," he said, turning up his collar when he got to the barn. "Do you more harm to ride them than it'll do them good."

"I'm not gonna melt," he said, flinging a blanket over Malomar's back. "Your turn to lead the pack," he said to the mare, patting her on the rump.

The old man was tough enough to hammer into hardwood, but Harry knew his joints had to hurt on a day like this. With a sigh, he nudged Nate out of the way and flung the saddle over the dark horse's back. "I'll take 'em out today," he said, and to save his father any embarrassment, added, "You can take them tomorrow."

"Sometimes you're just like your mother," Nate said, the tone anything but a compliment. "Subtle as bricks, the both of you."

"Dad, it's cold and wet. And you're sixty-seven and arthritic. I gotta go with you anyway, so what's the point in us both getting wet?"

"Well, Harry, you're thirty-eight and stupid, and it doesn't stop you from doing your work, so why should—"

"I ought to know better than to try to do you a favor." Considering his track record lately, he ought to know better than doing *anyone* a favor. He just couldn't seem to help himself. "It's raining, Dad."

"So you said." Nate led Malomar from the barn, Chuckie barely missing a trampling by the mare's legs.

Harry saddled up one of the new horses and opened the stalls on the six that hadn't been exercised the day before. Stupid old man, he thought to himself. Stubborn. He supposed his father was muttering the same thing about him outside on the trail.

One of the horses whinnied and poked him in the back. He gave the horse a shove with his shoulder and tightened the cinch on the new mare. Horses needed to learn manners, his father always told him, and so when the horse nudged him again, he smashed his elbow up against what should have been bare horse. Pain shot up his arm and he turned to find Malomar, fully saddled, dancing sideways against him.

"Stupid horse," he said. "Whatcha do with Nate? Leave him mending the gate?"

The horse nudged him again.

"Go on back out to Nate," Harry told her, slapping her rear.

The horse held her ground.

Harry grabbed up the reins and led the horse from the barn. "Dad!" he yelled. "Where are you?"

Down at the end of the path where the gate separated the corral from the trail, Chuckie was barking up a storm.

"Dad?" he called again, but again Chuckie's barking was the only answer.

And then he saw him, lying in a heap by the gate, the dog pulling at his jacket, and Nate making no response.

His hip was broken, but the doctor said that the break was clean and that in time he'd mend. Harry sat with him in the stark white hospital room, his hand on his father's upper arm.

"You need anything?" he asked Nate when the nurse came in. "Pain medicine?"

"You got a tranquilizer for my son?" he asked the nurse. "I think he's losing it."

"He seems all right to me," the nurse said, taking his father's wrist and checking his pulse. "You're a lucky man to have such a caring son. Why, if I told you the things I've seen . . ."

"Tell the kid I'm gonna be fine, will you?" Nate told the nurse.

"Tell the old man he's gonna have to take it easy," Harry answered back.

"Tell him I broke my hip, not my head," Nate said, pulling his arm out of the nurse's hand.

"Tell him he's gonna have to have a nurse at the house or I'm putting him in a home," Harry threatened.

"Tell him not to threaten me if he knows what's good for him," Nate countered.

"Now *you're* threatening *me?*" Harry bellowed. "You're flat on your back and *you're* making threats?"

Nate reached for the trapeze that hung over his bed. The nurse held down one of his shoulders. Harry followed suit and held down the other.

"If you want to exercise this morning, Mr. Woolery," the nurse told Nate, "you can start by exercising a little restraint. Then maybe we can move on to exercising your bladder." She lifted the plastic bag at the foot of the bed. "Are you drinking any water?"

"She's looking at my pee, for Christ's sake!" Nate whined.

"It could be worse," Harry said, and Nate's eyes rolled and he shook his head with disgust.

"A practical nurse is a very good idea, Mr. Woolery," the nurse said, flicking the IV bag that hung beside Nate's bed and adjusting the control. "I'm afraid you're going to be incapacitated for quite a while."

"Then you don't know me very well," Nate said, squinting at the nurse's badge and adding, "Miss Po."

"I may not know you," she conceded. "But I know broken hips, and I know doctor's orders and I know what happens to men like you when they try to get up without any therapy."

Nate's hands clenched. Harry was sure that his father would like to wring poor Miss Po's neck on his way out of the hospital.

"I'll get some fresh ice packs for your hip," she said sweetly, as if she were used to crotchety old men like Nate. "And I'll bring a list of nurses that the hospital recommends for aftercare."

"I don't need—" Nate began, but Miss Po was out of the room before he could finish. "Look, Harry—"

"I can't take care of you, Daddy," Harry said. It was the first time he'd called him that since he was a little boy. It felt funny on his tongue, like one of his mother's cookies might taste after all these years—familiar and bittersweet. "I've got a job to go to every night, and now my days—"

"—are full of the widow," Nate said, his lips turned down.

"I was going to say that I've got to see to your stupid horses," Harry said. Not that Nan hadn't been at the back of his mind, the time they'd spent together, the way she tasted, and sounded, and felt in that room with her mother's braid and her father's frame on the wall. He felt the smile creep onto his lips, and it made him grin all the broader for the warm feeling Nan gave him with just a thought.

"You feed 'em this morning?" Nate asked.

"Have I left your side?" Harry answered. "They'll survive until this afternoon."

"You haven't fed 'em since yesterday?" It was more a judgment than a question.

"They'll be okay," he assured his father. At least he

hoped they would, and Chuckie would, too. And anything or anyone else who was depending on him. "As soon as I make arrangements to hire one of the nurses on that list, I'll go on back to the farm."

"I don't need a fu—"

Miss Po's perfect timing had her walking in and cutting off his father's foul words. The man was ornery, but he was an ornery gentleman, and a gentleman didn't swear in front of a lady.

"Here are several nurses' aides that the hospital routinely recommends." Miss Po handed him a preprinted list. "They aren't all available, but I'm sure you'll find one."

Harry looked over the list. One name jumped out at him. "You know if Eleanor Springfield is available?" he asked.

Miss Po smiled. "I hear she's thinking about taking a leave of absence," she said with a shrug. "But you can check with Home Care. Their extension is at the bottom of the list."

"Maybe if she knows it's for me," Harry said, and wondered if that wouldn't make her run even faster in the other direction.

Jennifer Po shrugged. Clearly she was a person who minded her own business. A wise and rare woman, Harry thought. "You'd have to ask her," she said with a warm smile that encouraged him.

"I take it she's related to your widow woman?" Nate asked.

"She's a good nurse," Harry said, pretending that having Eleanor around wouldn't be one more tie to Nan, one more way to get closer, so that when he told her who he really was, it would be that much less important because their lives would be intertwined in so many ways.

He made a quick call to Home Care while Miss Po gently packed Nate's hip in ice, and asked them to hire Eleanor for him if she was available, and then told his father he'd be back in a few hours.

"Take as long as you need," Nate said, but he was sucking on his white moustache as he spoke, a sure sign he was nervous as hell.

"The dog . . . the horses . . ." Harry started to explain. "They've all gotta be seen to."

"Bet he crapped all over the house," Nate said. He didn't shoo Harry out.

"Locked him in the barn with the horses while they were getting you into the ambulance," Harry said.

"He's a smart boy, my son," his father told Miss Po. "Even if he doesn't look it."

"I'm going now," Harry said, pretending to be angry at his father's words.

"So go," his father answered in the same tone.

Harry stood by the door.

"Go," Miss Po urged him. "Your father and I have some private business to attend to."

Nate winked at him. "I haven't gotten an offer like that in twenty years." He looked at Nurse Po, all of twenty-three if she was that old. "So you had to wait until I was flat on my back for this?"

One small piece of Nan Springfield's memory tape kept playing and replaying her mother's warning words about what men wanted and the virtues of waiting for that ring on your finger. It wasn't a memory tape, but an LP, she decided. And it had a definite skip at *Did he call? Did he call? Did he call?*

So when the phone finally rang on Friday afternoon, she had a distinct edge to her voice that even she could hear.

"Hello?"

"Nan? It's Harry." He sounded like he was doing ten other things when he should have been lying on his bed fantasizing about her.

"Hello, Harry." She was cool. In control. No accusatory *Where have you been*s between sobs.

"You okay?"

What did that mean? *You're not pregnant, are you?* Fine time to ask how carefully she tracked her cycle. Not that that would be assurance enough. Heaven help her, until she saw the proof, she'd worry.

"Nan?" Now there was silence in the background.

"I'm here, Harry." Where else would she be?

"Something wrong?"

"No."

"Oh, Jeez! You thought . . . You didn't think . . . ? Nan, did you think I was . . . ? My father broke his hip. He's in the hospital. It happened yesterday morning and I've been with him every minute since."

"Oh, Harry! How awful. How did it happen?" God, she was so self-centered! Thinking only that he didn't love her, and not that anything could have gone wrong in his life.

"I should have called."

"It's all right," she said. "How bad is it?"

"I think it isn't as bad as it could be, but you know doctors. They never give it to you straight. I'm sorry I didn't call."

"Don't be silly," she said, but she was hugging herself just the same.

"I thought about you," he said softly. "All the time."

"All the time?" she asked, pulling the phone cord as far

as it would reach so that she was out of anyone's hearing range.

"Well, most of the time. There was the surgery, and—I'm opening the can, Chuckie. Relax!"

"So you're back at the farm?" she asked. She loved thinking of him there in his boots and jeans, at home with the horses and the pines.

"Had to come home to feed the animals," he said. She heard the rustle of papers. "And pick up a few things before I go back to the hospital and the station." The tone in his voice had changed.

"Is he going to be all right?"

"Nate? They say he'll be fine, but he's going to need a nurse to rehabilitate him."

"That's the kind of thing Eleanor does," Nan told him.

"I know. The hospital recommended her. They're gonna check with her and see if she's really going away or not."

"She has a lot on her plate, Harry. It's complicated. But she just might welcome staying at your place for a while."

"I'd like to see you again, Nan," he said, and his voice went husky and her knees went weak.

"When?"

"I'll call when I can."

She held the phone against her breast long after he'd hung up, until Rachel asked her if when she grew up, her boobies would be able to hear, too.

"No," Nan told her. "But your heart will."

Eighteen

When Nan was a little girl, her father used to tell bedtime stories to her and all the other children that were always moving in and out of their house. Sometimes the stories were from the Bible. And sometimes he would try out his sermons on his youngest congregation.

Once he told them that there was a great castle in the Kingdom of Happiness. He described the castle and its occupants in minute detail. Of course, that might have been in response to all the questions about what everything looked like, what everyone wore, and whether they had weapons of mass destruction or a giant with one eye on the premises.

Her patient father answered all their questions and explained that more important than the gold and silver and gems, were the king's five daughters: Kindness, Generosity, Understanding, Forgiveness, and the littlest princess, Curiosity. And there were his sons: Bravery, Honesty, Loyalty, and Piety.

Her father explained that such values had to be protected at all costs. And the king brought more and more good citizens into the castle to keep them safe, and then he had a moat built around the castle so that all of the new occupants, too, would be safe.

But eventually word spread of his glorious kingdom, and an awful dragon, Evil, and some lesser dragons—Greed, Envy, and Duplicity, took up residence in the moat, and everyone had to be on guard because inside the castle was what everyone wanted most—Inner Peace.

Later, in Nan's early teenage years, her mother claimed she saw three new trolls under the drawbridges—Laziness, Sloppiness, and Carelessness, and warned Nan about ever letting them into the house.

When things began to sour with Phil, Nan found she needed to work even harder to keep the good things in and the bad things out, because now there were new enemies on the attack—Spitefulness, Anger, Doubt—and it seemed as if she was the only one guarding the gate.

Still, it was comforting to think that she could control her own happiness.

Foolish, but comforting, even now, after all the bad years with Phil, and then his death. She should have known better.

Trying to do your best was just no guarantee that evil, or injustice, or plain stupidity wouldn't leap over the moat and grab you by the throat.

And it shouldn't have hit her so hard when it did.

Especially since she knew it was coming. Still, she couldn't help crumbling when she got the letter from Social Services that Vanessa Elburn was being released from the state prison in Lucasville, and she would resume custody of her daughters, Robin and Rachel, in just over a week.

It was 1:30 P.M. Harry was probably at the hospital—if he wasn't sleeping. Eleanor was holding the hand of some patient she expected would die before the end of the week. Besides, Nan wasn't looking for a shoulder to cry on . . . all right, she wasn't *only* looking for a shoulder to cry on.

She wanted help to fight off the dragons that were getting ready to storm the castle.

Reluctantly she opened her phone book and dialed Vernon's number. It was better than rolling over and playing dead.

"Nan, good to hear your voice!" Vernon said when his secretary finally agreed to put her call through. His apparent joy was definitely unnerving. "How've you been? I've been meaning to call . . ."

"I'm fine," she assured him, surprised that he cared. Maybe she'd been selling him short all these years. "But I need your help."

"Of course," he said expansively. "Anything I can do for Phil's wife. Anything."

"Social Services wants to take Robin and Rachel back. Their mother is getting out of jail and—" She took a breath and tried to collect her thoughts. The truth was, she didn't know what she expected Vernon to do about it. There really wasn't anything he could do.

"I could ask your lawyer to look into it," he offered. "I don't know that there'd be any grounds to stop them from giving a mother custody of her own children, but I could certainly ask him to make a few calls on your behalf."

"My lawyer?" Nan heard her voice squeak.

"Dick Meltzer," Vernon said. "The guy who's handling your suit against Tweed. I should have called you last week when I heard you'd signed the papers. I don't know what you were waiting for, but it's done, so no matter."

She'd forgotten she'd even signed the papers, stuffed them into an envelope, and left them in the postbox for the mailman to take.

There was a heavy silence, and then Vernon said, "You

know, Nan, if you win this suit, you'll be a very wealthy woman."

"Vernon, I don't think that I—"

"And a wealthy woman is a powerful woman. A woman with the resources to take on the establishment, to fight for what she wants or believes in. Do you think for a moment that Social Services would be jerking the chain of a millionaire?"

She thought about the cost of D.J.'s therapy. Visions of more children, a minivan, birthday parties with pony rides, all danced in her head. "I really don't think I could make a man, even *that* man, pay—"

"He doesn't pay, honey, though believe me, I wish he did. His insurance pays for it. The station pays for it. Best we can hope for is that he loses his job over it all."

"Do you think that the lawyer can do anything about Robin and Rachel? It's not like I just want to keep them," she explained. "I'm worried about their safety. Robin has scars and Rachel had nightmares for months after she came to me."

"Nan, the man expects to make about a quarter of a million dollars from your case. He'll help. He'll damn well shovel shit with a sugar spoon if he has to. I'll call him for you now."

"Thank you, Vernon, for not poo-pooing me about this," she said. She hoped he didn't hear her sniffing back the tears.

"No one 'poo-poos' a millionaire," he said. "Least of all me."

Nan hung up the phone. She could be a formidable woman. A woman of means. A millionaire.

She picked up the receiver again and dialed.

"I'd like to have a bouquet of flowers sent to Nate Woolery at Mercer County Hospital." She gave the florist the details, and then, in a burst of pure lunacy, added, "And I'd like a beautiful, big, bright, springy bouquet sent to Mrs. Nan Springfield at 159 Robby Lane. . . ."

He'd managed to catch a few hours' worth of sleep, feed Chuckie and the horses, still get to Josh's game in time to see the boy score an easy goal, give him a high five and a hug, and have a good twenty minutes left to stop by Nan's. After that he'd stop by the hospital and check on Nate and head for the station.

Somebody else would have caught a few extra minutes' sleep in his car, but somebody else didn't have Nan Springfield waiting in her house. Jeez, if it was anyone but Nan, he'd have found himself pathetic.

Her face lit up at the sight of him standing on her doorstep. A welcome like that could get a man home through a hurricane.

"Harry!" It was a song in her voice—a symphony. God, he had it bad. Bad? No—terminal.

He leaned down, intending to give her a sweet peck on the cheek, but something—her perfume or her warmth or the softness of her lips—made him so hungry that he greedily kissed her lips. And she was giving as good as she got, her lips parting for his tongue to trace them, allowing him to cross the threshold and taste the sweet warmth of her mouth.

He ran frantic fingers through her hair as if he needed to reassure himself that she was real—such goodness, such softness—he always worried when they were apart that he'd imagined it all.

But now he was sure, with Nan in his arms, and he

maneuvered her into the hall, kicking the door shut behind him.

"Thought I'd just take a chance that you were home," he said as they sort of fell into the house and he noticed the flowers on the living room table. "It's not your birthday, is it?" He'd hate to miss her birthday. Why didn't he know when that was? Why didn't he know everything about her?

She looked embarrassed when she shook her head.

"Who sent them?" he asked, trying to sound nonchalant.

She worried her bottom lip. Who the hell was sending Nan Springfield, *his* Nan Springfield, flowers? And why was she accepting flowers from some other man?

"Well," he said, checking his watch, "I guess I ought to be getting to the hospital."

"Are you jealous?" she asked, her eyes as wide as saucers, her smile dazzling.

"Should I be?" he asked coyly. Jeez, he'd slept with the woman. Didn't that make her his?

She couldn't look him in the eye.

"I've gotta check on my father and get to the sta— work."

"I sent them," she mumbled, her bare toes playing with the fringe on the rug.

"What?"

"I was celebrating," she said.

"You sent yourself flowers?" he asked, trying not to smirk. He loved those naked toes of hers, loved her shyness and her impetuousness and the way she embraced life. Not to mention the way she embraced him.

She shrugged as if she just couldn't have helped it.

"And what are you celebrating, if I might ask?"

She took a deep breath. "Okay—this starts out awful,

but I just know it's going to have a happy ending. Robin and Rachel's mother is getting out of prison next week and Social Services wants to 'reunite' the family."

Harry grunted. He didn't see much cause for celebration in that bit of news.

"But I spoke to my lawyer and he is going to challenge the decision to return them on the grounds that she abused them before and she hasn't proven herself fit and he'll move for her to be required to complete a parenting program and by the time she does that, I should have my money, and then he figures if he can't work any more legal magic, maybe I could offer her "

"Back up about half a dozen steps," Harry told her. "I don't even want to touch the stuff about the lawyer and the money, but it sounds like you're talking about buying the girls."

"I know," she said solemnly. "And I know you think that's wrong."

"Not just wrong, but illegal."

"You think the law cares?" she asked. She looked wise and confident. Defiant, even.

"What makes you think that their mother would even consider—"

"Oh, of course not. A mother would never do that, would she? A mother wouldn't be willing to sell her daughters' bodies for crack, and take a Magic Marker and write the prices she wanted next to each of her daughters' orifices."

Harry swallowed the bile rising in his throat. Ragged nails bit into the flesh of his palm.

"And the legal system wouldn't say she was 'rehabilitated' and had 'paid her debt to society' and give her back those girls—"

He couldn't breathe, couldn't take in air. He held on to the doorframe, afraid that if he let go he might just slide down to the floor.

"Rachel?" was all he could manage to utter. "Robin?"

"Little Robin," she agreed. "And if it hadn't been an undercover cop, she and Rachel would have been raped and sodomized and God knows what else, so that their mother could get another vial of crack."

"They weren't . . . ?"

She was breathing heavily, but to her credit she held back the tears. It made her stronger, but softer, too, as if she wouldn't take away from the children's pain with any of her own. "The doctor found burns and cuts but no signs of—how did he put it? *Invasion.*"

"Yes, but they aren't going to send those girls back to a woman convicted of child endangerment," Harry said, and even to his own ears he sounded naive and unsophisticated.

"Oh, those charges were dropped," Nan said, as if it were the natural end to the story. "Entrapment by the officer. They put her away for possession of crack and crack paraphernalia."

"Still, they wouldn't turn those two sweet little girls over to some crackhead fresh out of jail."

"Would you like to see the letter?" Nan asked. "Would you like to know about the other children I've loved and let go of? Tony, the one who disappeared off the face of the earth two days after I let them pull him from my arms? Would you like to know how D.J.'s parents tried to stop him from banging his head against the wall?"

"There's got to be a way to stop them," he said, his big hulky frame suddenly counting for nothing. It wasn't a monster after the girls—not a bear or a bad guy that he could fight off. It was the justice system—*justice?* Ha!

"That's what I'm doing," she said. "I'm fighting with the legal system working for me, and if that doesn't work, I'm fighting dirty. She wanted money for the girls—I'll give it to her. Plenty of it, if she'll give me custody."

"We'll get the money," he told her, wondering what else he could sell now that the Shelby Mustang was history. Would his father still keep the horses now that his hip was broken and old age was setting in?

"I'll get it from Harris Tweed," she said, crossing her arms over her chest.

"What does Harris Tweed have to do with what happened—or, thank God, didn't happen—to the girls?"

"You're kidding, right? All of this started with Harris Tweed defaming my husband. If he hadn't, Phil never would have gone tearing out of here that night and had an accident. And if Phil were still alive, we could go to the judge and make him choose between a minister and his wife keeping the girls and some single mother ex-con with nothing to offer them. Ministers get a lot of respect, Harry. A judge would think twice, at least, before taking the girls from him—especially after what happened with Tony."

"But you're still," Harry started, then let the words *the minister's wife* die on his tongue. She wasn't. And she was right about that at least being Harris Tweed's fault.

"If Phil were alive, the judge would be taking two sweet girls out of a loving, stable environment and risking their well-being with an ex-junkie prostitute. Would you want to be the judge that had that ruling all over the local papers?"

"Maybe if Tweed got the word out about it, if he told his listeners—"

"I know that the man feels guilty about what's happened, but I don't think that a judge would be likely to listen to some cynical disk jockey who's already told his listeners what he thought of my husband. I don't think it would help for him to say that the wife of the man he called an embezzler—from his own church, no less—should be the mother of two impressionable children. And, Harry, to be honest, I don't want anything to do with Tweed. It still smarts that you came here under false pretenses and let me believe that the church had sent you."

"Don't sue Tweed," Harry said after a big sigh. "He never meant you any harm."

"Please don't defend him to me," she said, rubbing her arms as if she couldn't get warm.

"It was just a joke on the radio at your husband's expense. Happens a million times a day on a million radio stations—"

"Only this time it cost a man his life, cost a woman her husband, cost a boy his father, and cost three other children a safe haven from a terrible world. Why should *we* pay?"

She didn't need some lawyer who would take a cut of the spoils. She could argue the case herself and he'd fork over the money.

"Tweed didn't make him hit that tree," Harry said softly. "That was God, or fate, or simple carelessness."

"Phil Springfield was an excellent driver. If he was careless, it was because he was too upset to think straight." She swiped at the tears on her cheeks, tears that Harry wanted to wipe away for her, tears that Harry wanted to erase. "Upset with Harris Tweed and what he'd accused him of. I know in my heart that was why he was so upset."

Upset enough to aim for the tree? Harry wondered. Upset, ashamed, cornered and facing disgrace, did he really miss the turn and go skidding into the tree? If he did, where were the skid marks? Harry hadn't seen them when he'd returned to the station the next day.

"Don't sue him, Nan," he said. "Nothing good can come of it. I'll find a way to get you money, and help keep the kids, all of them, and I'll—"

"Harry, you can't help me. I need money and power and respect, and suing Harris Tweed is going to provide me with all of those."

"It won't make you happy, Nan," he warned.

"My happiness isn't important," she said.

"Nothing in this world is more important," Harry said sadly. "And suing Harris Tweed is going to open a wound that may never heal."

Nan stood on her toes and kissed his cheek. "It's sweet of you, Harry, to care so much about me. But I'll be fine. Really. This is something I have to do. For my girls."

Harry thought about the prices written in Magic Marker on Rachel's and Robin's bodies. He wondered about D.J.'s parents stopping the kid from banging the wall. And his own happiness didn't seem as important as sand in the desert. "Do what you have to do, Nan," he said, kissing her forehead and ruffling her hair.

"Call me tomorrow and let me know how Nate's doing," she said as she opened the door for him. "And give him my best."

Nate didn't deserve quite that much. No one did. Especially not Harry.

Nan stood by the kitchen radio just after midnight. All day she'd fought off the feeling, argued herself out of it, pushed it from her thoughts.

She couldn't ignore her suspicions anymore.

Don't sue Tweed.

Harry was quick to offer Tweed's services. Too quick.

And while she had nothing against maintenance men, Harry just didn't strike her as one.

She'd considered the possibility before, always dismissing it as ridiculous—the product of a persecuted mind, a victim mentality. And she didn't want to be guilty of possessing either.

Flicking on the knob would tell her.

Don't be an ostrich, Nan, she could just hear her father say.

Don't borrow trouble, she could hear her mother advise.

There's nothing worse than a fool. That was Phil talking.

"Oh, for pity's sake." She said the words aloud, startling herself.

But then, the longer she just stood in the kitchen, resisting the radio dial, the longer she could go on loving Harry Woolery.

The light flicked on in the hall. "What are you doing up?" Eleanor asked her from the doorway.

"Have you known all along?" Nan asked. Her hand rested on the top of the plastic radio, but still she hadn't turned it on.

Eleanor glanced at the clock. They always said that about guilty people—that their eyes darted to the crime scene. *Yes, Ellie, it's after midnight and Harris Tweed is on the air.*

"Let me guess. Tonight he's talking about how Social Services wants to take away Rachel and Robin," she said.

Eleanor said nothing.

"Should I turn it on? Hear his voice?" Nan asked her.

Eleanor shook her head. "Ignorance is bliss," she said softly.

"And what is deceit?" Nan asked. "What is lying and backstabbing your brother's wife?"

"I never backstabbed you," Eleanor said. "I just thought that the man deserved a chance to do right by you and you wouldn't give him one."

"And when I let him go through Phil's papers, the intimate details of a decent man's life, did he have a right to that, too?"

"That may have been a mistake," Eleanor admitted. "But the fact that he didn't find anything—"

Nan was surprised that no tears came. She felt calm and perfectly in control despite the fact that the two adults she held most dearly had betrayed her. She had welcomed them both into her home—lowered her drawbridge for them to get over the moat meant to keep the likes of them out.

"Well, it's not as if I meant to hurt you, Nan." Eleanor took a step toward her, and Nan backed up until she felt the counter pressing into the small of her back.

"That's the second time tonight I've heard that," Nan said. "And it doesn't hurt any less coming from you."

"Nan, he loves you. I love you."

"How can you lie to someone you love? How can you keep them in the dark when you know that the truth will eventually come out and hurt all the more for your part in it?"

"Nan . . ."

"I may have betrayed Phil unwittingly by allowing Harr—*that man* to look at Phil's records, but you did it knowingly. You betrayed your brother, and you made me betray him."

"You've never betrayed anyone," Eleanor said. "Listen to me, Nan—"

"No," Nan said, putting up her hands to stop Eleanor's words. "I don't want to listen to you. I don't want to talk to you."

"I'm sorry," Eleanor said softly as Nan brushed past her on her way to the hall, holding back tears that she was afraid she would drown in.

"I wish to God that helped any," she said softly.

She wished to God that anything would help at all.

Nineteen

Eleanor found Harry in Nate's room at the hospital. Harry introduced her to his father and explained that he needed as many hours as she could give him.

"How would twenty-four seven be?" Eleanor asked.

"Twenty-four hours a day, seven days a week?" Harry asked. She could see the concern all over his face. She supposed he wasn't drop-dead gorgeous, but his face was warm and open and friendly, and she had no trouble understanding how Nan had fallen so hard, nor why she felt so betrayed. A face like Harry's said, *Everything I am is here for you to see*, while his words were full of lies.

"I need a place to live," she said simply. She had no idea how much Nate knew of the situation between Harry and Nan.

"What does that mean?" Harry asked. "What's wrong with where you are right now?"

"Nan and I both need some breathing space," Eleanor said cryptically. "I had thought about maybe traveling, but if you want me to, I could move in with you while your father needs me."

"I don't need a nurse," Nate said, but Harry ignored him.

"There's plenty of room at the farm if you don't mind a sloppy dog and a bunch of horses."

"Would I be sharing a room with any of them?" Eleanor asked, attempting a smile.

"Only if you want to," Nate said. "That pup has a way of worming herself into your heart."

"Heartworms?" Eleanor said, trying to make a joke of it. Harry wasn't buying any of it. His eyebrows were low over his eyes, his forehead a mass of wrinkles. He studied her from head to toe.

"What happened?" he finally asked. "Something wrong at Nan's?"

"She found out something last night," Eleanor said cryptically.

"About the kids?" Harry had leaped to his feet. He didn't seem to know what to do with his hands.

Eleanor shook her head. With a gesture of her chin, she indicated the news was about Harry. "I didn't tell her," she said, raising up her shoulders to indicate that she had no idea how Nan had found out. The radio hadn't been on. She just didn't know.

"Well, if this is as good as you can keep a secret," Nate said, looking from her to Harry and back again, "then it's no wonder she found out who you really are."

"I really am Harry Woolery, for Christ's sake! Harris Tweed is an act, a character I play. I'm not him. I'm me."

"Don't tell me, son," Nate said. "Tell her."

Eleanor shook her head. "She's so upset that she won't even talk to me. I'd wait a bit if I were you."

Harry sat down heavily and dropped his head into his hand. "All those times I screwed up, Dad," he said to his father, "were all just practice for the big one. I sure learned good."

"No, you never learned," his father said, shaking his head. "That's your problem."

She slammed the door in his face.

"Could I just talk to you?" he shouted through the door as rain dripped down the collar of his coat and onto his neck, sending shivers down his back while he waited.

There was no answer.

"I could ring the bell again and Topher would open the door and let me in," he warned.

She opened the door a crack, the security chain still in place. "Go away!" she whispered at him, shutting the door once again.

"I can't. I think I'm in love with you."

Silence again.

"Nan?"

"You're a liar, Mr. Tweed. Go away."

"Eleanor is staying with us, in case you want to get in touch with her," he yelled.

"Yeah, well, birds of a feather," she shouted from inside her house.

"Don't blame Eleanor," he said.

" 'Don't blame Eleanor,' " she repeated as she cracked the door open once again. " 'Don't blame Harris Tweed.' Who do you want me to blame?"

"How about the system?" Harry offered halfheartedly as he stared into sad green eyes.

"Did the system make you lie to me? Did the system make you look over personal records that belonged to my husband? Did the system make you . . . the other night . . ." Her cheeks reddened and she looked down at his shoes. "Was that the system's fault?"

"That was my fault," he admitted. "But I didn't think it

was a fault. I thought it was a good thing." Blame for the other night? He wanted credit, not blame, for both of them.

She looked up then, eyes wide with disbelief. "A good thing? To trick me into the bed my parents slept in? The bed Phil and I slept in? To not even so much as protect me from pregnancy?"

"Open the door. Take the chain off or I swear I'll just kick it in with my foot before you can get the police over here." He took several steps back, preparing himself.

She closed the door and he listened to the chain sliding out of its groove, waited while she opened the door and let him push his way in.

Her body was stiff and rigid, the Nan he'd seen at her husband's funeral. "I'm not pregnant," she said softly. "So you can stop worrying."

"I wasn't worrying," he said. The fact was that he was so in love with her, he hadn't even thought about it until this very moment. And when he thought of it now, well, all he could say was, "I was wishing."

She blinked at him. "I should have known from the beginning who you were. You sure do have a way with words, don't you? I hope they pay you a lot at that radio station. You are a gifted talker."

"I mean it, Nan."

"Would that be Harry or Harris?" she asked. "The maintenance man or the talk show host? Santa Claus or . . ."

"You wouldn't let me help you," he said. It sounded lame now. He'd had months to tell her the truth, months he'd treasure now, he supposed.

"And so you showed me the decent, kind, honest person Harris Tweed is by lying and tricking and deceiving me?"

She clutched the collar of her shirt closed, as if she thought he was going to ravage her on the hallway floor. Not that he didn't want to, even with her furious at him.

"We'll get through this, Nan," he said. He wasn't sure even he believed it.

"No, I don't think we will. We couldn't have even before you lied to me. But now—my God, I slept with the man whose words sent my husband out into the night never to come home. I slept with that man in the bed I shared with my husband. How can I ever get over that? Har—You know, I don't even know what to call you. . . ."

"Harry," he said. "I'm really Harry Woolery. Harris Tweed is just a character I play, a fictitious loudmouth on the radio. It's an act. I leave him at the station door like Arnold Schwarzenegger leaves the Terminator at the studio."

"I think Maria Shriver knows who he is when she lets him get into her bed," Nan said.

"Would you have let me into your bed if you knew?" Harry asked.

"You know I wouldn't have. That's why you lied to me. Was I a good lay, Harry? Was I worth the lie?"

Her eyes were sharp, and he felt his own welling up with tears. "I never meant to hurt you," he said again, a feeble answer to a monumental affront. "I couldn't stay away. I knew I should, but I couldn't. I can't."

"If I have to, I'll help you," she said, and pointed toward the door. "Come back here again, and I'll call the police."

"Nan—"

"I don't want a scene in front of the children," she said firmly.

He had been about to warn her of the same thing, but she stole the threat from his arsenal.

"Go. Now. Let the children remember you as a nice man."

"I am a nice man," he said. He couldn't even look at her. She shook her head, and her eyes glistened in the light.

"What did I ever do that was so bad? I saved your house. I got help for D.J., I—"

"If only I could forget the rest of it. If only I could forget how you made me betray Phil, how you made a fool of me. How you made me hate myself."

Calling him a murderer hurt less. "I did all the wrong, Nan, not you."

"I was a very willing accomplice. And I have to live with that. Please, Harry, go."

There was nothing else to do, nothing else to say. "If there's anything else I can do for you or the children—" he began, backing out the door, wishing he could at least hold her tightly if only just to say good-bye.

She smiled a phony smile that didn't fit her face. "Yes, well. I guess my lawyer will be in touch."

Over the next three days he called her at least a dozen times. Each time she would replace the receiver without acknowledging him, sigh, and throw herself into cleaning the house as if she could scrub away his existence, his memory, from her safe haven.

Well, she'd say this—she had a mighty clean house. Cleaner than her conscience.

When she finally took a break and sat down at the kitchen table, the children were all over her. Rachel handed her paper flowers that they'd made, Robin kissed her heart, and D.J. stood close enough by for her to touch him if she needed to, even while he waved his cape behind him.

"What's all this?" she asked guiltily. Oh, she'd played

with them, dressed them, fed them, but her mind was a million miles away, and now she could see that they weren't such babies that they hadn't known, hadn't felt, hadn't worried.

"Are you sad?" Rachel asked her.

Robin pushed against the sides of Nan's mouth, forcing a smile where apparently one had been missing.

"How could I be sad when I have all of you around me?" she asked, studying all their faces, memorizing them, shutting out the thought that there would likely come a day after which she'd never see them again.

"Can we make cookies for Uncle Harry?" Rachel asked. There was an edge to her question, as if the question were hypothetical, as if she wanted to know *if* they could, not whether.

"How about we make a special treat for Topher when he gets home from school?" she suggested.

Rachel exchanged an I-told-you-so look with her sister.

"We could make a field of dreams," Nan suggested. "Nine baseball players on a green baseball diamond."

D.J. began banging his head against her lap. She'd been awful about him, just loving him and letting him be. But then, that wasn't really loving him at all. She had to do what was best for him.

"Stop, D.J.," she said softly. "We're going to bake now. You're going to have to stop so that we can bake. Lift your head up now. That's my boy. What a good boy! Stop banging, D.J."

She stood, pushing his weight onto his feet, and took him by the hand.

"We're going to bake some cookies," she said. "Can you get your apron from Rachel and bring it to Mommy?"

In the bottom drawer in the kitchen were three aprons

for her three helpers. Rachel passed them out and each child presented their back for her to tie their strings. Apron strings. How soon would she be forced to cut them? How much time could Dick Meltzer buy her? How much time would a million dollars buy?

And how many times would Harry call her, she thought, as the phone rang yet again. And how many times would she hang up?

"Stop calling me!" she shouted into the phone, then lowered her voice and added, "Please."

"Mrs. Springfield?"

There were just days—weeks—when nothing went right.

"Hello?"

"This is Nan Springfield," she admitted sheepishly, while the little voice in her head was begging her to pretend it was a wrong number.

"It's Patty Price," the voice said. "Is everything all right?"

"Everything is fine, Mrs. Price," Nan said. *Fine if you don't mind the world crashing down on your head.* And she doubted Mrs. Price was calling to make things better. She pointed with her free hand at the canisters, and the children carried them to the table. Thank heavens for Tupperware seals, she thought, as D.J. all but bounced the sugar to the table. "I'm sorry. I've been getting some prank phone calls."

"Don't those hooligans even take a break for lunch?" Mrs. Price said sympathetically.

Nan said nothing.

"Well, I was just calling to congratulate you on your wonderful news," Mrs. Price said.

"What news?" Nan asked, a smile already on her face at

the hope of wonderful news. Her mind raced. The girls! D.J.! "What news is that?"

"Well, I suppose it's a whole bundle of good news, isn't it? Of course, none of it is certain yet, but after your fiancé called and told me about the therapeutic riding and his father's horse farm, I just don't see how the Santiagos can possibly resist giving up custody. I mean, you two have so much to offer D.J., and they know they just can't handle him and the four others they have, what with Mrs. Santiago on dialysis and—"

"My *fiancé* called you?" Nan asked when she could find her voice.

"That man could charm the whiskers off a kitten, couldn't he? I was not supposed to give him any information, you know. But when he told me about what D.J.'s therapist said about the riding, well, I—"

"My . . . *fiancé* . . ."—she nearly choked on the word—"spoke to D.J.'s therapist?" Harry had spoken to Dr. Winston's friend about D.J.? She and D.J. hadn't even seen her yet. What the hell was the man doing? *Hell?* Just look at the depths he was dragging her down to, even thinking in nasty words like *hell*. Worse words threatened to spill off her tongue.

"His interest is extraordinary," Mrs. Price continued. "He's quite the take-charge man! It seemed to make a world of difference to Mrs. Santiago that D.J. would be in such a loving home. Between you and me, I think her health is failing and she's afraid she'll leave all the children with Mr. Santiago, who is just too overwhelmed with their girls to give D.J. the extra attention he requires."

"Well, it's certainly a loving home," Nan agreed, measuring out the flour while she balanced the phone against her shoulder.

"I can't make you any promises, Nan," Mrs. Price said. "And I don't think the department appreciated that lawyer calling them about Mrs. Elburn, but if you at least got to keep D.J. . . ."

"I want them all, Mrs. Price." She handed the big wooden spoon to D.J. and whispered to the girls to tell him to stir, stir, stir.

"You know that isn't how foster care works, Mrs. Springfield." So she wasn't "Nan" anymore. "We've always counted on you to understand. Here the fact that your fiancé is able to offer so much in the way of specialized care for D.J. could possibly tip the scales, but—"

"You know, it's an uncertain world out there," Nan said, dragging out her words. "If, heaven forbid, I were not to remarry, do you think that I would have to give up D.J.?"

"Nan, listen to me. What happened to poor Reverend Springfield is not going to happen to your nice Mr. Woolery. You know what they say about borrowing trouble . . ."

The thought of Harry dead was sobering. Maybe she didn't want him in her life, but she didn't want him dead. God forbid! Please, God forbid!

"I just meant that I wouldn't have to wait until I was actually married to get custody of D.J., would I? You see, Mr. Woolery was married before and I don't know how long until his divorce is final—although they've been separated for years," she added quickly. The last thing she needed was Mrs. Price thinking she was running around with a married man.

"Oh, I don't believe that Mrs. Santiago is interested in seeing the license or anything," Mrs. Price laughed. "All she'd have to do is talk to that Mr. Woolery of yours for five minutes and she'd know he meant every word he said about marrying you."

"I'm sure," Nan agreed. No one knew better than she did how convincing Harry could be. She was still reeling from that fact, wasn't she? "So I could get sole custody? I mean in the meantime?"

Mrs. Price sighed. "I certainly wouldn't stand in your way. And I'd hate to think that the department would, but then with the Elburn girls and all the trouble . . ."

"Don't ask me to trade one for my other two," Nan said bitterly.

"They aren't yours," Mrs. Price reminded her. "To trade or to keep. Personally, I think your lawyer's suggestion was a good one, and Vanessa Elburn has agreed to start the parenting classes as soon as she is released. I expect she'll have those girls back in less than six weeks. If I'd been smart, and less of a softy, I'd have moved them out months ago, before you got so attached to them."

Mrs. Price had the uncanny ability to make the girls sound like puppies that were going back to the pound. Nan pulled out the big wooden cutting boards and the rolling pins and let the girls start rolling while she poured out the milk for the pudding and helped D.J. open the little box.

"Now I hate to take them, with all the celebrating you're looking forward to," Patty Price said.

"The celebrating?" Vanilla pudding dust settled like a cloud on the kitchen table as she juggled the phone on her shoulder.

"I think it's the loveliest idea to take out each of the people that mean a lot to you both instead of having one big party."

"What exactly did Harry tell you?" she asked, wondering

if she could cook the cookies with the steam that was coming out of her ears.

"Well, I asked about an engagement party and he told
me your idea. I think it so suits you! Quiet evenings with
friends. I'm honored to be included, Nan. I really am."

"Quiet evenings," she repeated feebly.

"I was touched by the things that Mr. Woolery said you
told him about me. I've always tried to bend the rules for
you because I could see how much you loved each of the
children. It's not easy being the bad guy, and I . . . well, I
thank you for understanding."

If she ever saw him again, which would follow hard
upon the melting of the polar ice caps, she would kill him.

"He thought that Thursday night was good for the two
of you."

"Isn't that just like a man?" Nan asked, thinking he'd
have to do better than that. "He forgot all about our theater
tickets."

"Theater tickets? That's funny, he said to tell you that
the people you were supposed to go out with couldn't make
it and so you were free. He didn't mention the theater."

"He gets confused," Nan said. And little wonder, with
all the lies he told. "We'll have to get back to you on which
night."

"He suggested next Tuesday if he'd forgotten some other
commitment on Thursday."

"Did he?" Words she'd never used popped into her head.
Words her father would wash her mouth with soap for even
thinking if he were still alive. "You had quite a talk with
him, I see."

"He's very easy to talk to."

She remembered that about him and felt bereft all over
again. She'd lost not only the man she loved, but her friend.

"Well, you let me know which day is good for the two of you. I'm almost always available, being a widow and all. It'll be nice not to have a meal alone."

"I can have dinner with you on Tuesday, Mrs. Price," Nan said before she could stop herself. Then she added, "But it's highly possible that Mr. Woolery won't be able to join us. He works nights, you know."

"Yes, he mentioned that he works at WGCA. Isn't that exciting?"

"Well, it was certainly a surprise when I found out," she answered.

"You're a lucky woman, Nan Springfield. It looks like it's all coming together for you now."

D.J. hit himself in the head with the wooden spoon. Nan tried to take it away and wipe the pudding from his hair, but he pulled free and ran to the hall.

"Not again," she called after him, her hand over the receiver.

She could hear D.J. hitting his head against the wall.

"Oh, yes. Everything's coming together," Nan repeated. "I've really got to go now, though."

"Well, congratulations, and have a great day!"

"Right," she said sarcastically after she hung the phone up and headed for the hall. "Stop doing that, D.J. I need you to help me pour the pudding into the tray to make the ball field. Stop banging and come back into the kitchen."

"Is Uncle Harry coming over tonight?" Rachel asked. "Should we make extra for him?"

"No, Mr. Woolery is not coming over tonight. And he is not your uncle, and you should not make him cookies. Come on, now. Let's make Topher's dream field."

No sooner were they back in the kitchen than the phone rang again.

"Hello?"

"Nan? Don't hang up. I can explain."

She wanted to tell him to go stick his head into the oven. She wanted to tell him to just let her be. Three pair of eyes watched her, waiting.

"I'm sorry," she said, barely choking out the words. "But I think you've got the wrong number."

Harry softly replaced the receiver in the cradle. Mrs. Price hadn't wasted any time, as he'd suspected she wouldn't. Apparently, Nan wasn't amused. Nor was she grateful that his quick thinking might very well get them D.J. in the end.

"Hang up on you again?" Nate asked him while Eleanor fussed over the hospital bed that now dominated the living room.

"She's softening," he lied.

"She's wounded to the quick," Eleanor said. "She needs time to heal."

Harry nodded. He didn't want to talk to Nate and Eleanor about Nan's pain. His own wounds stung, too, and the knowledge that he'd been the cause of both their suffering was almost more than he could bear.

"Whatever she feels about me, I'd still like her to know about the riding therapy that Jordan's friend thinks might help."

"And while you're at it, you want her to know that she can bring the boy here," Nate added.

"If she wants," he shrugged.

"Son, they could use you for a storefront at that new Kmart."

Eleanor looked puzzled, but Harry knew just what was coming.

"You're goddamn big and everyone can see right through you."

"Thanks, Dad," he said, shoving his hands into his pockets.

"You ready to start your exercises?" Eleanor asked Nate, taking the warm towels off his hip and reaching for the trapeze until she'd made it low enough for him to grasp.

"I don't need to pull at some damn bar," his father said. "I need to get up outta this bed and see to my mares."

"The horses are fine," Harry assured him. "And I'm not carrying you out there in this rain so that you can see for yourself. It's time you sold the horses off and retired, anyway. What do you wanna go busting your butt for at this stage in your life?"

His father shook his head at him and pulled himself up with the bar. The muscles in his arms shuddered and he let Eleanor steady him. And then he spoke. "I'm a horseman. It's not a job, it's me, who I am. If I stopped raising the horses, I'd be nothing, no one. Can't you understand that yet?"

The radio had never been that for Harry. It had been a goal, one he thought would make him happy, fulfill him, but it hadn't happened. Nothing had ever made Harry feel complete. No, that was wrong. Nothing had ever made Harry feel complete *before*.

"I understand," he said, their eyes connecting. He knew now who he was, with or without Nan's permission. He was her other half, until the day he died. Even if she never forgave him, even if she never took him back. Even if she fell in love with someone else and married the man and had ten kids. They would all be a part of him. Everything about her would always be a part of him. Whether that part ached or thrilled was up to her.

Eleanor watched him lumber over to the door, grab his woolen shirt, and head out to see to his father's horses, Chuckie at his heels.

"Boy's got it bad," Nate said after Harry had shut the door.

"My fault," Eleanor said, handing him two painkillers and a glass of water.

"You're a rare bird, Eleanor," Nate said as he gulped the pills greedily. "Most women—hell, most people—don't want to be blamed for anything they've actually done, and here you are, taking the blame for something that's none of your doing."

"I wish that were true," she said, gently rolling Nate onto his side to check for bedsores and thankfully finding none. "I knew all along who your son was—knew when he showed up as Santa Claus—and never said a word to her, never warned her, never stopped her from falling in love with him."

"You can't stop the spring from coming, honey," he said with a grimace, watching her as she took the pulse in his feet and checked their color. "You'd do as well to stand in the river and try to stop it from flowing."

"I could have stopped two hearts from breaking. And speaking of hearts," she said as she raised his back off the pillows until he could grip the trapeze, "let's get yours pumping."

"It's not like you did the lying," Nate rationalized for her.

"How do you men do that?" she asked, genuinely amazed. "Just compartmentalize the wrongdoing and then distance yourself, or anyone else, from it?"

"Think I'm letting you off on a technicality?" Nate asked.

She'd been down this road before—the straight and narrow one—before she'd veered off into the great abyss. Staunchly she'd refused to abort her child, and then she'd turned her back and let Vernon give it away, take the responsibility for it. Take the blame.

But it hadn't worked. And no matter how fast she ran, she couldn't escape it. Somewhere there was a girl named Marissa Jane Broder who was looking for her. And who wouldn't care how hard Vernon had made it for Eleanor.

"How can you hold yourself responsible for what Harry did?" Nate asked. Ah, but what went around came around, didn't it?

"I called the station and planted the idea of Santa in Harry's ear."

"Well, with manure for brains he had plenty of fertilizer close by," Nate said.

She put the stethoscope's earpieces in place. "Shh. Just nice easy breaths now," she told Nate, making sure that he wasn't retaining fluid in his lungs with all the lying around. If there were no complications, she'd have him sitting at the edge of the bed by the afternoon, and tomorrow she'd introduce him to the walker. By the end of the week she'd probably be chasing him out to the barn.

"You think you can talk her out of the lawsuit?" Nate asked when she eased him back down onto the pillows. He looked exhausted and she revised her opinion of just how soon he'd be up and around.

"She's furious that I'm here with the two of you. All I can get out of her is that the kids are all right."

"Get some rest now," she said, fussing at the sheets to make him more comfortable.

"Everybody worries about their kids," he said groggily, the pills beginning to work their magic.

She patted his shoulder reassuringly. "Don't you go worrying about anyone but yourself," she cautioned him, rubbing a bit of lotion into his arms to keep the circulation going.

"Don't worry? It's a million dollars," he said, his speech slurred now. "Slander, she says. If it's slander, what's that key to then, I'd like to know. Why would he have a second deposit box key that his wife doesn't know about?"

"What key?" Eleanor asked, but behind his thin eyelids, Nate's eyes were drifting and she knew she'd lost him to sleep.

 Twenty

"So, how are the wedding plans progressing?" Mrs. Price asked Nan once they were all seated at La Viola.

Nan tried a smile. When that didn't work, she waved her hands vaguely. She'd managed to keep Patty Price distracted all the way over, giving her directions for a shortcut out of the neighborhood and commenting on the rain. But now there was no putting her off.

"Well, we haven't been able to finalize anything just yet. Things are kind of hectic at the moment without my sister-in-law's help. Just getting out of the house these days requires a full-scale strategy," she said, avoiding the question rather deftly, she thought.

"Maybe I shouldn't have taken up your evening," Patty Price said apologetically. "If you two want to be alone . . ."

She was an awful liar—which was to say that she did it so infrequently that she never quite got the hang of it. If it hadn't been for D.J., she'd have fessed up and run from the restaurant already.

"We two?" Nan asked, realizing that it was certainly a fair assumption on Mrs. Price's part to think that she would be spending time with her *intended*. "Don't I wish! But with Harry's schedule and mine, it'll be a wonder if we ever see each other again."

"Well, wonder of wonders," Mrs. Price said, and raised her hand to wave. Nan felt her heart sinking and didn't bother to look toward the door. "He didn't want me to tell you just in case he had to disappoint you."

It wouldn't be the first time, she thought.

"Sorry I'm late," he said, his voice coming from behind her, his hand gently touching her back, warming her like hot maple syrup on a cold morning. He dipped his head and kissed her hair. "I missed you," he said softly.

She bit her tongue rather than say *Not by enough.*

"This is a very nice place," he said, pulling out the chair beside her and easing into it. His leg pressed against hers. She shifted slightly in her chair.

"I feel terrible about horning in on your time together," Patty Price said. "I bet you two have so much to discuss."

"Actually," Nan started, hoping to ditch both Harry and Mrs. Price with one blow, "I have a slight headache and—"

"I'll take you home," Harry said. He brushed a few hairs away from her face and took a hard look at her. She refused to meet his eyes. "I'm sure Mrs. Price won't mind if we make it some other time."

She didn't want to get into a car alone with Harry. She didn't want to hear him say he was sorry, or that he loved her, or that he wanted to make it all up to her. She didn't want to risk softening, letting down her guard only to be hurt again. If she waited until Mrs. Price left, she could just call herself a cab.

It would be easier to be with Harry and Mrs. Price, than with Harry alone. Maybe she could make clear to him in public what she was afraid she might forget if they were together in private—that she didn't love him, couldn't love him, could never, ever love him. Better to stay. After all, she could make it through an evening of meaningless niceties and lies. "Maybe a little wine might make me feel better. I hate to ruin everyone's evening."

"Waiter!" Harry raised his fingers and a man appeared. "We need some champagne here, if you please."

The waiter nodded, produced a wine list from midair, Harry chose, and the evening was off. They ordered salad and Nan asked for a big basket of garlic bread. Anything to keep some distance between them.

"So, have you set a date?" Mrs. Price asked. Harry's foot was nudging Nan's.

"As soon as I can get Nan in front of a judge," Harry said, covering her hand with his own. A judge. Of course he wouldn't ask for God's blessing. He didn't deserve it.

"Well, don't forget that pesky little lawsuit," she said, leaning over the table and saying quietly to Mrs. Price, "Harry just has a little legal matter to take care of. Nothing major, but we both want to get it out of the way before making any plans."

"Oh," Mrs. Price said. "I'm sure your Mr. Woolery won't let that get in your way."

"Well, that's probably his plan," she answered with a smile so sickeningly sweet that Harry took his hand back and fumbled with his silverware. She refused to feel sorry for him, or to miss the warmth of his hand over hers. "Harry's always got lots of plans and he doesn't like to let anything get in his way."

"Speaking of plans, have you gotten D.J. up on a horse yet, Mr. Woolery?" Mrs. Price asked.

"Not just yet," he said. "And please call me Harry."

"Or just *Har*," Nan suggested as the waiter put the basket of hot bread in the center of the table. "It's so much less confusing."

Harry's hand slipped beneath the table and squeezed her leg. Maybe he was trying to warn her. Or maybe he thought she'd be willing to pick up where they left off.

In answer to both, she reached out for the garlic bread and somehow—oh, quite by accident, to be sure—knocked his glass of ice water into his lap.

"Thanks," he said, mopping at the mess and shooing the waiter away. "I needed that."

Mrs. Price laughed while Nan felt her cheeks glow, and then she suggested that Harry go to the men's room and dry his trousers with the hand dryer.

After he'd excused himself, Patty leaned over the table and whispered, "He could have *I love you* tattooed on his forehead and it wouldn't stand out any clearer!"

"Don't suggest it," Nan said, diving into her salad with a vengeance.

"So, when are you two going to—"

"We haven't set a date yet," she said. "My life is very complicated right now, as is Mr. Woolery's, and—"

"I was going to ask when you two are going to try putting D.J. on a horse," Mrs. Price said.

Nan was at a loss. She'd seen therapeutic riding mentioned in passing in the literature she'd been devouring about autism, but until she settled her lawsuit, she didn't know how she could possibly pay for private lessons for D.J.

"According to that very nice therapist you've got the appointment with, he's at just the right age for it to make a world of difference. How lucky you are that Harry's father raises horses!"

Nan nodded. She'd be damned if she'd spite D.J. just because she wanted nothing to do with Harry Woolery-

Tweed. If she thought of him as Woolery-Tweed, she'd not be so likely to forget when she looked at him—like now as he came back from the men's room with his face all red—who he really was and what he'd done to her.

"Warm," he said, sitting down gingerly and fanning his lap with his napkin as he replaced it.

Nan squelched her smile.

"If by some miracle it's not raining, can I try the riding with D.J. this weekend?" he asked her. "I spoke to the therapist that Dr. Winston recommended and she put me in touch with this woman, Dori, who teaches the handicapped and—"

"You've done all that already?" Mrs. Price asked.

"Perhaps D.J. could see her," Nan suggested. She had to admit that he was trying.

Very trying, she reminded herself.

"Well, she thinks that at least to begin with we might have more luck with D.J. if he wasn't in any kind of a group, and she doesn't have any openings to fit him in."

Nan wondered if that was true. She wondered if anything Harry ever said, or had said, was true, like that he cared about her, that he loved her. Not that it would matter. Harry was not a possibility in her life.

"Dori's been letting me work with her all week, sort of training me so that I'll be able to work with D.J., and I think that I'm ready to try him on one of Nate's older mares." He looked like one of her kids, eyes all wide and wishful, just waiting for her permission to do something so special he could hardly sit still. "If it's all right with you."

"D.J. on a horse?" The idea scared the living daylights out of her. "I just don't know if he could possibly—"

"He could," Harry said simply, but his eyes were dancing. "They use the therapy on all kinds of handicapped kids—kids a lot worse off than he is. Dori says that most of the kids can pay attention for the whole session. She says that this one kid, Bobby, I think maybe he's got Down's syndrome, wouldn't speak above a whisper before he started riding. God, you should see him, Nan! Telling the horse what to do, calling me to see him make the horse turn this way or that—"

It was as if the words weren't enough. He used his hands to gesture, his whole body to emit a rush of excitement that seeped into her own.

"And she's got some sort of funding so that she can do a lot of it for free. It's incredible. These kids who can't even sit up in their wheelchairs get onto these horses and control them. I—"

"Saturday," she said. "The girls have dance lessons and Topher has a practice game. I could drop him off at eleven."

"Why not wait until after the game and then bring all the kids back to the farm and—"

Nan shook her head. "I wish I could," she said. But the kids had gotten too attached to Harry as it was. Maybe she had no choice but to allow Harry to help D.J..

But that was as far as she could let it go.

Mrs. Price was wonderful about taking a hint. After Nan dodged every question about their wedding, Harry was relieved when his constant watch glancing led to the inevitable *It's getting late*s and the party broke up.

Ross had agreed to host the show without him, and he had as long as Nan would give him. From the way she was nestled against the door in the car, it didn't look like she'd give him a moment past stopping at the curb. In fact, he'd be lucky if she didn't jump out when he slowed the car on her block.

And so he took the longest route possible back to her house, telling Nan that there was an accident on the highway and he was just avoiding traffic.

"Oh, really?" she asked, obviously doubting his veracity. He could hardly blame her.

"Jackknifed tractor-trailer across three lanes," he said. "Turn on the radio if you don't believe me."

He glanced in her direction.

"Fine," he said when it was clear she didn't believe him. "Would you rather I took the highway?"

"Don't you see how awful this is? I can't even trust you to tell me the truth about the traffic."

"Then trust me," he said. "It's as simple as that."

"No, it's not," she said, shaking her head. "And it wouldn't make any difference. The bridges are burned, Harry. There's no going back."

"I made a mistake, Nan. Haven't you ever made one?"

"I made a big one," she said. "But I'm trying to rectify it. Or at least not compound it."

"I'm not the one making it worse, here. Granted, I made a terrible mistake, but people do, and the world goes on. I didn't set out to hurt you," he said, reaching out to cover her hand with his own. "You left me no choice but to deceive you."

She pulled her hand away. "It's my fault?" she asked incredulously. "In that case, don't forgive me. Turn right here. You can cut through the school's parking lot."

"Can't we get past this? Can't we start over and do it right?"

"Like telling Mrs. Price we're getting married? Would that be on the new, clean, honest slate?" she asked. "It wasn't bad enough when you were lying to me? Now you're involving me in your lies?"

"That isn't necessarily a lie, Nan," he said, pulling over to the side of the road and putting the station wagon into Park, turning off the wipers so that the rain slid down the windows like tears. "All you have to do is say yes, and I won't be a liar anymore."

"Very clever," she said, busying herself with her purse.

"Need something?" he offered, reaching for his hankie as she pulled out a small package of tissues.

"No," she said, her nose in the air as if she were very proud at herself for being self-sufficient. Of course, the pride seemed a bit tarnished when she wiped at the tears that dotted her cheeks.

"Damn it, Nan! This isn't easy to say, but I'm in love with you. You and those kids and those braids on your bedroom wall. I would treasure them all—treasure you—"

"Oh, Harry," she said, her voice cracked with pain. "Do you think it comes easy to say that I could never trust you?" She was hugging herself in the seat, rocking gently.

"Oh, but you have no trouble trusting Phil to the grave and beyond. He couldn't have done anything wrong. And I can't do anything right." The key in his pants pocket burned, like a child's penny yearning to be spent.

"Don't bring Phil into this," she said. "This is between you and me."

"That's ridiculous. There's nothing that happens between us that doesn't have your saintly husband smack in the middle of it."

"There are some things," she said, deep green eyes glistening in the dark and meeting his. "Or at least there were."

"And what if you're wrong about Phil? What if in this lawsuit of yours it comes out that Phil was a liar just like me?"

She sighed. "You certainly don't think much of my ability to judge character, do you? Not that I've given you good reason, falling for you."

"Have you fallen for me, Nan?" he asked.

She swiped at a tear. "I'll get over it," she said.

He hoped that wouldn't happen, but sat silently.

"I suppose that you think I'm easy to hoodwink. That a man could share my bed, my life, and I'd be blithely ignorant to the evil lurking within him. Well, everyone isn't rotten to the core in my world. If they were, I wouldn't want to live in it."

God, she was beautiful there in the moonlight, so righteous even if she was wrong. "Am I the only bad guy in your world?"

"You're not evil, Harry. Just wrong for me. And the sooner you see that, the easier it will be for both of us to go on with our lives."

"You don't think I'm evil, but you're suing me for a million dollars? You'd never do that if you didn't think I was one of the bad guys." Not even, he thought, for Robin and Rachel's sake.

"You did a terrible thing, maligning Phil on the air like that without even knowing who he was or the kind of good life he led."

"Ah, yes. The saint. The man who never did anything wrong. Mr. Perfect Husband."

He watched her stiffen, knew he'd hit a nerve, knew he ought to just shut up and take her home. But he couldn't.

"Well, the rest of us aren't so perfect. We make mistakes. We say things that we shouldn't, do things we shouldn't, and find a way to live with the results.

"Or maybe we just die and leave others to clean up our messes," he added.

"My husband was a good man," she said.

"So am I. And maybe you can never have with me what you had with him—that utter devotion, that trust, that incredible firstness or whatever the right word is for never having been burned before, never having lost before. Maybe I can't give you what you had with him, but it's a big sky, Nan, and there's room for other stars in it."

"But we only revolve around one," she said.

"Do you know how much I wish I'd been Phil? That I'd been the one to take you in my arms at night and see that face of yours first thing in the morning? To watch you grow with a child of mine in your belly? To just sit across the table from you and share a cup of coffee and tell you how my day went and ask you about yours?"

"It wasn't the way you think," she said softly. He supposed it wasn't. He knew very little about God and spiritual love and doing good. The only part he could imagine easily was how she must have inspired Phil to do his best.

Was that why Phil had stolen? Had he put that money away in case she needed him to come to her aid the way Harry was trying to do now?

"Could you please take me home now?" She was digging in her purse and this time he forced his hankie on her. "Thanks."

"Did Phil carry a hankie?" he asked. It was a stupid question, but he was hoping the answer was no, and was pleased when she shook her head. In some small way he was seeing to her needs the way Phil never had.

"Home?" she asked again.

"You're never going to forgive me, are you?" he asked before he put the car in gear.

"Is he ever going to come back in my door? Am I ever going to be able to have one last conversation with him? Take back things I shouldn't have said? Tell him one last time that I loved him, despite it all, despite everything, I still loved him?" She leaned her head against the window and her eyes glistened in the moonlight.

"He knew that," Harry said. "I don't know much about God and stuff, but I know that wherever Phil is, he knows."

She stared blankly out at the night, silent.

"And husbands and wives say stupid things all the time that they don't mean. He couldn't have doubted that you loved him, Nan. Not ever."

She met his gaze, sober, hollow.

"So, you didn't kiss him good-bye," he said. Some small piece of him was glad of it. She'd been another man's wife, borne his child, and still Harry wanted to think of her as his own. "Did you fight? Was that it? Did you do one of those if-you-leave-now-don't-bother-coming-back jobs? A man never takes that sort of thing seriously. If they did, they'd never leave."

"And how do you suppose they take 'I want a divorce'?"

He put the car in gear and pulled away from the curb slowly, his hands gripping the steering wheel. "You asked Phil Springfield for a divorce?" he asked, throwing a quick glance her way.

There was no response.

"And you think I upset him?"

It was a low blow, and he'd have torn out his tongue to take it back when he heard her soft sobs. Still, she'd put him through hell and back laying all the guilt on him, when at least a part of it was rightly hers.

Hell, if she'd been his wife and she'd asked for a divorce, he'd have driven off the nearest cliff.

What right did she have blaming him? Suing him?

When she mumbled, "I can't tell him I'm sorry," he had his answer.

Twenty-One

There was a break in the rain on Saturday despite Nan's praying otherwise. Not that she didn't want to take D.J. to Harry's place. Not that she didn't want to see Nate, and even get a glimpse of Eleanor. She just couldn't bear the thought of facing Harry.

Not now that he thought it was her fault instead of his own. He was wrong. She'd gone over that night a thousand times and was sure that Phil would never have left if it hadn't been for Harris Tweed's accusations. They'd have talked about their problems, maybe even ironed them out. He'd have realized that they couldn't go on the way they were, and, faced with loving her or losing her . . .

"Why can't we go to Uncle Harry's with D.J.?" the girls asked for the millionth time.

"I could skip practice," Topher added, in case she might have somehow missed the fact that the kids wanted to see Harry and the horses. "Josh's gonna go back to the farm after the game, and he and I could—"

"This is D.J.'s time," she explained yet again. "Mr. Woolery is going to teach him to ride, just like Mrs. Lewis is teaching you girls to dance and Mr. Bonino is teaching you to hit the ball."

"I'd rather learn to ride," Rachel said, to a chorus of *me toos*.

"You can't wear a tutu to ride," Nan said, fastening the net skirt around Robin's waist. "And riding is going to be D.J.'s special thing."

"Because he's *special*," Topher said. Nan didn't like the tone in his voice.

"Each of you is special," she said, looking pointedly at Topher while she fastened a yellow dishtowel to D.J.'s shirt and agreed with him that he was Super Big Bird now.

"Yeah, but he's *different*," Topher said.

"And the rest of you are all the same?" Nan asked. "There's no difference between you and Robin?"

Topher frowned. He knew that she was purposely misunderstanding him. "Yeah, but he's . . . *you know*," Topher tried again.

"I know that D.J. sees the world differently than you and I do. And I know that people look at him, and at other children with difficulties, like they aren't quite perfect."

"Well?" Topher asked. "He's not exactly . . ."

"In whose opinion?" Nan asked. "And, for that matter, whose opinion counts?"

"Mine!" Robin said, raising her hand up.

"Okay," Nan said, wishing she knew the right way to go about this, to teach her children the value of every person, not just the ones who might become nuclear physicists or great novelists. "How many people here think that Chuckie is a cute dog?"

Topher's hand shot up. Robin watched Rachel. Nan put her hand up. Robin's and Rachel's followed suit.

"Mr. Woolery doesn't think so. Neither does Josh's mother. Does that change how Chuckie looks?"

The children looked at her like she was crazy.

"What if everyone in the world agreed that only white dogs with long hair were pretty. Would that make Chuckie ugly?"

They shook their heads.

"If I said she was a pretty silly looking dog, would that change how she looks to you?"

They shook their heads again.

"So what other people think really isn't important, is it? I mean, it doesn't change the value of things to us, does it?"

"No, but it's not just other people, Mom," Topher said, and she supposed he was right. "He *is* different."

D.J. pulled away from her and watched her struggle with the answer. There was no getting around it.

"Yes, he is," she admitted reluctantly. "I guess you must be growing up, because you're noticing things more now. And I guess you've also noticed that some things are harder for D.J. than they are for you. Lots of noise upsets him, for example."

"And he bangs his head," Robin added.

"And we want to help him," Nan said. "Right?"

The girls and Topher nodded their heads vigorously. D.J. ran out of the room with one finger up, his signal that he'd be back. "And one way to help him is this horse riding," she continued. "I know you're jealous, but if it will help D.J.—"

"You're gonna go riding!" Topher told D.J. as soon as he came back into the kitchen. "Uncle Harry'll help you and you're gonna like it a lot!"

"And you can tell us all about it when you come back," Rachel added.

"And we'll teach you how to dance," Robin said, balancing on her tiptoes in her tutu.

D.J. put a drawing of what Nan assumed to be a horse,

on the table. He took a crayon and carefully, meticulously wrote something at the top of the picture and then drew the stick figure of a man on the horse's back. When he was done, he handed it to Nan.

"What's this?" she asked him and then looked carefully at the drawing. Against the sky in five neat blocks were five carefully written squared-off letters.

H A R R Y.

"What does it say?" Robin asked.

Topher and she exchanged amazed glances. Only Rachel answered.

"It says *Love.*"

Nan didn't want to admit it, but she supposed that Rachel was right.

Harry looked out the window waiting to see Nan's car come up the gravel drive. He'd been ready since the crack of dawn; Bimbo had been saddled and out in the corral since nine. He'd chopped logs until he'd broken a sweat, and stopped then only because he didn't want to smell when she finally showed up.

Not that he expected her to stay. Not that he even wanted her to. Damn woman, putting all the blame on his shoulders, making him sell his Shelby Mustang and get a stupid station wagon like some henpecked husband, turning his radio show into the *Evening Charity Extravaganza* and taking all the bite out of it, making him eat his gut with guilt while she merrily stomped on his too-easily-offered heart.

He wasn't waiting for her. He was waiting for D.J.. She could drop the boy and go, for all he cared. He hoped she would.

He should have just sent a car for the kid and avoided

seeing her at all. That would have been better, he thought as he pulled a small piece of tissue off the nick on his neck.

"Time for my pill yet?" Nate asked when Harry looked at his watch yet again. If she didn't show up in the next ten minutes, she'd be late. He hated it when women were late, as if they weren't ruled by the same clock as the rest of the world.

"Another twenty minutes or so," Eleanor said, patting Nate's arm gently and helping him turn onto his side. "Can you hang in there a little longer?"

Harry tried to find a way to blame Nate's accident on Nan. He decided to be mad at her because it wasn't her fault and he resented her pure innocence in yet another instance. He was worried about Robin and Rachel. Each time he thought of them, he felt sick to his stomach. The idea of taking them—and all three of the boys and Nan— piling them all into that lame wagon of his and heading for the border loomed appealingly.

Well, maybe not taking Nan. That wasn't at all appealing.

"Pace where I can see you," Nate ordered him.

"Does watching me make you feel better?" he asked, moving to within Nate's range of vision.

His father gave him a smile. "Well, you know what they say about misery . . ."

"I'm not miserable," he said, checking his watch again. Eight more minutes and she'd be late. Maybe she didn't care whether the riding would help D.J., but he surely did.

"Oh, anyone can see that," Eleanor said. "How about I put on a fresh pot of coffee? By the time I'm done, she'll probably be here."

"Like I care," Harry said. He sounded like an eight-year-old kid.

"I do not want to sell the farm, Harry," his father said after Eleanor had gone off to the kitchen.

"You mean you don't want to *buy* the farm," Harry corrected. His father was less and less sure of his words, and while Eleanor assured him it was just the medication, it seemed to Harry that Nate had aged twenty years in just over a week.

"No," his father said. "I mean to pay for the lawsuit. I don't want to lose everything I worked for my whole life, everything your mother worked for . . ."

"Dad, the lawsuit is against me, not you. Your farm is safe even if she were to go through with the suit, which she won't."

"You'd have to leave the station, leave Ohio. I'd go on public assistance, lose the farm, have to follow after you and live in a crummy residential hotel with drunks in the hall . . ."

His father was picking at lint on his white cotton blanket, shifting his weight with painful effort.

"Listen to me, Dad. Nan Springfield is not going to go through with this lawsuit. She's going to marry me. We're going to have a bunch of kids and make you a grandfather a half dozen times over."

"What if she wants to sue you and not marry you?" Nate asked. "You weren't exactly irresistible before she found out that you're the man she thinks killed her husband."

"Then she'll learn to live with that. I'm not going to let her ruin everyone's lives because she can't face her own part in all this." There was Rachel, Robin, even Topher would be hurt now. And for what? Because she was stubborn? It wasn't as if she weren't in love with him, no matter what she might say to the contrary. "She won't sue me, Dad, because she's going to marry me, and a woman doesn't sue her husband for all he's worth when she's already gotten that by marrying him."

Eleanor came back into the room carrying an insulated mug of coffee with a straw attached to it for Nate. "She's here," she said gruffly, as if she were annoyed that he was in love with Nan.

"Tell the old man he's got nothing to worry about," Harry said, rising and pushing his hair back as if that could put order into his life.

"Nan wouldn't hurt you," Eleanor said to Nate as she put down the mug and helped him pull himself up with the trapeze. "She's not the kind of person who would hurt anyone, ever, unless they damn well deserved it."

"Let it go, Eleanor," Harry warned as he headed for the door. "All that's just water under the bridge."

"Maybe," Eleanor agreed. "And maybe that bridge is to Chappaquiddick."

She pulled up in front of the house and turned the car off. For the entire ride she'd told D.J. all about the horse he was going to ride. She told him everything she knew about horses and saddles and barns and owls and whatever else she could come up with to keep his mind active and his body still.

So it was only because she was so very tired and weak that Harry looked maybe a little good striding toward the car, his flannel sleeves rolled up to his elbows, his jeans a little too snug, his boots sinking into the mud and making sucking sounds.

"Hi." He stood by her window waiting for a response, but no words seemed to come.

And then a million words wanted to flood out—that she missed him, that she hated him, that she loved him. *How* *could you*s fought with *I should have*s and *want*s fought with *won't*s. In the end she said nothing, and he went around the car and opened D.J.'s door.

"You ready to go for a ride?" he asked, crouching beside D.J.'s seat while he undid the car seat buckle that kept her boy safe. "You want to sit way up tall on that brown horse over there and tell her to giddyap?"

He let D.J. wiggle out of the seat himself, understanding that the boy didn't like to be touched, but his hand was out there to steady him, to make sure he didn't trip or fall. Once he stood back up, he shut the door and leaned down so that his face filled the window opening.

"You wanna watch?" he asked. The invitation was there to take or leave, as she wished.

She nodded, still unable to talk to him, still afraid of what she might say, and he nodded back and offered his hand to D.J., who followed him toward the horse.

Nan caught up with them in the corral.

"This used to be my saddle." He spoke quietly, just to D.J., holding the saddle low so that the boy could touch the leather. It was a tiny saddle, and the initials *HTW* were carved into the skirt. She tried to imagine Harry's big body ever small enough to fit into a child's saddle, and the picture of a young Harry stung her heart. What a shame that Josh looked so much like Suzanne. Not that it didn't make for a handsome child, but to see a miniature Harry—that would be a sight to behold.

"He has a big eye," D.J. said, nearly poking the horse's eye with his finger.

"Two of them," Harry agreed. "Brown and soft and you can tell just what she's thinking when you look at them, can't you?"

Just like Harry's eyes—brown and soft and you could tell

just what he was thinking. Or so Nan had thought, anyway, once upon a time.

"She's thinking that she'd like you to climb up there and tell her what to do," Harry said, all his attention focused on D.J. for the moment. "You think you can do that?"

D.J. nodded, his eyes wide and bright, and reached for the saddle.

"I'm going to have to lift you, and you can't scream out, D.J. That will scare the old girl and she won't like it. Can you let me pick you up?"

Nan watched D.J. struggle with himself and, in the end, nod. She let out the breath she hadn't realized she was holding.

"You need to do just as I tell you," Harry warned him, putting him onto the big horse's back and adjusting the stirrups to fit D.J.'s little legs.

"Go!" D.J. told the horse.

Nan felt the panic rise inside her, but the horse seemed to look at Harry for direction and hold her ground despite D.J.'s repeated commands to "go, go, go."

"Hold on to the pommel," Harry told him, placing D.J.'s hands on the front of the saddle. "I'll walk you around the ring a few times, and then, if you're ready, I'll let you go yourself, okay?"

"Ready!" D.J. said, but when the horse took her first few steps, D.J. let out one of his howls. Nan stepped forward to take him, but Harry signaled her to stay where she was, and stopped the horse.

"Are you afraid?" he asked D.J., who continued to scream. Harry raised his voice and said, "Screaming can scare the horse, so unless you're frightened and want me to take you off, you have to stop."

Miraculously, D.J. stopped. He turned, a tear glistening

on his cheek, and called out to Nan, raising his hands to her.

"Mommy can walk beside you," Harry said, "but if you take your hands off the saddle, you can't stay on the horse."

D.J.'s hands grabbed the pommel again.

"I am so proud of you," Harry said. "Look at D.J. up there, Mommy, doing just as he's told!"

And then, somehow, very naturally, Harry took her hand and she fell into step beside him, making a slow circle with D.J. and the horse inside the fence ring.

"Tell the horse to walk slowly," Harry told D.J. while his thumb made little circles on the back of her hand.

"Slow!" D.J. commanded. The horse slowed her pace to a crawl. Harry's thumb eased slowly across her knuckles, back and forth, back and forth.

Without stopping, he told D.J. that the horse's name was Bimbo and that he should tell her "Good Bimbo!" To Nan, he said, "Sorry, I didn't name her," while D.J. shouted out compliments to the big brown horse with the awful name.

D.J.'s eyes glowed with a fire Nan had never seen in them. He held the reins with purpose. He ordered the horse to stop and cheered himself when Bimbo came to a halt. "He looks so happy up there," she said. "He looks . . ."

"Focused," Harry supplied for her, his eyes as bright as D.J.'s. "You should see some of the other kids—you'd just love Dori and her group."

That uncomfortable feeling in her stomach was indigestion— she'd rushed breakfast— and not jealousy. After all, why would it matter to her if Harry Woolery-Tweed thought that some woman named Dori was wonderful?

"Something wrong?" he asked. "You look . . . I don't

know . . . annoyed?" His eyes shifted up to D.J. and then back to her. "He's all right. Really."

D.J. was fine. Nan could see that a lot more clearly than she could see what she was doing there in Harry's corral with Harry so close that his jacket brushed hers.

"I really ought to go," she said, backing away from him and struggling not to wish she could stand just where she was forever, in the shelter of Harry's shadow, watching D.J.'s face twist with concentration as Harry handed the reins over to him.

"Remember," he told D.J.. "You want her to go slow near the house and stop by the gate. Can you tell her when to go slow and when to stop?"

D.J. nodded. Harry continued to walk beside the horse, one hand on the reins up near Bimbo's mouth where D.J. couldn't see, and despite herself and her better judgment, Nan kept pace beside him.

"I've really got to get back soon," she said, but she let him put his arm around her, and agreed that it was chilly out when he offered that as an excuse.

"Topher playing ball today?" Harry asked. She'd seen Josh when she'd dropped off Topher, and it occurred to her that Harry was missing Josh's game to give D.J. this ride. He had suited her schedule and she hadn't taken his into consideration at all.

"Why didn't you tell me that Josh would be playing? I could have brought D.J. some other time so that you wouldn't have had to miss his game."

He shrugged, as if it weren't all that important, complimented D.J. on remembering to slow Bimbo, and then looked at her sheepishly. "I didn't think you'd be too happy when you found out that Josh was on Topher's team again."

"You mean I might think you were manipulating

things?" She pulled away from his embrace far enough to look at him, and wished she could trust the warmth of those big brown eyes.

"Bad habits die hard, I suppose," he said. "And I did arrange it. It wasn't easy, either. They don't like making team changes in Little League, you know."

"But that didn't stop you," she said, trying to show an annoyance she didn't really feel.

"I won't let anything stop me," he answered.

What kind of woman would be stupid enough to fall for a line like that? What kind of woman found a statement like that flattering? Maybe one who'd waited in vain for ten years to hear words just like those, and who would have settled for a lot less. And now here was a man with all the words she'd been waiting for, and she couldn't accept them from him.

"Wouldn't it be nice to have all the kids up here some day?" he asked before reminding D.J. he needed to tell Bimbo to stop.

"You mean some Saturday or Sunday?" she asked. Was it *some day* he was talking about, or *someday*, as in forever? And just how nice would that be? How possible? She felt as if she were stringing him along and knew it had to stop.

"Maybe after church?" he asked.

"Harry, nothing can ever come of you and me. I can see you are a nice man at heart, really I can, but I would feel as if I were dishonoring my husband if I got involved with the man who. . . ." She left the words unsaid. They both knew what Harry had done, and neither of them needed the pain of hearing it put into words. "Can you understand that? Can you see what I'm saying?"

"I'm in love with you, Nan. And you love me. And to

throw that away would be a sin as surely as it would be to steal and lie and kill."

"They aren't the same, and you know it. You play with words and throw them at me and expect me to see things in the most convenient—and not the truest—light. I can't do that. Not now."

"I can wait," he said simply.

"There's nothing to wait for. This isn't something I can 'get over.' I've lived my life so that I can feel sorry for all the poor lost souls on Oprah and Sally Jessy Raphael. I don't want to be one of them—Women in Love With The Men Who Killed Their Husbands. I can't do that. And now, on top of that, I'm going to have to call Mrs. Price and tell her that we are not getting married," she said. "I can't live a lie."

"Don't let it be a lie. Marry me," he said. "We won't tell Oprah, and if you don't fall in love with me in a hundred years, you can divorce me. I'll probably be too old to do the things I want to do to you by then anyway."

She couldn't help but smile, but it was a sad smile.

"Will you at least think about it? And hold off telling her for a while? Until things are settled with D.J. and the girls and all? For their sake, if not for mine?"

"Stop!" D.J. ordered the horse. "Mommy, did you see?"

She wondered if Harry would take D.J. riding once he went back to his real parents.

"Look, Mommy! Slow! She's walking again!"

"I see that! What a horseman you are!" She turned to Harry, who was leading the horse over to the rail and taking the reins from D.J.. "We've really got to go," she told him.

"D.J.'ll help me take off her saddle and put her back in the barn. You wanna say hi to Eleanor?"

Nan looked at her muddy loafers. Every night she cleaned them and the next day it would rain and ruin their shine all over again. Some things were just hopeless.

"I know she'd really like to see you," Harry continued. "She's a lonely woman, Nan. Don't punish her for my mistakes."

Nan said nothing. She wasn't trying to punish anyone. She was just trying to put one foot in front of the other, make it through each day and get on with her life. And being with Harry wasn't making it easier to do that.

"I'm sorry I didn't tell you who I was from the start. Or if not at the start, then as soon as I knew what was happening between us. I just never expected it to go this far. I thought I'd do something nice for Christopher and then maybe set up an account to pay for his college—put in a few bucks every week, and be on my way. I guess Ellie thought the same thing."

"She turned back the covers on the bed," Nan said, and she felt her eyes grow watery. "She knew who you were and she didn't warn me. That's hard to forgive."

"You're big enough," he said, tossing the words off as he pulled D.J. from the saddle and put him down on the muddy ground. "You can do it."

D.J.'s eyes devoured every step Harry took. He held on to the stirrup that dangled near his arm as Harry carried the saddle to the barn, leaving Nan alone in the corral with Bimbo.

"Don't give me that look," she told the horse. "I'm going. I'm going."

Eleanor had watched most of the doings from the window in the Woolery's kitchen. Oh, she'd given Nate some lunch, checked for bedsores, for circulation problems, for infection at the surgical site, and helped him sit up, but she'd glanced out the window every chance she got, wondering whether she should tell Nan what she'd overheard.

When she saw Nan heading for the house, she told Nate she'd be right back and met her at the front door.

They stood facing each other in the foyer for a minute, Nan asking after Nate, Eleanor giving the correct medical answers.

"I've been worried about you," Eleanor said, studying Nan's sad face. "I was hoping you'd look better by now."

"The woman from Birthright called. I told her you were away for a while."

"Thanks," Eleanor said. "At least you didn't have to lie for me."

Nan reached out and ran her hand down Eleanor's sleeve. "I've missed you," she managed to get out before the two of them were in each other's arms. "So much. I've missed you so, so much!"

"I was so afraid you'd never forgive me," Eleanor said, and Nan stiffened in her arms. "Not that I deserve forgiveness," she added.

"I don't believe you ever meant to hurt me," Nan said, leaning back so that they could look each other in the eyes. "But you kept something from me that I had every right to know."

Eleanor told herself to forget the exchange between Harry and Nate. She told herself that Harry loved Nan and that to raise Nan's suspicions just when she seemed to be healing, and for that matter, softening toward Harry, would be a mistake.

"It was wrong to keep it from me," Nan continued. "And it made me feel as if you thought I couldn't make the right decisions on my own."

Well, that was giving Eleanor no choice. "Listen," she said quietly, pulling Nan closer to the door and away from the living room where Nate lay resting. "I know it doesn't mean anything, and I don't want to stir up trouble, but I overheard something this morning . . . I know it's nothing, but—"

Nan's big innocent green eyes stared at her, waiting.

"Nate is really worried about this lawsuit," Ellie said. "And I heard Harry tell him not to worry about losing the farm because Harry was going to get you to marry him."

"Oh, Lord!" Nan said. She looked like she'd swallowed a bite of apple only to find half a worm left in it. She eased herself down into the chair by the phone.

"I'm only telling you this because I know I should have told you who Harry was the minute he walked through the door, and I'm not about to make that mistake again. Now, I don't believe for a second that he's after you just so you won't sue the pants off him, but I guess you have a right to know that he said he wasn't going to let you ruin it for everyone. And then he said, 'She won't sue me, Dad, because I'll marry her before she sues me, and a woman doesn't sue her husband.' "

"Why does he keep saying that?" Nan asked. "I told him it isn't going to happen and he just won't let it go."

"Nate's afraid they'll have to sell the farm. Harry already sold his car because of all of this . . ."

"What do you mean, 'because of all of this'?" Nan asked her.

"I'm not supposed to know," Eleanor admitted. "And Harry would kill me if he knew I was telling you, but Nate said that Harry sold that car of his so that he could make up the difference between what he'd collected and what the Prills wanted for the house next to the church."

"Oh God." Nan put her head down into her hands. "I wish he hadn't done that."

"But you got to keep the house."

"Every day I'm more in debt to that man, Ellie. And that's the man that drove Phil to his death. How am I supposed to reconcile that?"

"Maybe if you did drop the suit so that Nate doesn't lose the farm—"

"Nobody's going to lose anything. My lawyer says that Harry's insurance will pay the claim if he loses. You ought to tell him and Nate that he's much better off not marrying me because he'd get all my debts and obligations if he did, and it won't cost him anything since he's not."

"His insurance will pay it?" She thought about how sure Harry had sounded when he'd told Nate he would marry Nan. A smile split her face. "I knew it! He is really, truly, in love with you! Oh, Nan! Someone who loves you the way you deserve!"

"Ironic, huh?" Nan asked, pushing off her knees and standing up. "My mother always used to tell me there were plenty of fish in the sea. So who comes along but the whale who swallowed Philip?"

The phone was ringing when Nan and the kids poured through the front door, wet from the late afternoon rain. It had been like some sign from above that the short time that they'd needed for D.J. to get in his first ride had been dry. They'd been the only dry hours in a spring that all but had mold growing behind the children's ears.

"Take off your wet clothes," she shouted after the kids as she grabbed up the phone and said, "Hello."

"Nan? I've been calling you all day."

"I was out, Vernon," Nan said, feeling instantly guilty

about where she'd been, who she'd seen, even though it had all been perfectly innocent. "Is something wrong?"

"I'll have Marshall Field's send you an answering machine on Monday. I'll just tell them to deliver it to the only house without one."

"Fine," she said, not biting. *And I'll call the papers to report the first time you decided to help me out.*

"Spoke to your lawyer yesterday," he said. He sounded very happy. She could almost see him at the other end of the line rubbing his hands together doing that greedy little hand dance. Well, she really didn't think that she could bring herself to sue Harry even if the money wasn't going to come out of his pocket. The man had such goodness. To hold him to one mistake . . .

"And?"

"And the asshole never informed his insurance company that he might have opened himself up for a lawsuit." He was nearly cackling.

"So?" Nan didn't like the game Vernon was playing. She wanted him to just tell her why he called and not make her party to his obvious glee.

"So he's on the hook personally for the million dollars!" Vernon said.

Nan waved the children back toward their rooms and pulled out a chair to sit down on. "I don't understand," she said when she could find her voice. "Mr. Meltzer told me—"

"He hadn't spoken to their lawyer yet. Seems that his policy requires timely notice of possible liability when the slander takes place. The insurance company is disclaiming any liability beyond the cost of his defense."

"What does that mean?" Nan asked, remembering what Eleanor had told her about how frightened Nate was of losing the farm. Remembering, too, that Harry had told him there was nothing to worry about because he would marry Nan before he'd let her sue him.

"It means that should that SOB lose—and he will—his insurance won't be paying the judgment. Harris Tweed will be on the hook for one million dollars. Now, there's justice, for you. Philip will have his revenge, and you'll be on easy street for the rest of your life. Better still, when we're done with him, he won't have a pot to pee in. He won't have—"

Nan was sure Vernon had a whole list of things that Harry Woolery wouldn't have, but she wasn't listening to him anymore.

He wants to marry you so that you won't sue him. I heard him tell Nate that a wife wouldn't sue her husband.

There was one thing she'd like to add to Vernon's list of things Harry wouldn't have. But how could she take back a memory?

Twenty-Two

"She's requested an immediate hearing," Brianna Conneely told him when Harry called her back on Monday
afternoon. "That would mean a mediation board."

"An immediate hearing?" What had happened since
he'd seen Nan on Saturday? For Christ's sake, he had been
so sure that he had a goddamn ring in his pocket. "You're
sure she requested a hearing?"

"An *immediate* hearing, at the court's earliest conve-
nience."

"Would she do that if she wanted to just drop the case?"
Harry asked hopefully.

"Mr. Woolery, if she wanted to drop the case, she'd do
just that. This is an escalation. Dick Meltzer, her attorney,
says she's out for blood. He's a straight shooter, and if he
says she's pissed, I'd say it wasn't posturing."

"I'll talk to her," Harry said. "Don't do anything yet—
don't agree to—"

"Mr. Woolery, I'm advising you as your lawyer . . . no,
strike that. I'm *ordering* you to stay away from Mrs. Springfield. Leave this to me, because any efforts on your part, no
matter how innocent, would appear to the court to be coer-
cion. After all, here's this poor sweet widow lady, all alone
and struggling, and along comes the big bad nasty-

mouthed radio guy trying to intimidate her without benefit of her lawyer. You'd do irreparable harm."

"Look, Ms. Conneely. Mrs. Springfield and I have a relationship. She . . . that is, I . . . There's a good deal of affection involved here," he said lamely.

"Well, then think of this as the divorce without benefit of marriage," Conneely said. "It's less complicated."

"It is not less complicated," he shouted into the phone. "This is as complicated as it gets."

"Mr. Woolery, you are obviously very upset, and I don't blame you. A million dollars is a lot of money, even for a radio personality like yourself—"

Harry couldn't help but laugh. "This is great. It took a million-dollar lawsuit to turn me from some no-account talk show host into a 'radio personality.'"

"Actually, the station tells me that your ratings are going through the roof. They figure this lawsuit will boost listener interest even higher."

Everything they said about lawyers was true. Here he'd told his attorney that he was in love with the woman who was suing him, and all the lady could get out of it was dollars and cents. "Well, we all know how important the ratings are. Hey! Maybe I could commit suicide. I bet that'd shoot my ratings through the ceiling!"

Ms. Conneely laughed.

"Or maybe I could kill someone."

Ms. Conneely laughed again.

"Maybe my lawyer . . ."

"Now, Mr. Woolery. I'm sure we'll come to some equitable settlement once Mrs. Springfield has calmed down some and been made to see the reality of your financial situation. Why don't you come down here later in the week and we can go over some of your financial records—"

"That's it? You're folding? Is this a woman thing? You're just automatically on her side? Just give her whatever money I have and you're outta here? Where's my defense? Where's freedom of the press and the First Amendment? Where's poetic license and lack of intent and cause and effect and—"

"I'd just like to get some idea of numbers for when the time comes. I'm not throwing in the towel by any means. We're just dealing with a sympathy factor here that puts you on the hot seat and hangs a halo over Mrs. Springfield."

"Nan wouldn't do this. It's got to be that brother-in-law of hers. And Social Services. They're in this up to their necks." He sounded like a raving lunatic, even to himself. "This is—"

"Harry? May I call you Harry?" Ms. Conneely didn't wait for an answer. "I've got to put you on hold for a minute. Don't let that stop you from ranting or anything. You just go right ahead and I'll be back to you as soon as I can."

"I'm going to call Nan—" Harry started.

"No, Mr. Woolery, you're not. Not if you want to be represented in this case. There is no good that can come of your contacting Mrs. Springfield. You'll simply hurt your case if you do that. From now on, I will convey any messages you have for Mrs. Springfield through her attorney. You will have no contact with her, or my firm will be relieved of its burden to defend your outrageous accusations which caused the Reverend Philip Springfield to go blindly into the night and lose his life."

Harry looked at the receiver as if he could see the lawyer there in the phone. "Well," he said slowly. "It's a comfort to know that you're on *my* side."

"That's my point, Mr. Woolery. What I just said was

merely a taste of what Mrs. Springfield's lawyers are going to do to you when they present their case. But clearly you can see how a case can be made by the other side. So believe me when I tell you that you've got to do as you are told. I know you're not used to it. My clients never are. They'd all like to be the one calling the shots, but this is my ballpark and you've got to play by my rules.

"No contact with Mrs. Springfield."

Harry was silent.

"Of any kind."

So the phone call was out.

"No missives."

And the note.

"No gifts."

Ditto the flowers.

"No promises."

Harry fingered the ring in his pocket. What the hell had happened to his life?

Mrs. Price did not take the news of the postponed wedding well. She implied that Nan was dragging her feet and not showing sound judgment if she wasn't leaping down the aisle to join her life with someone as—how had she put it?—*generous-spirited* as Mr. Harry Woolery.

Nan always knew Patty Price was an idiot, and this was just one more example of the woman's inability to tell the good guys from the bad ones after the cowboy hats came off. Not that Nan herself was taking home any blue ribbons for judgment herself.

"But the riding went well?" Mrs. Price asked.

Nan peeked around the doorjamb and surveyed the goings on in the kitchen, then stretched the phone cord back into the hall and said, "D.J. loved it." She didn't say that she could never take him back to Harry's place. "I've got a call in to Dori Winters to see if I can get him into a program there on a more regular basis."

"I see," Mrs. Price said, drawing out the words as if they were inevitably bringing her to some conclusion Nan didn't want her to draw.

"She runs that therapeutic riding academy," Nan continued. "She's gotten some incredible results . . ." She stopped, picturing the dancing lights in Harry's eyes as he'd told her about one child or another and the progress they'd made.

"I suppose that's a good idea," Mrs. Price said, but her tone said that she wished D.J. would be at Harry's farm.

She came back into the kitchen and carried the children's plates to the sink, handed each child a cookie, and whispered to them to go get their raincoats and galoshes on. Topher, bless him, took charge of D.J. and told him they were getting ready to go out, told him they were going to the closet, told him every step of the way.

Mrs. Price was talking on the end of the line, prattling about the wet weather, for the most part. Nan wished she'd just get to the point and let her get on with the day. She had to get herself and four children to church. And she needed every minute she could spare for all the prayers she was offering up these days.

"The reason I'm calling is that I saw Vanessa Elburn yesterday," Mrs. Price finally said, and suddenly Nan was in no rush at all—the clock had stopped. Her heart had stopped.

Rachel complained that Robin was wearing her sister's boots. Topher said that his sneakers were waterproof. D.J. pulled his sleeve up his arm and pushed it down again. And up again. And down.

"Nan?"

"I'm very busy," she told Mrs. Price. "Services start in a few minutes and I hate being late. Phil always said— Well, it doesn't matter what he always said, does it?"

"The social worker says she's doing very well."

"Wonderful," Nan said with as much feeling as she could feign. "I hope she has a wonderful life without her girls."

"I feel very badly about this," Mrs. Price said.

Nan waited silently for the bottom to drop out of her life. Stupid things flashed through her mind—smuggling the kids out of the country, holding off Mrs. Price with a sawed-off shotgun.

"I'm picking up the girls tonight," Mrs. Price said. "I think they need an interim step between you and going back to their mother."

"Tonight!"

"You wouldn't like it tomorrow or the next day any better, Nan. It was my mistake, letting them get so attached to you. They need a more neutral environment before they go back home, and I can't put Vanessa Elburn off long."

Nan hummed to herself, as if drowning out the words would make them go away. The children lined up in front of her in their shiny plastic jackets and their shiny yellow boots.

"Otherwise there's a good chance they'll hate their own mother for taking them away from you. We can't have that."

Topher buttoned the top button for D.J. Rachel buttoned Robin's.

"This way they can remember you fondly and hate the poor woman who takes them in until next week."

"But we're a family," Nan said.

"I'll be by just after dinner," Mrs. Price said as if Nan

had said nothing at all. "I'd suggest you just pack them an overnight bag and I'll get the rest of their things tomorrow. It's too traumatic to pack all their things and ship them off in one—"

"If I . . ." Nan started, but their was no way to finish her sentence. There were no alternatives.

"About seven?" Mrs. Price asked.

Nan nodded, not caring that Mrs. Price couldn't see her. And then she put the phone back on the receiver and picked Robin up into her arms.

"Let's go," she said softly, choking back her tears.

"I'm not a baby," Robin said, squirming in her arms to get down.

"Just for today," Nan said. "You can be my baby just for today."

Twenty-Three

A week had passed with no contact between them. Harry had struggled through every hour of it, cursing himself, cursing his lawyer, cursing fate. Once, he'd actually broken down and called Nan, been surprised to hear her voice on an answering machine, and called back three times since, always when he knew she'd be out, just needing to hear the sound of her voice. The first time he left a message, telling her to call anytime, day or night, if she needed him.

Apparently she hadn't. Didn't. Wouldn't.

And so he'd made the trek in the rain to the Bat-o-Rama, knowing all the kids were taking batting practice and wondering all the while whether she'd show up with Topher, and feeling about as lame as a grown man with a Godzilla-sized crush could feel.

Josh took a few practice swings before stepping into the batting cage. Harry watched him cut the air and gave him the thumbs-up sign. He had as much right as she did to be there, if she showed up with Topher. Two parents just watching their kids. Let her, or her lawyer, try to make something out of that.

He thought he'd feel her presence the moment she walked in, like in a movie or a book, but she must have been there awhile when he finally spotted her with D.J. in the next to last row of the small set of bleachers meant to accommodate parents or girlfriends on a Friday afternoon at Bat-o-Rama.

Her hair was damp and clung to her face. He watched her unabashedly, admiring the way she kept up a steady stream of conversation with D.J. while she waved at Topher before he took his place in the batting cage. He took a few steps in her direction, saying hi to the parent of another teammate before putting his foot up on the bleachers and bending to tie his laces.

It was a good ploy, or would have been had he been wearing anything but loafers. He looked up at her sheepishly, knowing she'd see right through his ruse, hoping she wouldn't look right through him.

Her eyes were focused on the distance, if they were focused at all. The rims were red, and she blotted at her nose with a well-used tissue. It had been a mistake to leave her alone for even a minute, never mind the several days his lawyer had already demanded and the several weeks that would necessarily follow. All anyone had to do was look at her to see how much she missed him.

"Hi," he said.

She nodded at him, acknowledging his presence, but didn't say a word, didn't take her eyes off Topher to look at him.

"Hey, Butch," he said to D.J.

The boy crawled onto Nan's lap.

He climbed up the bleachers and took a seat a few feet away from them on the riser just below theirs. "Wow. I see he's letting you hold him," he said. When she didn't answer him, he said, in what he supposed was a stage whisper, "I'm not supposed to talk to you, either."

Nan looked down at him. Her eyes were bloodshot and she sniffed and dabbed at her nose with the remnants of her tissue. *Pathetic* would have been a compliment. He couldn't help but feel good that she was lost without him, that she missed him, that if he'd left some old sweater at her house, she'd have spent the night with it wrapped around her.

Okay, it was kind of rotten of him, but he felt flattered that the rift between them had her in tears. After all, it had been her decision. He hoped she was good and sorry now and ready to pick up where they'd left off.

"It's time to drop this, Nan. You miss me, I—"

"Go away, Harry," she said abruptly, shifting D.J. on her lap so that it was a wonder the boy could even breathe. "And leave us alone." She shifted her eyes back to the batting cage even though he could see that Topher was over in a huddle with his coach.

"Right," he said. "And then you can do your crying over me in peace?"

"I'm not crying over you, Harry. I'm not even thinking about you. There are other—" She stopped herself and bit at her lip, blinking furiously to keep the tears at bay.

Oh, no.

Oh, no, no, no.

"Where are the girls?" he demanded. God, he was a stupid fool, thinking that she was mooning over him. He took a deep, shuddering breath and repeated his question.

Nan struggled—he could see her fight the tears, hold back the sob. It didn't leave her with any words to answer him.

"Tell me they didn't send them back to their mother," he begged, watching for the shake of her head, and holding his breath until he saw it.

"Interim," she managed to get out, then clenched her eyes shut and pursed her lips.

"Interim what?" he asked, tamping down his fears. They'd never take the girls away from Nan. They couldn't be that stupid, that cruel—not to Nan, not to the girls.

And not to him. How much harm could one stupid conversation over the radio cause? And how could he repair it?

She sniffed and he offered her his hankie. Instead of taking it, she dug deeper into her pocket and pulled a nearly disintegrated tissue out. She blew her nose into it and shoved it back into her pocket.

"I wish I could undo all of it," he said softly, laying the hankie on her lap without touching her no matter how hard he wanted to, no matter how his arms ached to hold her and pet her and comfort her. "All but knowing you."

"The glib Mr. Tweed," Nan said, slinging arrows at his heart with one hand while she held on to D.J. with the other. "Always the perfect words."

He grabbed up D.J. and straddled him across one leg, bouncing him like a horse would. "Hold on," he told the boy and shifted so that his shoulder was pressed against Nan's thigh. When she went to pull away, he stayed her with his hand. "Tell me about the girls," he said. "Tell me what I can do."

Nan shook her head. "They're gone. Mrs. Price took them last week and placed them with someone less possessive. The only thing that's stopping her from doing it again . . ." She took D.J.'s hand in hers and let him use her fingers as the reins.

He nodded his understanding and waited for her to explain what was stopping Mrs. Price from taking D.J., too.

". . . is that she believes in the riding."

Harry'd stood on his head to convince Patty Price. It was good to know someone believed him. "Will you bring him again?" He didn't dare add *soon*, let alone *ever*.

"No, Harry, I won't. And if I can't get Topher's team changed, I'll take him out of Little League so that I don't have to see you again."

"Come on, Nan. Enough already. Put it behind you, behind us. You know in your heart I never meant you—"

"—any harm," she finished for him. "You ought to get that tattooed on your forehead like a warning label. *Approach at your own risk. Not responsible for any resulting damage.*"

"Look, I love you, Nan Springfield," he said. "More than anything in the world. And I will go on loving you until I die. But I've taken about as much of this as I can," he added, shifting D.J. so that the boy sat across both legs as he munched on a round cookie that had been hastily decorated to resemble a baseball. Even in her sadness she couldn't disappoint a child. Even in her sorrow she couldn't diminish someone else's joy.

"No one asked you to come and see me," she said. "It'll be bad enough when I have to face you in court."

"Then don't," he said. "Call the whole farce off. Don't go after me because you need to convince yourself that you believed in Phil. You can't make up now for what you thought then."

He saw the hurt flash in her eyes and felt guilty for using what she'd admitted to him against her. But he didn't think for a second that suing him was going to make her happy in the long run, and if he had to choose one or the other, spare her now or lose her later, well, there wasn't much of a choice there, now was there?

"He'll be vindicated, and—"

"And then will you be happy? Will that make up for the fact that you asked him for a divorce?"

Shit. He shouldn't have said that. But she pushed all his buttons, frustrated him so, that he couldn't help himself. And now he'd gone and opened wounds that still hadn't healed over.

"I'm sorry," he said, putting his hand on D.J.'s back and giving the boy a gentle rub because he'd wanted to hold him for a long time and D.J. had always resisted.

"What if I swore I'd never lie to you again, Nan?" he asked, holding up two fingers to signify Scout's honor.

"It wouldn't matter," she said, keeping her eyes glued to the batter's box rather than look at him.

He let his hand slide down D.J.'s back until the edge of it was resting on Nan's thigh. "You make me crazy, you know that?"

"You give me too much credit," she said, pretending not to notice that he was touching her.

He wanted to ask her if she remembered their night together, if the feel of his skin against hers haunted her the way it haunted him. He wanted to ask her if she dreamed about him, too, and woke in a sweat of desire, bereft that he wasn't beside her.

He moved up a row and sat next to her. Close. Close enough to study the little gold daisy earring on her lobe. Close enough to ache from not being any closer.

"I called your friend Dori," she said, fussing with D.J.'s hair. "So this fella can go riding again."

"He can go riding at the farm any time he wants," Harry said.

"I wanna ride," D.J. chimed in. Harry could have hugged him for the words alone, but the little pout on his face would have melted a heart of stone.

Is that what Nan had? His soft, sweet Nan? Had he hardened her heart with all the trouble he'd caused?

"Dori is trying to find a time to fit him in," she said. She looked him in the eye and with a sad smile said, "I can't take him to your place anymore. I can't have anything to do with you anymore."

"Because of the lawyers?" he asked. "Because we can call them off, call off the whole damn thing and start—"

"No, Harry, we can't." The angry Nan was back—the Nan of the stiff back and the tight jaw and the sharp eyes. "And all your sweet words won't change my mind. You tricked me once, but—"

"I didn't trick you," he said, frustrated and annoyed and tired of beating a dead horse. "I didn't force you, I didn't seduce you. All I did was love you and all you did was love me back. And maybe you're sorry, Nan Springfield, but I'm not. Maybe you'd take it back, but I'd give ten years of my life to be with you again, and believe me when I tell you—"

She looked at him with something that was uncomfortably close to pity. "I can't believe you. My father used to say, 'Fool me once, shame on you. Fool me twice, shame on me.' Well, I'm ashamed of myself many times over. But I can't let you fool me again. I can't drop this case; I can't leave a cloud of suspicion over my husband's head."

"And how I feel about you, about the children—that means nothing to you?"

"Of course it means something. But it doesn't take away what you did. And it doesn't stop the hurt from growing." She sniffed and straightened her back.

"Whatever happened to 'Erring is human, forgiving divine'?"

"I leave the divine stuff to the Lord," she said softly.

"And 'Vengeance is mine, saith the Lord'? I see you're willing to turn that job over to your lawyer."

"Well, we mortals do depend on the court system. And I'm content to leave it in a judge's hands." She looked at him with such sadness that all the fight went out of him.

His lawyer was right. He was about to be taken to the cleaner's for all he was worth.

But then, he wasn't worth a tinker's damn without Nan.

Sometime around noon, Eleanor tiptoed past Harry's bedroom door on her way to her room. She could hear him tossing and turning on his bed, the headboard creaking, the pillows being punched, the heavy sighs of a man knee-deep in misery and sinking fast.

She'd heard him call Mrs. Price and yell at her for tearing Rachel and Robin from Nan's safe haven. She'd heard him scream at his lawyer to do something, anything, to forestall the hearing. She'd heard him beg someone named Dori to find room for D.J. in her riding academy.

She found her sweater and, wrapping it around her shoulders, headed back downstairs to give Nate his afternoon dose of Percocet. She found him doing his exercises and chastised him for not waiting for her.

"Wanted to impress you," he said, winking at her as she eased him back down against the pillows.

A man hadn't winked at Eleanor in nearly twenty years. Unless you counted the guy who got an erection while she was bathing him after he'd had both his legs operated on. And he was flying so high on Demerol he'd mistaken her for Julia Roberts. The memory made her giggle like some schoolgirl.

"You're pretty when you smile," Nate said, cupping his hand for his medication.

"And you're drunk on pain pills and feeling no pain today, huh? Maybe we ought to lower your dosage."

"I'm stone-cold sober, young lady, and I think—"

"Young lady?" Eleanor said with a laugh. "Now I know you're flying."

"You remind me of my wife, a little," he said, a faint smile playing at his lips.

"Why is it that patients always fall in love with their doctors and get soft spots for their nurses?" she asked, fussing with the pillows and feeling more self-conscious than she had in years.

"Who says I've got a soft spot?" he asked, but his voice wasn't gruff, and his eyes held a twinkle Eleanor hadn't seen before.

"Okay, you don't," she said, pretending that she wasn't just a little bit flattered that a man like Nate, a man who had lived by the sweat of his brow and had not just survived, but prospered, had found her worth noticing.

"I think I do," he said, the surprise in his voice matching the wonder on his face.

"Too much Percocet, you old coot," she teased, backing away slightly. She was too vulnerable. It had been too long. And as soon as he was well, he'd be back up in his saddle and she'd be spooning clear broth into some old lady's mouth. And he wouldn't even recall her name.

"I've got all my senses," he said. "And maybe I am old, but I'll be damned if I let you call me a coot, since I don't even know what one is."

The phone rang and she rushed to get it, hoping that on the off chance Harry had actually fallen asleep, it wouldn't wake him.

"Woolery residence," she said as professionally as she could with Nate looking up at her with those goo-goo eyes that she was surely reading something into that wasn't there. Interest, maybe. Fancy that!

"Eleanor, that you?" Vernon asked.

She put her hand over the receiver. "This is a coot," she whispered at Nate. "Yes, Vernon. It's me."

"You sound like a maid," he said.

"You sound like your usual self," she answered in return.

"Disappointed?"

"Perpetually."

"Likewise, I'm sure."

"I'm working," she said. "Is there a reason beyond harassment that you called?"

"I heard the damnedest thing from my lawyer today," he continued.

She refused to ask him what he'd heard.

"About Harris Tweed . . ." he continued.

She held the phone with her shoulder and picked up Nate's wrist to check his pulse, doing her best to ignore Vernon. Nate slipped his wrist from her hand and patted the side of the bed, indicating that she sit, his face knotted with concern.

". . . and Harry Woolery."

"Well, how does it feel to be the last to know?" she asked Vernon, satisfaction surging through her blood.

There was silence on the other end of the line, and her bravery waivered a little, slipped into mere bravado.

Nate took her hand and squeezed it gently. It was the kindest act a man had done for her in as long as she could remember. Kind enough to remind her of the best in men, something she had forgotten a long time ago.

"Leave it alone, Vernon," she said as her heart raced within her chest.

"I'll have his head on a platter for this," Vernon said.

"For what? For helping out your brother's widow when you wouldn't do it? For saving her home when you'd have her in some little apartment on the west side of town? For teaching your nephew how to hit a ball and . . ."

"I want you out of that house tonight, Eleanor. I won't have you sleeping under the enemy's roof."

Eleanor looked at Nate. She thought of the hell Harry was going through, how he'd tried and tried and hadn't given up yet. And what had Vernon done? What had he ever done but make the people around him, the people he was supposed to care for, miserable?

"Did you go to bat for her with Social Services? Bend the truth a little to protect her girls?"

"What do you suppose it looks like with you working for—" Vernon started, but Eleanor was on a roll. Years of withheld rage came bursting to the surface like some behemoth whale hungry for air.

"Did you think ever about what was good for Nan? What would make her happy? Do you care that she glows when Harry comes to the door? That after all she's been through, there's someone that can make her smile—does that matter to you?"

"Well, he's gonna put a genuine smile on her face when he signs that check for damages."

"That'd make *you* smile, if it happens, but not Nan. Not that you care. It's always been dollars and cents and the principle of the thing with you. Never what would make someone else happy. Never what would make me happy."

"You think you'd have been happy if you'd kept the kid? Been an unwed mother and brought up a bastard child?"

The words stung, even after all those years, and still she wanted to protect her baby from the likes of Vernon and anyone else who'd blame a little girl whose mother had made the fatal mistake of letting her brother control her life. Even if her baby was now old enough to have a baby of her own.

"Mitch would have—"

"Pathetic, Eleanor. You sound like one of those old ladies reliving that one brief moment when life seemed to hold promise. Worse. You *are* one of those old ladies."

Nate lay on the bed beside where she sat, no doubt hearing every word. It was too late to move away now, and there was a look in his eyes, a warmth that might not carry across the room, might vanish if she even moved.

She was tired of the guilt, the shame, the loneliness. She was tired of Vernon using her poor judgment as a weapon he wielded every time she had an opinion. She was tired of being a willing victim, an accomplice to her own unfulfilling life, her own empty future.

"As your brother, as Nan's—" Vernon began.

"Vernon," she said evenly, despite the racing of her heart. "I don't have a brother. I never did. I had a keeper."

It felt wonderful, liberating. It felt like pulling the shades open to find that the sun was shining gloriously.

"Keep out of Nan's life," she warned Vernon, the first warning that she could ever remember giving him. "Stay away from both of us."

"How sharper than a serpent's tooth," Vernon recited.

"I'm not your child. And thanks to you, I have no child."

"Well, there's something to be grateful for—on your child's part."

"That remains to be seen," Eleanor said. She smiled and took Nate's weather-beaten hand, letting him infuse his strength into her.

Maybe she'd tell Nan to ask for a phone number where she could reach the Birthright people. Maybe she could find out some more about Marissa Jane Broder. Maybe even write to her, someday, when she had her life together and was someone that her daughter might be proud of.

Twenty-Four

Harry had admitted long ago that he was paranoid, and while he went through all the motions of donning the Best's Cleaning uniform and borrowing their truck, he never really believed that anyone gave a hoot about the comings and goings of the not very popular Harris Tweed.

Until this morning.

And Ross's comment about the sudden increase in loiterers hadn't really rolled off his back the way he'd pretended.

If someone was looking to settle a score, it would have to be an old one. For weeks, old Harris Tweed had been about as menacing as a declawed pussycat. And wouldn't you know that his ratings would be climbing with every show? Who would have thought that the world was ready for a guy who bled for someone else's pain?

Deftly he had managed to avoid the reporter from the local Fox station as he and Ross had left the WGCA building. He'd gotten into his Volvo a mile away and driven to Josh's, dropping the boy off at school with not much more than a ruffling of his hair and a kiss in the air before he placed his Best's cap on the kid's head to keep him dry.

And then he'd headed for home. The rain, only a drizzle when he'd left the station, gathered steam and hit the windshield in heavy, unrelenting drops. He turned the wipers on faster, and cracked open the window to clear the foggy windshield.

It was never going to stop raining, and things were never going to stop getting worse. And waiting at home were his father and Eleanor, with their disappointed faces, and he was having himself one heck of a pity party.

He'd been there before when he'd lost Suzanne. A few weeks and he'd be his old acerbic self again and the world could just watch out for the likes of Harris Tweed. Nan Springfield would be just another memory filed away in a closed box that he wouldn't dare open for years.

Nan. She was in every compartment of his mind, every cell of his body. Unbidden, her scent would creep up and envelope him. Pink sweaters in advertisements undid him. Little girls with braided hair closed his throat. Even well-worn black pumps like she'd had on the first time he'd seen her, choked him up.

One sorry dude, that's what he was, and if he didn't come up with some plan, he was going right down the toilet. And Nan Springfield and her lawyers were hell-bent on flushing the handle and waving good-bye.

The road to his father's farm was rutted from all the rain, and Harry took it slow, not because he was a cautious man, or because he cared about the Volvo wagon, but because he was in no rush to get home. Fifty feet behind him a truck pulled into the drive, and he wondered what had gone wrong now—a burst pipe? TV cable out?

There were three cars and a second van up near the house. Through the rain and the wipers, Channel 7's logo was visible on the side of the white van. Ah! The old "When it rains, it pours" theory of life. A woman, dressed in a raincoat and carrying a red umbrella, all but leaped from the van, followed by a less enthusiastic cameraman. From each of the other cars, men in trench coats emerged, and a camera flash attempted to brighten Harry's already dandy day.

He lowered his window and gave his best unconcerned smile. "Can I do something for you guys?" he asked. He nodded at Christine Chapman, who did the local scandal news, and added, "And lady?"

The questions came fast, and every one of them hurt. Some were asked into microphones, which were then thrust at him for the answers. One of the men was writing furiously on a steno pad that he tried to protect from the rain by holding it under Christine's umbrella.

"Is it true that you're really Harris Tweed from WGCA?"

"Are you really involved with Philip Springfield's widow?"

"Is it true that you deceived her as to your real identity and that she was unaware of your connection when you began seeing her?"

"How is that going to impact the lawsuit she's filed against you?"

"Do you go to the Old Deburle Church, and did you always, or were you just trying to get to know Nan Springfield?"

"How serious is your relationship?"

"Were you and Nan lovers?"

That one was from Christine. Only a woman, Harry thought, would ask a question like that. A gutteral "What?" escaped his lips.

"Mrs. Springfield says you are no longer involved in any way. So just how involved were you two?"

"And were you involved with her when you ran that telethon to save her house?"

"I understand you aren't seeing Nan Springfield anymore. Are you angry with her for filing suit against you?"

"My lawyer has advised me to have no contact with Mrs. Springfield while the suit is pending," Harry replied. "I'm not angry with anyone." Man, he had a black belt in lying now.

"Was your affair the reason they took her foster children away?"

"Is it true that your sons play on the same Little League team?"

"Does Christopher know who you really are?"

"Does Joshua?"

A lifetime of trying to keep the people he loved safe, and it was washing away in torrents down his father's gravel drive.

"Don't you guys have any real news to cover? There must be some other story going on, even in Ohio."

"There will be, as soon as the Scioto River crests," one of the men said. "But for now, there's a human interest angle here that's hard to beat. People are taking sides and fighting like they know all the details. Maybe you wanna just straighten them out. Tell your side of it, since they're all pulling for the poor widow. . . ."

They were baiting him, and despite his big mouth, he was no bass, and he wasn't going to bite.

"What about the lawsuit?" the woman in red asked. "Is she really suing you despite the fact that you're involved?"

Harry closed the window and waved them all back from the car so that he could open his door. He got out and stood as tall as he could, towering above them.

"*Were* involved," he stressed, looking toward the porch

and watching Eleanor waving him in. "And I'd say the suit is due to that," he added, blinking the rain out of his eyes.

He had to call Suzanne and warn her to protect Josh until he could explain everything to the boy. He had to call—no, clearly the Widow Springfield was well aware of the media circus her lawsuit had created.

Were involved. The deepest of wounds. He fought the urge to strike back. After all, he could compromise her forever with three little words: *her husband's bed.* He could tell them how she'd been happy to receive him, how the covers had been turned back in anticipation, how she'd tricked him into loving her so that he'd help her with her finances and her mixed-up life.

"Harry!" Eleanor yelled to him. "Come in out of the rain!"

"Leave the children out of this," he warned all of them, wondering if they would, if there was a way to make them. "It's between Mrs. Springfield and myself."

"Our sources tell us that you used the children as a way to get Mrs. Springfield to diffuse the lawsuit. Is that true?"

Harry looked down at Christine Chapman. Everything about her was harsh, from her red umbrella to her red lips and sweater and nails. Well, maybe that way the blood didn't show when she drew it.

"I have nothing to fear from this suit," he said, crossing his arms and tucking his hands up into his armpits so that the Best's Cleaning logo was hidden. Inside the jacket he wore, he felt the rain running down his neck. It was cold and unwelcome, but then, so was life. "I'm going in."

"Just one more thing," one of the men—Harry thought he might be Jack Burns from the *Columbus News*—asked. "What about your accusations that the Reverend Springfield stole money from the Old Deburle Church? Can you prove those allegations?"

Used the children to diffuse the lawsuit. Were involved. Yeah, probably he could. After all, he had the key to the whole damn case, if he wanted to use it.

"Watch and see," he said, smiled, and slogged his way through the mud to the house.

He knelt down to take his boots off and waited to hear the closing of car doors. Out of the corner of his eye he could see them inching toward the porch.

"Are you Eleanor Springfield?" Christine asked. "The reverend's sister?"

"Take your boots off inside," Eleanor snapped at him, pulling at his sleeve as if he were a five-year-old, and slamming the door behind him before he was all the way inside.

The doorbell rang.

"Ignore it," Harry said. "How's Nate?"

Was that color rising in Eleanor's cheeks? "He's sleeping and I don't want him disturbed." She went back to the door, swept her hands through warm brown hair Harry had never noticed before, and pulled it open. With her hands on her hips she announced, "There is a man in here recovering from surgery. He needs his rest and I expect you all to respect that. If you fail to, I'll call the police and have you removed from here. Is that clear? You can hound Harry beyond the gate if you must, but you will not step foot on this porch again while I have a patient in this house."

Harry wanted to yell "Yeah!" like some child who'd found the safety of home and whose mother was routing the bullies who had chased him there.

Eleanor waited while the vultures backed off the porch. Quietly she closed the door and leaned against it.

"You ever teach at Saint Agnes's Boys Prep?" Harry's

father asked, coming slowly in from the living room with a metal walker.

"Look at you!" Harry said, but it didn't seem to him that his father even knew he was in the room.

"Quite a mess you've made," Nate said to him, his eyes still on Eleanor Springfield.

"*I* made?" Harry shouted. "*I* did? Did *I* sue? Did *I* call the papers and the five o'clock news? Did I do anything but try to help that woman and those children?

"I didn't slander Phil Springfield and you know it as well as I do," Harry said sharply before he realized what he'd said.

"What does that mean?" Eleanor asked. "Did Phil really steal money from his own church?"

Harry shrugged, and exchanged a look with Nate that warned him that they were treading on shaky ground.

"Son of a moralizing, two-faced, holier-than-thou—" Eleanor took a breath and went on. " 'Pray for your soul, live with your mistakes, shame on the family.' Oh, but Phil was quick to say all that. Can you prove it?" she asked Harry.

Again, Harry shrugged.

"Why would you protect him? If Nan knew, she would be free of him once and for all and maybe she could move on with her life—with you," Eleanor said and looked between him and Nate. "Why don't you just go back outside and—"

"Because it would hurt Nan and Topher. And what difference would it make? She doesn't want me, and it's hard to blame her. I'm no more trustworthy than the reverend was. So what would be the point in telling the world that Topher's dad was a thief? That the man your sister-in-law loved and respected stole from the congregation that adored him? I'm a lot of things, Eleanor, but I'm not spiteful."

"This has nothing to do with spite. This is a matter of truth," Eleanor said.

Harry shook his head. One, he had no right to go pointing fingers at liars and thieves. Two, he hadn't any real hard proof—not in hand, anyway. And three, Nan would be crushed. After all the hurt he'd done her, he just couldn't bear to do any more. No matter what it cost him.

"It's me," Dee Richards said when Nan finally answered the phone. She reached for the light beside the couch where she'd decided to rest for a minute or two. Obviously the minute had stretched to darkness.

She looked at her watch. It was nearly seven o'clock. She put her hand over the receiver and called out. "D.J.?"

"You must have been worried sick!" Dee continued.

"Is Topher all right?" Nan asked. Dee was supposed to have dropped him off hours ago. Just about the time Nan had finally sat down on the sofa and let the rain lull her into oblivion. Again she called out for D.J.

"Oh, the boys are fine—loving every minute of this, really. They've closed all the roads by the river. Believe me, I tried them all. There's no way to get in to you. Didn't they tell you to evacuate?"

D.J. came into the living room. He had one side of an Oreo cookie in each hand, and a filthy face.

"Nan?"

"I don't know. I fell asleep, actually. D.J. and I lay down for a nap, and the next thing I knew, you were calling." Nan looked out the window. It was hard to see anything in the darkness, but there were no headlights moving on the street.

"I think you should call the police or the fire department or something," Dee said. "They could come get you out of there."

Nan stretched the phone cord into the hallway. From there she could see brown wafer cookies floating across the kitchen floor. Where she stood, the carpet was squishy. "I've gotta go," she said, thinking of all the precious things scattered about the main floor of the house. "I've gotta move stuff into the attic where it'll be safe."

"Never mind the stuff," Dee said. "You need to get out of there. They're saying on the TV—"

There was a crackling sound on the line, and then the house went dark. "Great. We just lost our power! I've gotta find a flashlight. Can you hold on? Dee? Dee?"

Except for the rain against the windows, there was only silence. The line was dead.

"D.J.?" she called out. "Don't be scared. Mommy's here. Just stay where you are and talk to me so that I can find you."

Wind accompanied the rain like some big bass drum might try to drown out a piano. D.J. said nothing.

"Can you clap your hands?" Nan said, holding the terror at bay by humming and making a list in her head of everything she would move as soon as she found D.J. "Can you stomp your feet?"

The flashlight. Where the heck did they keep the flashlight? There was one in the cellar, of course, but if the kitchen was flooding, she wasn't going down into the cellar in the dark with D.J. wandering around upstairs on his own.

"D.J., this isn't funny," she said. "Mommy can't find you if you don't make any noise."

All the progress they'd been making seemed to come to a dead stop in the dark.

"Mommy's going to find some candles," she said, trying to reassure D.J. as best she could. "I'm going into the dining room. Can you hear my feet slopping on the carpet as I go?" *Can you hear my heart thudding in my chest?*

Thank the good Lord Phil hadn't had a romantic bone in his body and they'd never burned the candles she'd bought from Stacey Miller and her daughter Jamie at the church bazaar. Matches were another thing altogether.

"D.J., you're making Mommy nervous because she can't see you. Could you please, please say something?"

"Something." It was a little voice, filled with terror, but even Topher's first word wasn't more welcome.

"Good boy! Say it again," she begged, feeling her way toward him in the darkness.

"Not again!" he said, his voice and tone mimicking her own.

"Yes, again!" she said, bumping into the side table that had been in that spot all her life.

"Not again!" he said, and laughed as her arms came around him and she scooped him up and kissed his cheek.

"It's dark," he told her.

"We're not afraid of the dark. We have each other."

"We need Uncle Harry," D.J. told her, burrowing against her breasts.

"What we need is a book of matches and a lot of energy so that we can move lots and lots of things upstairs."

"I want Harry," D.J. said plaintively.

"Well, I don't," she said, glad that the darkness hid her face from D.J.'s. Who was she kidding? Even her three-year-old could see through her. And in the dark, yet. But she didn't want some man to save her from a little rain, she wanted him to save her from herself—from the life she was going to live, that safe life that she'd always led, hiding from the real world in her circles at the church, closing her eyes to the problems in her marriage, keeping her heart reserved for the children in her life. Maybe Phil had been right. Maybe she was interested in the children to the exclusion of him.

It wouldn't have been that way with Harry. She was sure of that. As sure as that it would never be Harry. It would have to be a man she could trust, a man who had no secret, dark side. A man whose motives she would never question.

After searching blindly through drawer after drawer in her mother's old breakfront, she finally found a small box of matches.

"See, we can take care of ourselves very nicely," she told D.J. as she lit the tapers and the room took on a soft warm glow.

"My feet's wet," D.J. said.

Nan slipped her foot from her shoe and touched the floor. The water had made its way into the dining room. "Okay, we'll just grab a few things and take them up to the attic with us," she said, wishing she could just take D.J. up there and leave him while she gathered her treasures. It was lucky nothing had happened to him while she was sleeping. She wasn't about to press that luck by leaving him in the attic with a burning candle.

He followed her into the bedroom, where she took the framed braids off the wall. There were several inches of standing water lapping at her mother's bureau. Her bedskirt danced on the surface, spreading out like white clouds against a dark sky.

Photos! She grabbed the framed wedding picture of her parents and piled it atop the braids. The picture of Topher's second birthday went on top of that. The entire Morrow and Eastman clan at a reunion in Van Wert, all framed in something that looked like bread dough, balanced unevenly on the others.

"Follow me," she told D.J., racing toward the living room with its mantel full of still more pictures. "Hold on to my shirt," she said, bending so that he could get hold of the stretchy bottom of her cotton turtleneck.

They were slogging now, the water rising almost perceptibly.

"My toys?" D.J. asked.

"Next trip," Nan promised, grabbing the picture of Robin and Rachel; the little heart frame from which Tony, the child who had disappeared with his mother, stared out trustingly at her; the photo of her and Phil on their wedding day. "I can't hold any more. Let's just get these upstairs."

At the foot of the stairs to the attic, the door fought her, the water weighing against it, but using her shoulder, she managed to get it open. She felt the pull of her turtleneck against her neck lessen, and then D.J. began shrieking.

"We are not going to yell or cry," she commanded herself as well as him. "We are going to put these things where they are safe and—" She eased them out of her arms and onto the third or fourth step without burning herself on the candle. As she turned to lift D.J., she heard the pile tumble.

D.J. quieted. They both stood and stared at the picture of Phil staring up at them from under an inch or so of water.

All the years of convincing herself that he was a good man, that he meant well, that he really did love her and the children, that he could do no wrong, bubbled up around the sinking picture, caught in the swirls of water that threatened the house.

Nan looked at the half smile on Phil's face, caught by the candlelight. It was the most he had ever given her, given their marriage, given their child—half a smile, half his love, half his heart.

And he had refused to accept any more than that from her.

Quite deliberately she laid her foot across the eight-by-ten glossy reminder that she was a very poor judge of men, and stepped down hard enough to hear the glass crack. She hated Phil; maybe she had for a long time, and maybe it was hard to face that about herself, that she could hate her dead husband.

"D.J., do you think you can wait at the top of the steps for Mommy? I'll keep talking to you, but I have to go faster to move things to where they won't get wet. Can you do that?"

D.J. was staring at her foot. She lifted his chin with her free hand.

"I want you to climb the stairs where you'll be safe, okay?"

He banged with the side of his head against the wall, his eyes not meeting hers.

God help me, she thought, pulling him away from the wall and sitting down on the second step with him standing in front of her.

"Not now, D.J. I can't . . . You're all wet. I'll bring you some dry clothes if you wait at the top of the stairs." She stood and took his hand, but he refused to follow, rocking his head as if the wall were still within his reach.

Impatient now, she lifted him up and carried his rigid

body up the stairs. *I lift up mine eyes,* she thought, heading for the attic with D.J. in her arms.

"You'll be fine here, honey," she told him. "I have to get you some dry things and find Topher's baby album and my mother's wedding dress and Nanny Annie's cookbook and . . . Stay here!"

She headed back downstairs. Somewhere a car alarm was ringing. She looked out the window.

Please, God . . .

Every house was dark.

Twenty-Five

Harry sat in front of the television set, phone in hand, calling Nan's number for the fourth time. Chuckie lay beside him on the couch, her head resting on Harry's knee. Absentmindedly he scratched the dog behind her erect ear.

"Nothing?" Eleanor asked. Then as if to reassure herself as much as anyone else, she added, "Well, they've evacuated everyone. If she isn't answering the phone, it means she isn't there."

The signal echoed in his ear. "Busy. How the hell can her phone be busy if she isn't there?" Harry demanded. This time instead of redialing, he called the operator, told her Nan's number, and said he'd been getting a busy signal for hours. After all the lies he'd told, what was one slight exaggeration?

"That line is out of service," the operator told him. "There are lines down in that area."

On the television some idiot reporter stood knee-deep in water at an intersection in Deburle, pointing toward the river. "Power has been cut off to the homes west of Meadowfarm Road. I understand that the phone lines are out as well, and all homes have been evacuated as Paint Creek rises about six inches an hour. Temporary shelters have been set up in the Deburle High School, the library, and the new indoor tennis stadium on Fort Hill Road."

"See?" Eleanor said, pointing toward the television that they had all been worshiping since six o'clock, when he should have just gotten in his car and gone down there, lawyer's warning or not. "They're all evacuated. Nan's probably holding Children's Hour at the library, don't you think?"

The television showed people huddled in groups in a high school gym. Thankfully, Suzanne had called and told him that she and Josh were high on a hill at Charles's parents' house, well out of the path of the floodwaters. Of course, Nan hadn't extended him the same courtesy. As if she didn't know he'd be worried sick about her and the kids. As if!

Nate flipped off the TV with the remote. "You can't go down there," he said flatly. "Lawsuit aside, all the roads are closed. You saw the water. You'd never get through."

How could he say that he had a feeling in his gut that she needed him? Talk about hokey! How could he explain that he simply had to know that she was safe—that breathing, swallowing, keeping his fists from balling, were all impossible? That sitting there in his father's warm, dry house was impossible?

"Where are the keys to your truck?" he asked.

"If she's still in the house, which she isn't, she's safe up in the attic," Nate said, and looked at Eleanor. "She's got an attic, doesn't she?"

Eleanor was standing over the TV, working the buttons on the cable box to restore the picture. She nodded, stood back, and watched as a porch gave way to the river's tug and collapsed, fine old balustrades floating atop the mud, being carried along with other debris and finally buried under.

"I could take the wagon, but the truck's higher," Harry shouted toward the living room as he pulled the green rubberized boots he used for mucking out the barn from the front closet. "So where are the keys?"

"Harry, listen to me," Nate started. "You could get yourself killed going out in this, only to find out that she's perfectly safe and playing tennis right now."

"Well, if that happens, you can put *Here lies a fool* on my headstone, okay? You've probably already gotten that much carved."

Eleanor came into the hallway holding the truck keys in her hand. "Thanks, Harry," she said, putting up his collar like his mother used to. "Please be careful and please call us as soon as you know anything at all."

"You'll hear me yelling at her all the way up here when I find her," Harry assured her, kissing her quickly on the cheek.

Someday, when they had family meals at their place—his and Nan's—it would be nice that Eleanor would be there. When they were together and the world was right, it would be nice to be sharing it with Eleanor, and Nate, and . . .

"I gotta go," he said.

Eleanor just nodded at him and offered him a worried smile.

"I'll find her," Harry said.

"I'm sure she's safe," Eleanor added.

"Me too," Harry said.

And then they embraced, probably, Harry thought, because when you're lying it's better not to look in someone's eyes.

———

D.J. had followed her right back down the stairs, and Nan had been forced to carry him in one arm and drag things that mattered to her back up the stairs in the other. Because she had no free hands, she did all of this in the dark. One candle still burned on the stairwell to the attic. She had no clue where the other one was, only that it had gone out and that this taper was nearly done.

All the photos in the basement were surely ruined even though she'd learned early on to keep them on the highest shelves. The Christmas ornaments she'd fashioned with her mother when she was a little girl, her father's sermons. All no doubt gone. There was a highchair down there that Papa Noah had carved just before the turn of the century.

She climbed to the top of the stairs with D.J. and a box she hoped contained Topher's baby shoes, and sat down on the top step. D.J. was exhausted, cranky, and she held him in her lap and rocked him, humming softly and apologizing to all her ancestors for breaking the chains that had bound them to future generations.

D.J. got heavier and she knew he was asleep. She could see the reflection of the candle in the water and watched as the water rose to snuff it out. For the first time she began to wonder if they would be all right there in the attic. Surely the water couldn't rise that high. She could hear things thudding in the kitchen, pots rattling. Somewhere in the house, boards were groaning, and she clutched D.J. against her and began to quietly recite the Lord's Prayer. "Our Father who art in heaven, blessed be Thy name." *Please, God,* she thought, *He's just a little boy. There's so much ahead of him. And I've hardly done anything with my life.*

She was wet, and cold, and beneath D.J. her leg had fallen asleep. Leaning her head against the stairwell wall, she closed her eyes and pictured Harry's face. "If only," she whispered against D.J.'s hair.

Shivering now, she wondered what she'd done to deserve so much grief. It seemed, looking back on it, that her life was one long line of good-byes, starting with her mother's death when she was just a teenager, and ending with finding out who Harry Woolery really was and having to put him behind her.

New noises. Groans and bangs and finally the tinkling of glass breaking.

"Nan? Are you in here?" a voice called out.

It could be she was just dreaming—some sort of aural mirage.

"Harry?" she answered back cautiously, afraid to scare the dream away.

"Hello? Is anyone in here?" he yelled again. *Harry* yelled. *Her* Harry.

"Harry! I'm in the attic with D.J.," she hollered, standing up with D.J. in her arms as the flashlight beam crossed the doorway.

The light nearly blinded her when he aimed it up into her face. "What the hell . . . what are you doing here? You're supposed to be at a shelter. They evacuated the whole area. I've been everywhere looking for you. Where's Topher?"

"He's at a friend's. He's safe. How bad is it out? I lost power and I couldn't find a radio with batteries, and I—"

"Bad enough. The roads are all closed. The creek is six feet above flood stage and isn't even cresting yet. What the hell are you doing still here? Why didn't you leave? I had to walk from Meadowfarm Road in thigh-deep water. I finally found some guy with a boat—he's waiting outside. I thought you . . ." His voice trailed off.

"I didn't hear the evacuation," she said. "I fell asleep and when I woke up there was water in the kitchen and I tried to save everything and . . ."

"You get the braids?" he asked.

Tears filled her eyes, spilling over. D.J. fought to get out of her arms and head for Harry, and she eased him down and let him go. "Yes," she said softly as Harry scooped up the little boy and aimed the flashlight on the steps.

"Well, get 'em and let's go," he said gruffly. "For Christ's sake, I'm soaking wet and this guy isn't gonna wait forever."

"Don't yell at me," she said, cocky now with relief. "I didn't ask you to come get me, you know. In fact, I never asked you for anything."

"Except a million dollars," Harry said, mounting the stairs.

"Why are you coming up?" she asked, backing away slightly from the stairwell.

"To get my million dollars' worth," he said, huffing on each step as he carried D.J., his boots sloshing and squealing as he came closer and closer.

"What?"

He leaned over and kissed her softly. D.J.'s hand rested against her cheek as he did. "Fifty cents," Harry said, shifting D.J. so that he was able to press his body against hers, to kiss her more deeply, more thoroughly, more fully than she could ever remember being kissed. "Buck and a half," he said, and leaned into her again.

"Are you crazy? The water's rising," she warned him as he closed in on her, warmth rising from his body as he let D.J. slide down his side. "And the man's waiting."

"I moved heaven and earth to get here and I want my proper thanks."

"Are you bargaining with me?" she asked, touching his

face, tracing his nose and brows with her hands to assure herself that he was real.

"Just tell me one thing and we'll go. Do you really think that I used the children to get to you?" His words were warm against her forehead; his breath heated her temples; his nose touched the tip of her ear.

"Well, you did get Topher on the same team as Josh," she said, tipping her head so that his lips grazed her brow.

"Do you think I meant to hurt you, Nan?" he asked, pulling away just slightly and taking the flashlight back from D.J. to shine it at her face. "Ever? Do you think I ever meant to hurt you?"

Nan shook her head. No matter how mad she'd been at him, no matter how deeply he'd deceived her, even counting the night they'd spent together—no, she didn't think he had ever meant to hurt her.

"Do you think I ever would?" he asked.

Before she could answer, before she could tell him that learning to trust him was the hardest thing she could ever do, but that she was willing to try, a horrendous groan, as if the house were giving up, sounded beneath them.

"Come on, in there!" a voice called from downstairs. "We gotta get going before it's too late."

"Where are the braids?" he asked, grabbing up D.J. and shining the flashlight at the pile of her life that sat by the top of the stairs.

"I can't leave all this," she said, looking down at the white satin Bible she had carried down the aisle, as her mother had before her. "It's my home. It's my life."

A second groan, a wrenching, sorrowful cry, came from deep in the house as if it felt the same way she did.

"I'm leaving!" the man called from downstairs.

"We're coming," Harry yelled back. And then softly,

tugging at her arm to make her stand beside him, he said softly, "It's only a house. These are only things. Will you forget how your mother looked on her wedding day? Will you forget Topher's goofy smile?"

"I don't want to lose all this," she sobbed, trying to gather all of it into her arms. "I want more than the memories. I want to go back. I want to—"

"Take what you can carry over your head," he told her. "And know that we may even lose that."

"I can't just leave everything. My father's whole life is in this house." She bent down and picked up a tattered composition notebook with two skaters pictured on the front. "Nanny Annie's recipes," she said, flipping open a page and holding it out for him to see the old-fashioned writing and the newspaper clippings it held.

"They're in your head, aren't they?" he asked.

"I can't wait any longer!" the voice called.

"Be right there!" Harry shouted back. "You'll write 'em all down at home for the children."

"I am home!" she shouted. "Take D.J. and go. I'll wait out the storm."

"The hell you will," he said, lifting her right off the ground and carrying both her and D.J. down the wet stairs.

"Put me down," she shouted, but she didn't dare wiggle or move a muscle for fear that all three of them would go tumbling into the wet darkness that waited at the bottom of the stairs.

"I'll go, I promise, just put me down."

At the bottom of the steps, he eased her onto her feet and steadied her. The water was up to her thighs, and she bit at her lip to stop from crying out. The force of the water pushed her against the wall. As he grabbed her hand and pulled her along with him, he promised to come back and save anything that was left when it was all over.

They went out the window through which Harry had entered, the man in the boat maneuvering it so that they had only a few feet of water to cross. Harry handed D.J. up to the man, then picked up Nan and set her feet into the boat. He walked the boat a few feet away from the house and then managed to climb into it himself.

While Harry helped propel the rowboat down Robby Lane, D.J. burrowed himself against her. He began to cry softly, and she hummed to him whatever came into her head.

"Row, row, row your boat," Harry sang out. He smiled at her and D.J. and raised a wet blanket over them like a tent. He pulled the flashlight from the pocket he'd stuck it in and handed it to D.J. "Here, you better hold on to this, big fella," he said. "My dad always says life's an adventure and you've gotta be prepared for it to ambush you every now and then!"

They'd found the truck under a few more inches of water, but it was sound enough to drive, and though the roads were flooded and the driving was slow, they managed to get back to the farm in one piece. It was a soggy piece, but Harry doubted anyone had ever been as warmly received.

Eleanor had Nan in the shower and D.J. in a warm tub before Harry had his jacket off. Chuckie was dancing circles around his legs, and Nate was limping around the kitchen with that walker of his, staring at the frame full of waterlogged braids on the table, the spread pages of Nanny Annie's journal, and his son.

"She dropping the suit?" Nate asked.

"We didn't discuss it," Harry answered, making a big pot

of coffee and looking in the cupboards for some hot chocolate for D.J. He pulled out two of his mother's fine white
china cups and saucers and set them by the Mr. Coffee.

"You didn't discuss a million-dollar lawsuit?" Nate
asked, eyebrows raised to the ceiling and beyond.

"We were busy trying to stay alive," Harry said.

"And is she grateful enough to drop the suit?" Nate
asked.

"I don't know," Harry said. He supposed she was. He
supposed she was just as head over heels in love with him as
he was with her. All right, maybe not just as much, but
those kisses he gave her were well returned.

"Does she know you could prove that the good reverend—"

Harry heard voices from the living room and hushed his
father up. "Not yet."

"Tangled web," his father said with a shake of his head
as he headed out the doorway just about the time that Nan
was heading in.

"What's that?" she asked, having thankfully missed exactly what Nate was saying.

"Well, aren't you lucky to be alive?" Nate said.

"It seems a lot scarier now," she said softly, and Harry
could see that she was shivering despite the heavy sweater
Eleanor had lent her.

"Sit down, I'll get you a cup of coffee," he offered.

"Coulda died if it weren't for Harry," Nate said. "You
and the boy."

Nan looked whiter than his mother's fine china.

"Maybe you'd like a little wine?" Harry said.

She rubbed at her arms without answering.

"Scotch?"

His father shook his head and banged out into the living room.

"Think you could have a little tiny glass of Scotch? It'd warm you right up and calm you down some." He reached for the bottle in an upper cupboard. "I could put it in your coffee, if you like."

"You trying to get me drunk, Mr. Woolery?" she asked, a little color returning to her cheeks as she joked with him.

"Would it get me anywhere?" he asked.

"Depends where you want to go," she said coyly, then gave the pretense up. Sitting down at the table, she fingered the wet pages of her great-grandmother's journal, the faded ink blurred and running across the page in wavy blue circles. "I was so scared, Harry! I thought that the water would just keep coming up the stairs and that D.J. and I would have to climb out onto the roof, and that I'd fall asleep and he'd roll off the roof, or that—"

"Shh," he said, coming over and crouching down beside her. "You and D.J. are safe now."

"But what if you hadn't come? What if the house just slid into the river and—"

"I came," he said. "Didn't you know I would?"

She shook her head so sadly that it nearly broke his heart. "No, Harry, I didn't. I don't know how you really feel about me. I thought I did, but when I found out who you really are, I realized that you lied to me, and people don't lie to people they . . . well, people they really care about."

It was hard to make sense of what she was saying, to even understand the words between the sniffles and sobs. She blew her nose and continued.

"And then I thought I did again, and I found out that you lied to me again about the lawsuit, and that you could have to pay a million dollars if I didn't drop the suit, and now I just don't know who you really are at all. But then, I suppose I never did."

"You've always known who I am, Nan. I'm the man who'd risk his life to find you."

"That was nice," she said, a little smile touching the corner of her lips. God, how she was fighting it all. How badly she didn't want to love him, to trust him, to hope that something in that life of hers might turn out right.

"Nice?" he said, pretending to be cut to the quick as he rose and filled the shot glass with the whiskey. "I wade in water up to my privates calling out your name all over Deburle like some lovesick cow and you call it nice?" He put the shot glass of Scotch down in front of her and nodded at it.

"It was more than nice," she agreed, sniffing at the amber liquid and squinching up her nose.

"*More than nice.* I was cozy and warm here at home, lying around before I had to leave for work, and instead of napping and heading off for Columbus, I risked life and limb—"

"It was . . . noble," she agreed. "And appreciated," she added, fingering the rim of the shot glass but still not drinking the Scotch. Despite her playful words, she still seemed on the verge of tears.

"I think it'll do you some good," he said, nodding at the drink.

She took a small sip and immediately her eyes watered and her cheeks went crimson. Coughing and sputtering, she stared at him in disbelief. "Is that poison?" she asked when she could finally talk.

"Of course. That was what I saved you for—to poison you. Don't care much for the taste, huh?"

"My chest is on fire," she said, gulping in air. "So that's why they call it firewater!"

"You've never had Scotch before?" he asked, watching as she shook her head, reminding him that she had led a mighty sheltered life before he'd barged his way into it.

"Finish it," he said, coming closer and handing her the glass.

She looked scared, and he knew she was.

"I'll check on D.J. and the others," he said, trying to keep the huskiness out of his voice. He was through with acting like friends when what he wanted was to be her lover, her husband, her safe haven in the storm. "Finish that before I get back."

He would tear her walls down, stone by stone, until she had no choice but to let him in. And once inside, he would build new walls around them and the children, keeping all of them safe within his love.

Nate was snoring in the living room, still unable to climb the stairs. Harry took the television clicker from his hand and turned off an old *Bonanza* rerun.

Upstairs, Eleanor was putting D.J. to sleep in the bed she'd share with him. She told Harry that she'd be turning in too, as soon as the boy was asleep.

He checked his room. Eleanor had obviously straightened it up while he was gone. The covers were turned back just as they had been in Ellie's bedroom all those weeks ago. Good old Eleanor! And he'd been so conceited, he'd thought it an invitation from Nan.

She was in the kitchen at the table, just where he'd left her, but the Scotch was gone. She'd managed to get the braids out of the shadow box and laid them on her napkin to dry. The composition book was most likely beyond salvaging.

"You doing okay?" he asked, coming in and pulling out the chair beside her.

She nodded, but he wasn't stupid enough to think that the gesture was any more than bravery.

"You don't have to keep a stiff upper lip for me." He traced her bottom lip with his finger, trying to still the trembling there, only making it worse.

"It's like the river," she said quietly. "I'm afraid I'll drown if I let go."

"I'll save you," he said, pulling on her chair so that it was snugly against his. "As many times as it takes, I'll save you, I swear."

He could see her fighting the urge to lean against him, to open up to him, to let him in.

"You can trust me," he said, gathering her against him, kissing the top of her freshly washed hair.

She pulled back and looked at his face, gauging his sincerity. He just let her stare, let her look beyond the things she held him accountable for, beyond the lies he'd told her and the deceits he'd played upon her, let her look at all he was and was ever likely to be.

"I know, I know," he said, his thumbs tracing her cheekbones softly. "I don't have the best track record, do I?"

Another half smile sent his heart soaring with hope.

"You gotta trust someone, Nan. You weren't meant to go through life alone."

"I'll never get my girls back," she said, and the dam that had been holding back her tears broke. "My house is probably floating down the river with every picture of them in it. Everything is wrong, Harry . . ."

The rest of her words were lost in his flannel shirt as she buried her head in his chest and sobbed up a storm that dimmed the one going on outside. Shoulders shaking, chest heaving, breaths coming in gasps, she let the demons out while he held her in his arms and felt his own heart break.

He caught words here and there, when she reached for the napkin on the table to wipe her nose, when she shifted her position against him, when she took a shuddering breath and blurted something out before continuing to cry. "I don't understand," he heard her say. "Why do I have to be tortured by dreams about the girls and tested at every turn? I've been good. I did what I was supposed to do. I just don't understand."

If there were any words of comfort to offer her, he didn't know them. And so he just held her and let her rail at the injustice of it all, rail for the both of them, and hope they could put it all behind them.

"I'm so tired of being brave," she said at last, and he felt the full weight of her against him, like when Josh used to fall asleep in his arms. "Of being on guard."

He stood with her in his arms and made his way toward the door. With his elbow he shut off the light, then whispered, "I'll keep the dragons at bay."

She shifted against him, as if she were trying to see his face in the darkness. Then she settled for nuzzling against his chest with a sigh that seemed to cleanse the air so that they could start anew.

He carried her up to his room without asking her if it was all right. He kicked the door shut behind him and then laid her down on the bed, all still in silence, still in darkness. He sat down beside her on the bed, his back to her supine body, his hands in his lap.

"I could leave you now and go sleep on the couch in the living room," he said. "Or I could make love to you and keep you in my arms all night. But there's no middle ground here."

Her hand ran down his back.

"I mean it, Nan. If you don't ask me to leave now, I'm going to take you in my arms and never let go."

She tugged at his sleeve.

"I mean it, Nan. Never. Do you understand what I'm saying?"

And then he felt her unbuttoning the cuff of his shirt.

He wanted to give her one last chance, but the words refused to come out of his mouth. Instead he stretched out on the bed beside the woman who had been in his dreams every night for months.

She opened his shirt, pulled the tails from inside his jeans, and pushed up his undershirt so that most of his chest was bare. Without saying a word, she repositioned herself so that her head rested against his bare skin, her breath teasing his nipples as she sighed.

"I'm sorry I need someone to slay my dragons," she said softly. "I know that I should be capable of taking care of myself and my children and that I—"

"Everyone needs a dragon slayer," he said, his fingers playing with her hair and enjoying the intimacy of talking to her in the darkness. Oh, he'd enjoy all that was still to come—and he wouldn't be able to bear these quiet moments if he wasn't sure that the fire burning in him would be sated—but talking like this felt like being married to Nan. He smiled in the darkness. "Don't you know you've been mine for months now?"

She crawled up him, her body dragging against his and setting all his nerves on fire, until she reached his face. Her hands rested on each side of his head as she touched her lips to his, softly, tenderly. "Love me, Harry," she whispered against his cheek, and if more sensuous, more arousing, more erotic words were ever spoken, he'd never heard them.

He rolled her off him and laid her on her back, fussing with Eleanor's sweater until, with Nan's help, he'd gotten it over her head. Beneath it she wore no bra, and he ran his hand down the side of her breast.

"It's still damp," she explained. "My bra. I wouldn't want you to think that I go around—"

He kept his laughter low. Just next door D.J. and Eleanor were sleeping, and he didn't want either of them to hear him and know that Nan was not alone. "If I'd known, we'd have been up here an hour ago," he said, while his hands explored the soft flesh of her breasts, her midriff, while the fingertips of one hand burrowed into her waistband and pushed her sweatpants down toward her hips.

"They're Eleanor's pants," she said. "I usually wear—"

He stopped pushing against the pants. "Do you want me to go?" he asked.

"No," she said quickly. "I'm just—"

"Nervous," he finished for her.

"Don't be silly," she said, her voice a little higher than usual.

"I'm not being silly," he said, trying not to sound impatient when he added, "I'm not the one talking about bras and sweatpants and the price of tea in China."

She took a deep breath and her body softened beneath him. He hadn't even been aware of how stiffly she'd been holding herself until she let it go. "I never mentioned tea," she said, her hands pulling his shirt down his arms.

"Don't," he said, slipping his hands out. "Mention tea, that is."

"I won't," she said, working at his belt buckle.

"Good." He threw the shirt across the room and lay back

so that she had easier access to his belt, and button, and zipper, and whatever else she might be looking for, which at this point would not be at all difficult to find.

"Harry, I—" she started. He wanted to ask her if they couldn't talk later, after, when he could think, but this was hard enough for her. He wouldn't ask anything more of her than she wanted to give.

"Mmm?" he asked, prompting her to go on, when all he wanted was to touch every inch of her with every inch of himself, to learn what made her happy and what excited her, and where and when and how fast and how deep.

"Could you turn on a light?"

"What?"

"I want to go into this with my eyes open, Harry. I want to read your eyes and I don't want either of us to be surprised by anything later."

He rolled over and switched on the bedside lamp. The glare was harsh after the darkness, and he squinted at Nan and she squinted back in return before climbing out of bed, finding his shirt, and laying it over the lamp so that the light was softer.

She sat down on the bed beside him, stark naked. If his ardor had cooled any from the interruption, it was restored at the sight of her pale pink nipples, the slight fold of skin at her waist, the pale brown curls that were almost hidden from his view by one of her thighs. She reached across him and grabbed a pillow, clutching it against her and hiding her sweetness from him.

"You scare me to death, Harry Woolery," she said, her eyes dipping down toward his waist and snapping back to his face.

"It's not all that big," he said, feeling proud as a peacock as he pulled out the pillow from behind his head and covered his privates with it before getting serious. "You scare me, too."

"Why?"

"Because I could lose you. And if I did . . ." There weren't words he could put to it. To say he would be empty wasn't enough. He'd lost Suzanne and felt alone. This would be like losing a piece of himself. The best piece.

"Please don't lose me," she whispered, letting him take the pillow from her hands, her eyes still locked with his. "I don't want to be lost anymore."

It was all he wanted to hear, all he needed.

He pulled her toward him, watching her face as it came closer to his, watching to see her eyes finally close when he kissed her with all the love he had been stockpiling for his whole life. All defenses down, he whispered, "I love you," against her lips and then tried to bind them with his kiss, but she pulled her head back.

With wide eyes she studied him, taking her time, taking his measure. And then, just when he began to think that maybe she'd changed her mind, she smiled the softest of smiles. "I love you, too, Harry," she admitted, the smile broadening until they hardly needed the lamp on to make the room glow.

"Yeah?" he said, teasing a nipple idly. "You gonna prove it?"

Nan supposed there were more romantic things that Harry could have said. At the moment, with him kissing her neck and with one finger barely touching her breast, she couldn't think of any. And when his mouth dipped lower and captured her breast, and his hand crept lower still and began to fondle her feminine curls, she couldn't think at all.

He was everywhere at once, filling up all her senses,

making her forget whatever it was that had kept them apart. There was nothing before Harry as he touched her intimately, erasing with his touch years of pain that were buried deep in her heart. He was in no hurry, it seemed, as he rolled her onto her stomach and kissed her back, the dimples in her bottom, the sides of her waist. He lifted the hair off her neck and whispered words of love, punctuating them with kisses that slid down her spine and heated her belly.

When he'd thoroughly loved her back, he turned her over and started in again on her front, kissing her face, the space between her breasts.

And when she couldn't stand it anymore, when she lifted herself against him and whispered for him to love her, he eased apart her legs and took his love home.

Somewhere people went about their business. They ate and slept as if the world were still on course.

But in the small bedroom where Harry was sharing his love with her, Nan knew that the world would never be the same, that it had stopped its rotation and everything had, just for a moment only, stood still. From now on Nan would always know why the earth was just a little closer to the sun—because she and Harry had reached for the stars.

Reluctantly he finally slipped from her body and put his arms around her, holding her close, as he'd said he would.

"Happy?" he asked, fitting her into the curves of his own body, enveloping her with his arms and his love.

She nodded against him, too emotional to speak. Who'd have ever thought that a thirty-two-year-old widow could find a man who would lay down his life for her?

In the next room she heard D.J. banging his head and Eleanor's soft voice calming him down. In the morning she'd tell Ellie where things stood, but for tonight she would just revel in the warmth of Harry's arms and listen to the even sound of his breathing—louder and stronger than the doubts that reverberated faintly in her head.

He'd whispered something about getting breakfast and tiptoed from the room almost before Nan's eyes opened to the semidarkness. He'd told her to look through his drawers and find something to cover what he called her delectable body, claiming that he couldn't be responsible if she didn't, and winking at her. And then he'd taken a pillow and a blanket with him, to make it appear as if she'd spent the night in his room alone.

She threw back the covers and looked down at her naked body. He had loved her as she had never been loved before. And she didn't just mean in the physical sense, though surely that was true as well. But he had loved every part of her—her too tender heart, her too weak backbone, her too soft stomach.

There was a robe at the foot of the bed, and she wrapped herself in it. There was fabric enough to go around her twice, and it smelled of a manly scent. Of Harry.

Jeesh, but she looked awful! Her hair was sticking straight up on one side, and there were creases on half her face. It didn't stop the smile she saw in the mirror as she studied what a night of Harry's lovemaking had left her looking like. *Thoroughly loved*, she supposed, from the red cheeks and the bright eyes.

Still, while Harry might find that attractive, she had no desire to raise Nate's or Ellie's eyebrows. Not that she was ashamed of what she'd done with Harry.

Well, not completely.

Even if she should be. Love like that deserved the sanctity of marriage. *Mrs. Harry Woolery.* Good heavens! What would Vernon say? What would the entire congregation of the Old Deburle Church think of the reverend's wife marrying Harris Tweed? She looked in the mirror and tried to appear shocked with herself.

"I know how it looks, Mr. Royce," she said with her nose raised high in the air, "and I am so, so sorry. But the fact is, I simply don't give a rat's patoot!"

And then she opened Harry's top drawer in the hopes of finding something she could throw on after her shower—his shirts would fit her like a dress, but Eleanor was probably still asleep and she really didn't want to bother . . .

In the top of the drawer was a big manila envelope with the address of Harry's lawyers in the upper left-hand corner. She'd gotten two letters from them herself, before her lawyer had demanded that they correspond only through him. *Important Papers* was written across the front in Harry's usual broad handwriting.

Wouldn't Vernon be disappointed to learn that now that she was going to marry Harry, there would be no lawsuit after all. No million dollars for him to "help her invest."

She closed the drawer and opened the one beneath it, pulling out one of Harry's shirts and holding it up against her chest, the papers to the lawsuit on her mind.

She should just leave the envelope where it was. Or maybe she should toss it in the garbage. After all, she wasn't going to sue Harry now. Maybe they should make a roaring fire and burn the papers. Or . . .

She'd heard of people rolling around in money, and she smiled at the twist she had in mind. She could rip up the complaint in a million little pieces and sprinkle them in the bed for Harry and her to roll in. When he came back with her breakfast she would be covered only in little strips of her soon-to-be-dismissed lawsuit.

Rushing to the bed, she threw back the covers, centered herself perfectly on the bed, and dumped out the contents of the envelope so that she could start ripping. The summons and complaint were there. So were several pages she had shown him from Phil's ledger. There were other papers too, but she wasn't interested in them, wasn't interested in anything but a cold safe-deposit box key that rested on her bare thigh.

Dangling from it was one of those small cardboard cards Phil attached to all his various keys. In his clear, small hand were written three little words: *National City Bank.* Below it, in Harry's bolder writing, was *Box #1072.* She flipped it over. On the other side, still in Harry's hand, *Washington Ave. Columbus Branch.*

A second, secret box, just as Harry had suggested. Well, of course he had. He'd known it all along. Checked it out, too, from the looks of it. And kept it from her. One more lie.

Trust me, Nan. I would never hurt you, Nan.

And she'd believed him. Despite everything, she'd believed him when he'd said he would never lie to her again, that he would never hurt her. The man didn't know how to tell the truth. And she . . . what a fool she was. But not half so foolish as Harry, if he thought she'd marry him now. Or drop her suit.

Or do anything that would please him, ever, ever again.

Dispassionately, dry-eyed because she'd already been to the bottom of the well, she got up and threw on the clothes that Eleanor had loaned her. When she was dressed and carefully returned Harry's papers to his drawer, she tiptoed into Eleanor's room and gently shook her.

"I'm leaving," she said. "Can I borrow your car?"

Eleanor blinked at her and extricated herself from D.J.'s embrace. "Where are you going?"

"Can I leave D.J. with you just for today?" she asked.

"Of course you can," Eleanor whispered. "Just tell me where you're going."

She'd have answered her if she'd known, but instead she ignored the question. She'd figure it out later, when the pain stopped and she could think.

She took the keys that Eleanor held out to her.

"Tell Harry . . ." she said, and then she shrugged. She didn't know what to tell Harry.

She just didn't know anything anymore.

Twenty-Six

"I'd like to get into Box 1072," Nan told the officer at the desk when he raised his eyes to her.

No doubt she was a sight, her eyes bloodshot, her nose running, standing there in Eleanor's sweatpants and sweater, soaked after running from the car in the rain.

"My house is flooded," she explained, fishing for a tissue in her pocket, stepping back so that the rain didn't drip off her and onto the man's desk.

"We've been fortunate here in the city," the man said sympathetically, pretending not to notice that two droplets from her hair had landed on his stack of business cards.

"Well, I haven't been exactly lucky out in the sticks," she said bitterly, thinking it was the understatement of the century right along with *Perhaps I haven't been exactly wise* . . . Although, with her shock subsiding, she had to admit that Harry had been good to her and the children. Very good. He'd saved her life, and D.J.'s, too.

And she'd gone running out of his house without so much as asking him why he had the key. What kind of faith did that show?

Did running mean that she didn't trust him, or that she no longer trusted Phil? And did it matter when both of them had lied to her?

"Your key?" the man asked, turning to flip some cards in the safe-deposit file drawer. Before she could hand it to him, he looked up at her quizzically. "You did say 1072?"

"Yes," she said, realizing for the first time that she might have trouble getting into the safe-deposit box without Phil's signature. Didn't they seal boxes when people died? "It's my husband's, actually. That is—"

"I'm sorry, ma'am. I'd like to help you, especially since you came all the way over here in the rain and all, but—"

"Listen," she said. "I have to get into that box. You can watch that I don't take anything out. I just need to see what's in there."

"You don't need the key for that, ma'am," he said with a sad little smile. "That box has been closed since last summer. It's empty."

"Closed?" she asked. Maybe, just maybe, Phil hadn't really done anything wrong. Maybe he'd undone it. "But why do I still have the key? And when exactly was it closed? Does it say there?"

The man looked up at her, tilting his body slightly to see beyond her. Nan turned, too, and saw the bank was nearly empty.

"I can check for you," he said. "But you might get more information about it from your husband. I'm sure he—"

"I'm sure he's explaining it to someone much more important than I am," she said, looking toward the ceiling.

"No one could be more important to him than you, I'm sure," the man said kindly, hitting some keys on the computer in front of him.

Nan waited, a million scenarios running through her head, searching for innocent reasons that Phil could have had a secret safe-deposit box. For example, he could have been saving money for a gift for her and was afraid that if he hid it in the house . . . she abandoned that one quickly.

What if, she wondered, someone gave him something important to hold? A minister was a confidant, wasn't he? What if one of the women in the church—

"Are you Mrs. Springfield?" the man asked.

She swallowed the bile that rose in her throat. "I'm Nancy Springfield," she said, and for the first time in her life she was ashamed to be associated with the Reverend Springfield's name.

"Well, that explains why you have the key, anyway. Your husband never turned it in. But the account was closed on August tenth."

August tenth. The day before Phil had died. She looked at the key in her palm. The writing on the card was smudged and the ink ran off the paper and onto her skin like a tattoo.

"I'll take that key now," the man said. "There's a ten-dollar key deposit that I can have mailed to your home within seven business days."

"My home is floating down Paint Creek," Nan said flatly. "Mr. Springfield is dead. My children are all over the state and my shoes are full of water and they squish when I walk."

The man tilted to his side again and raised his eyebrows in some sort of apology. Nan looked behind her to see a line of three people waiting impatiently. She handed the key to the man behind the desk.

"I need the refund now," she said, turning to look at the people behind her. "In a rush?" she asked with more than a touch of sarcasm. "Having a bad day? My problems aren't yours?"

A young man in his twenties looked at her sympathetically. What did he know about life, anyway? The woman behind him diverted her eyes, while a small child tugged at her hand.

The man rang a teller and instructed her to bring over ten dollars. Behind her, she could hear the woman tell her little girl that they had to wait because the woman at the front of the line had a problem. She didn't know the half of it.

Nan took the ten dollars from the teller and looked the woman in the eye. "There but for the grace of God, lady," she said.

And then, very loudly because no one in the bank seemed to be making a sound, she slurped out of the bank, each soggy footstep louder than the one before.

It was still raining hard outside.

No one even noticed when she raised her hands up toward the sky and shouted "Is this ever going to end?"

"How could you not ask her where she was going?" Harry demanded for the third time since Eleanor admitted giving her the keys to her car.

"I did ask," Eleanor told him again. "But she didn't tell me."

"That's the same thing," Harry said, flopping down heavily on the couch.

"She didn't appear to be in the mood for talking." Eleanor wiped D.J.'s chin and sent him into the living room to see what Nate was doing.

"She was fine when I left her," Harry shouted.

Eleanor poured him another cup of coffee and put away the whiskey that was still on the counter from the previous night.

"It's a goddamn monsoon she's out in," he said. "If she

had to go somewhere, why couldn't she let me drive her? Or take the truck?"

"Harry," Eleanor said. "Calm down. All your yelling and screaming is probably what drove her out of here in the first place."

Harry's jaw dropped. "Drove her out? I drove her out? What are you talking about?"

"I don't know. But she ran out of here like her tail was on fire."

"Maybe she was just going to get Topher," Harry suggested. "Or maybe she needed to get something at the drugstore."

"A little late for that, I'm guessing," Eleanor said. "You can't get morning-after pills over the counter, you know."

Harry looked ill.

"Did she say something, *anything* else? Did she say when she'd be back?"

"I told you. She said 'Tell Harry' and then she just shrugged," Eleanor said. "I took that to mean she'd be right back."

"Well, it's been four damn hours."

"She asked if I'd mind watching D.J.," Eleanor added.

"Until when?" Harry demanded. "Until tonight? Tomorrow?"

"Well, I'm sure she'll be back for the hearing," Eleanor said. She was going to add that she was sure Nan would want to drop the suit, but before she could, Harry was ranting on.

"That hearing isn't for three days," Harry shouted. "Where the heck is she going in the meantime? What about the kids? She isn't just going to leave them, is she? Does she have a credit card? Money?"

Eleanor noticed he didn't say a bloody thing about the

hearing. It was as if it wasn't even a concern to him. "What if she went through with the suit, Harry? What if she went through with it and won?"

"Then she'd have some money eventually," he said, standing up and peering out the window. "In the meantime did you give her any money? I don't remember her taking her purse yesterday. How is she going to eat? What if she runs out of gas on some highway?"

"There's twenty dollars in the ashtray," Eleanor said. "Emergency money."

Harry paced the kitchen. "Is this an emergency?" he demanded.

Eleanor thought it might be. She thought that love was always an emergency, and if it wasn't seen to, you stood to lose everything.

"You know where Topher is? Maybe I can call there," he said, reaching for the phone.

"She'll call me about D.J.," Eleanor assured him.

"But she won't call me?"

"I don't know," Eleanor admitted. "I don't know why she didn't find you and tell you where she was going. I only know that she looked crushed when she left."

He leaned his forehead against the freezer door.

"I'll talk to her," she promised. What she really meant was, she'd pound some sense into the girl before it was too late.

"You'll talk to her when she comes back," Harry added, as if he wanted the reassurance that she would.

"Yes," Eleanor said. "Or when she calls."

"From where?" Harry asked, as if she were keeping it a secret from him and he could trick it out of her.

"I don't know. How far can she get on twenty dollars?"

———

The car was going on fumes when Nan pulled into the driveway of the stately house on Parkview Road in Fox Chapel. She'd been lucky that Interstate 70 still had two lanes open, and that the gas station attendant happened to know where Parkview Road was.

She had no hope that her luck would hold out and that Vernon would be happy to see her. Especially with the news she was bearing.

Adele opened the door. "Nan? My word! You look like a drowned rat!"

"Thanks, Adele," Nan said, waiting to be invited in.

"I only meant," Adele started, apparently couldn't think of anything kinder to say, and took a step back into her foyer. "Well, come on in out of the rain. Did Vernon know you were coming? He didn't mention—"

"No, I didn't even know myself until this morning. Is he still down at the plant?" The trip had taken her five and a half hours with the rotten weather and Eleanor's old car. Still, it was only a little after four.

"No, dear," she said condescendingly, as if Nan ought to know Vernon's habits. "He never works past four at the plant. He's in his office." She nodded toward the back of the house.

"Could I just use your bathroom first, Adele? It was a very long drive." And a cup of coffee would be nice, too. And some dry clothes, maybe?

Adele pointed toward the guest bathroom down the hall. "There are some towels in there," she suggested, looking at the puddle that was growing on the marble tiles beneath Nan's feet. Nan wasn't sure whether Adele mentioned the towels so that Nan could dry herself or the floor. Before she could apologize for the mess, a voice rang out from down the hall.

"Adele! I've been calling you for the last five minutes! Where the—" Vernon shouted, coming out from his office and stopping in his tracks at the sight of her. "Nan!" he said, as if he were thrilled to see her, rushing forward, hands outstretched.

"Hello, Vernon," she said, letting him take both her hands in his to welcome her.

"Nan's here," Adele said, earning a look from Vernon that would have curdled milk.

"I can see that," he barked at her, then softened his tone as he addressed Nan. "You're freezing cold, for God's sake. And wet. What did you do, woman, walk here?"

"Almost," Nan said, trying to laugh. "I took Eleanor's car."

"The one I gave her? You're all right?" Vernon asked, stepping back to look at her.

"Does she look all right?" Adele asked, *tsk*ing at the shape she was in.

"She looks wonderful," Vernon said. "A regular water sprite. Christopher okay? Where is he?"

It felt good to have someone look at her as if she wasn't carrying a plague. It felt wonderful that someone cared.

"Topher's at a friend's, who luckily isn't in the path of the river," she said.

"Still calling him that?" Vernon asked. "Well, I'm sure it'll pass. Things like that always do. I remember when Philip wanted to be called Lip. He got over it, and Christopher will, too."

Lip? So many things she never knew about Phil. And now she knew one too many.

"Vernon," she said, cutting him off. "I need to talk to you about Phil. I found out something that—"

"Adele," Vernon said, stopping her mid-sentence. "For

the love of God, make Nan some coffee. And take her
upstairs and give her some dry clothes." He shook his head
at Nan sympathetically. "You take a shower, honey, and
pull yourself together and we'll talk at dinner. You like Chinese? There's a great new Szechuan place that delivers."

"The children don't like Chinese," Adele said. "I'm
making veal."

"You like Chinese, don't you?" Vernon asked again, ignoring his wife. Before she could answer, he added, "Good!
I'll order in for us while you get comfortable."

"Vernon, you aren't going to feel like celebrating when I
tell you about this," she said.

"Christopher's safe?" Vernon asked, obviously avoiding
the subject of Phil. "We could go down and get him in my
Lexus. That truck will—"

"It's better if he isn't here for this," Nan said. "He's fine
with his friend, and D.J. is with Ellie."

"And those girls? You're still looking after them?" he
asked.

"Not right now," Nan said and rubbed at her arms.

"You're cold," Vernon said. "Which is right where we
started, isn't it? Go on up and take a nice warm shower.
Maybe Adele can find something nice of hers that won't be
too big, and you'll feel like a million bucks by the time
you're done." He winked at her.

"Don't count on it," she said, following Adele up the
double-wide staircase.

"Were you planning on staying overnight?" Adele asked
before they reached the top of the stairs. Nan had no idea
what she was doing, or even why she'd come to Vernon's.
Except that she just couldn't face Harry now, admit that
yes, Phil probably was a thief, but that didn't give Harry

the right to be one, too, to steal the key from wherever he managed to get it and then to keep it from her.

"Of course she's staying the night," Vernon shouted up. "She can stay as long as she likes."

That was a bit of reassuring news, since, when she thought about it, she had nowhere else to go.

"Of course you can," Adele said with so little sincerity that Nan, even as eager as she was to believe it, wasn't fooled.

"I'm sorry," she said softly, laying a hand on Adele's arm. "I don't mean to put you out."

There was a flash of something in Adele's eyes—boredom? As if she were telling Nan that she was not about to be put out. Nan let it pass. If Adele wanted to be annoyed at Nan's visit, it suited Nan fine. Let a little reality trickle into Adele's life and see how well she bore up.

Heck, Nan would like to see her break a fingernail and still function.

It didn't matter once she was in the shower. The warm water was heavenly, and then there was the heat lamp that came on in the bathroom as she stepped out of the shower door. And the towel that was plusher than the ones at the Palmer House in Chicago, where she and Phil had spent their wedding night. On the counter there was a fancy dish of powder that smelled heavenly. Next to it Adele had left a bottle of roll-on deodorant, a hairbrush, and a blow-dryer. Nan felt herself begin to relax, felt the knot in the back of her neck loosen.

In the guest room, Adele had laid out one of those exercise outfits that whistled when the legs passed each other. She didn't know those things could wrinkle, but this one must have been rolled in a bag and left under a Mack truck. On top of the very pink outfit was a pair of lacy underpants, a pair of socks, and a bra that would fit Nan only if she put the socks in the cups instead of on her feet. There was no shirt, so Nan pulled the zipper up nearly to her chin. Despite the clamminess of the material, she was powdered and dry and actually did feel a million times better. Which meant that she could swallow again, take a breath that didn't shudder in her chest, and feign a smile.

And that, she thought as she made her way down the stairs to the main floor, where Vernon would be waiting for her, wasn't anything to sneeze at with what was going on in her life.

Adele was setting the table in the dining room, candles and silver and every dish the woman owned, and declined any help from Nan.

"The girls will help me as soon as they're done with their homework," she said.

"Are they home?" Nan asked. "It's so quiet that I thought they must still be at school."

"Vernon needs the house quiet so that he can work," Adele said.

"Phil was like that, too," Nan said softly, remembering how he hated the chaos that reigned before dinner.

"Yes, well, Vernon's made quite a success of his life, this way," Adele said. "And I've helped him. He and I understand the value of a fine home and well-behaved children, and we've both made the necessary sacrifices to get where we are."

"And the children, do they understand?" Nan asked, thinking of her nieces working in silence up in their rooms with their doors closed. If she had the money at Christmas, she'd get the girls a big stereo system and some heavy-metal tapes. That ought to irritate the heck out of Adele and Vernon.

"The girls are very happy. Children need routine. They thrive on it. Every psychiatrist says so." She looked at her watch. "You'd better go in and see Vernon. He likes to eat promptly at six o'clock, you know."

"Well, I certainly don't want to upset anyone's schedule," Nan said. *Just because my home is gone, my love life is over, and my lawsuit is horse manure.*

"I'm sure you won't," Adele said. She bit at the side of her lip and then gestured with her head for Nan to follow her into the kitchen.

Once inside the spotless, stainless steel-clad kitchen, Adele turned to face Nan, apparently weighing things in her mind and coming to a conclusion.

"I think a woman is just as capable as a man, don't you?" she asked.

Capable of what? Nan wondered. *Lying? Stealing? Building a bridge?*

"I mean, she can sign a check as well as a man, pay her own bills, buy her own car . . ."

"Certainly she can," Nan agreed, wondering where this was going.

"Like Eleanor, for example," Adele said. "She could have afforded her own car, but Vernon insisted on giving her ours."

"It was very nice of him," Nan said. She left out the part about the fact that it was six years old, in need of repairs, and that Vernon was probably embarrassed to trade the thing in on his first Mercedes.

"Now, I don't know why you're here, dear," Adele went on. "And we're always happy to see you. But with Phil gone, you are just going to have to learn to manage your own affairs eventually, and to come running to Vernon every time you need something is . . . well, it doesn't set a good example for the children, Nan. It makes it seem as if you can't manage things without a man to—"

Nan cut her off. "I came to tell Vernon something that was better discussed in person than over the phone. I don't need his help or his advice, and if I'm putting you out—"

"Don't be ridiculous. We love to have you. It's just that at this moment money is a little tight here and I can't put off paying for the girl's teen tours . . ."

"I haven't come to ask for money," Nan said. Though she wouldn't even be able to leave without another twenty dollars or so for gas to go home.

Home. Now that was a problem she was going to have to deal with, and real soon, from the looks of things.

"I know it would be simply to tide you over. Vernon says you're going to be a very rich woman. But maybe a bank could advance you—"

"I'm not going to be rich, Adele. But I will get by. I have not come to take the food out of your children's mouths." *Or the teen tour out of their summer, just so my kids can wear shoes on their feet.*

"There you are!" Vernon said, coming into the kitchen with a smile on his face. "Come into my study and we'll talk a bit before dinner."

"It's almost six," Adele said. "I was just about to call the girls."

"Well, you and the girls go ahead and eat that veal you were making," Vernon said. "Nan and I have some business to discuss and we can have the Chinese later."

"Vernon," Nan said, "I'd love to have dinner with the girls and Adele. There's no need to go to the extra expense or bother—"

"I thought there was something you needed to discuss with me," he said, putting his hand under her elbow. "I'm sure it would only bore the girls, and I'd like to put your mind at ease so that you can enjoy your food. You've lost a lot of weight since Phil died. Not that it doesn't look wonderful on you, but tonight you can go off the diet a bit, don't you think?"

She looked over her shoulder at Adele as Vernon led her from the room. Her sister-in-law was sharpening a carving knife, looking at Nan as if she were a side of beef.

He closed the door to his office behind her, and Nan thought how thrilled Adele would be with that. It was one more reason not to dawdle, not to prolong the whole ugly mess.

"Phil took the money," she said as soon as they were both seated, Vernon behind a massive mahogany desk, she in a leather wing chair.

"Ridiculous," Vernon said. He wasn't outraged, wasn't curious. He was merely adamant.

"He had a safe-deposit box in Columbus," she said, the words leaving a bitter taste in her mouth.

Vernon grimaced. "A box in Columbus? Have you been in it?"

Nan shook her head. "It was closed the day before Phil's death."

"So?" Vernon asked, one eyebrow raised as if the fact that Phil had a secret safe-deposit box meant nothing.

"So why would he have a box that no one knew about?"

"I don't know, but certainly it would be best left that way. You haven't told anyone, have you?" he asked.

"Harry Woolery knows. He was the one who had the key," she mumbled.

"You mean Tweed? Shit. I knew Phil didn't have as much brains as a box of rocks, but— How do you know Tweed has this key?"

Nan wasn't sure how to answer that one. "I know he *had* it," she said.

"*Had* it?"

"I took it," Nan said.

"Probably planning to use it in court to show that it wasn't slander at all—that Phil did steal the money and stashed it in that box."

"He wouldn't do that," she said.

"What do you think he had it for, Nan? Tell me what else he was planning to do with it?"

Nan clasped her hands and tapped her thumb against her chin. "I don't know."

"Of course you don't. Because there is nothing else he could want to do with the key. It was evidence, but now it'll disappear." He held his hand out as if he expected Nan to turn the key over to him.

"I don't have it. I turned it in at the bank. But Har—Harris Tweed knows the number. Not that it matters. I can't sue him now."

Vernon looked at her blankly. "Because . . . ?"

"Because thirty-five thousand dollars is missing and Phil had a secret safe-deposit box in another town."

"And what was in the box?" Vernon asked, pretending to be baffled.

"Thirty-five thousand dollars. Less the price of Phil's new car, I'd assume."

"Nan, with the box closed, there's no proof at all, even if Tweed had that key."

"It doesn't matter. Because I know the truth now." She supposed she'd known it all along, from the moment she'd seen Phil's face as he listened to the radio show that awful night.

"The truth? The only truth I can see is that Tweed was

lying yet again. Withholding the key from our attorneys and on a course to slander your husband again. But after the suit I don't think either of us will have to worry about him anymore."

"The whispers about Phil are just dying down, thanks to Reverend Michaels," she said with a sigh. "If I open them up again, I'll be the one to ruin Phil's reputation. Let me assure you that my knowing is bad enough. That and that someday I'll have to tell Topher. I certainly am not going to sue Harris Tweed now."

"Oh, you'll sue him, Nan. And you'll win. You'll mop up the floor with him and clear your husband's reputation once and for all. And the church will return your money to you, and the court will assess damages at a million dollars—"

"Harry doesn't have a million dollars, Vernon. He doesn't have anywhere near that."

"Well, whatever he has, he'll be giving you a piece of it for the rest of his life. And that's how things should be."

"That isn't how things should be, at all," Nan argued. "I can't sue Harry knowing that he was right about Phil, even if he didn't know it then."

"And there's the key to the whole thing, forgive my pun. But even if you have so little faith in the man you married that you would believe the worst about him—and that disappoints me greatly—the fact is that Harris Tweed had no reason to believe that Phil was guilty of anything at the time he slandered him and that but for his comments, my brother—your husband—would be alive today."

Nan said nothing. Maybe Vernon was right. She was so focused on proving Harry wrong that she had been overlooking the obvious. Harry didn't know it was true, and Phil was dead because of the things that Harry had said.

And on top of that, even if he had taken the money, he didn't deserve to die for it, did he?

There was a knock at the door. "Dinner's ready, Daddy," one of her nieces said.

"Then eat it," he shouted back before continuing their conversation.

"Can you pay for Christopher's college the way you would have been able to if Phil were still alive? What about the counseling that boy is going to need? What about all the other children you give your heart to? Can you afford them? For God's sake, Nan. Can you afford to feed yourself and Christopher? Is Social Security enough for you to raise that boy the way Phil would have raised him?"

Of course not—but then, Phil was stealing to raise him.

"But that's not Harry's responsibility, now is it?"

"Tweed? He didn't start this whole chain of events? He didn't send Phil out into the night? He didn't come then, lying to you about who he was? He didn't hide that key from you? Look at you. Have you got a place to stay? Thanks to Tweed you'd be out on the street if it weren't for me."

"I think Mother Nature had a hand in that," she said, not ready to blame God for forsaking her. "And I don't believe for a second that he meant to hurt me," she added.

"He let you see that key to make you happy?" Vernon asked. "To ease your mind? Or did he let you see it to make you back out of the lawsuit?"

The truth was worse than that, but she couldn't bring herself to tell Vernon that Harry hadn't come clean about the key. That she'd simply found it . . . in Harry's bedroom . . . after they'd made love.

"The man meant to hurt Phil. He meant to hurt you,

and *Topher*, and he'll keep hurting other innocent people if you don't stop him."

"Don't be melodramatic," she warned him. Things were bad enough.

"Have you ever listened to him, Nan? To the show? He insults, he accuses, he degrades—and all to make a buck. At best, the man has no moral compass—doesn't know right from wrong."

Maybe Vernon was right. After all, Harry had hidden the key from her. He'd lied to her. What made her think he was telling the truth about loving her when he lied about everything else? Did a man lie to the woman he loved? She didn't think so.

But if he didn't love her, why had he risked his life to save her? Why had he helped with D.J. and the girls? Why did he trade his beautiful car for that station wagon?

She didn't know. She just didn't know.

"He's been very good to me and the children," she said almost apologetically. "D.J. and I might have died in the floods last night if Harry hadn't saved us."

"Guilty conscience," Vernon said. "Just goes to prove how responsible he feels—he *is*. Why else would he be looking after you?"

Because he loves me? And that brought her right back to the fact that Harry had lied to her over and over again. And that a man didn't lie to a woman he loved. And if he did, he wasn't a man that a woman could love back in return. Not this woman, anyway.

"Look at it this way, Nan. You'll tell the judge your side, honestly. And he'll tell his. And the judge will decide what's fair, calmly, rationally, the way it ought to be. You're much too upset about all this to be thinking clearly. If you're right and Harris Tweed bears no responsibility, the judge will simply rule in his favor. And I'll eat my hat, because no sane person, present company excepted, could possibly think anything but that Tweed is covered in guilt."

Vernon came and sat on the arm of her chair, putting his hand on her shoulder. "It'll be all right. You'll see. You'll stay here until the trial. I'll send Eleanor's car back to her and have Christopher picked up if you like." Well, surely she couldn't stay at Harry's anymore. Not now. Maybe not ever.

"I'll call Dcc and ask her if he can stay with her. It's only a couple of days. Will you call Eleanor and ask her to keep D.J. for me?"

Vernon smiled like he was the Pope himself. "Of course," he said. "You're right not to call her now. Not while she's staying in that man's house. I'll take care of everything."

"Thank you," she said softly. As if things could be taken care of with just a phone call. As if anything could ever take back what had happened, what Phil had done, what she'd done, where all of it had led to.

"Now, wouldn't some General Tsao's chicken taste good?"

Nan smiled politely, sure that anything she ate now would taste like sawdust, and that she wouldn't care that it did.

"Everything is looking up," he said, taking her hand and leading her toward the door to his study. "You're going to be happy again someday, Nan. And ironically, Harris Tweed will provide you with the means. He tooketh away, and he'll giveth. To his eyeballs."

Funny, it seemed like Nan wasn't the only one who was confused about just how important Harry was in her life.

Twenty-Seven

Harry sat in the courtroom which was rapidly filling up, his back to the door despite how much he wanted to see Nan the moment she walked in. The three days she'd been gone had been agony. Eleanor had gotten a call from Vernon saying that Nan was there and asking her to watch D.J. until the hearing. So he knew she was safe, at least physically. She refused to speak to Eleanor, let alone him. Or at least that was what Vernon said. Who knew what the truth was in Pittsburgh?

In Ohio, the truth was he was hopelessly in love with Nan Springfield. And Harry's father, his lawyer, and the object of his affections, all couldn't care less.

If it hadn't been for Eleanor, Harry thought his father probably would have gone and had a stroke about his refusal to turn over the goddamn key to his lawyer. For a man who'd preached morality all his life, he seemed to have lost the map to the high road at a mighty inopportune time.

His lawyer was still seething over the fact that not only had he failed to keep his distance from Nan Springfield, but he had pursued her, taken her to his home, and, in Ms. Conneely's words, taken advantage of the woman's devastated situation. The fact that he'd saved her seemed to have gotten lost somewhere when Harry refused to answer her questions about whether he'd actually slept with Nan.

"Great," Ms. Conneely had said sarcastically.

Only Eleanor had understood, offered sympathy, help, and prayers. She'd promised to do anything she could, and she'd vowed not to let Vernon ruin Nan's life the way he'd ruined hers. That was less than comforting, knowing that Nan was vulnerable, at the man's mercy, and dependent on him for a roof over her head at the moment.

Behind him a reporter leaned forward and poked at his back. "Do you think you'll lose your job if you lose this case?" he asked.

"I think I'll get a raise," he said honestly. "And a better time slot and a larger audience. What do you think?"

The man laughed. "I think you're probably right. Is that why you're doing it?"

"I'm not doing anything," Harry argued. "I'm the defendant in this suit."

The reporter handed him a copy of the morning paper, as if Harry hadn't seen several already—as if Nate hadn't waved one under his nose that read THE SUIT'S SUIT.

In this one the headline read A HARRIS TWEED SUIT. The article recapitulated the details of the allegations he'd made on the radio—if you could call a goddamn joke an allegation. It included a list of all the charitable and good works that the Reverend Springfield had overseen as minister of the Old Deburle Church, what an upstanding citizen he was, how his wife was a pillar of the community and loved by all.

He had no quarrel with that, at least.

"No interviews," his lawyer said, coming up the aisle and taking her seat beside Harry at the defendant's table. "You better not have said squat," she warned Harry.

"Did I say *squat?*" he asked the reporter who'd handed him the paper.

"Not even *crouch*, or *bend at the knees*," the reporter said with a wink, jotting something down in his notebook, which caused Ms. Conneely to wince.

"You must be a very wealthy man," Brianna Conneely said quietly. "Not to take a million-dollar case seriously."

"I've got money," Harry said, when the truth was closer to *You can't get blood from a stone.* "I'm just morally bankrupt."

The lawyer looked over Harry's shoulder. No doubt their reporter friend was getting every word.

"Just shut up," Ms. Conneely said. "I don't want a word to come out of your mouth unless the judge asks you, specifically *you*, and not just the defense, a question. Got that?"

Harry saluted.

All he wanted was to see Nan. Let her have his money—he was willing to give her everything he owned anyway. All he wanted was five minutes to say his piece.

"And don't even think about addressing Mrs. Springfield directly," she added. "You'll do any talking to her through me."

Harry ignored her, his eyes on the back door.

Vernon was on one side of her, Adele on the other. She supposed they were not going to take any chances that she might run. Why should she? She hadn't done anything wrong in all of this.

"I am so proud of you," Vernon said as the walked down the high-ceiling hallway. "You look wonderful."

She should. Vernon had bought her a new dress—not too flashy (after all, she should look needy but well kempt)—new shoes, and a handbag that was stuffed with tissues. The one directive Vernon had given her that she thought she'd have no trouble following, was that she could cry all she wanted to.

They stopped at the metal detector to wait their turn, and watched while two policemen led a handcuffed man around the barriers and into one of the courtrooms. The man's head was down, his eyes on the floor. Nan wondered if he was a murderer.

"Criminal cases are down here," Vernon explained. "Where I wanted Tweed. We're up on the second floor," he added.

Nan hummed softly to herself, wishing she weren't in the courthouse, picturing herself on a beach in the south of France. All right, she had no idea what a beach in the south of France was like, but she figured it had sand and the people had wonderful accents and it wasn't raining, and there was no doubt in her mind that she'd rather be there than here in rainy Columbus about to see Harry's face again.

"Nan?" Mrs. Price's surprised face came into focus. Nan was definitely not in the south of France.

She smiled politely. For D.J.'s sake. Truth was, she hated Mrs. Price, even if it wasn't her fault that Rachel and Robin still haunted her dreams.

"How lucky to run into you here! I tried to call you several times, but the lines are down near the river."

"So are the houses," Nan said bitterly. "I suppose you want D.J. now, too?"

"How is he doing?" she asked.

"This is Phil's brother, Vernon Springfield," Nan said. "And this is his wife, Adele."

"A pleasure," Mrs. Price said. "And I'm sorry for your

loss. The reverend was a good man and we all miss him very much."

Vernon puffed out his chest and said something like "Yes, well." He seemed impatient to get to the courtroom. Nan, on the other hand, could have waited for hell to freeze over.

"Can I speak with you privately for just a moment?" Mrs. Price asked, trying to take Nan's arm.

"Of course." Nan shrugged out of Vernon's grasp and followed Mrs. Price toward a recess in the hallway. When they were fairly sequestered, Nan said simply, "Do you really think that with the floods and all, D.J.'s mother is ready to take him back?" She made it clear from her tone that she did not.

"Nan, I'm here in the courthouse because Vanessa Elburn is about to have her parole revoked," Mrs. Price said. "They caught her doing crack downtown."

"The girls?" Nan asked, her heart lodged firmly in her throat. "Are my girls all right?"

Mrs. Price smiled and patted Nan's hand. "So then, if I can get the court to terminate her parental rights, I take it you'd like to raise them?"

Nan put her hands over her mouth to keep the shriek inside. Tears slid down her cheeks as she nodded vehemently.

"I know that you and Mr. Woolery have parted ways. He assures me that it's only temporary, but that's hardly enough to go to the judge on. I don't know what's going on between the two of you, beyond what I read in the papers, but I need to know that you'll be able to afford to keep them. You will, won't you?" Mrs. Price asked her. "I mean, I can tell the judge that they'll be financially secure as well as loved?"

Nan nodded, too emotional to speak. Her girls! She was going to get her girls!

And damn it all, but her first thought was to tell Harry. Wasn't that a kick?

Nan had on a blue dress that Harry had never seen before. She looked like a stranger from the neck down, all tailored and tucked and businesslike. But the softness was still there in her face, and she hadn't managed to tame the wisps of blond hair that bounced as she came down the center aisle flanked by Vernon and his wife. Without so much as a look at him, she took her seat beside her attorney.

"Would you give this to her?" he asked Ms. Conneely, pulling out a carefully folded piece of paper and handing it to his attorney.

"What is it?" she asked, eyeing it suspiciously.

"None of your business," Harry replied. "But if you don't give it to her, I'll make a paper airplane out of it and sail it over there." He didn't really want to make that many creases on it, but nothing was keeping that paper out of her hands. He'd promised, and, contrary to what everyone seemed to think of him these days, he was a man of his word.

Brianna Conneely took the paper, rose, and instead of handing it directly to Nan, stood talking to her lawyer as if the message would turn the entire case on its ear. Solemnly they turned the piece of lined paper over and over on the table while Nan stole a glance at him.

It was the opening he needed. He gestured toward the paper and nodded his head. *Go ahead. Take it. It won't hurt you.*

She crossed her arms over her chest.

Good. She'd feel like an idiot when she finally opened the stupid thing and realized what it was.

"What's in the note?" the reporter behind him asked, but Harry ignored him as Ms. Conneely came back to the table and told him that Nan's lawyer wanted to open the note first.

Harry merely shrugged his approval.

The lawyer unfolded D.J.'s drawing carefully, no doubt with the hope of gaining new evidence of Harry's depravity. He handed it to Nan with the hint of a scowl, and Harry watched her trace the boy's crayon drawing of a man on a horse. At least that was what Harry thought the boy had drawn. It didn't make much sense if it was a dog with a bicycle helmet and rollerskates on its back, which it looked as much like.

Vernon took the drawing, folded it on the same lines so as not to crease it further, and put it into his suit pocket, leaning toward Nan and whispering something she apparently agreed with.

Another look his way, a hastily mouthed thank-you as if she didn't want anyone to see, and then her eyes were focused straight ahead once again.

"That from her kid?" the reporter asked. "How'd you get it?"

"Long story," Harry replied, thinking how convoluted their lives had become.

Finally the judge came out of the side door. He climbed the two steps and took a seat behind the huge desk with the Ohio state seal emblazoned on the front of it. He had to bang his gavel twice before anyone besides Harry paid him any mind.

"Morning," he said in a no-nonsense-will-be-tolerated voice. "I see that these proceedings promise to be as unorthodox as the defendant in this case." He grimaced at Harry.

Brianna Conneely grimaced at Harry, too.

They were all smiles across the aisle.

That is, if one didn't count Nan, who was biting a ragged cuticle, her eyes on the table in front of her.

"I'm sorry to disappoint all you folks in the peanut gallery, but there will be no show today. Because the parties to the suit requested an immediate hearing, the case has been scheduled for a mediation session. What that means, for all you reporters who were looking for some sound bites for the five o'clock news, is that the parties and their attorneys will repair to a private room with a mediator. In this case, that would be retired justice Stephen Schlissel, who has already received briefing papers on the case.

"These papers are held in the strictest confidence and will not be disclosed to the other parties in the case, their lawyers, or even to the court. Any leaks to or by the press will be prosecuted to the full extent of the law. Clear?"

He eye'd Harry over half-rimmed glasses. Well, his lawyer had warned him that he'd be dog meat. He'd just expected that it would take a little longer. Harry nodded. What did he care, anyway? He'd already given her the only thing he valued his heart so what did he care if the court ordered him to give her the rest?

They filed out of the room, two reporters trying to make dates to see him after the session, and entered a door at the end of the hall. The room was set up to make people feel, and, Harry supposed, act, civilized. Dignified. High burgundy leather chairs surrounded an enormous table that was too big to reach across to wring someone's neck.

Which, as Vernon solicitously pulled out Nan's chair for her, was definitely tempting.

"Judge Schlissel! Good to see you," Nan's lawyer said, shaking the mediator's hand. "It's been a long time. Wish you'd consider coming out of retirement."

Harry wanted to gag.

"Mr. Meltzer," the judge said, acknowledging him and then extending his hand to Brianna Conneely. "Still working hard, I see, young lady. Always an uphill battle for you."

Harry extended his hand, introduced himself, and then sat sullenly back in the soft leather chair across from Nan. Except for saying that he had never meant to hurt Nan Springfield or her husband, he planned no defense.

"This is a confidentiality statement," Judge Schlissel said, opening up a file that was waiting on the table. "It covers all written and oral communications made in connection with the mediation process."

He handed copies to the lawyers, who gave it cursory looks and then handed one to Nan and one to him. He signed his without reading it.

"Now, when this goes to trial," Vernon said, "it's no longer private, is that right?"

"Let's make that *if*," Judge Schlissel said. "And no, what is said here remains here. And if you wish to stay, I have to insist that you sign the statement as well."

Vernon nodded and signed with a flourish. He suggested that Adele leave, as if he didn't think she knew how to keep her mouth shut.

Harry wanted to tell his lawyer that Vernon probably wanted Adele to be free to tell the world anything that went on in these chambers and not be bound by some statement that would never interfere with him telling his wife what had happened. But then, Harry was a suspicious man.

Once Adele had left the room, Schlissel told them all

that he had read the briefing papers and admitted finding the case very interesting. Harry doubted that was a good sign. But then, if he was hoping that the court would help Nan see that he was not responsible for Phil's death, he thought he had a long, long wait. He just didn't get what it was that was spurring her on. Her guilt at not standing by her husband? Her guilt over what she'd done with Harry?

"This is not a trial," the judge said. "And I have no decision-making power. The full responsibility for the settlement remains with you and your lawyers. But I will remind you that the wait in this county is at least eleven months for a trial date, and with that in mind, I will try to help you settle this case between the parties."

"But if they don't agree, then she gets her day in court, am I right?" Vernon asked.

"You're the Reverend Springfield's brother?" the judge asked. Mr. Meltzer apologized and did the formal introductions.

"Yes, Mrs. Springfield will have her day in court if she so chooses. I would like to suggest that she already has an attorney, who I'm sure is being well paid to represent her interests. You, Mr. Springfield, might be called 'a hand to hold.' I think you'll probably do her the most good with the least interference."

Harry purposely reached out his foot as far as he could. When he touched Nan's foot, she pulled back, sat up straighter, but said nothing.

"Shall we get started?" the judge asked.

Harry shifted in his seat. "I never meant to hurt you, Nan," he said, wanting that out on the table before anything else was said. "And I thought you knew that. I just don't get what happened."

Before he could continue, or Nan could respond, her

lawyer put up a finger to signal Harry to wait. "Your honor, I think it would be in the best interest of all the parties if they were to speak to and through their respective attorneys. There are extenuating circumstances here that make exchanges between the parties painful for my client, and I—"

"You don't want me to talk to you?" Harry asked. For God's sake, Meltzer's client wasn't the only one in pain.

"Your honor? Could we set the ground rules here to include that Mr. Tweed—that is, Mr. *Woolery*—not address Mrs. Springfield directly?"

"I'm sorry," Harry said. "In general. Ms. Conneely, would you be so kind as to ask Mr. Meltzer to ask Mrs. Springfield if she wishes for me not to talk to her?"

Nan blinked furiously. "Harry, don't make this harder."

He could have mentioned that what was good for the goose was good for the gander and if he couldn't speak to her, well . . . but he melted at the sound of her voice, and was silent.

"Mr. Meltzer, I assume you would like to present your case?" the judge asked.

Meltzer began with a recitation of facts that Harry already knew too well, colored by Nan's view on each of the issues.

She firmly believed, or so Meltzer said, that Harry's intentions were malicious and small, and that his remarks were intended to embarrass the reverend and injure his standing in the community.

Harry asked when it would be his turn to answer the allegations.

"Did Philip have a turn?" Vernon shouted. "Did you give him a chance to defend himself, or did you just spread lies over the airwaves like some Nazi—"

"Last time I *asked* you," the judge told Vernon. "This time I'm *telling* you. You are present to give Mrs. Springfield any emotional support she might need. This is not your vendetta. If you can't be helpful to the process, I don't want you part of the process."

Vernon backed off, patting Nan's hand solicitously. "I'm sorry, your honor, it's just—"

"Don't," the judge warned. "Leave it be."

Vernon nodded.

"Ms. Conneely, would you like to state the facts as your client sees them?"

Harry's gaze locked with Nan's while Brianna Conneely explained that Harry's job was to poke fun at institutions— the church, the government, the system at large. She belittled his job, said she personally had no sympathy for him, but the truth was that Harry had no knowledge of the Reverend Springfield, and therefore could not have wilfully inflicted harm upon him.

"But he did it anyway," Nan said softly. "Not knowing who he was, the kind of man he was, the kind of minister— he said awful things, not caring who they would hurt and what harm they would do."

"It was a joke, Nan, and you know it," he said before Brianna Conneely put a restraining hand on his arm.

"Here's the thing about it," Ms. Conneely said. "It was a joke but it didn't roll off the reverend's back, now did it? And why was that?"

The look on Nan's face turned his gut. The possibility of Phil's betrayal had been bad enough for her. He wouldn't be party to yet another betrayal.

"Because he didn't have a sense of humor," Harry said quickly, yanking his arm away from Conneely's hand. Phil's guilt was not a place they were going to go, not even if it meant that he'd have to concede the suit. Of course, if he did that, he'd be guilty in Nan's eyes forever, and that would ruin any chance they had for a future. This wasn't a rock and a hard place he was between—he was in a trash compactor with a Kleenex to brace the walls.

They bantered more, the lawyers, flinging about words like *chronology of events* and *knowledge of possible consequences* and the fact that the radio station phone lines had been busy that night. Meltzer accused him of having taken the phones off the hook so that the reverend was not able to get through, and Conneely countered with the phone records of incoming calls.

And all the while, Harry stared at Nan, memorizing the tiny lines that radiated from the corners of her eyes. He caught the slightest whiff of her perfume and inhaled it into his memory. He thought of the way she laughed and the way she cried and wondered what her life had been like with Philip. Was she as stifled with him as she seemed to be beside Vernon?

They moved on to what the judge called the "critical legal issues." While the legal mumbo jumbo went on, he mouthed "How's Topher?" at Nan.

How's Topher! She sat there, scared to death that at any minute he was going to mention Phil's second safe-deposit box, and he smiled at her and asked *How's Topher.* She stared right through him, tamping down memories that would hurt for a lifetime and then some.

He tapped at her foot with his. A better woman would have just tucked her feet under her chair and ignored him. But a better woman wouldn't have gone and slept with Harry Woolery twice, now would she? And so, gauging where his leg was in relation to hers, she slumped slightly and then kicked him in the shin for all she was worth—for seducing her, fooling her, making her love him and breaking her heart.

"Ow!" he howled, obviously more surprised than hurt. "What was that for?"

"Oh," she said as sweetly as she could. "Was that your leg? I'm so sorry. I never meant to hurt you."

You could have heard a paper clip hit the carpeting in the conference room.

"What did I do?" he asked. "What?"

"Your honor, could you please remind Mr. Woolery that—" Mr. Meltzer began.

"I don't need reminding," Harry shouted, pounding a fist on the conference table. "I need explanations. I need a goddamn map for the landmines this lady's got planted. I need to know what I did that was so—"

"You killed her husband, for Pete's sake!" Vernon shouted, coming to his feet beside Nan's chair and leaning over the table to wave his finger in Harry's face. "You estranged her sister-in-law. You orphaned her son. You—"

"I made a joke at her husband's expense," Harry said evenly. "No one but the reverend took it seriously."

"The whole church did," Vernon corrected. "The elders, the Session. The trustees actually accepted money from Nan to replace—"

He stopped himself there. Nan looked at the judge and at the lawyers. The truth was that no one was going to help her. She looked at the conference room ceiling. It appeared to her even He wasn't interested.

"You know darn well, Mrs. Springfield," Harry said, staring down at her as if he could see right through to her soul, "that this has nothing to do with my comments on the radio or what happened last summer. Does it?" he demanded.

"Last summer Mrs. Springfield was happily married to Christopher's father. She had a houseful of children and knew her place in the world. Now none of that is true. What of that do you think you're not responsible for?" Vernon asked. "Her church circle tiptoes around her and whispers behind her back. Last summer they were busy preparing to celebrate the tenth anniversary of the reverend's coming to the Old Deburle Church. Now there's resistance to a memorial service."

Nan held her breath, waiting for him to refute Vernon's words, tell them all that her marriage hadn't been happy. That on the very night he'd died, she'd asked her husband for a divorce.

"I'm talking to Mrs. Springfield," Harry said to Vernon while he bored holes in her soul with his eyes and his words. "What happened, Nan? What did I do?"

The judge spoke, his voice soft compared to the angry shouts that filled the room. "Mr. Springfield, sit down, please. Now, Mr. Woolery, you've been accused of slandering the Reverend Springfield. Whether his widow likes you or not is irrelevant. Whether you like her, and I've performed wedding services for bridegrooms that seemed less smitten than you, is also not relevant. Now I—"

"Your honor," Harry said, "This isn't the kind of thing a man finds easy to say. Especially not in a courtroom full of lawyers, but I'm in love with her. Head-over-heels, tongue-hanging-out, can't-catch-my-breath in love with her. And I don't want to hurt her."

"This is not about hurt," Nan said, folding her arms across her chest to hold herself together. "This is about last August, when, with no knowledge of me, or my husband, or our son, you told everyone within the range of WGCA that he stole the scholarship money from the church. You said that he had a house in the Caribbean and you also said that he never slept with his wife." She fought to hold the tears at bay. "What right did you have to do that? What right did you have to then barge into my life, my grief, and use my children as tools to get to me?"

"I never—"

"You disguised yourself as Santa Claus. You had Topher put on Josh's hockey team. You involved yourself with D.J.'s treatment." She stopped short of saying that he had gone through all Phil's belongings. After all, any minute now he would bring that up himself and there would be no defense to Phil's opening up a second safe-deposit box.

"Your honor, I thought we agreed that it would be best if Ms. Conneely and I did the talking in this case," Mr. Meltzer said with a heavy sigh.

"This is a mediation," the judge replied, his head resting on the back of his interlocked hands. "It's less formal than a hearing and I think that your client is doing just fine for herself. I think I've got a good picture of the—"

"No, you don't," Harry said. "You're seeing it in black and white, and the color makes all the difference. There are things that you don't know about this case, things no one knows, that—"

"When you accused my brother of stealing, did you have any reason to believe that he had stolen so much as a dime from anyone?" Vernon demanded. "Yes or no? Just answer the question."

"Now you're a lawyer?" Harry asked. "The D.A.? Why not just charge me with murder?"

"I tried it, damn you," Vernon said. "But they wouldn't prosecute. Do you think I want your money?"

"Actually, I thought Nan was suing me, not you," Harry said. "Or are you expecting Nan to fork over some portion to you for all your help and understanding? Not to mention the money that Phil owed you, and the fourteen percent interest rate you were charging your own brother."

Vernon coughed and sputtered as he rose, his chair flying out behind him to hit the wall. "This mediation is over. I'll see you in court, Mr. Harris Tweed." He opened the door to the room and stood waiting. "Come on, Nan. I want you out of here."

A piece of her wanted to go. Really, it did. But the rest of her was tired of being told what to do. And she didn't want to take her case to court, where without the confidentiality statement the whole world would find out what Phil had done. "You go ahead," she told Vernon.

"No," he said, wavering at the door. "I'll wait."

"Do that in the hall," the judge suggested. "In fact, why don't you lawyers wait in the hall, too, while the parties and I—"

"No, your honor," her lawyer said. "I can't allow my client to discuss her case without my representation. It would be unethical and unprofessional and—"

"And I don't think it would be in my client's best interest to deal directly with Mrs. Springfield, either."

"Please just drop the suit, Nan," Harry said simply. "I'll give you what I can, but I—"

"Your honor, that was not a bona fide offer," his lawyer said quickly. "Mr. Woolery has a valid defense and just wishes to spare Mrs. Springfield the emotional distress that this case will necessarily cause her—"

"Because he's already caused her enough emotional distress," her lawyer said.

"I want more than you can give me, Harry," Nan said, hearing the hopelessness in her own voice.

"I can't change the whole world for you," Harry answered. "But maybe I can right your little piece of it."

"Your honor," her lawyer drawled out, exasperation dripping off each word.

"Ladies and gentlemen," the judge said, addressing both attorneys. "I think we'll break for the day. I can see that your clients are feeling the stress of these proceedings, and before things are said that shouldn't be, I'd like to recess and begin anew in the morning."

Another night without Topher, without D.J. and the girls. Nan leaned toward her attorney. "Could you ask that D.J. be brought to my hotel room this evening?" she whispered.

The attorney repeated her request, and added to it, "by a third party."

"I'll have Eleanor bring him," Harry said. He smiled at her, that soft smile that had warmed her through one chilling moment after another. "He misses you."

"I miss all the children," she said quietly, rising and brushing out the wrinkles in the dress Vernon had purchased for her. She couldn't say that she missed Phil. And she wouldn't, not for anything, admit that she missed Harry almost more than she could bear.

Twenty-Eight

Eleanor had just given D.J. and Nate dinner when Harry came through the door looking like he'd been hit by an eighteen-wheeler. His shoulders sagged, his step faltered, and when he threw his keys down on the table and sat down in the kitchen chair, Eleanor just wanted to throw her arms around him and tell him it would all be all right.

Only she wasn't sure that for him it would ever be.

"Nan wants you to bring D.J. to the Hyatt Regency in Columbus," he said. "I'll drive you in on my way to work, if you like."

Like? She wanted desperately to talk to Nan, to tell her she was thinking about Marissa Jane and to ask her what had made her run away—and to Vernon of all people. Eleanor really needed to warn her about Vernon and his high motives. "What are you doing back, anyway?" she asked. "Why didn't you just hang around, have dinner and then just go over to the station?"

"We got any coffee?" he asked instead of answering her.

She poured him a cup. "You look like you just lost your best friend."

"I did," he answered.

Nate came into the room, his walker clunking against the worn linoleum floor, D.J. following behind at a safe distance. "How'd it go in court?" he asked before Eleanor could signal him that things were obviously sliding downhill faster than a runaway sled on ice.

"Well, she hates me. The judge hates me. And Vernon, well, Vernon would like me tarred and feathered and run out of town on a rail—after I fork over the million he thinks I have stashed somewhere, of course." D.J. clambered up into Harry's lap and cuddled against him. There had been an incredible transformation in the boy.

"What happened when you told them about the key?" Nate asked, ruffling D.J.'s hair.

Harry was silent.

"I asked you what happened when you pulled out the key to the guy's safe-deposit box." Nate repeated, taking a seat at the table across from Harry.

"Whose safe-deposit box?" Eleanor asked. "Phil's?"

"Dad, would you just let it go?" Harry asked, buttoning up D.J.'s shirt.

"It's a million dollars, for Pete's sake," Nate said. "How the heck am I supposed to just let it go when you've got proof—physical evidence—that the guy was a crook."

"It's no proof, Dad," Harry said. "It's not any kind of evidence and it doesn't prove anything. It's just a damn key."

"What key?" Eleanor asked.

"He found a key to a second safe-deposit box," Nate said. "And he hasn't even told Nan about it yet. Have you?" he demanded of Harry.

"I will when the time is right," Harry said, setting D.J. on the floor and coming to his feet. "You want a lift into the city?" he asked Eleanor.

"They'll garnishee your wages for the rest of your life," Nate warned him.

"It's looking to be the only way I'll ever get to help her, Dad," he said.

"That's sweet," Nate said. "I'm sure her second husband will appreciate it no end. They'll vacation on your money very happily."

"Go suck a pain pill," Harry said, heading out the door with D.J.

Eleanor guessed they were getting a ride.

Nan called Dee from the Hyatt Regency as soon as she got rid of Vernon. Of course, she really wasn't free of him, but she'd firmly locked the adjoining door, kicked off her shoes, and dialed up Dee, asking if she could bring Topher to Columbus.

"Are you all right?" Dee asked.

"Sure," Nan said, as brightly as she could. "I'm fine. I'd just like to see Topher for a little while—give him a hug and a kiss. You know."

"Well, I was just giving the kids dinner," Dee told her. "And then they were going to watch a videotape."

"Is he all right?" Nan asked.

"First he loses his dad," Dee answered. "And the girls. Then his house goes floating down the river and his mother takes off for the better part of a week. How do you think he is?"

"Let me talk to him," Nan said.

"Is this going to be one of your 'Hey, kiddo, everything all right? . . . Well, good . . . be seeing you' talks? Because he cried for half an hour after the last one and he seems okay at the moment, so—"

"Then bring him here."

"For a half-hour visit, and then take him back home

with me again? I don't think he'd do real well with that, Nan. I really don't."

"Then put him on the phone," she said. "I need to speak to him."

"You sure do," Dee said. "But if the two of you could stop being so brave and start being honest, it might do you both some good."

Nan waited for Topher to come to the phone. She could hear Dee coaxing him, telling him she'd pause the tape, as if Topher didn't want to be interrupted by his mother, even if he hadn't seen her for days. Well, whose fault was that? Certainly not Topher's.

"Yeah?" he said into the phone.

"Hi, honey. It's Mommy."

"Yeah, Aunt Dee told me." Flat. Uninterested. She bet he was biting at his lip.

"I miss you, sweetheart."

"We're watching a movie."

"Topher, I wish I could just come get you, but there's somewhere I have to be tomorrow. I'd drive out there tonight, but I'm waiting for Aunt Eleanor to bring D.J. over and—"

"—and he's more important."

"No! No one is more important to me than you. It was just the way that things worked out, and D.J. doesn't have school tomorrow the way you do, so he and Aunt Eleanor can stay over and then—"

"He's gonna stay at the hotel with you?" This wasn't going very well.

"If Aunt Eleanor doesn't want to drive back," she said, hoping that D.J. could stay with her, wishing that Topher could, too.

"I gotta go," Topher said. "We wanna see the movie."

"Christopher, I love you," she said, her words reaching out to hold him when her arms could not. "I want you here with me and I'm doing everything I can to make that happen."

"Is Harry there?" Topher asked.

"Here in the hotel with me? No, of course not."

"Josh's mother said Harry has the hots for you."

"Josh's mother told you that?" Nan crushed the phone cord in her hands.

"No. She told Josh's dad—you know, Charles. And Josh heard her. What are 'the hots'?" He sounded so little, so innocent.

"It means that he likes me," Nan said.

"In a boy-girl way, right?" he asked.

"Yes, it means that, but Josh's mother is wrong. Mr. Woolery and I are just friends, Topher."

"If my dad got killed in an accident, like you told me, how come Uncle Vernon says that some man killed him?"

"This isn't something we can really go over on the phone," Nan said, seeing for the first time that her baby wasn't immune to all the turmoil going on around him, seeing that the world was closing in on him just as it was on her. "But I'll tell you all about it tomorrow night, I promise. In the meantime, don't you worry about what Uncle Vernon says, or what Josh's mom says, or anyone else. The important thing is that I love you and after tomorrow we'll be a family again. You and me and D.J. and the girls, too."

"You can't be a family without a dad," Topher said. "And I don't have one."

"We can be a family," Nan said softly. "I promise."

"Uncle Harry called me," Topher said. "He said he went to see the house and there's nothing there anymore. That it all got washed away."

Nan swallowed hard. Some piece of her had really believed that her father's house would still be standing when she got back to it. Maybe not ready to be lived in—she wasn't a fool—but salvageable. "Is that right?" was all she managed to get out.

"Where are we gonna live?" Topher asked.

Nan let out a big breath. "Don't you worry about that," she said, having no better answer to give.

"They're starting the movie," Topher said. "I gotta go."

"Tell Aunt Dee that I'll be there for you tomorrow night." She wanted to add *come hell or high water*, but the expression hit too close to home.

"Bye," Topher said, and the phone went dead before she could even tell him, one more time, how much she loved him.

By the time she heard the knock on the door, she'd had herself one good cry and had determined it was the last of her tears. She'd determined that before, but she supposed the supply was replenished by all the floodwaters, because she surely had plenty left for this last bout of self-pity.

"Ellie," she said, opening up the door. "I'm so glad—"

But it wasn't Eleanor standing in the doorway. A thinner, older Stan Denham stood in the hall, his eyes darting at Vernon's door. "Hello, Nan," he said, his voice so low she could hardly hear him. "Can I talk to you for a minute?"

"How did you know I was here?" Nan asked him.

"I still have a few friends around," he said. "Not many, but you're pretty big news. Can I come in?"

Nan didn't know what to say beyond the fact that she wasn't in the habit of inviting men into her hotel room.

"We could go somewhere for a cup of coffee," he suggested. "Or maybe some dinner, if you haven't eaten already."

"I don't think so," Nan said. "Ellie is on her way over with D.J. and I've got to wait for her."

"Then could I come in? What I have to say isn't for the hallway." Again he looked at Vernon's door.

"Vernon did come with you, didn't he?"

"Yes," she said, her eyes darting to his door as well.

"Is he in there?"

"I think so," she said. Vernon had offered to take her to dinner, but she'd declined for the same reason she'd given Stan. He'd told her to order up some room service if she liked and he'd check back with her later. And he'd warned her not to take any calls from Harry, then called the desk and told them not to put any through to her room. After he left, she'd called them back, told them she had finished her nap, and said they were free to put through any calls that came in.

At the moment, she was in need of Vernon's financial help, but that didn't mean that she was going to stop being an independent person just because he was picking up the tab for her hotel. After all, clearly Vernon had a stake in this outcome, too. If she won, she'd be in a position to pay back the six thousand dollars Phil still owed him. With interest.

She opened the door wider and gestured for Stan to come in.

"Mind if we turn on the TV?" Stan asked. "I don't want Vernon to—"

Nan switched on the TV, putting the volume up slightly to cover their conversation. "I know about the safe-deposit box," she said. "I found the key."

Stan closed his eyes and let out a ragged sigh. "I'm glad.

I didn't know how I was going to tell you, but I thought you ought to know before this lawsuit goes any further."

"How did you know about the lawsuit?" Nan asked. "I thought you were living in St. Louis now."

"I read about it in the paper. It's the kind of thing that makes the news, I guess." He reached into his pocket and pulled out a long envelope. "I haven't known what to do with this since Phil died."

Nan took it and opened it. Inside was a stock certificate for fifty shares of D-LINC, and another for one hundred shares of CSR Electronics. Both were made out to Phil Springfield.

"He gave them to me the day before he died and told me to sell them for whatever we could get."

"Why?" she asked. Phil had never cared much about money. Not enough to break a commandment, she didn't think.

"Because time was running out," Stan said simply.

Nan shook her head. "I meant why did he take the money in the first place? He did take it, didn't he?"

"He owed it to Vernon," Stan said. "So when Vernon suggested—"

Nan reached out for the wall and steadied herself against it. Stan, his face white as a sheet, pulled out the desk chair for her and guided her into it, apologizing for upsetting her as he did.

"Vernon suggested that Phil steal from the church?" Nan asked, wanting to be sure she was following exactly what Stan was saying.

The accountant nodded. "Only he convinced Phil that it wasn't stealing. He said he'd done it for years, borrowed money from his father-in-law's company without the old man knowing it, kept half, invested the other half and returned it when the stocks got high enough."

"And that isn't stealing?" Nan asked. "You and Phil thought that wasn't stealing?"

"For just an instant, and then the guilt got to him. But he couldn't just sell, because the stock was going down and there was no way to replace the money. Vernon was always on Phil's case about the money he'd loaned him, and I had Caroline's braces to pay off, and it was going to be a piece of cake, the way Vernon told it. And it seemed so harmless."

"Vernon knew?" Nan repeated again, unable to get past that part of the confession. He'd been so eager to blame Harry. But then, so had she. Now it seemed like there was enough blame to go around for all of them. Phil included. Especially Phil.

"Don't go getting angry with Vernon," Stan said. "If it hadn't been for him, I'd probably be checking groceries at Krogers."

"He got you the job in St. Louis?" Nan asked. *Get him out of town. Get him out of sight.*

"Had to call in a few favors, I think," Stan said.

"And you came here tonight because . . . ?" Nan asked.

"I wanted to be sure you knew the truth before it came out in court or something," Stan said. "I thought that maybe, if you had the proceeds from the stocks, that you'd give up the suit and then—"

"I thought these were worthless," she said, holding out the certificates to him.

"The stocks have doubled," Stan said. "Just like Vernon promised. You can cash them in and—"

"Why didn't *you* cash them in?"

"These have Phil's name on them. The executor of his estate needs to cash them."

"You had some in your name?" Nan asked.

Stan nodded.

"You cashed them in?"

He nodded again.

"You realize, of course, that I paid the church back for all the money that was missing."

Stan pulled out his checkbook from the inside pocket of his suit jacket. "I'll give you my half of the—"

"Oh, no," Nan said. "You'll give the church that money. And you'll tell them exactly what you told me. And if they decide to prosecute you, well, you'll have to deal with that, won't you?"

"But Phil—" Stan began.

"Phil paid with his life. You're getting off easy." She wondered what Vernon would pay with, how she could make him pay.

"You don't want me to do that, Nan," Stan said. "The truth coming out would hurt everyone. Think about Christopher. The whole congregation would think that Phil was a thief."

"He *was* a thief," Nan said. "And he risked everyone's happiness for a few dollars that Vernon probably never missed. The lies stop here, tonight. If you don't go to the church, I will."

"But—"

Eleanor's knocking interrupted them. This time she was sure it was Eleanor because she could hear the softer thud, thud, thudding of D.J.'s little cowboy boots against the bottom of the door.

"That's Ellie," she said. "Thanks for coming. Thanks for being honest with me, whatever your motives."

"I can't—" he began, but she opened the door and lifted D.J. into her arms, kissing his cheeks and his forehead and the top of his head. It felt as if she hadn't seen him in years.

"Stan was just leaving," she told Eleanor. "Come on in!"

"Stan?" Eleanor asked, obviously surprised to see him there.

"I'll tell you all about it later," Nan told her as Stan squeezed out the doorway and scurried down the hall.

"We need to talk, Nan," Eleanor said, hesitating in the doorway. "Is Vernon with you?"

"He never was," Nan said. "He never was."

"Oh, so you finally noticed?" Eleanor asked.

"It always seemed to me that he was good to you, Ellie," Nan said as she fussed with D.J.'s jacket.

"Well, appearances are deceiving," Eleanor said. "Listen, I'm thinking about calling Birthright. I talked it over with Nate—he's quite a special man—and he told me to wait just a day or two and then to go ahead and talk to her."

"Oh, Ellie!" Nan said, hugging her, D.J.'s arms wrapped around both sets of legs.

"So then you think it's a good idea?" Eleanor asked. "I'd have to explain to her why I gave her away when I loved her and her father more than anything on this earth," she said, pushing Nan away from her so that she could watch her face. "I'm going to have to tell her that I let my brother chase off her father before I knew I was pregnant and that when I knew, I couldn't find him. And that I let my brother convince me to give her away for the good of the family's reputation."

"He chased him off?" Nan asked, wondering how this little detail was never divulged by her husband in the re-counting of Eleanor's disgrace. She lifted D.J. up onto the bed and told him it was all right to jump on it while she kept an eye on him.

"He was a trucker. Vernon convinced him that he wasn't good enough for me—that I was going to be a doctor someday and I'd be ashamed of him. It was awful. He wrote me this letter about how he'd think of me wherever he was and be proud of all I had yet to accomplish.

"So now I empty bedpans and I have a daughter I've never even met."

"Watch!" D.J. shouted, falling on his tummy and bouncing back to his feet.

"You're a circus act!" Nan told him. To Eleanor she said, "Couldn't you find him? I mean when you found out?"

"I was so stupid," Eleanor answered. "I let Vernon and Phil look for him. I was busy throwing up and hanging on by my fingernails—watching my scholarship get given to someone else—so I left it to them. It wasn't for years that it occurred to me that they might not even have looked."

"Vernon wouldn't—" Nan started, but then she stopped herself. Maybe Vernon would have. Maybe Phil would have, too. "I'm glad you're going to finally contact her."

"I'm still not completely sure. If only there was a way to know what she thought before I opened up all that hurt again."

D.J. bounced against her and fell back onto the bed.

"I've got some cookies, D.J.. You want one?"

D.J. scrambled off the bed and sat down at the desk. "And milk," he announced.

"I'll call room service," Nan said. "You want anything, Ellie?"

"Think they have any crow?"

"What?"

"You could use a serving about now," Eleanor said. "It's

time to drop the lawsuit, Nan. Harry loves you. More than you could ever imagine."

Nan smiled politely. She didn't want to fight with Eleanor. She didn't want to fight with anyone. She just wanted to pick up the pieces and move on with her life.

"Did you know Phil had a second safe-deposit box?" Eleanor asked.

"So?"

"So Harry was right about Phil all along," Eleanor said.

"He could have told me that, Ellie. He could have come to me at any time and been honest about everything."

"Oh, and you'd have listened? I think not. You didn't want to have anything to do with him, remember?"

"It would have been better if I'd never had anything to do with him, don't you think?" Nan asked.

"No, that's not what I think at all. He's got the key, you know. To the box."

"Does he?" Nan replied. If he thought so, he'd never even looked in his drawer, never pulled out those papers, never mounted his defense.

"Nate and he had quite a fight about it this afternoon. Seems Nate's been pressuring him to produce the key and Harry won't do it."

"Why not?"

"Because he doesn't want to hurt you," Eleanor said simply. "Not even for a million dollars."

"If that's true," Nan asked, "then why didn't he tell me when he found the key? Why did he keep it a secret and why does he still have it?" Or *think* he does.

"He said you didn't want to know the truth yet. And surely you didn't want to hear it from him."

Nan sat down on the bed. D.J. came over and jabbered

at her. She couldn't make sense of what he was saying any more than she could process what Eleanor was telling her.

"Even if that was true, if he was trying to protect me," Nan said, "why did he hold on to the key?"

"He was hoping that someday you'd be ready to hear the truth, and that when you were, he could provide you with it."

"Vernon says Harry is playing me like a violin," Nan said softly.

"Vernon ruined my life. Don't let him ruin yours."

Twenty-Nine

Harry walked out of the station manager's office swinging his arms forward and back in sync, so that he sort of clapped as he went. It was, as far as he was concerned, his last argument with anyone. He was done. He'd had it.

He gave Ross the thumbs-up sign and watched his friend shake his head and grimace at him.

"You got her on hold?" he asked. When Ross indicated the flashing light on the phone, Harry mouthed, "Just let me call Nan while you get my dad."

Ross dipped his head in question and Harry put his hand up to the side of his face in imitation of phoning.

Ross rolled his eyes, but spoke into the mike. "We've got something really special coming up after this next commercial, so stay tuned because you won't want to miss the crap that's coming down the pike. Back in two."

And then he signaled Ray to play the commercial.

"Don't do it," he said as Harry picked up the phone and dialed Nan's hotel.

"You wouldn't want to disappoint all those listeners, would you?" Harry asked.

"We do it all the time," Ross said just as Harry put up his finger to indicate that he'd reached the hotel.

"Mrs. Nancy Springfield, please," he said and tapped his heels as he waited for her to pick up the phone.

"Hello?" Her voice was soft and groggy.

"Did I wake you up?" he asked.

"Harry? What time is it? What . . . ?"

He didn't have time to explain. He'd be back on the air in a minute. "Listen, turn on your radio to ten-fifty," he said.

"Harry, I—"

"Please, Nan. I'll never ask you to listen again."

And then he hung up the phone, praying that she would turn on the radio and hear what all his other listeners were about to hear.

The station manager cued him. He shook his head and gestured to Ross.

"Well, here's a first for *Tweed After Dark*," Ross said while Harry prayed that Nate had done his part like they'd planned and that Eleanor was listening. "There's a young lady on the phone who is looking for her mother. She's hoping that there is a woman out there who will hear her story and give the station a call. Miss Broder, are you there?"

"*I'm here*," Marissa Jane Broder said, and her soft voice filled the glass room that he and Ross spent every night in.

"And you were born in . . . ?" Ross asked.

Marissa filled in the particulars. And then, in that same soft voice, she spoke directly to Eleanor. "*I just want my mother, my birth mother, to know that I don't want anything from her. I have a wonderful life. If anything, I want to thank her for giving me up so that I could have the parents I have and the sisters and brother I love.*

"*I'm married to a wonderful man, and this past summer*

our first child, our daughter, was born. I really am very happy . . ."

"But . . . ?" Ross cued her.

"There's just this piece missing. I could pretend that I want to know my health history for Sarah's sake, or that I want to know why, but the truth is that I just want to know where I fit in this world—what my birth parents were like, whether they are still alive. . . . Have I looked into my mother's face and not known? Is she the woman at the bakery? Is she my doctor or the woman who sits next to me in church? When Sarah was born, I looked down at this little girl and thought, 'She looks like me!' It's the first time in my life that I've ever felt that . . ."

"There's a caller on line one," Ross said, nodding to him that it was Eleanor. "You there, caller?"

"Marissa? It's your mom."

There was dead silence in the studio. People came out of their cubicles. The station manager hung in the doorway. A sob swept through the air, but whether it was Marissa's or Eleanor's was anyone's guess.

"I'm sorry I didn't let you find me sooner. I was so afraid that you would hate me for letting you go."

There was a long pause, long enough for Harry to wonder if he'd done the right thing.

"Are you really my mother?" Marissa asked.

"Yes." It was a simple word, but it brought tears to Harry's eyes and clogged his throat. *"Your eyes were slate blue in the hospital. The nurses said that they would change. Did they? Are they still blue? Like mine? Or did they turn darker like your father's?"*

"They're blue," Marissa said, her voice cracking so that she could hardly get out the words. *"So are Sarah's."*

"Well, I'm sure all you voyeurs want to hear the rest of

this conversation, but it seems to be rather private to me, and besides, I have a news flash just handed to me. Sad news coming out of Columbus. It seems Harris Tweed was laid to rest tonight after a career that spanned half a dozen cities in a dozen and a half years. Tweed was known for his acerbic style, his insulting humor, and his unrelenting nastiness. For years he peddled his anger and disappointment and found that it struck a chord with disenchanted listeners. He leaves behind a string of angry listeners and one partner who won't know what to do without him."

Sad music began to play—his manager having a flare for the dramatic—and Ross launched into a eulogy for the newly departed Harris Tweed.

Had Harry known how good it would feel, he'd have killed off his alter ego years ago.

He wondered if Nan had heard, if she cared. He wondered what he'd do with the rest of his life if she wouldn't let him share hers. Whatever it was, he wouldn't be hiding behind someone else's identity, wouldn't be sneaking around in the dead of night.

Quietly he stood up and slipped out of the broadcasting booth with a wave to Ross. He was in the elevator before he realized what he was doing. With a laugh he headed back to the booth, opened the door, and threw the Best's Cleaning cap in Ross's direction.

"Call me a cab," he said. "I'll be waiting outside."

Ross took the cap and put it on with the brim toward the back. "Any cabbie in the vicinity of WGCA, wanna stop by and pick up a fare?" he said into the microphone. "Good. That's done. Now if anyone wants to explain to me why the Cubs can't seem to win two games in a row, would they please give me a call? I swear these guys are jinxed.

And would the Mets fan with the voodoo doll give it a rest? I mean . . ."

Harry shut the door silently and headed out into the breezy night. The sky was clear and the stars were shining. And there was something on the wind that made him smile.

He was back at the courthouse at nine, a sea of reporters waiting for him. Harris Tweed's death was big news, and the fact that he was Harris Tweed wasn't a secret anymore.

"So what's the deal?" a reporter asked. "You get a better offer somewhere else?"

"Not much of a publicity stunt," someone else said.

"What are you hoping to accomplish by this?" a woman reporter asked, putting the microphone to a small tape recorder against his left nostril.

"Anonymity," he said, pulling his head back.

"So you're saying you just want to be some average Joe?"

He ignored them all. He didn't owe them any statements. What he wanted was to be left alone. To be a private citizen and live a private life.

They were waiting for him in the conference room—the attorneys, the judge, Vernon, and Nan.

"Good morning," Harry said. "I hope I haven't kept you waiting. I've been working on a proposed settlement and I was just trying to fine-tune the details." He handed the paper to his lawyer.

"Before that—" Nan began.

"Please," Harry interrupted. "Let me get the offer on the table before you refuse it."

"Look—" she began again.

"Let him offer, Nan," Vernon counseled. Nan shot him

"Your honor? Do you still have the authority to conduct marriages?"

"Oh, no," Nan said. "Just because I don't want it to be in the church doesn't mean I'd settle for a civil ceremony. I want you to promise to more than just a judge that you'll love me forever."

The judge stood and shook Harry's hand. "I think this concludes our business, ladies and gentlemen. Quite nicely, I might add."

"Just a minute," Nan said. "There are still some numbers we need to talk about."

Vernon, scowling till then, crossed his hands over his chest and smiled. Meltzer, who had risen to shake Harry's hand, took his seat once again.

"What numbers?" Harry asked.

"How many children?" Nan asked, as if the question were an obvious one.

"All of them," Harry agreed. "Topher and the girls and D.J. and Josh whenever we can have him. Five."

"And?" Her eyebrows disappeared behind her bangs.

Harry leaned back in his chair and imagined Nan's belly stretched to bursting with his child. "And as many more as you want to have," he agreed.

"Good," she said, standing up and coming around the table to within his reach. "Because I want a houseful."

"I guess it'll be a breeding farm," Conneely said to Meltzer.

Vernon looked miserable.

But Harry couldn't wait to get started.

a look that would have dropped a horse. Vernon's head actually snapped back an inch or two.

Ms. Conneely passed the settlement offer to the judge. "Offer it," the judge ordered.

"My client has offered to support Mrs. Springfield and any and all children in her care for as long as she lives," Brianna Conneely said, hands raised as if it were a very simple matter.

"On the condition that she drop the suit," Meltzer finished for him.

"That's not actually the condition," Conneely said. "Though of course, that is a given."

"What's the condition?" Meltzer asked, hands folded against his chest as if he weren't about to give away anything.

His lawyer looked around the room. Her eyes settled on Nan. "She's gotta marry him," she mumbled.

"What!" Vernon shouted. "Of all the unmitigated gall . . ."

"People who live in glass houses, Vernon, can't afford to throw stones. If you want to talk about unmitigated gall, you might want to make sure your own ass is covered," Nan said.

Vernon's jaw dropped. Harry supposed his did, too. He'd never heard a swear word out of Nan—didn't think she even knew one.

She whispered something to her lawyer, who stared at Harry as she spoke.

"We need a recess for a few minutes, your honor," Meltzer said.

"Take all the time you need," Harry said, happy that at least she wasn't rejecting his proposal out of hand.

"You can use that side room," the judge indicated with a nod of his head. "We'll wait here."

Vernon rose along with Nan. "I don't think so, Vernon," Nan said a bit too sweetly. "Don't worry. You'll get everything that's coming to you."

While Nan and her lawyer were gone, Brianna Conneely and the judge talked about golf. Harry had trouble thinking about anything but what could be going on beyond the oak door to the judge's left. That and what had transpired between Nan and Vernon. The balance of power had obviously shifted overnight.

They came back in, Nan looking at her feet as she walked. His life was hanging in the balance. What the heck did she have to be nervous about?

"Well?" the judge asked.

"Against the advice of counsel," Meltzer began, "my client will agree to drop her lawsuit on one condition."

Harry was sure she'd ask that he never darken her doorstep again.

"That Mr. Woolery not rescind *his* condition."

Harry jerked up his head. Nan was smiling shyly at him.

"You'll marry me?" he asked, unable to quite believe what he was hearing.

She nodded.

"I won't allow it!" Vernon said. "I won't hear of it!"

Nan looked him straight in the eye. "Oh, you'll be too busy explaining to Adele and her father how you embezzled funds from their company to worry about what I'm doing," she said, dismissing him with this adorable little jerk of her shoulder as she turned back to Harry. "I want to adopt the girls."

"Absolutely," he said, unable to keep the smile from his face.

"And I want to learn to ride horses," she said. "So I can help with D.J.'s therapy."

"Of course."

"And I'd like to know how you expect to support me without a job."

"Well, best laid plans," Harry started. "I really did mean to quit. But I got a call this morning from the station, and they're offering me a daytime slot, under my own name, if I'm willing to take on some more lost causes. I said no, but they made me a heck of an offer, which also gives me the chance to get the farm going again," he said, surprising himself along with everyone else in the room.

"What did you tell them?" Nan asked.

"I told them I'd have to check with my boss," Harry said, gesturing with his head to her. "What do you think? It'd give us enough money to maybe start a therapeutic riding academy of some sort at the farm."

"Are we going to live at the farm?" Nan asked, her arms crossed as if she were one tough cookie, but her eyes twinkling and giving her away.

"I thought so," Harry said hesitantly. "That is, I didn't really think otherwise . . . Truth is, I didn't expect you to say yes quite so soon."

"That's your tough luck," she said, and then turned to her lawyer. "This is a binding deal, isn't it?"

Dick Meltzer laughed. "Nothing's been signed, but you do have several witnesses to his offer here."

"Saturday," she said.

"Or the deal's off," Harry warned.

"With all the children," she added.

"At Old Deburle?"

"Too many memories. At the farm."

Thirty

The rest of the week was a flurry of activity for Nan. Harry went with her to speak to the Old Deburle Church trustees, who unanimously agreed that the stock certificates belonged to Nan, since she'd already repaid the church the money that Phil had taken. They told her that Stan had come to them and asked for forgiveness, donating to the church all his ill-gotten gain.

And Reverend Michaels agreed to perform the ceremony at Harry's house, which Nate sold to Harry for the sum of ten dollars on the condition that he (and his horses) would be allowed to stay on for as long as they all lived. Nate also mentioned, with a wink to Harry, something about requiring Eleanor's services for a good long time.

As a result, Nan and Harry spoke to a local builder and made arrangements to add several bedrooms to the house, more than they needed right now, but Harry apparently had very high hopes.

Dee helped her find a dress, which she snuck into the house without showing Harry or the children.

With Eleanor, she cleaned the house from top to bottom and cooked up a storm for the guests they had invited by phone to the wedding.

By Friday they had all of the children under Nate's roof.

And in all that time, she had slept alone in Harry's big bed, waiting for their wedding night, apologizing to God for ever doubting that He was watching over her.

"What about a honeymoon?" Eleanor asked late Saturday afternoon as she and Nan fussed with their hair in the small bathroom on the second floor. "Marissa and Sarah aren't coming until next week, and Nate and I would be happy to watch the kids so you can—"

"No honeymoon," Nan said. "Harry and I talked about it and we just want to start our real life together. All of us."

"But you would be starting," Eleanor said. "It'd be like kicking it off with a bang. And Nate and I . . ."

"Where would we go that would make us happier than here?" Nan asked. "And don't I want to share all that happiness? We're going to be a family, a family that enjoys each other, that plays and eats and grows together. I can't wait another minute for that."

There was a soft tap at the door.

"I think your wait may be over," Eleanor said, and cracked open the door.

"Is she ready?" Nan heard Harry ask.

"I've been ready my whole life," she said. "Go downstairs. I want to make an entrance."

"I'll be waiting, but don't take long," he said. "Remember, As long as you've been ready, I've been waiting."

"Go," Eleanor said, pushing him out of the doorway. "I'll have her down there in a flash."

Someone from Nan's congregation played a violin, and she struck up the wedding march as the woman he loved came down the stairs. She was a vision, just this side of an angel. She had something soft and pale on, but all he could see was that face, that incredible, loving face, smiling first at her guests and her children and then turning just to him, smiling a special smile for him alone. He escorted her to where Reverend Michaels stood waiting in front of the fireplace, and tucked her hand in the crook of his arm.

"Dearly beloved," the minister began, and Harry thought that the words had never been more fitting, had been written just for the two of them. She was his dearly beloved Nan, and he would always be her Harry.

The ceremony was lovely, although it lacked the frills of the church, the pomp, the circumstance. And yet it was perfect for them, for they needed nothing more than their love to fill the night.

There were plenty of well-wishers and a pile of gifts. There was Chuckie in the midst of everything, and a whole lot of children, and lots of toasts made with cookies and milk.

But mostly, there was Nan—smiling, hugging guests, seeing to children and throwing smiles his way that just obliterated everything and everyone.

He had second thoughts about the honeymoon. Even if it had just been to a hotel in Columbus, at least they'd be alone now. But Nan wanted to wake up in the morning with a house full of her children, and Josh was staying over, too, and Harry had agreed that nothing sounded better than starting their new life together as soon as possible.

Unfortunately, that precluded something else he wanted to do as soon as possible. Hell, the woman was his wife now, wasn't she? And a husband had a right . . . a duty, even. He'd even sworn as much—in a court of law.

And the more he thought about going up to their bed, the longer the evening became, until he thought about showing her the horses out in the barn and getting some hay in her hair.

"Well, time for us to be going," someone finally said.

"Yes, it is," he agreed so readily that several people turned to stare at him. Their surprise turned to understanding and the house cleared out as fast as if someone had yelled "Fire!"

And Eleanor and Nate saw to the little ones, and the bigger ones saw to themselves, and Harry helped Nan put the dishes and cups in the kitchen and waited for the house to quiet.

Nan yawned. "What a perfect, perfect day," she said, stretching her hands out and then wrapping them around herself in a very satisfied hug.

"It's not over yet," Harry said, scooping her up and heading for the stairs. It was a wonderful feeling, her head resting against his chest, listening to the thudding of his heart, knowing that it beat for her as he climbed the stairs to their new life as man and wife.

He stood her on her feet beside the bed and reached around her, unzipping her dress down the back while he embraced her. "My wife," he said possessively. "Imagine someone like you loving someone like me."

"It's not hard," she said. "Loving you."

"I'm boorish," he argued, pushing the dress over her shoulders and kissing just beside the strap of her bra. "Not refined."

"Hardly," she argued. "You're down-to-earth." He slipped his finger under the bra strap and pushed it off her shoulder. "I like that. Being down-to-earth, I mean."

"I've a sarcastic streak as wide as the Mississippi," he said, reaching around and looking for the hook in her bra, tracing beneath her breasts on his way back and unfastening the front clasp.

"I have stretch marks," she admitted.

"The hair on my chest is turning gray," he said.

"In a man, that's distinguished," she said, tilting her head back so that he could kiss her neck and moaning as he did.

"I'm not really good enough for you," he said, pushing her dress down until it fell to the floor. "You're so perfect."

"Only in your eyes," she said.

"Who else has been looking?"

She waited for him to finish undressing her, to push down the slip and the pantyhose and the pink silky panties she'd bought for just this moment. Instead he just stood in front of her, his hands resting gently on her shoulders.

Finally he whispered, "I think I'm scared, Nan."

She backed away from him slightly, sat down on the bed, and patted the mattress beside her.

"Of being married? Or of being married to me?"

He laughed and shook his head. "I'm afraid that you're going to come to your senses. That you'll realize that you couldn't possibly love me and I'll—"

"That won't ever happen. I'll never stop loving you. Not for as long as I live. Even if you stop loving me."

"Stop loving you? Don't you know how crazy I am about you? Woman, I sold my car, I quit my job. I'm actually looking forward to shoveling horse manure for the rest of my life just so that I can spend that life with you."

"What if that grates on your nerves and you turn around one day and wonder why you ever married me?" Hadn't Phil done that? Hadn't Harry's first wife?

"Never happen," he said, his hand idly making circles on her shoulder. "Not in this lifetime."

"What if you—"

"What if the sky falls in? What if the sun doesn't come

up tomorrow? Some things you just have to take on faith. I'll be here, Nan. Always."

She turned and looked at his sweet, kind face, full of love and understanding and infinite patience. Faith was something she could understand. "Where are those gray hairs?" she asked, running her fingers over his chest and letting her breath tease his skin as she pretended to look for signs of his aging. "Here?" she asked, placing a kiss on his breast. "Here?"

And then the teasing was over. Oh, sometime after he'd fought with her pantyhose and won, he'd made some mention about looking for stretch marks, but before long the kisses became earnest, and she had no doubts about Harry's love as he tasted and touched and loved inch after inch of her breasts, her midriff, her belly.

And she kissed him back, and roamed his body with her fingers, encouraged him with her moans.

And they sealed their pledges with their bodies, and he wrote *I love you* deep inside her womb, where she would keep the message safe for all the years they had to come.

It seemed to her that he had all the time in the world, while she was hurrying to reach some place she'd never been before, a place that belonged only to her and Harry.

When she got there, he was waiting.